The Sacrifice

■■■ *Macmillan of Canada/Toronto*

The Sacrifice

Adele Wiseman

Dedicated to my father and mother

First published 1956
First Laurentian Library edition 1968
Reprinted 1972, 1973
This edition 1977

ISBN 0-7705-0253-9

Printed in Canada for
The Macmillan Company of Canada Limited
70 Bond Street, Toronto, Ontario M5B 1X3

The Sacrifice

Chapter One

———◄●►———

The train was beginning to slow down again, and Abraham noticed lights in the distance. He shifted his body only slightly so as not to disturb the boy, and sank back into the familiar pattern of throbbing aches inflicted by the wheels below. A dim glow from the corridor outlined the other figures in the day coach as they slept, sprawled in attitudes of discomfort and fatigue. He tried to close his eyes and lose himself in the thick, dream-crowded stillness, but his eyelids, prickly with weariness, sprang open again.

Urgently the train howled the warning of its approach to the city. Facing him, Abraham's wife seemed to seize the same wailful note and draw it out plaintively as she sighed in her sleep. Her body huddled, strained and unnatural, on the faded green plush seat. He could feel the boy, slack and completely pliant, rolling to the motion of the train. The whistle howled again, the carriage jolted, and his son lurched heavily, almost lifelessly against him.

Enough! With a sudden rush of indignation, as though he had been jerked awake, it came to Abraham that they had fled far enough. The thought took hold in his mind like a command. It came alive in his head and swept through him angrily, in a wave of energy, a rebellious movement of the blood. It was as simple as this. Enough. He must act now.

He sat up carefully, shifting Isaac's limp form into another position, fired in his new determination by the boy's weak protesting mumble. Slowly, he stretched, feeling his joints crackle, willing the cramp out of his body. He looked about him impatiently.

As though summoned, the conductor entered the coach. Abraham turned his head and beckoned imperatively.

"Where are we?" he asked in Ukrainian, tentatively, his red-

3

rimmed eyes gleaming with excitement, his loud voice muted to a hoarse whisper.

The man stooped, his face polite, questioning, and to Abraham offensively vacant in its noncomprehension. "I beg your pardon?" he said in English.

"Where are we stopping, please?" Abraham asked urgently in Yiddish, speaking slowly and patiently so that the man must understand.

The conductor shook his head. "No speak, no speak," he said, pointing to Abraham's mouth, then to his own, with a deprecating gesture.

Abraham looked at the man with irritation. Was there anyone on the train who could do anything but make faces and smile? "Why does the train stop?" he asked suddenly, hopefully, in Polish.

The conductor shook his head helplessly.

Abraham leaned forward and gestured wildly toward the window to where the lights blinked in the distance.

The conductor, as though realizing something, smiled a broad, reassuring smile, shook his head vigorously, patted Abraham lightly on the arm, and made as if to move on.

"The train! stop! why? What city?" roared the Jew in exasperation, spitting out the words in broken German.

At the sound his son jerked suddenly awake, frightened, and looked blindly about for a moment. Other passengers groaned, stirred their numb bones, and mumbled in protest. The conductor swayed on down the car, shrugging apologetically at drowsy faces.

"Animals here," muttered Abraham, subsiding and turning helplessly to his son. "They can only gibber and gesticulate."

"What's the matter, Pa?" Isaac yawned. "Can't you sleep?"

"*No!*" With a gesture, he flung aside the overcoat he had used as a cover. "The train is stopping. We're getting off."

"But we have two more days."

"Who awaits us?"

There was no answer to this that the boy knew of. Who awaited them? What awaited them? It did not really matter whether they stopped here, blindly, or went blindly on to the other city for which they had bought the tickets. Isaac crouched for another moment and watched his father, who was collecting their bundles. His own limbs were so knotted that it took him a moment to gather the strength to get out from under his warm coat and stretch.

The conductor called out the name of the city.

"No; enough, I say," said Abraham. "Fifteen months and eleven days. If I had to spend more days and nights worrying about a new beginning I would not have the strength to begin. Two more days and nights in this position, and this whole human being that you call your father will make sense only to an upholsterer. I do not know where we will sleep tomorrow, but at least our beds will lie flat and we will rock no more."

"But our tickets—" Isaac rubbed his eyes with numb fingers and shook his head to clear his thoughts.

"Ah, our tickets." Abraham scratched the itching skin under his forked beard reflectively. "Well, it's senseless trying to explain anything to that fellow. Listen to him. Me he can't answer a simple question, and now he wakes up the whole train with his shouting up and down. Well, I suppose he can't help himself. Would I have understood him even if he had understood me?"

Strength and humor returned with his decision. He moved around and stretched; his blood began to circulate again. Like a young man entering deliberately into an adventure, he felt excited at making a positive gesture in the ordering of his fate.

"In fact, come to think of it, we'll be saving money. If we get off here we save the rest of our fare, so just in case they're not clamoring for a butcher and I don't get a job here right away, we'll save that much more money to live on in the meantime. That's why it's such a good idea to get off here. You see, your father has not lost his common sense. In fact, it's a wise decision I have made with God's help. And we can see about our tickets in the station."

Lights flashed by; at the other end of the car a young couple were gathering their belongings.

"The important thing now," Abraham continued, "is that we must stop running from death and from every other insult. We will seize our lives in these scarred hands again." He paused to consider his words with pleasure.

"Come, boy, we must wake your mother—but gently. How weary she is."

When the train grunted to a halt Abraham and his family, his wife blinking and shivering with sleep, stood among the few waiting with their bundles in their arms. The conductor, noticing the group assembled to leave, rushed up to them.

"No, no, no!" He shook his head and reached for Abraham's suitcase. "This isn't your stop!"

Abraham brushed his arm away firmly.

"Shalom," he said politely, yet with a certain fierceness that prevented the conductor from persisting. They descended to the platform. The conductor stood shaking his head in exasperation over these immigrants. Abraham cast him a last, forgiving glance. As though it were written, he could see what they must do. First, to find the immigration barracks—to sleep, at last, without the artificial pulse of engines to remind them even in sleep that they were wanderers. Then, with the new day, to settle themselves gingerly on the crust of the city, perhaps someday even to send down a few roots —those roots, pre-numbed and shallow, of the often uprooted. But strong. Abraham felt strength surge up in him, excitement shaking the tiredness out of his body. No matter what is done to the plant, when it falls, again it will send out the tentative roots to the earth and rise upward again to the sky. The boy was young, the boy was blessed, the boy would grow.

Isaac shifted his bundle uncomfortably under curious stares and raised his eyes upward and ahead in imitation of the oblivious purposefulness of his father. He moved stiffly, aware of the difference in dress between these people and himself, and listened, lonely among the strange rhythms about him, for voices of warmth.

That morning they had found a place to live, and now they were bringing their belongings to install in the room. Isaac thought of the new home with trepidation, perhaps not so much in spite of but be-.

cause of the fact that the landlady had told him happily that she had two daughters just his age. What would two native girls think of him? What if they were like their mother—two garrulous girls with sharp noses, the tips moving like rabbits', incessantly up and down as they talked?

Sarah, Isaac's mother, who had lived for months as in a dream, found herself hypnotized, watching the face of Mrs. Plopler as she talked. When the woman addressed her persuasively, woman to woman, reiterating the merits of this furnished room with its bed, its couch, its bureau, its chair, and its big window, she merely nodded up and down, unthinking.

The landlady was a thin, flat-fronted woman with nothing to draw the eye from her hyperactive nose other than a head of tightly grizzled hair that started upward from her head in stiff, small waves. As she talked she examined her prospective roomers and saw that they were no longer young, this straight-backed Jew with his beard thrust forward, as though starched, away from his chest, and his wide-eyed, unresponsive wife. Still talking, she swept her eyes over their pale adolescent son, who stood looking at her in a way which she found vaguely irritating. Her eyes took in their portable belongings. She concluded that they were lucky to get her room, and, reminding them again that they would have the benefit of a furnished room with a bed, a couch, a bureau, a chair, and a big window, as well as kitchen and bathroom facilities, which they would share with her family, she asked for her rent in advance.

Half an hour after they were securely installed and she had their rent pinned away warmly, their landlady was telling a neighbor how she had taken a poor immigrant family into the house, practically right off the train, and how she had made them feel immediately at home. "Why, they're taking baths already."

Shortly afterward she met her adolescent daughters at the door with the whispered news that she had rented the room to an immigrant family with a son of about sixteen, who, however, didn't look like much, but that they would nevertheless have to stop running about the house half-naked in the mornings. She added that the tenants had taken baths already, three separate baths, and that she had served them tea in the kitchen and had gleaned that the father was a butcher. At present, she told the girls, they were asleep after their long trip.

Leaving her daughters at home—two overgrown girls who began to wander up and down outside the room, pausing to listen and giggle at the door of their tenants—she went off to shop for supper. At the grocery she mentioned that she had taken an immigrant family into her house, people she knew nothing about, that they had taken baths already, that she had served them tea, that the husband was a butcher, that they were resting at present, and that it was hard for two families to share one bathtub.

When her husband came home she told him that they had finally rented the furnished room to an immigrant family, that the husband was a butcher who didn't have a job yet, though they'd paid rent in advance, that they were at present asleep in their room, that they had taken baths already, and that she wondered how often they intended to take baths during the week, all three of them.

"You have to show them that we have a bathrub right away," said her husband, who was a joker and a jolly good fellow at a party but surly, with secret grievances, at home.

"Well, it's by the toilet," she defended herself. "They would have found out anyway. And besides, it's because of the long train ride that they bathed. They're greenhorns; they won't want to bathe very often. You know how filthy these people are apt to be."

"We have too much hot water for you," he grumbled.

"She served them tea, too," chimed in Gertie and Goldie eagerly, happy for some diversion after having palpitated around the house all afternoon in vain.

The Ploplers waited to get a glimpse of their tenants, but Abraham and his family slept on until the evening. Then the Ploplers noted that the lights went on and heard their voices murmuring, the man's louder than the rest. But they couldn't catch the words. From the moving about they assumed that the new tenants were unpacking and putting the room in order. Possibly, even, they were eating something from one of their outlandish bundles. Then the lights went out.

"Certainly sleep a lot," commented their landlord. "Why you didn't knock on the door and ask them if they want anything is beyond me. I think I have as much right to see them as you have. I go out in the morning and come back to find half my house rented away, and nobody thinks to introduce me to my new tenants. Nobody thinks fit to ask me if maybe in my opinion they're not suitable for tenants in my house. Who rents a room just like that?"

"Why didn't you tell me when the lights were on to knock on the door?" said his wife. "You'd think they'd come out by themselves to be sociable. They know I have a husband."

"Thank you for telling them you have a husband. What are they hiding themselves away for?"

"Maybe they're tired," suggested one of the girls.

"I'm tired too," said her father. "So what?"

"What does the son look like?" asked the other girl, who had heard at least half a dozen times before. They both listened eagerly while their mother described how thin and wretched-looking a boy he was, but not, for all that, entirely ugly. The landlord resigned himself sullenly to waiting till morning.

Maybe they're whispering that we might want some water during the night. Isaac lay, sleepy and thirsty, conjuring up this fanciful hope because he was ashamed to venture out of the room in his bathrobe among all those feminine voices that whispered in the kitchen. It seemed to him that he had not had any water for a long time. The taste of salt herring was in his mouth. He got up and brushed against the chair, making a noise so that the whispering in the kitchen held its breath for a moment. His father's deep, open-mouthed breathing continued to purr and chortle from the bed, and his mother lay silent, curled up under the bedclothes. Isaac found an orange to suck and lay back down on the couch with it.

It was different when they had changed boats and were in England for a short while. There it didn't matter that his clothes were

different. He could walk with his hands in his pockets, knowing he'd
be leaving soon, and pretend he was a tourist—wealthy, idle, indo-
lent, even perhaps at times a bit supercilious. He saw himself back
in London when he had stood for a long time watching people buy
bananas, wondering what was done with them. Yet he had not let
on, just cocked his head carelessly to one side and whistled a short
snatch of melody, as it were absent-mindedly, as though speculating
on some subject far off from these petty transactions.

At last a man and a little boy had bought some of the bananas,
and the little boy peeled one of them and began to gobble greedily.
So Isaac had bought and peeled to take, tentatively, taste. . . .
Pleasant . . . Floating in to confront his parents. Mother's gasp.
"What are you eating?" Father: "Raw!" . . . Isaac, enormously
sophisticated, wearing no clothes at all, prowling a strange house with
raw girls, whispering, "It's a fruit to gobble greedily in English."
Tasting-sipping-drinking deeply. Suddenly, his brothers' heads
crowding among the immigrants. Moses: "Like water." "No, like
herring." Jacob, the learner, in the darkened room. "Like watered
herring"—definitively. "Like water." Moses, the singer, adamant.
"Raw water." "Can't get water from a torn bathrobe"—contemptuously.

The orange didn't help much, ventured Isaac. She still wagged
her yellow nose.

As Isaac slept.

After lunch, when Isaac went to the English-language course that
had been organized in the district high school, Abraham left the
house with him. Isaac pointed at objects, enunciating carefully the
English names.

"Tree. Sky. Cloud. House. Mountain."

Abraham would repeat, fingering the syllables clumsily with his
tongue, but with immense satisfaction listening to the sound of his
son's apparently adroit mastery. When they parted, the young voice
continued to repeat itself in his head, raised, clear, ardent, for to
Abraham his son's voice must be ardent. Nothing grows but by desire.

Sky. Houz. He stopped in front of a tree, frowning at it demandingly. Now what did he call this?

His beard jutted out in vexation, and his eyes traveled up the trunk in search of a clue.

Boim. Isaac's voice, speaking cheerfully in Yiddish, came to his mind.

"*Boim,*" said Abraham out loud to the tree with satisfaction and proceeded toward the busy avenue.

The little leaves are falling from the trees. Abraham expanded his scope, carefully enunciating his thought mentally, as though it were an elementary language lesson, thinking in Yiddish, but laboriously, so that he could feel pleasantly as though it were the English equivalent.

He stopped as he reached the avenue and pulled out his little snap purse to look for the address the butcher had given him that morning.

Today I may find work. Then we will go to night school. It may be that there are new thoughts in English. The Russians, too, have very clever sayings.

The chill autumn winds ruffled the hair on his face, outlined his bare cheeks where they met his beard, and crept, clean-smelling, into his nostrils.

Isaac will yet do something fine. He was not spared for nothing.

He looked into the shop windows as he passed and checked the numbers above their doors.

The butcher had said, looking at him in a sly way, "Polsky might be needing a new man now that he's opened up again. His business is booming. The women can't resist nosing around now that he's back. You know how women are."

Abraham had asked for and written down the address of this Polsky's shop.

"Quite a man, Polsky," the butcher had begun again. "And when the women get hold of something like that their tongues run ahead of them. Can't talk of anything else."

"Yes," agreed Abraham, who only half heard. "You think perhaps that he might need someone?"

"Never can tell. He's got a pretty big place there. Used to have someone to help him. And now that he's just back from his little holiday, as they say, and his mind probably isn't altogether on his work yet—well, he probably needs someone." The butcher chuckled wisely and winked. "Only you'd better watch; it may be catching. How does your wife feel about that sort of thing?"

Abraham saw himself already on the way. Immediately after lunch he would go. It was no good to go with a hungry look. He thanked the butcher and left, leaving the man to look after him with some annoyance, the frustrating taste of an untold story on his lips.

That was a strange man, that butcher, full of funny looks and hints. But maybe this man will really need me. Abraham paused before two large windows, aware that he was nervous and anxious. He looked about him at the preparations nature was making for winter.

If I get work we will walk in the park this evening, he promised himself as he opened the door to the store. The large bell tinkled distantly in his ears. He closed the door behind him carefully. If not —we will walk in the park.

He straightened up and walked through the sawdust to the counter, where the butcher was waiting on a customer. Standing a little to one side, his hands behind his back, he waited tensely till the man should be through.

Isaac walked to school, studying signs and faces, learning the contours of the city, wondering what was to come for him. The city rose about him, planted on an undulating countryside that seemed to have spilled over from the ridge of dark hills in the western distance. The life that he remembered wavered uncertainly forward to meet the life that he seemed just about to live. In the morning he had wandered around in the flats of the city, the crowded, downhill area in which he lived. The flats scooped down toward the edge of the brown river with a sort of lilting quality, as though the earth had lifted a shoulder and the houses had slid closer together and the factories had slipped and jostled one another to the river bank.

Westward, above the flats, grand houses spread themselves. Their rocky gardens and many trees prepared, with an autumnal festival of color, for the austerities of winter. Along the edge of the sharp incline which, like a small cliff, separated the heights from the flats, the streets lit up brightly at night and were crowded with people. In the day they were filled with traffic and the commerce of the city.

Beyond the river to the east, and beyond the township and truck gardens that dotted its farther bank, was another gradual rise, which gathered breath for several miles and heaved up finally with a tremendous effort to a double-crested hill that dominated the eastern landscape. To Isaac the land seemed like a great arrested movement, petrified in time, like his memories, and the city crawled about its surface in a counterpoint of life.

He was aware of the hill to the east as he walked. When he didn't look at it, it seemed to crowd up closer, as though it were watching, absorbing every gesture in its static moment. He looked sideways and back toward it, and the mountain assumed its proper proportion, the sweeping double hump carelessly mantled in splotches of autumn color.

The mountain reminded him of how he had asked the giggling daughters of his landlady the source of the lights that peered at night from behind its first hump. They had crowded close beside him at the window, Gertie and Goldie, the younger one right up against his side. The older one had held her finger to her ear, described a circle with it several times, then pointed to the lights. The younger whispered, "Crazy-house," giggled, and shuddered fearfully closer to him. This was why it was called Mad Mountain—a strange name to call a mountain that looked so intimately on all the affairs of the city. Strange to think of the people that it had gathered up to live with itself. It was not a thing to laugh and giggle about as these girls did. But with women it is always so, Isaac told himself sagely. What they said meant little. It was merely to draw your attention to the other things that their eyes and lips could tell you.

It was because of a girl that his brothers had discovered one night that he sometimes stayed awake and listened to them talking. How young he had been then! That night back in the old country returned to him now with a vividness that banished the warm immediacy of the sun and the keen-smelling breeze from his senses. He had lain awake as he had intended, hoping to hear another argument about God, so that he could finish explaining to the incredulous Menasha Roitman across the street why some great thinkers thought that maybe there couldn't be a God. He had forgotten, because of Menasha's interruptions and arguments, the lofty line of reasoning that Jacob had followed some nights before. Now he listened, puzzled, while his brothers crawled into their places on the huge stove beside him and whispered about an ordinary girl.

Minutely they debated whether the carpenter's daughter had really spent all afternoon picking flowers in her front yard solely because Moses himself had spent all afternoon walking back and forth past her house.

"You say she was picking flowers for two whole hours?" asked Jacob, the thinker, man of reason. "She must have picked a good many flowers in that time," he continued thoughtfully. "And what would she do with all of them?" It followed, obviously, that the flowers were only an excuse. And what other reason could she have?

"Do you really think so?" Moses had asked in such a pathetic voice that Isaac had wanted to giggle. And Moses tried to remember out loud what kind of flowers and how many flowers she had picked, and whether that was all she had really been doing in the garden. He went carefully over the many times that he had wandered back and forth down the street, pretending to be immersed in thought, until the smell of hops from the brewery two blocks down, combined with his excitement, had nearly overcome him. He recalled that she had kept slightly turned toward the walk, that when he glanced her way he had caught her eyes several times lowering hastily to her work in the garden. Once when he had passed she actually raised herself up and stretched, with one hand on the back of her hip and the other wiping across her lovely brow and fine black eyes. But even though her lips seemed to be smiling she might just have been shading her eyes from the sun and not really looking at him. Thus reasoned

Moses the singer, humbly, his voice filled with emotions that Isaac
had never heard there before, except, perhaps, when he sang one of
those love songs that his mother liked with so much feeling that the
neighboring women gathered around to hear. The desire to giggle
surged up in Isaac again, and he stiffened against it.

But Jacob was alert and serious in his brother's behalf. "How
could she have been shading her eyes from the sun? You said that
it happened in the late afternoon. If it did, since her house is on the
west side of the street, the sun would be behind her and shining toward you, so she couldn't have been shading them; she was just pretending. She must have been looking at you. The sun would be in
your eyes. Do you remember if you had to squint when you looked
at her?"

"Squint," said Moses brokenly. "I love her."

Isaac snickered, choking over the piece of bedcover that he was
stuffing into his mouth.

There was a moment of utter silence, during which Isaac tried
desperately to fall suddenly asleep. Then Moses pounced.

"Pest! You were listening! What did you hear? What did you hear,
little devil?"

Isaac, though he was a little frightened, tried to sound innocent
and injured and sleepy with Moses breathing heavily over him, but
the question itself seemed so silly that his voice broke on a quaver-
ing giggle. "You like girls."

Now it was afterward, with another sun and a breeze that smelled
of laying the old earth to sleep. How old had Moses been then? His
own age; and it did not seem so silly now to want a girl to look at
him. He thought, as he awoke to the pattern of the stone high-school
steps that he was ascending, of what Jacob had said after he had res-
cued him from the "lesson" that Moses had begun to teach him.

"Wait, wait, little knacker, you'll grow up yet."

Who could have dreamed then that they would not wait with him?
Sometimes the very thought that it was he who still lived frightened
him. It made him now, as the high-school bell rang, rush into the

classroom and, without even seeing the welcoming smile of his friend who sat beside him, sit down quickly and bury his mind in the grammar book.

During the absence of her men Sarah stayed in the house and made a home of their room. Gentle as a nutcracker, Mrs. Plopler took her under her wing. She introduced her, with significant looks, to the neighbors. She accompanied her to the grocer's, and introduced her with more significant looks to the grocer and the customers who were waiting to be served. The significant look was a staple in the social equipment of Mrs. Plopler. She considered herself a past mistress in the art of talking between the lines. So she let Sarah know, or thought she let Sarah know, that this was the grocer about whom she had already spoken and would speak again as soon as they returned home. At the same time she let the grocer know with expressive movements of the nose, eyes, and lips, that this was the immigrant of whom she had spoken, and that there was much to be said further about her. Back home, she laid open the lives of the grocer and his customers and the neighbors before Sarah in a constant flow of Yiddish.

Sometimes Sarah felt as though the nibbling face were pursuing her. Unobtrusive though she tried to make herself, standing in a corner by the sink, preparing a meal for her men, her mind still in its customary reverie, Mrs. Plopler would appear, hair and nose over her shoulder, holding forth on how she herself preferred to prepare that particular dish. Almost invariably, just as Sarah was ready to cook her dinner, the landlady managed to reach the stove and plunk down a kettle on the only empty element. Then Sarah had to wait and listen to the endless flow of words. Sometimes the words seemed to recede and become like little human cries that pierced into the back of her mind. Then Sarah would look up, startled into sympathy, with her dazed brown eyes full on Mrs. Plopler's face. And Mrs. Plopler would feel the warm reassurance that somehow this silent woman recognized that she too had a soul.

But Mrs. Plopler's soul was a voraciously sociable one. She would follow Sarah into the bedroom hungrily, talking. Sarah had to listen, clasping and unclasping her hands, looking one way and another to avoid the peripatetic face. Why did she have to talk so? Why did she have to beat upon the air with sounds? And those things that she said sometimes that were not from the mouth of a friend.

"You know," said Mrs. Plopler one morning, "you have the room very nicely arranged, but I'm afraid you haven't got enough floor space. In all the interior decoration books nowadays they talk about floor space. Just the other day Gertie and I were reading in a magazine with pictures, how floor space gives a room a new look. Maybe you don't need the chair. It clutters up the place."

Sarah roused to what she sensed was a threat to the comfort of her men. "We need the chair. Isaac studies his lessons on the chair by the bureau."

"Oh, I thought you could do without it. Why should he study here? Will we bite off his head if he sits in the kitchen?" asked the landlady, who did not particularly want Isaac in the kitchen but thought the boy held aloof from her daughters. Not, of course, that she would approve if they got too friendly. As she told one of the neighbors, it was enough of a worry to her just to have a strange boy in the house. A mother has to use her eyes. Mrs. Plopler let the neighbor know that she was equal to the task.

"Thank you," said Sarah. "But he likes to work by himself where it's quiet."

"Oh," said the woman. "I didn't know it was so noisy in my kitchen."

And she told her husband that night that their roomers didn't feel that the house was quiet enough for them, that they were complaining already. Her husband grunted what did she expect, with her taste in tenants. Mr. Plopler slept turned away from his wife, and she had to lean forward to catch his mutterings. Sometimes he did turn to her but completed his attentions with a brusque dispatch that left her quickly alone again, like a used utensil.

Mrs. Plopler had married for love. But never from the first day of her marriage, in spite of the fact that she had brought with her such a nice dowry, had she been able to please her husband. She lay back again. "Cuff for kindness," she concluded, was all you could expect from these people.

Abraham paced home over ground that met his strides firmly, as though he had just learned to walk. Before the man, Polsky, who had finally given him a job, there had been a variety of butchers who looked at him, estimated his age, added five years for his beard and the furrows between his eyes, and five more because he spoke no English, and shook their heads. His employer looked to be a good-natured man, large and ruddy and as rudimentary as the red meat that his arms slung so easily on and off the hooks on the wall.

"So you're a butcher." He looked Abraham up and down. "In the old country they turn out even the butchers like rabbis, ha-ha-ha, eh? Don't take offense. I'm a man who doesn't blow in lace handkerchiefs. I say a girl should know what a pinch is for. Straight and to the point, ha-ha-ha, eh? One thing I know about an old-country man. He knows his craft. You can pickle meat?"

"Of course," said Abraham loudly, for his voice was loud and strong.

"Of course. Well, I need a man who knows the subtleties. I always throw in a little bit too much of this, of that. I'm more of a business man myself," the butcher continued with pride. "We'll get along, eh?"

Abraham was grateful to this man—a rather coarse fellow, from the way he talked, but a man who in his own way seemed to have a heart—and some discernment. He had, after all—rather rudely, of course, in keeping with his nature—noticed that he, Abraham, had a certain air about him, that he had the appearance of a holy and a learned man. Well, hadn't that been the dream of his father? And if his father hadn't died so young, leaving him with a mother to take care of and five sisters to worry about, would he have been a butcher? And his own sons—did not a man take on dignity from their achievement, their near-achievement of his dream? But what would another care about this? What did it matter to them that he had had a son who would have been a great cantor and another who was a scholar already when yet a child. Did other men care that he had had a son miraculously returned to him? This was for time to tell the world. Now they looked at the furrows about his eyes as though he were the trunk of some tree and shook their heads. And he himself could rely only on his powerful voice, which resounded so in his own head, and on his upright bearing to show that he had still the strength of a young man.

What did it matter to destiny, the age of a man? A God who could pluck the fruit of a man's desire when it was scarcely ripe and strangle such seed as could have uplifted the human race did not think in terms of days and years.

But I am not—his steps paused with his mind's anxious scruple— angry with You, Lord, any longer. One son at least shall not precede his father to the grave.

"Tree." It came to him suddenly, out loud. Tree. This means *boim* in Canada. Abraham beamed at a stranger who passed him. We will surely walk in the little park by the river this evening. And I will buy bananas. He had become inordinately fond of the new fruit his son had discovered. Isaac should be home soon from the English school. He himself would come in, carrying a bag with bananas, and maybe something else, something else that was good. Perhaps he would wait for a little while before he told them. Yes. They would know by the bananas and the other something that it was not bad news. So he would hold it in for a while and wait for the right moment to tell them that he had found work, that they were on their feet again.

Just thinking about it as he walked along, and then while he bought the bananas and the other treat at the grocery—the very thought of it made him feel so enthusiastic about the prospect of coming in and making them wonder a little about what had happened to him that somehow he couldn't help himself. The minute he stepped over the threshold, his face beaming, he announced that he had found a job. Without even waiting to put down the bags that he carried, he told them everything—where he had been, what had been said, and that he had already worked a few hours just to get used to it.

"Polsky! Him! Not *him!*" Into their eager discussion erupted the ecstasies of the landlady. "But he's just the man I was telling you about yesterday." She turned on Sarah vivaciously. "And this morning—no, wait—yes, I think I must have mentioned him to you this morning too. As though it were fated!"

Sarah looked up at her blandly. "Yes." She didn't remember, but it seemed likely that within all that Mrs. Plopler had said this Polsky, who had given her Avrom a job and had enabled him to relax now for the first time in so long, should be included.

Abraham recalled, as he had recalled in those anxious moments of waiting while Polsky dealt with a customer, how the other butcher had sounded as though sending him to this man was something of a practical joke, almost as though Polsky might be dealing in not strictly kosher meat.

Mrs. Plopler, who saw happily that she wasn't going to get any help from Sarah, plunged into her story.

Polsky was a scandal. One day, suddenly, with no warning, he had walked out of his shop, closed up and disappeared. But that wasn't it, that wasn't it at all. Polsky was a married man with a wife and children—a sloppy wife and scruffy children, but that wasn't the shame of it. The shame of it was that Polsky had a customer, a married woman, a woman who was not so young as she made out and certainly not as attractive as some of the men made out, although he, Avrom, would no doubt have the chance to judge for himself. This Laiah had a husband who was a nice quiet young man, who made her a living. And of course, now it began to appear, who knows how many other men she had as well? Such a woman seems to know well enough how to prevent herself from having children and having to remember how many fathers each child has. So she was free to run around turning other men's heads. Although what kind of man her husband could be was hard to understand. A man who could stand around and let his own wife make—they should excuse the expression—a public urinal of herself. *But.* That was the beginning. Without anybody even suspecting, this Laiah had been carrying on a relationship with this Polsky. Only such things can't be kept from the eyes of the world for long. When Polsky locked his shop that day and disappeared, Laiah also walked out of her house and disappeared— with Polsky.

The landlady paused, surveyed them significantly, and went on that they might not interrupt.

People talked, of course. People were horrified. Here was this wife, here were these children. What was to become of them? Who would have imagined that Polsky, laughing and joking with the customers, would someday desert his wife and children? What was going to happen? The whole world knew that this was not the end. Then one day, just about two weeks ago, after a whole month— pouf! They're back. All of a sudden a big wagon of meat pulls up outside of Polsky's shop, right there on the avenue. Polsky jumps out and opens the place for business. But that's not all. Where is Polsky living? With his wife! They say he brought her presents, and the kids presents, and they're living the same as before. One thing is certain, that no man could stuff Sonya Plopler's mouth with presents and sneak in the back way. And that one, his paramour? Pooh pooh! She's back with her husband. With her own eyes Mrs. Plopler had seen them parading around together at the Free Loan Society banquet. They say she has the nerve to show her face in the butcher shop too. God, what's happening in the world? Mrs. Plopler took a long, deep breath and exhaled emphatically. "He must be doing good business too," she added as an afterthought, "if he can afford to take on help again after being closed for a month."

During her recital Mrs. Plopler had ignored the fact that Isaac was present. Abraham thought of this with disapproval as he noticed that his son was leaning forward with his mouth open, apparently anxious to enter the conversation. He tried with a frown to catch Isaac's eye.

Mrs. Plopler looked at Abraham. It was time for him to break the significant silence which she had allowed for her information to sink in.

"I suppose," ventured Sarah, who was, as always, vaguely distressed to see two human beings perish in the jaws of another, "we don't know exactly what—" she trailed off lamely, made aware by Mrs. Plopler's stare that she had not risen to the occasion.

"But how do people know," said Isaac cleverly, bubbling with his brother Jacob's favorite dialectical approach, "that they were together? Just because they were gone at the same time doesn't mean—" His voice faded away as he caught his father's eye.

Mrs. Plopler's ardor, though dampened, still flickered. To Isaac's bewilderment, after she had progressed from damning Polsky and Laiah through all the people who by their passivity condoned such affairs, she darted suddenly to the conclusion that it would be only decent for her to patronize the place where her tenant worked. Tomorrow she would go herself to make an order. "I'll help you to pay your rent," she concluded in high good humor.

Later on, when they had escaped from the house and were sitting together on a bench in the little park by the river with few words passing between them, each one made his own silent voyage into the past and the future. Sarah remembered with a certainty in her mother's heart her intuition that Moses had had his eye on a girl already. Isaac watched the double-crested mountain, towering in front of them, and was aware of it even as his mind jumped from thought to thought. It was strange that, no matter where his mind went, the hill remained there, solid in his vision, every time he looked up. It was a comfort that it didn't change, like the people he had known and the other things that had once stood rooted, it had seemed, forever. It was like the sight of his father's face when he had opened his eyes for the first time after the fever, towering over him, claiming him.

Now that Abraham thought of it he determined to buy permanent seats at the neighboring synagogue for himself and his family as soon as possible. After all these sorrows, God had chosen to set him and his family down in this strange city to await what further He had in store for them. Very well.

Chapter Two

———◆——————◆◆◆◆———

That first year the winter descended very close on the autumn leaves. The city huddled in its own warmth among the piled-up snow. Although, with a certain fondness for their native landscape, the citizens claimed that Mad Mountain sheltered them from many a violent wind, the winds had apparently learned to circumvent this hazard and blew most persistently from the undefended north.

In the evenings, caged in the square room with the chair, the bed, the couch, and the other landmarks that the landlady had so minutely detailed, Abraham paced restlessly as his past years in their fullness forced themselves over him. Strength, he knew, strength was what was required of him now. His part was to accept, to rebuild, and to wait. It was no use to dwell too much on those memories that came at a man unawares, with bitterness. The main outlines were clear. Nowhere was it said that it would be a honeyed life—not here, in these alien lands. But how strong the gall had been, how bitter when it came. Still there had been the miracle, the reiterated promise. How would he have stood it else?

Isaac, still weak from the typhus that had forced them to halt their flight temporarily in Poland, seemed to fall prey to every common cold that made its way from breath to breath in the city. From the window of their room he watched now the snow piling up in warm, rounded, shadowy heaps.

"Come away from the window," growled Abraham. "You coughed all night last night. Don't think we didn't hear you. The landlady and her big window," he continued as Isaac turned back to his homework. "From every big inch of it a big draft." He peered out at the shadowy back yard, holding his hand at the same time to where the sharp chill that had made its way through the hole in the storm window filtered through the frozen rags that were stuffed into the cracks of the inside frame.

"What are you standing in the draft for, then?" Isaac challenged over the newspaper that he was deciphering.

One son, Abraham was beginning to realize, was as hard to bring up as three. "I haven't got a chest cold. I don't cough all night," he retorted righteously. But he did not linger with his usual pride on the fact that he had so neatly made his point. There was real concern in him for the boy.

He came and looked over Isaac's shoulder at the newspaper. For a while, twice a week in the evenings, he and his wife had gone to the English classes. Sarah had sat shyly, and blushingly couldn't answer the questions that were put to her by the young teacher, who spoke neither Yiddish nor Ukrainian nor Polish nor Russian nor German, but had nevertheless attained an appalling fluency in the English tongue. Abraham fidgeted during the class and came privately to the conclusion that, beyond the parts of speech, the teacher did not seem to have much to tell him. In the end, what with Sarah's indifference and his own overtime at the butcher shop, he had decided that they could teach themselves. So he contented himself with looking knowingly over Isaac's shoulder at the newspaper and making great leaps across sentences, pouncing on an odd word or two, from which he constructed privately plausible meanings, from some of which Isaac had the greatest difficulty in dissuading him.

Sarah kept Mrs. Plopler company in the kitchen. Mr. Plopler, in the American style, was on his weekly night out with the boys. The landlady probed into their past. She asked about the town they had come from, the state of the country, their business, their home. Sarah spoke a little, and when her words blundered toward her sons she remembered her four men when they had been most fully hers. Four straight backs, waiting for her at the dinner table, the shoulders of the boys gracefully molded, hard and vital under the clean shirts. She began to cry silently. Mrs. Plopler, in sympathy, began to cry as well, tentatively at first, then with great sloppy sobs, rocking herself from side to side and moaning intermittently over the terrible fate of Jewry.

When Abraham emerged in some alarm from the bedroom, Mrs. Plopler at once became terribly brave. She spoke touchingly to them of the new world, new friends, a new life. It seemed to Abraham at times that she was not so uncongenial as she appeared at other times. Perhaps, in the incomprehensible woman's way that draws courage from tears, she might be able to help his wife to accept their fate. But no. A moment ago Mrs. Plopler had been weeping with Sarah, watering a wound that was far deeper than she could understand. Now, with the tears scarcely dry, the last traces of moisture highlighting the ardent curiosity in her eyes as she leaned forward, with casual eagerness—"This Laiah, you've run into her at the shop? How does she strike you? What sort of a type is she?"

Abraham fought back the twinge of impatience. Isaac had come into the kitchen and had pulled a chair close to where his mother sat. The boy put his arm around his mother. Abraham fingered his beard and frowned seriously at Mrs. Plopler. "A type," he said, "that likes corned beef, pastrami, lamb chops, chuck." He cast a sly sidelong glance at Sarah and Isaac. Isaac was smiling. He continued seriously. "Leg of mutton, veal, wieners, ribs—"

"Yes, yes." Mrs. Plopler leaned forward again. "But besides that, I mean, what is she like? I've seen her once or twice myself; she was pointed out to me, but myself I can't see what they make such a fuss about."

"You can't?" said Abraham. "The first time I saw her she awakened desire in me."

Mrs. Plopler's eyes widened, and she cast an indescribable glance at Sarah.

Abraham's eyelid scarcely flickered. "I said to myself, With only half the pelts in the fur coat that woman is wearing, my wife could have a fur coat that would keep her warm for ten, maybe fifteen years.

"And her hair!" He was inspired. "You wouldn't believe it, but that hair is thick and auburn, just like the coat, brown and lustrous.

Do you know that at first I could not tell where the hair left off and the coat began? I thought to myself, This must be either a very hairy woman, or else when the coat comes off the hair comes off with it, and she is entirely bald."

Isaac laughed out loud.

Abraham sighed. "I wonder how much such a coat would cost."

"You needn't worry," broke in Mrs. Plopler excitedly. She felt that she had unearthed a mine of information. "That coat didn't cost her anything, nothing she isn't used to giving." She widened her eyes and distended her nostrils significantly at Abraham. Abraham returned her stare with an equally intense significance in his own.

"What," cried Mrs. Plopler joyously, "does she behave like in the shop—I mean when she comes in?"

"My dear friend, what can I tell you?" He looked again at his son and his wife. "They say that a cow will stand in a green field and wave its tail and show its rear to every passing bull. Who knows?" And that was enough. He felt a sudden annoyance at having indulged himself so far, even jokingly. What did he have to do with that woman, that he could take it upon himself to bandy her character around with such a one as Mrs. Plopler? What could she have to do with them, with her body that seemed to have difficulty keeping still inside of the luxurious fur coat, and her hoarse, low voice with its persistent animal call? She was what she was. The world was still the same. There were those who felt that, with God's mercy, if they stretched their bodies and their souls and created and built and grew, who knew what heights they, or their sons, or the sons of their sons might not reach? And there were those who preferred to go through life in other postures. It was not for him to laugh at her because he had chosen to live another life—not, especially, while he could still understand the animal call. No, it was an unworthy thing. A man may choose the sunlight, but he has no right to pass casual judgment on the shadows.

He would have to be more polite to Laiah the next time she came in to make an order. Isaac was still grinning broadly at his father's wit, but Abraham knew that, although Sarah smiled automatically, she only half listened, her mind elsewhere.

There were some women—Mrs. Plopler was still talking, not willing to drop the subject so easily now that she had caught her tenant in such a sympathetic mood—that didn't know what decency meant. Yes, and they seemed to think that all the rest of womankind didn't follow their example and act like animals because they had never had a chance to. They couldn't understand that some people kept themselves clean and decent because they preferred it that way. Take herself, for instance. You might not think so now—Mrs. Plopler laughed—but she had been a very popular girl in her youth.

Abraham, looking at Mrs. Plopler's face, lost track of her words. It was certainly warmer here in the kitchen than it was in their bedroom. It was no use, Abraham knew, to think about their own kitchen with its smooth mud walls that he had so frequently whitewashed himself. And their oven—but that was an oven! In the winter there was no fear that your boys would catch cold with that broad, warm oven to sleep on.

Decent, Mrs. Plopler emphasized; she had always kept herself decent—like her daughters, who were even now out having a good time. Mrs. Plopler looked accusingly at Isaac.

Sarah leaned her head against Isaac's shoulder. He had lengthened out during the last few months, but he had gained very little weight since the typhus. What was this new world that they had come to? Avrom was here, thank God; and Isaac, by some miracle. There was this woman who talked and talked, sometimes with little barbs in her words. Her own eyes grated together when she blinked them, and ached so. When she cried it was no longer as though she cried with tears. The ocean had drained away, and she cried now with only the pebbles on the beach.

Men had wanted her, Mrs. Plopler testified. She had been considered not unattractive. Ah, but she had danced in her day! Mrs. Plopler scraped her feet on the linoleum, and the sound made a variation on her voice.

Isaac listened. He wondered why his father didn't again break out of the humming coil of the landlady's eloquence. Had he himself been Jacob he would have picked up his father's joking vein, and together they would have so entangled Mrs. Plopler that she would still be struggling to find her way out. And then Moses would have sung a funny song that he had made up on the spur of the moment, all about what was happening. It seemed to Isaac that Moses had been capable of that. He himself and his mother would have sat and laughed and joined in sometimes. The whole would have been a riotous evening, and they would have all gone to bed afterward, liking Mrs. Plopler and well contented with themselves. Instead they sat still and listened to her with irritation, or pretended to listen, for the look on his father's face was not that of a listener. Was he too thinking of what a night it would have been? Why hadn't he himself been able to think of something clever to say? What was it that he had said the other day that had had his father roaring with laughter?

His mother's head rested very lightly on his shoulder. Perhaps she was afraid to lean on him too heavily. He pressed her closer to him, to get her to lean more heavily. She had grown so small.

Discarded suitors, Mrs. Plopler revealed. One hadn't looked right to her; one didn't attend closely enough; one—out of pure caprice. Mrs. Plopler pursed her lips and smiled.

Outside the window the snow was falling, banking up comfortably against the window ledge. Soon, Abraham realized, would be Chanukah. And a different celebration it would be from that of last year, he promised himself—last year, when every word and ritual act had been accompanied by a little irony inside of himself that had made it a mockery. He knew now that he had been punished, but he knew too what mercy meant. Nevermore, he told himself fervently.

A clever girl knows, with a word and a look, how to put a boy in his place, opined Mrs. Plopler.

"Amen." Abraham, stirred by his own thoughts, rumbled his conclusion aloud.

Mrs. Plopler laughed. She allowed herself, caught by the mood of the moment, to lapse into silence. Her husband swam into her

thoughts. What was it that he found so attractive about his night out
with the boys? God forbid that she should ever ask him again to
give it up for one week. That one time had been enough to close up
her mouth on the subject forever. This immigrant had not yet picked
up the habit. Of course where he came from they had never heard
of such a thing. Old-country Jews. Mrs. Plopler smiled to herself in a
superior way.

The snow fell more heavily. The kitchen light grew more yellow
in its effort to combat the encompassing night. A silence had fallen
over them, so that Isaac could almost hear the falling of the snow as
he watched it, dropping ever so lightly and evenly on blue mounds
outside. Mrs. Plopler's eyes had taken on a slightly vacant look of
reverie, and her nose was almost still in repose. Isaac felt himself on
the edge of many worlds, intangible ones, that seemed to exist in the
silences and in the cracks and crannies of speech when a group of
people sat in a room together. Was there a mind free in the imprisoned silence, that could pry into their separate minds? Isaac looked
anxiously about him. No, none could read his thoughts, nor he theirs.
God? No. Isaac waited. The roof didn't fall. Only the snow fell, un-
disturbed.

Now winter was wearing thin; the frost on the butcher-shop windows was gradually turning to water and slipping its hold on the
glass, so that there were large circles of clear glass through which
they could see that the evenings were not as early as before.

"What time can bring! Who would have thought"—Abraham addressed Chaim Knopp and Polsky during a lull in business—"three
years ago that I would ever be in the new world, that I would be
wrenched out of my old life, that I would be working in a new place,
making new friends, with new people; that I would have learned a
new language." This last was not, he felt, so much of an exaggeration; the language no longer sounded so unfamiliar. He could exchange a few English words on the street, and even threw in an occasional English expression with his Yiddish, like a regular native. And
while it was not strictly true that they had made new friends right

and left, it all seemed at the moment quite imminently possible. Polsky, of course, was certainly not the type of a friend for him, and not only because he was considerably younger. And as for Mr. Plopler, there there was also little question of finding companionship, as he had discovered.

"It is written down in the statistics," Plopler's voice would prick at him while his eyes fixed Abraham with an accusing stare, his mouth forming the words primly, "in the statistics it is written down, that the wage situation has badly deteriorated since the recent heavy influx of cheap labor into the country . . ."

"You have a new Bible here then, these statistics?" Abraham's own voice would resound in his head.

And Mr. Plopler's voice, always elaborately precise and slow when it began an argument, would rise and quicken as it heated itself up. Once when Abraham, to change the subject, had asked him how long he had been in the country Mr. Plopler became offended and, turning away from his tenant entirely, launched into an elegant conversation with his daughter in broken English. That was Plopler, and there had been too much of Plopler unrelieved during the long winter months.

Abraham swept the sawdust more evenly over the butcher-shop floor. The pregnant tabby frisked around the broom like a kitten, playfully hurtling its enlarged body toward the broom, skidding gracefully by, sparring with one paw, and sliding on, cutting a wide swathe through the newly swept sawdust.

"Oi, cat, get away. I sweep, and she makes it nothing." The cat sparred with the broom that Abraham waggled at her.

"Any day now," said Chaim Knopp, looking at the round full pink belly and the rows of pendant, heavy teats. "Exercise is good for them."

"Here, you bugger," came Polsky's heavy voice. Polsky crooked his foot under the cat and hoisted it away, while it clung to his pant cuff.

"Watch out for the family," Chaim Knopp cautioned.

Bogger, thought Abraham, was no good. It must be rejected. One had to watch what one picked up from Polsky. Usually if it sounded like a good, strong, usable word, then it was a word decent people wouldn't use in any language, which was in a way a pity but perfectly understandable when you got down to the root of it.

But this finding of friends. It seemed now—of course it was early to tell,·but it seemed perhaps to be picking up. Isaac had brought home a new friend the other day. A fine looking lad, a native. There was this learned man, this shoichet, Chaim Knopp. He was ·beginning to reveal himself an interesting man, and friendly. Unmistakably he sat for longer intervals warming himself by the·wood stove than he had at first. The first time he had·acknowledged his introduction to Abraham by a few nervous nods of his beard, taken his orders for kosher slaughtered chickens, hastily declined Polsky's invitation to sit and chat awhile, mumbled a reply to Polsky's sly questions about the health of his wife, and was obviously glad to get away. But then one day when he and Abraham happened to be alone in the shop Knopp had rather hesitantly explained to him that his wife was very much opposed to his having business dealings with such an openly scandalous man as Polsky.

"She says," said Chaim, shrugging his shoulders in a characteristic gesture of his, "that she would rather starve than be pointed at. Who would point at her because I'm Polsky's shoichet, I don't know, but there you have these women. And why she should starve because of this I do not know either. But you know for a while you have to let them have their way—not to the point of letting them starve, of course, but just enough to keep them quiet."

Abraham, although he had had little experience with this sort of woman, agreed that the shoichet had taken the wisest course possible in not arguing the point with his wife but quietly going his own way.

"Of course," continued Chaim, "there is the question of whether it is right for a man in my position to continue dealing with such a man. But I do not honestly think that it is up to me to judge him. In his dealings with me he has always been fair. He is not a very elevated type, it is true, but I have also seen signs at times that he has not a bad heart."

"He took me in. He gave me work," said Abraham. "He is not the first man to make a fool of himself over women. At least he came back. He has some sense of responsibility toward his family. To some it may seem strange that a man in your position and with your education would still continue to deal with him, but those are the ones that, no matter what you do, somehow they will find you in the wrong. What good will it do him if decent people ignore him altogether? Then he would have no one to learn from. Let them look in on their own sins; then they will not have time to point at others'."

"That is true," Chaim agreed. He liked the way this man talked. "I can see that you too have studied a little."

"A little, by myself," said Abraham modestly. "My life has not allowed me much time for study. But what a man does not learn in the books he makes up for in his dreams."

Now the shoichet talked to him quite freely of things that were of interest and importance. This man looked to be someone that one could indeed bring home, provided that one had a real home to bring him to. And even if one didn't have a proper home, what difference? He did not appear to be a man with airs. That was what Sarah needed, people around her to talk to her, to force her out of herself. The sight of her sometimes as he turned and saw her sitting there, unmoving, her eyes distant and dream-haunted, wrenched his heart.

Perhaps if they had a real home of their own for her to putter about in, to clean and wash and work about, it might help. This question of a home had begun to bother Abraham. Maybe in the spring, or, at the very latest, in the summer. To leave without any ill will, any argument. Some second-hand furniture, two rented rooms and a kitchen, separate—that was important, private, so that they could get to know one another again. It was necessary to be a family, no matter how small. The house was not, after all, destroyed.

"You will be having your kittens tonight," said Chaim Knopp. "Your cat is having an early spring."

"Good luck to her, I say." Polsky chuckled. "It means she'll have a long summer ahead of her."

Chaim Knopp reverted to a topic that they had been discussing. As he spoke he watched thoughtfully while his diminutive black-shod foot traced delicate whorls and swirls in the sawdust. "Yes, it's true, when you first come to a strange country everyone else looks so big, so assured. And you feel yourself so small, so lonely, such a *pintele Yid*. I remember yet from twenty-five years ago, when I first brought my family over."

"And you've grown since you arrived, Chaim, eh?" Polsky, to whom the serious attitude of the two men toward questions of little importance to him was extremely amusing, laughed. He himself had come to the country when he was still a child, which made him practically a native.

The other day he had given Laiah a very funny description of a conversation between the two, imitating in turn Abraham's deep voice, his stance, his beard, which he tucked into his collar to avoid contact with the meat; and Chaim's singsong voice, his bright brown eyes blinking, and his pointed beard making jabs in the air as he spoke. Laiah had laughed and laughed and then shown her appreciation in another way that he found very gratifying. But the person that you make fun of or criticize or tell stories about is always a different person from the one you meet again next day, Polsky found with a twinge of unlooked-for embarrassment when he met Abraham's level stare again in the morning. Their laughter was not visible on him, had left no scars. There was something about Abraham, thought Polsky; yes, there certainly was. Nine more like him, and he'd have a real high-class *minyan* in his shop. That was something to tell Laiah, a good crack.

That Laiah, devil that she was, after hearing all his stories had begun to take a bit of an interest in his hired man herself. Now when she came into the shop she headed straightway for Abraham and stood there, flirting and rolling her hips at him. It was the beard, she told Polsky, the beard that she wanted to tangle her fingers into.

Whatever it was, Avrom wasn't biting. You'd think he didn't know what she was at. Come to think of it, maybe he didn't. It rather pleased Polsky to think that Abraham didn't know, or chose not to know. There were some types she didn't know about. But she didn't have much time to spend worrying about it. Their little escapade, through which they had both come impudently unscathed, had attracted the attention of men whose incomes stretched nicely across her imagination. Well, good luck to you. He felt the smugness of the early bird. They could have what he left over, Polsky decided generously. Chuckling away to himself, he turned his attention to his cash register.

He wanted to buy his wife a present. He prided himself that he never forgot those little attentions which keep a woman happy. The electric gadget that he had set his mind on had fairly recently come on the market and was quite expensive. The most unobtrusive way of collecting the money was to take an amount at random out of the cash register every few days, putting it down as expenses and forgetting about it. It was simpler and less troublesome than to wait until he had done his accounts and then deduct from his profits, which he always found harder to do. There were always other things that he wanted to do with the money then. Besides, his wife got a slice of his profits for running the household, and it seemed like too much to give her at one time.

"Do you know," Abraham said to Chaim, feeling, as he began, as he always did when he told about this, as though he were making an important confession, "I myself once had to slaughter an animal, and in the ritual way?"

Chaim looked at him in astonishment. "But you are not a shoichet."

"Ah," said Abraham. "That's just the point. Nor was I ever intended to be. I will tell you what kind of rascals there are in the world. It happened in our town, when I was yet an apprentice. At this time there was no shoichet living in the town. Whenever we needed meat we had to send to a town some twenty versts away for their shoichet. You can imagine that it was an expense. A man comes from twenty versts away, his journey costs him money, time, trouble.

Of course the butcher did not lose by it, he merely charged that much more for the meat, and so it went.

"Well, I had been out to the slaughter already several times. I had often enough seen the killing done. As an apprentice I was being taught how to clean out the carcass and divide the sections. You remember how it was in the old country—a butcher had to know everything. I would come with my master, and when the shoichet was through with an animal we would be waiting to do our work. Those were not the days I looked forward to. You know yourself how unpleasant it can be to mess about with the sticky warmth of a fresh carcass, and the smell.

"On this day my master and I took the tools and went down to the slaughter. When we got there there was an excitement. The cattle dealer was rushing up and down and tearing his beard. What were they to do? It was already late, and word had just been received that the shoichet had been waylaid and beaten up and robbed on the road, and had had to return home for treatment. My master and one or two of the other butchers stood together and discussed the situation. They wanted the meat. What could they do? Amongst the group of them my master stood out as the leader. It was he who spoke heatedly and longest. I stood off a ways, but I could see that he was driving some sort of a bargain, for finally they each one of them dug into his pocket and gave my master some money. Then they turned and left, calling out that they would be back in a little while to see if the shoichet had arrived.

"My master and I remained with only the helpers and the dealer. I stood there, puzzling it out, feeling a vague apprehension growing in me. Why had the butchers talked of returning to see if the shoichet had come, when they themselves had heard that he would not be coming?

"My master climbed onto the shoichet's platform. When he called me up to the platform I think I already felt what he was about. I trembled in every part of me.

"He took the knife and looked around him at the few of us who stood there. He was a man who was much feared in town as a fighter, and never had he looked more fearful to me, even though I had often before felt the weight of his palm.

" 'Perhaps it is written,' he said, 'that only a shoichet may slaughter an animal. That may be; of course I am not much of a reader myself. But I am as pious as any man. I too know the blessing, and I too know the ritual method. Who is to say that in the eyes of God I am not as much of a shoichet as the next man, if I please to be?' He looked around again fiercely, making a gesture with the hand that held the knife. Who, indeed, would gainsay him at that moment? For myself, I think I was paralyzed by the blasphemy and the knowledge of what he intended to do. I was not more than a child. Can you imagine what a moment this was for me? It would have been different if the town were desperate for meat. What may not a starving man do? But this was greed.

"I watched the life gush from the first cow. It died in precisely the same manner as others that I had seen that were slaughtered by the proper hands. He had not boasted unduly. He knew the words and the method. This was not unusual. I too was familiar with the prayer and with the method of the shoichet. I had seen it often enough.

"In this way he slaughtered two of the cows. Each time I stood beside him and wiped the bleeding knife and held it until he was ready. By the time they brought the third animal my master was in a jovial mood. All was going well with him. In one stroke he was making a fine profit. He had earned the shoichet's fee, and could still charge the same price for the meat when he sold it. And none who were present would dare to whisper of it, or if they dared to whisper none would dare to state it aloud. Who would risk the vengeance of the butchers? And would whispers affect the town's hunger? The Jews of the town would not eat the meat if someone came right out and said it was not kosher. But against the whisper of rumor their stomachs had a hungrier and a louder whisper.

"You can imagine how I felt, I who had been brought up by a pious mother to live in the way of the godly. But my trial had not yet begun. When they brought up the third beast my master turned to me as though to take the knife from my hand. Then I realized that he was looking strangely into my eyes, which were wide with wonder and fear. He started to laugh. I can hear him now.

" 'What are you afraid of? It's not hard. Come,' he shouted as though this idea had just come to him. 'You are my apprentice. You must learn this shoichet business too!' He seized me by the shoulders and turned me to face the animal. I looked back at him in horror, but I could see by the way he glared at me that he meant what he said. His hands clamped into my shoulders. Long afterward I could feel the bruises. 'You remember the prayer. Well, why should I do all the work?'

"I was afraid of my master, afraid to look back to where his eyes threatened and his fists clenched against his hips. I was afraid of his voice that commanded me. Perhaps it is wrong of me to think so, but I have always felt that that was my real Bar Mitzvah. When I had my Bar Mitzvah, in the synagogue, with half the town there facing me, and I choking the words in my throat, it was a great moment, and I felt that I was really becoming a man. But it was not until after I had been forced to take a life that I really changed and was no longer a child. Not only did I see in that moment the depths of baseness in a man, but when I turned, trembling, to face the beast, I approached another mystery. Who has to take a life stands alone on the edge of creation. Only God can understand him then. I looked about me for Him to deliver me. My master shouted at me to begin the ritual prayer. I could hear him dimly, shouting the first few words. His finger jabbed into my back. I started to whisper the prayer that I had heard so often from the shoichet. I felt as though I had suddenly been taken out of myself, as though this moment did not really exist and as though it had existed forever, as though it had never begun and would never end. Where had this happened to me before? I looked at the knife in my hand. Something in me pushed it away, pushed it away, but it lay there quietly, more real than any knife I had ever seen, the stains of blood already there, irrevocably waiting.

"As my tongue stumbled over the words of the prayer I blinked at the creature, trying to understand that it was going to die, and by my hand. I looked up, searching the sky that wafted down the pleasant air, and the sky crowded into my eyes piercingly, blindingly. Inside of me I could hear someone crying—so strange, so isolated. A living creature is different from the dead meat that I was used to handling. The difference frightened me. In front of me the cow was looking downward in a sort of modesty, with her eyelids covering her eyebulbs, which seemed so fine and large under their veil.

" 'Well, are you asleep?' my master shouted. The noise startled the cow, and she looked up at me. Her eye was large and brown and moist, and very deep. It made me dizzy to look. I closed my eyes and fell upon her. Will I ever forget that moment? It was as though I too were sinking with the knife. It was, as I have said, as though I were somewhere between living and dying. Not until I saw that the creature was dead did I realize that I was still alive. I have wondered since if that is what our forefathers felt when they made the sacrifices to renew their wonder and their fear and their belief, before they were forbidden to make them any longer. It is a mystery too deep for man."

Abraham broke off, and he and Chaim were still for a moment, while Chaim shook his head from side to side and Abraham nodded his up and down.

"Well, what happened?" Polsky leaned forward over the counter. "Did they catch him out or did the butchers get away with it? What difference did it make to the people," he answered himself, "as long as they thought it was kosher?"

"The villain," said Chaim. "The villain!"

"At first my master laughed at me because I stood there crying, with the knife bleeding in my hand. And then he began to shout at me to stop blubbering. But the dealer took my part and scolded him for forcing me to do the slaughter. Still, before I left he dug down into my shoulders again to let me know what would happen if I told anyone about this."

"Did you?" asked Polsky.

"When I went home I flung myself down and wept, and at first would tell my mother nothing. And when she asked me I shouted at her that my father had not meant for me to become a butcher.

My poor mother wept with me, protesting that neither would she have wanted it so. Finally I told her everything. We must go to the synagogue! We must denounce the butchers! But my mother would not hear of this. Who would protect us? What can a poor widow do? The butchers could kill us all and no one would raise a finger. She made me swear I would say nothing."

"Ah." Polsky looked relieved. "Well, what could you do? To those who ate it the meat tasted no different."

Chaim cast a reproachful glance at Polsky. "Of course, you could do nothing."

Abraham shook his head. "I don't know. I know that my master was punished. A few years later he had his skull split in an argument with another butcher. Perhaps God has punished me too for not denouncing the butchers."

"But what of your mother and your sisters?" said Chaim.

"That is what I felt." Abraham sighed. "Yet it is hard to know the will of God. And would the people have believed me? I have since learned a great deal about men. But that's the story. I have often wondered since then if a shoichet has any such feelings as I had when I killed that beast. Or was it merely because I should not have done it that I felt as though there were strange doors on the verge of opening for me. There are thoughts that draw a man in spite of himself. How often have I wished that I had a proper education. You are a fortunate man to know why you must do what you do. For me it was a terrible thing, but for you your work is a vocation with a purpose. I don't suppose that you, with your knowledge, could ever have felt this way."

"To tell you the truth, I don't even remember the first time I had to slaughter. It has become such a habitual thing," explained Chaim. "I know that each day when I wake up I will have to kill so many chickens, and, if not, what will I eat? I think that if you have to do it every day it is better this way. You don't waste time over it but cut cleanly, and it is over with. You were young, and it was something new and unexpected. I can imagine how you felt. Ah, those villains, God has repaid them, you can be sure of that. As for me, I was trained for it. It's my profession. Mind you I have always preferred to do circumcisions. It's more delicate work. Yes, I was trained to do circumcisions too. But people need chickens more often than they have sons, so economics have driven me to concentrate on chickens.

"Although, between you and me, I can't understand personally what people see in chickens. Myself I can't eat them. I can't stand the smell. You work around them all day, and they squawk you a headful; then to have to eat them at your meals too, it's just too much.

"I remember in the old country how my heart used to sink when a man would come to me and say, 'Here now, Chaim, I can't afford to pay you money now, so if you kill these five chickens for me you can keep the sixth one.' Well, can you refuse? So I'd kill the five chickens, and all afternoon I'd wonder whether I could sneak away and sell the sixth one to a peasant at the market.

"But my wife has eyes on her. She'd come into the shack as though she had smelled that chicken out, and she'd say, 'Chaim, and who's that chicken for, the one struggling in the bag?' And I'd say, 'What one? It's just a chicken.' And she'd say, 'Ah, Chaim, did someone pay you in chicken again?' And I'd have to nod my head.

"Sometimes I would ask her hopefully, 'Maybe you'd like to run down to the market for me, Bassieh, and try to sell it. We could buy meat.'

" 'Meat?' she used to say. 'What are you talking about, meat? Everybody buys meat. Even the poorest family buys a little meat occasionally. But they hoard their chickens for special occasions.'

"When you kill a chicken and the rest set up a din, everybody for miles around says, 'Those rich Jews, all the chickens that fellow has running around.' My wife, this makes her a *grande dame*, even if sometimes there's no bread to eat the chicken with. Everybody else eats chicken only on holidays, and we can have it nearly every day.

" 'Remember,' she used to say, 'anyone who walks into the house can see a table spread and a fine chicken laid out. Only yesterday the rabbi dropped in with his wife, that stuck-up, and I was roasting the chickens that Shloimehle left you, and believe me, this time she held her nose in the air for a different reason.'

" 'But Bassieh, I don't like chicken.'

" 'You're always saying you don't like chicken. But yesterday, when the rabbi and his wife let themselves be persuaded to sit down with us, you didn't say a word.'

" 'Maybe I didn't say a word in front of others, Bassieh, but I'm warning you, one of these days I'm going to set up such a crowing!'

"A lot of good it did me. If I didn't manage to sneak out to the market I'd choke on chicken."

"Well," said Abraham, who was rather surprised that such a dignified little man as Chaim should have such a wife, "and you still have to eat it?"

"No—sometimes, perhaps, the occasional spring. Now that her son's a manufacturer she's too busy learning the modern ways. She entertains now. You know, this entertaining. When I come home there are ladies with colds in their noses drinking tea. She serves them fancy little sandwiches and lets them know that her son's a manufacturer and that Lucy married a doctor and Paulia married a rich man's son. Mind you, she's a good woman, my wife—don't think I'm criticizing her, you've got to accept your luck—but she is apt to blow herself up a little, now that the children are doing so well."

He had educated children, this shoichet. Well, in that way Abraham himself did not have to be ashamed. But how did one tell a man who could say to you, "Look, this is my son, he does such and such, lives in such and such a place; here are my daughters, they are married to such and such"? How could one tell him of this son who already was and might have been, and that son who also was and should have been? There remained only one, and he was yet to be what had been ultimately intended for him. He felt himself very much drawn to this shoichet. They had much in common. How he would like to tell someone, to let it all come flooding out of him, to tell someone who might understand—and sympathize a little, perhaps. Much as he knew that no sympathy would be adequate and that he would remain as before, with the fullness of it only stirred about in his mind, the desire was on him to talk. To whom to talk? It was too easy to remind Sarah, to send her mind spinning back, too hard to make her forget again. And Isaac had a life to create ahead of him. One could not, because of one's own need, force a youngster on the brink of life to reminisce with the dead.

"Do you know," Chaim was saying, "that there is a trend nowadays against having the mohel perform circumcisions any more? There are actually doctors in town that went especially to learn the blessings."

"What?" said Abraham.

"Yes. It hurts that they don't trust us any more. Sometimes I feel like asking these young mothers, 'Did we do any wrong to your husbands?' They talk such nonsense. They say our instruments aren't clean. They say our beards get in the way. We have to live in fear that somebody might start a rumor that our hands shake. I've heard of a case. And once that happens—" Chaim shrugged. "But what's the use of talking? The ceremony isn't what it used to be, either. Remember how it was with us? A boy is born—we used to dance on the rooftops! When did they use to send a mohel away sober?"

"The mohel only?" Abraham laughed. "Three times in my life have I drunk the casks dry. Three births."

"Times have changed." Chaim sighed. "Places have changed. We must dance to the tune of the stranger."

Chapter Three

———◄●►———

Abraham looked the place over, inquired about rent, and made all the necessary calculations before he broached the subject to his family. It was an old semi-detached gray wood bungalow with a small open veranda, two feet of front lawn, a bedroom for himself and his wife, a living room that could be partly curtained off to make a bedroom for Isaac, and a kitchen. It already had a woodstove and an old wooden table in the kitchen. The woodstove they could pay for in installments. The table the landlord said he would throw in with the woodstove. There was a summer kitchen to store things in, and a small cellar that was reached by a trapdoor in the kitchen and housed the furnace.

The house, Abraham considered, was very low on the ground, and with no large cellar the cold would come up through the floors in the winter. But if he kept the furnace well stoked—and in addition there was the woodstove—they could make it do. To look at, it was shabby. The kitchen floor needed linoleum, and the whole would be pitifully bare at first. But gradually they could fill it in with furniture, paint a little bit, make it fresh. There were things a man could do himself in a place like this. And Sarah would find an outlet too, fixing and cleaning.

Before mentioning his plans, Abraham made a few visits to second-hand stores, priced one or two iron frame bedsteads, speculated about a new mattress, and carefully inspected an old davenport that didn't look too bright but seemed to have some spring left.

All in all, the idea seemed good. How much longer could the three of them squeeze their bodies and their personalities into Mrs. Plopler's big room? Of course it would run into a bit of money, but rent he would have to pay anywhere. So long as he was working—and Isaac too brought in a little money from his paper-carrier's route. Not that Abraham had spent a cent of it for themselves. Everything that the boy turned over went behind the counter into the bank. Isaac would need it someday.

The more he thought of it, the more he felt that it was absolutely necessary to move. Of late the landlady, for lack of anything else to occupy her mind with, had taken to watching Isaac and her girls. She had told both Sarah and Abraham on separate occasions, in conspiratorial whispers, that the youngsters were of an age where it was dangerous for them to be too familiar too much of the time. Doctors said—She didn't enlarge on what doctors said, but shrugged and sighed. "Well, it's nature."

Abraham had told her that Isaac was old enough to take care of himself, that he trusted his son, and that he hoped she could feel the same way about her daughters. Mrs. Plopler was horrified that he could think that she might mean such a thing. It wasn't that at all. Still, she managed to appear from unexpected places when Isaac was valiantly holding English conversation with the girls, and her smile and attitude paralyzed the boy's shy tongue into silence.

Abraham took his family to look at the house. The landlord occupied the other half of it, but there were separate front doors and separate verandas, with a solid veranda wall between that insured them a certain amount of privacy even on the porch. There was a back yard too, which could easily yield a small vegetable plot, once they had moved the garbage can farther back and cleared away the litter of wooden crates. The landlord's half of the back yard was almost completely occupied by a makeshift garage pieced together of boards, bits of corrugated tin, and old soft-drink advertisements. But he had promised to let them pile the crates on the garage if they wanted to. Crates and garage were necessary to his business, the landlord had explained importantly to Abraham, who now repeated it to his family, though he could not tell Isaac what this business was, since it had not occurred to him to inquire.

"Well?" Abraham turned cheerfully to his son as they paused for a second time to admire the window that was set in the front door. It was made up of pieces of colored glass cut in fancy patterns, and with the light from the outside shining on it, it threw colored shadows on the coat rack in the front hall. "What do you think, Isaac? Shall we take it?"

Isaac studied the window, aware that for the first time he was being asked to share the burden of an adult decision, and that the time was coming when he would have to make one for himself. "I think so," he said seriously.

Mrs. Plopler was not certain of how she should react. Sarah, with inspired tact, partly solved the landlady's dilemma by making her a partner in the decision. She was invited to an inspection of the new premises before they moved in. She was assured that she would always be a welcome guest. She was consulted as to the best type of coal for the furnace. By the time they left she had been won over and was even telling them why the move was a good idea.

"Of course, of course, I understand," she would repeat. "You are after all a family. One room is not enough, even though it's a very big room. It's not very nice for a grown boy to have to sleep in the same room as his parents. It's really a very nice little place you've found, even if it's not in such a good district. But what can you do? You can only afford so much, after all. And it's very nice that people who, after all, have not been in the country so very long, should be able to rent a little house for themselves. It was years before we moved out of our apartment into this house. Of course, we didn't want to move until we found exactly what we wanted. The minute I saw it, I thought how lucky you are. What if there are a lot of bootleggers around there? Do you have to have anything to do with them? Of course we can be just as good friends as ever. It's not so far, after all, although it's what we call the real old flats. And if I am a little bit afraid of walking through those streets in the dark, then your husband can take me up a ways."

Thus with a mixture of determined good nature and acidity Mrs. Plopler resigned herself to the loss of her tenants. All the same, she felt a little cheated, as though they had played a trick on her. It had all gone so smoothly, no disagreements, no arguments rising to a crescendo. It was almost as though the whole thing had happened behind her back.

When the time came and Abraham started to pull away at the borrowed handcart on which were piled the heavier of their recently accumulated belongings, while Isaac guided from behind, there were even a few tears from the landlady. Gertie and Goldie also watched from the steps. Isaac, with embarrassment, fancied what a funny picture he must make from behind as he leaned forward and pushed the clattering cart along. But he didn't care so much now. The girls were quite happy to be seen on the street with him, he knew, in spite of the fact that he was a greenhorn. He was no longer so green as before. They might giggle occasionally at his accent, but they were silent when he mentioned books that they didn't know.

Sarah carried the blessing of bread and salt into their new home and placed it on the kitchen table. Then they brought in their belongings. They left her to arrange things while they went with the borrowed handcart to collect first the davenport and afterward the dismantled frame bedstead. The new mattress was delivered later in the afternoon.

They brought in three boxes from the back yard to sit on while they ate their first meal in their new home.

"With my next week's pay," said Abraham gallantly, raising his glass of lemon tea, "I will invest in a chair for you, Sarah."

"And with my next week's pay"—Isaac, unable to contain himself any longer, followed suit—"I will invest in a chair for you, Pa."

Abraham looked at Isaac searchingly. "You'll have to sell a lot of papers," he said slowly, "to buy me a chair."

Isaac looked at his glass nervously. "If I have time after work I'll keep on with my paper route. But I think"—Isaac steeled himself to raise his eyes to his father's—"I might be able to give lessons in Yiddish and Hebrew in the evenings. My friend tells me that there are not many here who have studied as far as I have. I think I could even prepare boys for Bar Mitzvah if I keep on studying myself."

"You want"—Abraham picked his words carefully—"to quit going to the English school? What sort of work will you do?"

"The season is beginning now in the clothes factories. They are calling for boys to learn machining."

"A tailor."

"But I can study and teach in the evenings." Isaac trembled, and his heart beat more quickly, as it had begun to do at times ever since those days in the old country. "I can't"—Isaac gripped his glass violently and leaning forward, looked full into his father's face, his voice unnaturally high and dramatic—"I can't let you go on carrying me on your shoulders. It's not as though you were—as though things were—" Isaac choked on his words and rushed on. "I've already been to a place. I start work on Monday."

In spite of his displeasure at their content, Abraham heard the intensity in his son's words with a sensation of pleasure. My son, he could not help thinking with a flash of pride. Underneath the shyness, underneath the timidity, was the voice of strength that he could raise up. "On your shoulders"—he knew the right, the singing words.

Isaac had subsided but had not taken his eyes from his father's face. I'm old enough to make my own decision—he held these words in readiness, these and others, to back him up in his first big clash with his father. His face was slightly twisted from excitement and the feeling in his heart.

Sarah looked anxiously first at Isaac then at Abraham. But she said nothing and waited.

"Well," said Abraham after what seemed like a long time. "Well, I never thought that my son would be a tailor." Somehow he had known that the question would arise. How much could he do for them—alone, in the second half of his life, in a new country, working for another man? But he would have tried; he would have gone on working and hoping. He felt a bitterness arising in him again. After all his plans his son was to become a tailor in a sweat shop. But then, the Chassidim too had to work at other crafts while they studied. It was nothing new, this struggle. How ardent his eyes were, and stubborn. All his children were stubborn.

"It's nothing, nothing," said Abraham. "We don't have to be ashamed of having to work. My mother used to say, 'Work will sweeten your life.' 'It's a good thing that we have these sayings to remind us,' I used to tell her sometimes when I was tired, God forgive me.

"So you feel you must help? Well, this too is something fine. We will have a double celebration—a new house, and a new man in the house. What sort of place is it where you will work? You've been to see them, eh? Without consulting your father. Well, a new world. You knew I might not like it. What could I say? A man must make his own decisions, with God's help. They say, though, that there is much vulgarity in these shops. I don't know if you will like it. And shut in—they say it's hot working over those machines. See that you don't get to drinking too much cold water when you're sweating inside. But then in the evenings you will continue to study? Ah, there are many ways to reach an end. But your teachers in the English school will be very sorry to see you go. Who knows what they had planned for you? Such a promising student."

Isaac was surprised that the ordeal had passed, and so smoothly. He had braced himself as against a firm wall, and it had given way very easily, allowing him to fall into a new territory, a new part of his life. In his father's voice there was a new tone that Isaac heard with pleasure. He had done the right thing. Neither of his brothers could have done a more proper thing at this moment. He moved with a light step to comfort his mother, who was weeping silently. She always wept now, he thought dispassionately, laying his hand on her head. Whenever anything new happened, whether it was a good thing or a bad, she wept. It seemed to be the only answer that she had left to give to life when it made a gesture in her direction. But Sarah raised her head and smiled at him. "A new man in the house."

In the evening they had guests. Mr. and Mrs. Plopler and their family brought a honey cake. Polsky arrived with his wife, which turned the occasion into a major social event for Mrs. Plopler. She plunged joyously into a minute description of the composition of her honey cake and an intimate account of her own movements during the time she had been making it. The Polskys had brought a bottle of sweet red wine, and Mrs. Polsky, at the earnest request of Mrs. Plopler, described how she had prepared it. Chaim Knopp arrived. His wife, he explained, was visiting their daughter-in-law, who was sick in preparation for having her baby, but she had sent along a box of sweetmeats.

Sarah, flustered, ran into the landlord's next door to invite them to share the celebration and to borrow some cups and chairs. It turned out that Mr. Plopler and the landlord were business acquaintances. Plopler, Polsky, and the landlord wanted to play a game of cards, but since neither Abraham nor Chaim Knopp played they contented themselves with describing hands they had held. They went on to discuss card-playing mutual acquaintances, and from there to fights that they had seen develop over the cards. Chaim Knopp too told a story and soon the house was filled with animated conversation. Mrs. Plopler was in particularly good spirits, for several times she got the chance to make what she later described as "little thrusts" at Polsky, designed to put him in his place. But he, barefaced rogue, responded by practically flirting with her—how else to describe it?

Isaac's friend came over on his bicycle, and the two boys sat with the Plopler girls out on the front steps and took turns riding them around the block.

Abraham, when he got up to thank his guests, announced with pride Isaac's decision to share in the responsibility of the household. The guests congratulated him, and Mrs. Plopler especially was certain that the boy would make a girl a fine husband some day.

After the guests had gone the new house closed its silent walls around them. Sarah cleaned up. "Well." Abraham followed her into the kitchen. "So we have had a little party." There was surprise and something like apology in his voice. Sarah didn't answer but turned on the kitchen tap and began to wash the cups. "They wanted to wish us well," continued Abraham gently. "It was really very fine of them."

"Do you know what I fancied all evening?" Sarah smiled vaguely into the sink. "Singing. When was there a party in the house without singing?"

"My friend knows some people who might want their son tutored for his Bar Mitzvah," said Isaac quickly. "I told him sure I would do it. How do you like that?" They discussed the prospect of Isaac's first pupil, and Abraham advised his son in great detail until the time came for them to go to bed. Then Abraham lay helplessly beside his wife, waiting for her spasms to wear themselves out in exhaustion.

Chaim Knopp and Abraham were members of the same synagogue, the old white synagogue that was close to where Abraham lived. Chaim's wife preferred the new brick synagogue, which was attended by the more fashionable, but he was loyal to the synagogue that he had prayed in when he had first come to the country more than twenty-five years before. After the Friday-night service the two men sat on the bench outside and talked for a while. Chaim was not as happy as he might have been. He had reason to be happy—a son who was a manufacturer when he was only in his early thirties; two daughters married, one to a doctor, and one to a rich man's son; the third daughter already with a boy friend, not a doctor and not a rich man's son but a good, hard-working boy. His wife, of course, was not satisfied with the boy; he came under the water mark that the other girls had established; but this, Chaim felt, would straighten itself out. It was not this which made him unhappy.

It was his son the manufacturer. Things did not seem to go right with him. He was a good boy, although of course he was a boy no longer, but a man. Perhaps his trouble was that he was too clever, and of course he had got in with friends who were not friends but other rich men who knew too many pleasures. Not that his son did any wrong. People were always quick to say things about people who did a little better in the world than they. He was sure that his Ralph was not unjust to the workers—not the sort of boss, for instance, that Isaac had. He himself had heard Ralph mention Isaac's boss in a derogatory way. But Ralph grew richer. And this growing

richer is a thing a man should do carefully. Not that he, Chaim, had
any complaint. He was always welcome in the home of his son, and
Ralph often asked him if there was anything he needed. Not that he
would take anything while his own two hands could earn him a
living.

It was really the friends Ralph had. Of course in his business one
had to have plenty of liquor in the house. He entertained buyers and
influential people. If the others played cards—well, he had to play
too. It was understandable with a businessman. But he won a lot. It
was said that he had even won a share in another man's business.
But he had not said anything about it to his father, and there were a
lot of jealous people in the world who had nothing to do but talk.
Not that he discussed any of his business dealings with his father
any more. What would a shoichet know about finance?

It was really quite remarkable what being a businessman involved.
He often had to make trips out of town. They sometimes took him a
week—even longer. It was hard work, when you considered it. And
going to various places, stags with other businessmen; places where
they played cards and had entertainments to keep them good-
natured when they did business with each other. It was not the sort
of life that he had lived himself. Chaim's wife, of course, thought it
was fine. She liked to go to their house up in the heights and be
driven in their car. He liked to be driven in their car himself, though
not on Saturdays.

But lately this sad thing had happened, which Abraham already
knew about. His son's wife had lost her baby. And the doctors did
not think that she would ever be able to have another. Well, it was
true that they already had a little girl, a precious little thing. Still,
the news that they might never have a son was a blow to Ralph, a
blow to all of them. Of course, he, Chaim, personally did not believe
the doctors, but still, it was hard.

Abraham felt honored that Chaim had confided in him. Some of
what he said was not quite clear, although it was obvious that if the
son drove his car on Saturdays he was already one of those who did
not observe the rules of his religion as strictly as he should. For the

rest—well, if Chaim expressed himself so vaguely perhaps he wanted it so, to talk about it a little while without any disloyalty. Once a feeling has been expressed too clearly it can't be snatched back by the tongue. It becomes something else—an accusation, perhaps. And Chaim would not, Abraham knew, accuse his son in front of a stranger. Abraham, somewhere, had heard something about Chaim's son. But that didn't matter now. It was the other that was the sad thing, to lose a child and lose the chance of a son.

"I don't believe the doctors either," he told Chaim emphatically. "No one can make me believe it. What right have they to say it? Just because she had one difficult time. No, who can say that a son won't be born into the world? Only death is irrevocable." The feeling was in Abraham now, strongly, to talk. He had held off so far because he had not wanted to share it promiscuously with someone who might not care, who might change the subject afterward as though it were nothing and talk about the heat of the day. But Chaim had confided in him.

"Not for nothing," Abraham began, "did my mother use to say that everything in one is the property of none. A wise woman she was. Here you see it in your own life. Another man would say to you that you have every reason for happiness. And yet—there it is."

Chaim nodded his head and sighed.

"And yet"—Abraham made the plunge—"and yet there was a time, I think, when I had everything. Then I did not even think about it, but now, when I look back, I had at least the beginning of everything. God saw this and said it was too much. Chaim, I've never told you what happened, why we came over here as we did, nearly naked as we were."

"No," said Chaim. "I have often wanted to ask you. But I thought to myself, No; maybe it's something he doesn't want to talk about."

"It is a hard thing to talk about, just like that. Once I had three sons."

"Yes, I have gathered this."

"A small nothing, three sons. Well, you have probably imagined what happened. It is not hard for a Jew to imagine. It is only hard for a father to believe."

They sat on the bench outside of the synagogue. Isaac had already walked home with some friends, and the other men had long ago dispersed. They would be late for supper, but supper was always late on a Friday evening. Abraham felt a reluctance now that he had committed himself to telling, and at the same time a fierce desire to talk.

"They were not ordinary boys, my sons. I say this not because they were mine but because it was so. This was recognized by everyone. I have always known that something extraordinary was going to happen in my lifetime. I was born with this feeling, as though it had been promised to me in another place, another lifetime. If this were not so, why would I be alive to feel it? I had a difficult time in my youth. I was not a child for very long. But that does not matter. In my sons it seemed as though some augury were beginning to fulfill itself.

"Moses was the eldest. To tell you the truth, I cannot remember whether he sang in his cradle. It has always seemed so, but I do not wish to exaggerate where there is no need. He sang from the time when it is first possible for a child to sing, in a voice always so sweet and sure of itself that people would stop what they were doing and listen and wonder. He picked up tunes—it was almost as though he had gotten them himself, directly from the source of all music.

"Jacob was our second. As Moses was stocky, he was lean, with Sarah's slimness. He had—people said that his eyes were like mine. Before he was a few months old I can swear that he understood what we were saying. And before long he was answering us, talking almost like a man. To tell you the truth, we were a bit frightened. We did not know how much that child really understood. From day to day he learned more. Before he could walk properly we had to try to talk— When we spoke in front of him of things that a child shouldn't know, we had to speak in Ukrainian. Everything he saw and heard he had to know about. It did not stop him long, our speaking in Ukrainian.

"They were scarcely two years apart in their ages. They were very close to each other. Everywhere they went, two little men together. When Moses was five we wanted to send him to Chaider. It was time for his studies to begin. When the time came Moses wouldn't go without Jacob, and the two of them set up such a wailing that we thought, for a few days, just to quieten them down, we would let Jacob go with his brother. Well, at three years Jacob took to the books. He learned so quickly that the rabbi had to put him in a separate place to learn by himself. Not that they didn't have time for mischief too, my boys. When the rabbi fell asleep and the boys glued candy into his beard, whose boys were caned when the truth came out? To give you an idea of the kind of head that Jacob had, I must mention that by the time he was five he was already well in the Histories. The Histories—how many rich men celebrate with parties because their sons at the age of eight or nine have finally reached the Histories?

"These were the sons of Avrom the butcher. Isaac wasn't born until Jacob was three years old, nearly four. He was— Well, you see him now, a listening child, a wonderer. How he worshiped his brothers! To them he was a toy, to be taught, to be fooled with. He too learned quickly. Things go into him. He likes to consider. He does not let them out so easily. But when he does say something, then you can see the kind of a head that he's got. He is older than his years. But then, who wouldn't be?"

Abraham paused. It seemed to him that he had said much but told little of what really was. Words sounded like hollow boasts. He was thankful that Chaim said nothing.

"Well, the two boys studied until there was no more for them to learn in our small town. Moses was already known for miles around as a cantor. Still, he wanted to learn more music, to develop his voice. Jacob taught in order to continue his studies. They wanted, both of them, to go to the big city, where there was a seminary. Here Jacob could teach and continue to study, and Moses could continue to sing as a cantor in a big synagogue, and continue to study as well. They were willing to work, my boys. They did not just expect that their father should, in any way that he could, pay for them. They worked hard.

"After Isaac had his Bar Mitzvah they set out for the big city. They had been gone before to study and work, but only to the neighboring small towns and cities. They had always been home for the high holidays. Whenever Sarah felt lonely I could always send them a message. and they would come—young boys, on foot if they had not the money for the carriage, to see their mother. We never felt that they were really gone."

Abraham looked about him. The sky was beginning to darken around the edge of the mountain. How long ago was it? Four years? More? Less? It was as now. He was beginning to find it more difficult to talk. Something was beginning to pull painfully at the back of his throat. He leaned forward and scrutinized the ground in front of the bench, without seeing it.

"This year it is different. The house is more quiet. No ringing laughter and snatches of song. Isaac reads a good deal and is often by himself. Pesach is approaching, and we are preparing to celebrate the Passover. But it is to be a different Passover. It will not be such a celebration this year with the boys away for the first time. It is too far away for them to come back this year. There is not enough money. In the house it is beginning to be lonely. My wife goes about the house sighing because her children are growing up. Where will they celebrate? Who will take them in and make them at home?

"In the town the peasants and the townspeople are preparing for their Easter. They are beginning to be restless. The church bells ring more often, and the priests call them for meetings. Suddenly, from nowhere, a troop of cossacks appears. It is quartered in a neighboring village, but the cossacks wander about everywhere in the town. The goyim look at the Jews. The Jews start to look at each other. The air becomes harder to breathe. At night I crawl into my root cellar and bury my valuables, some here, some there, as my mother used to do. Everything that is small enough is hidden away. Other Jews that I know slip silently out of town, those that have a stronger premonition. We begin to be happy that Jacob and Moses are away. We barricade our doors at night and go as little as we can out onto the streets. We do not let Isaac out of our sight. Above the neighboring grocery store three families have gathered together and have already barricaded themselves in. There is a quietness in the town that is not of sleep. Still, Sarah prepares for Passover and we help her about the house, hoping that nothing will really happen this time. But in bed we lie awake and listen and wait.

"On their Good Friday evening the Christ dies. The church bells begin to clamor, and at the signal the cossacks come thundering into the town. The church doors burst open, and the goyim surge into the street, looking for Jews. Your neighbor is no longer your neighbor. A fiend has possessed him. Is this a man? No. He reveals what is inside of him, a beast.

"For three nights and days the church bells ring, and for three nights and days we hide. First of all the townsfolk lead the cossacks to the grocer's. The house is dark. They start to shout up at the Jews. They have been told that the families are hiding there. They make loud jokes and tease them to come out. Inside the house remains dark and silent. Those within—you can imagine how they clutch each other and pray. Then the crowd grows noisier. They start to shout and curse up at the house. Our neighbors, the townsmen, egg the cossacks on. A group of townspeople run to get kerosene and fagots. The cossacks set fire to these. All night the house blazes. Those inside are trapped by their own barricade. The night is filled with screaming. It vies with the church bells for an audience in heaven.

"That was the first. All night they go from house to house. What are our barricades to them? What are our lives to them? Barbarians. Mikhail Michlosky invited me to the wedding of his son. We drank wine together. They told me afterward that he was one of the worst of them.

"In the meantime we find our way to the home of a peasant with whom I have dealt for years. His wife takes us in and hides us in the vegetable cellar. For three days and four nights in all we are in darkness. From time to time the farmer or his wife brings us water. We eat dirty carrots and raw potatoes. But that is nothing. At least here we know, frightening though it is to spend all this time in darkness, breathing rank air—especially for the child—at least we know that we are safe for now. Then, on the fourth morning, they come to tell us that all is still. The Jews are beginning to return to the town. Christ is sated.

"We emerge from the cellar as from the tomb. We are alive again, but even the light seems hostile to us. For a while we are nearly blind. It hurts us to see. Perhaps, after all, now that I think of it, the light was our friend and wanted to shield us. I say a prayer because we have survived. We wonder how long it will take to get word from the boys that there has been no pogrom at the seminary. The streets of the town are nearly empty. The townspeople are sleeping off their orgy, or perhaps they are tired from their exertions and care only to stay within and fondle their loot. Who can understand the minds of barbarians? The cossacks, too, are gone. A few Jews like ourselves hurry back to see what has become of their homes. We greet each other but scarcely speak. There is still smoke in the air from the fires.

"On the way to the center of town we are met by a neighbor of ours. When she sees us she bursts into tears and runs past us. I call after her, 'Rachel, what is it? Whom have you lost?' She does not stop, does not answer. My wife begins to cry. My heart is suddenly heavy. As we walk toward the square we see a knot of people gathered. They are looking upward. On two long—I don't know what they were—poles, something is hanging, two bodies. Something in my heart gives a—a rip. I start to run toward the crowd. Ahh-h-h!"

Abraham moaned as though something were strangling him. He looked away from Chaim. His fingers worked convulsively in his beard. His throat was constricted and painful so that he had to speak slowly. His face was red, and there was sweat on his temples.

"Can you imagine what good boys they were?" There was an edge of pride in his voice. "To walk all that way. Money they didn't have. Their shoes were worn through. All that way to be with us for Passover. How fine, how fine. What could have possessed them?

Why couldn't they have stayed at the seminary this one Passover? Pesach comes—every year. Foolish boys. Oh no, not foolish, my sons—my fair fruit. To give us pleasure, to be with us. For one year we could have done without it, and still have that pleasure now. It's useless to argue. It's done, it's done. Can you wonder that she stands now, Sarah, in one place for so long, and forgets what and where? And for the boy to see this!"

Abraham got up. He wiped his hand across his face. He walked to the corner of the synagogue and stood for a moment, looking across the street toward his house. For a few moments he moved about aimlessly, quickly, back and forth. Sweat and tears ran down his face. His arms moved as though he had no longer any control over them. Chaim could think of nothing to say.

Finally Abraham sat down again. "We thought that my wife had died right then," he resumed in a voice that was, for him, quiet. "The women carried her away. I remained with the men to cut down my sons. For a while this problem occupied all of my thoughts: how to get them down without hurting them. As though they could be hurt any more. They had been clever to get them up so high. I don't know what happened to Isaac. I think he ran first to his mother and then back to me, and could not find a place for himself. I know that when we brought the bodies back to the house he was beside me.

"Well? Death cuts a gap in life. Suddenly you see nothing, the pit. A piece is wrenched away from you. An arm? A leg? No. These you can do without. A piece of your soul. A piece of what ties you to God. The death of a friend makes you think. It makes you look about you and wonder that your own life goes on. You must put your life together again differently, without his smile, without his hopes. When I was young I heard that a friend of mine had died."

Abraham spoke more quickly now that he was speaking impersonally. He was regaining control of his voice.

"A young boy, too. I had to remind myself time and again that now I must no longer ask, 'And what has become of Daniel? Has he learned to dance yet, or does he still knead the dough with his feet?'

He was not even a good friend. I didn't even like him particularly. Still, he was young. Who cannot pity the delicate green things that die? In the end I told myself that God knew best whom to take and whom to leave. It was not for me to argue His decisions. So Daniel gradually became just a boy who died. And after him there were others—sickness, pogroms. God knew best. My mission was my family, to bring up my sons. And what sons they were! What could not a great singer and a great scholar have done for our people?

"It was meant to be. We cut them down and brought them home for burial. We laid them on the floor that they had first crawled upon. In the next room my wife lay as dead. Isaac went from room to room. A friend wanted to take him home with her, but he would not go. Finally he fell asleep on the floor in a corner of the room with his mother.

"The house was empty. The furniture was broken. Some of it had been carted away. The samovar that I had tried to hide was gone, and so were clothes, cutlery, and, as I discovered later, some of the things that I had buried. Even the pictures on the wall, of my father and mother and sons, had been ripped. I saw all this clearly. My head was clear and empty. I saw all and felt nothing—nothing but an emptiness of the heart, as though my heart had gone to hide from what it had seen.

"What more can be said? To give such sons is to make a promise. To take them away again, and in such a way—I felt it was unholy. I was mad. I turned, in my heart, away from God. I felt that my soul was gone. All I had now was my frantic body. All I wanted was to move, to run run run. My body screamed to wear out all its movements in violence and to drop down in a heap, unfeeling, somewhere, anywhere.

"I started to sell everything that was left: my buried valuables, my little shop. Anything to get away. On the streets some goyim turned away when they saw me. Others wanted to make it as though nothing had happened. I said nothing. I looked at them. If God was not human, how could they be expected to be?"

Chaim looked up at him. "You turned away from God?"

"So," said Abraham, "but not now. When I speak of it my blood surges about. Another time."

For a few moments they were silent. Above them evening had dimmed the sky, and night was beginning to throw its long shadows. Isaac came around the corner, looking for his father. They watched him approach.

"My life," said Abraham. They rose and went to meet him.

Chapter Four

———◄◆►———

There certainly was a great deal of vulgarity in the shop, Isaac discovered; more than his father realized. The men and girls in the stuffy factory, which smelled of sweating bodies, were very free and easy together. Not that much was meant, in general. Sometimes Isaac himself thought of something to say that was clever and vulgar. But the vulgarity wasn't limited to the workers. Everybody in the shop knew that the big boss himself had only two joys in life: penny-pinching and fanny-pinching.

There were fights in the shop too, between the workers—sometimes over the work, sometimes over vulgarities that were said too sincerely and taken as insults. One of the girls had thrown a pair of cutting scissors at one of the men halfway across the room, because of something he had said. Luckily the scissors had only caught his scalp lightly, but there had been a big gash and much blood. They had had to call a doctor to treat the girl for hysterics. That was a month ago. Now the two were engaged to be married, and a collection had been taken up among the workers for a wedding present.

The work itself was not what he had expected. It was not as in the old country. There, when you learned a trade you learned it all. A tailor was a tailor, from the first snip of the scissors to the last button. Here he couldn't call himself a tailor. If he could have made a pair of pants, a jacket, it would have been something—out of his hands, something whole. But from the first day when he had sat down at the machine, months ago, to the present, he was on pockets. Sometimes, for a variation, it was belt facings—but mostly pockets. Isaac had a fantasy that had occurred to him during those months when the pockets had sped at an increasing tempo from his machine.

Someday I'll stand before God, and He'll say to me, "What can you do to get into heaven?" And I'll say to Him, "God, I can make You a pair of pockets." And He'll say, "I'm sorry, I'm a working man. I have no time to keep my hands in my pockets."

There were many thoughts that went through Isaac's mind as he worked. They came as though drawn out by the loud, whirring machine. Sometimes they set him smiling and chuckling to himself. Or else they were warm and promising and he'd glance up from his work, blushing. Then there were the gloomy thoughts that so often settled over him, those that went beyond laughter and love and that stopped and hovered over the uncertainty of life.

Of late he had taken to reading more and more books from the English library. That was something that his father approved of. Books were to make something fine of him, an educated man. The Hebrew and the Yiddish books weren't enough. They dealt with past things, old solutions. Perhaps these books could answer the questions about his life, about people, the questions that sorely needed answering. But the books, though they pulled him further and further into themselves, brought him no closer to certainties. Neither, when he turned from them to his life, was there any certainty. What new friend could yield him an answer to his unvoiced question, "You, are you good or bad?" What action could answer definitely to the demand, "Are you right or wrong?"

Good and bad, right and wrong had been connected with childhood. When had he been a child last? Reluctantly Isaac remembered Nikolai Korodin and his wife, Manya. In the middle of the night his father had knocked on the back door. The dogs had not barked at them when they entered the yard because they knew his father and the scraps of meat from the butcher shop too well. Without a word Manya, in her long nightdress and her cap, had led them in the darkness to the root cellar. She had let them in and closed the door behind them. Ah, but she had looked funny. In the cellar he had had long spasms of helpless laughter that exploded from between his clenched teeth and ran out of his eyes. His parents had thought that it was fear and hysterics. Perhaps it had been, a little bit. The cellar was blacker than night, because it was closed and night is open. It

was stuffy and cramped, and there was little air, but vegetable smell
and earth. Not until much later did Nikolai bring water and bread.

It was such a long time to be in the darkness. There had been only
the feel of his father and mother to protect him from all the shapes
he sensed. There were moments when the fear had made him feel
as though he were suffocating, unable to catch his breath, and had
put stitches in his heart. The air had grown worse and worse, as
though they were being buried deeper and deeper. Always there had
been the double hope and fear, the hope that Nikolai would come at
last and open the door, perhaps to bring food, or just to get some
vegetables. Carrots, Isaac had prayed. Let them want carrots. Then
when he imagined that noises approached there was the sudden stifling fear that it would be someone else, some monster come for
them. As the time crept by, another fear gradually grew in him.
What if Nikolai and Manya would never let them go? What if they
intended to keep them locked in here forever?

Nikolai or his wife came to them only in the night, for the neighbors must not know. When he opened the door Isaac strained past
him to see if there were really stars left, to catch a glimpse of something—any shapeless thing in the yard to try to focus his eyes on.
He took great rasping breaths of air that filled his lungs to the coughing point. Then Nikolai shushed him and he felt his father's hand
grip tightly his own. But it was so good.

On the fourth morning the door was wrenched open. "It's safe
now. Get out quickly!"

They crawled from the cellar, unable to move quickly, although
Nikolai urged them on. What a cramp his body was! How his eyes
ached—unbearable shooting pains from the sudden light! How
dazed, yet how good he felt! It was safe now, Nikolai had said. How
good Nikolai was, in spite of his gruffness and the rough haste with
which he had helped to pull them out of the cellar. As he walked
along the lane, a little behind his father, who was cautiously advancing, he had to keep pressing his fists in his eyes to ease the hurt. But
he thought of Nikolai and Manya, of how different they were from
the others.

Even after he had seen what waited for them in the square, after all of the terrible events had unfolded themselves, he had remembered Nikolai and Manya; at least they were good. He had clung to the idea. Why were they good? What was it that had made them different? On the street they looked no different. Nikolai was a surly peasant. They weren't half as friendly as Mikhail Michlosky, who, everybody said, had led the cossacks to the grocery store. Yet there it was. The thought of them remained like a streak of light in the darkness.

The darkness. In the middle of the night he had awakened and crept to the door of the living room, where his parents sat mourning on the floor by the bodies of his brothers. He did not want to go in to where his brothers, who had lain beside him, lay; but he was a man too, and this was his place. And besides, he did not want to stay in this room by himself with the broken furniture and the torn pictures and the walls that had also been mutilated in the search for plunder. He had crept into the living room and sat down on the floor beside his father.

As he watched, his eyes swollen and heavy, he caught his brothers breathing once or twice under the heavy velvet cloth. Aha! he thought—fooling me, pretending. Before he fell asleep against his father's shoulder he smiled at the sheets. Soon they would throw them off. They would stand up and smother the candles that threw horrible shadows on the wall and on the faces of those who sat beside them. When they laughed he would tell them that it was not a good joke. It was a time, even after they were buried, before he fully realized that there would be no more joking between them— not until after they went to say good-by to Nikolai Korodin and Manya.

There had been such an agitated, silent bustle of preparation to leave. He had scarcely even left the house by himself. His father didn't want him to. When he saw his friend Menasha it had been as though from a great distance. Menasha had looked at him with such timidity and respect that he had felt himself completely set apart. Menasha, he knew, had lost only an uncle.

Only once did he and Menasha get together again as of old, in Menasha's back yard. Menasha, to say something, had suddenly said a swear word. Isaac followed suit with another. Then together they solemnly called forth every curse they knew to fall on the heads of their enemies. It surprised them how many oaths they knew, and how easily they could say the ones they had always known but had never dared use before. But they dared now. So long as they didn't shout loudly enough to bring out Menasha's mother, who would have indignantly put an end to their cursing with a sharp flow of oaths of her own because she didn't want her son to grow up a *grobion*, a vulgarian, they were both safe. They stood there, facing each other, standing with their legs apart, as though to brace themselves against the shock the world would have at their words, and heaved their mighty oaths. The sound of their own words had a heady effect on them. Excited, they repeated themselves, elaborating their curses until it became a sort of contest between them. Finally, his ingenuity exhausted, Isaac burst into indignant sobs. Menasha, in sympathy, broke into tears as well.

That had been his farewell to Menasha, who was only a name now.

The day came when they went, all three of them, to see Nikolai Korodin and his wife, Manya. It was only right to take a ceremonious parting, although, of course, since they planned to steal across the border, not even Nikolai and Manya were to know that it was a parting. These people had saved their lives. Even though neither his father nor his mother seemed to care very much about this, still it meant something to show their gratitude.

Manya invited them into the house. Nikolai appeared from his orchard. They went into the living room, which was used only on special occasions. It had a stale smell that seemed to have been left over from a bygone celebration. The walls were painted with decorations in many colors. Peasants liked bright things. Their own was white with very little decoration. But of course they weren't peasants. That smell must come from what they eat, Isaac guessed —pork.

Isaac wondered if Nikolai and Manya understood that they were there to thank them, that the large slab of cow that his father had brought with them was a thank offering. Of course they must. Yet he felt that something should be said as well. It was a time for words, a time to break down the restraint that seemed to hold his father and Nikolai to the topic of crops and the fruit orchard. Maybe his father was waiting for the moment. Isaac listened to the conversation and waited too, letting his eyes rove over the flowery walls. That was one thing about colors and ornaments: there was always something to look at.

Then Manya went into the kitchen to prepare some tea. No more bread and water. Isaac idly watched her move into the kitchen. Would the smell become stronger when she opened the kitchen door? Then he'd know it was pork. Through the open door of the kitchen Isaac recognized with a shock their own samovar that had disappeared during the pogrom. He felt an involuntary shudder run through him. It stood on the sideboard in the kitchen, to the left of the door. It was unmistakable. It had been his mother's pride. It had stood her for a dowry when she had married. For a moment he felt panicky, as he had felt when he thought he heard alien footsteps outside the vegetable cellar. The room was suddenly filled with danger. He forced his eyes away from the kitchen. The bright walls began to close in on him. He tried to breathe, but his breath seemed to be caught on a jagged stitch in his chest. Had Nikolai seen that he'd noticed? He turned his head slowly around and glanced sideways at his father, who was listening to Nikolai. He saw in Abraham's eyes that he too had seen. But Nikolai was concentrating on the slow rattling of his own words, punctuating them with a flat forefinger on the table. Isaac breathed slowly, easing his breath over the stitch. His father's eyes, now perfectly blank, moved past his own, and he said something in answer to Nikolai. His mother was not looking at anything but sat still, her swollen eyes on nothingness. Isaac didn't want to look toward the kitchen again. But in spite of himself his eyes kept slithering toward the kitchen door.

Then, thank heaven, Manya closed the door. Isaac felt a prickling all over his body, a nervous urging to get up and go—quickly, to run if necessary. But his father sat, impassive and calm. Of course they couldn't go yet. It would give them away. It was as though they were the guilty ones and mustn't give themselves away, mustn't be caught knowing. He felt no indignation yet, nothing but fear and the automatic guilt of the prey.

Manya brought another samovar and served tea. Isaac's mind had ceased to function, but he could feel the formal little scene that was enacted with few words in a frightening silence. Ages passed for him before they got up at last and said their good-bys. Ages passed before the relief of the open door. And for some reason when they passed through the open door the relief passed as well. As they walked toward the gate, with Nikolai's dogs ambling along beside them, Isaac felt such a sudden sense of loss sweeping over him that it seemed that not until this moment had he really understood that his brothers were gone forever.

Perhaps for this reason he didn't like to remember that visit to Nikolai—for the memory of Manya's low-slung form in the bright dress disappearing into the kitchen, and the sight of the samovar; for that sense of desolation that came so vividly the moment he remembered the first breath of fresh air he had gulped when they left. That was where his father showed his superiority. Not even the mention of Nikolai's name had ever crossed his lips again since that day. He had not appeared surprised or broken his silence even to condemn. Isaac had often wondered afterward whether his father had really seen.

In the years that had passed Isaac had often found himself thinking about it—not wanting to, but unwittingly finding that his mind had gone back to that point in time. He had thought it out over and over again; he had not even flinched, finally, from the idea that if Nikolai had been abroad on the nights of the pillaging, then he might have been there at the murders as well. Might he not even have taken part? Then why had he protected them? Here thought broke down. How could he accuse Nikolai of goodness? Better, like his father, forget the existence of the peasant. But he found him everywhere, even in the books. They too worked out a question carefully, so that in the end it became two questions, or three.

Why couldn't he be like his father, keeping his eyes fixed somewhere, at a point, so that everything he saw had to mold itself to his perspective? Instead his eyes wavered from point to point, and nothing remained fixed under his stare but, moving, changed and revealed itself as something new. Even when he looked into himself, his own motives, the things he thought and the things he professed, he could see a thousand hidden sins. Thank goodness they didn't know what he was really like, his parents—what a sickly son had been saved for them.

But he had been saved; that fact remained. He was alive. At least he was here to feel the mystery of life, its contradictions; to discover, perhaps, its possibilities. If he was confused often, at least sometimes he could sense vaguely what his father seemed to know for a certainty; that he was not here for nothing. There was something in him that rose up sometimes, a feeling, a longing, a power, an astonishment. Was this what his father knew—that there was a purity somewhere, in spite of Nikolai, in spite of himself and his degrading thoughts? There was something in life itself that his father had drawn him back to, that waited for him. He must go on from there.

When the butcher-shop cat had kittens again Abraham decided to take one home to his wife. The responsibility would be good for her. She needed something to take care of; something lively would cheer her up. Abraham, Chaim, and Polsky examined the litter carefully, trying to find a he-kitten in the bunch. Polsky subjected each yowling baby to a rude examination in his big red paw. The mother cat, gratified, turned over on her spine, raised her paws up, and lolled about, letting them admire her brood. Polsky teased Chaim because, after all, he should be an expert in these matters. Were they circumcising Jewish tomcats nowadays? And Polsky laughed, not particularly disturbed that they didn't appreciate his belly-warmers.

They were still bent over the box when a customer came in. The customer pushed her bulk in next to Chaim. "That one's a boy; the other two are girls," she said immediately and positively.

"Of course." Chaim beamed. "That's what I thought." He arose and carefully dusted his knee. "Let's put a mark on him."

They named it Pompishke—a kind of dumpling. Sarah was pleased. Live things, Abraham told himself, certainly liven up a house.

The house was destined for even more livening up. Shortly afterward Pompishke brought home a scrawny little kitten that no amount of wishful thinking could prove to their now experienced eyes was a male. They called it Knobble, which is garlic. "You can't have pompishkes without knobble," said Sarah with a sudden flash of humor that made Abraham feel that if there were ten cats they'd keep them all.

"To say that I lost my faith is not enough." Weeks had passed since Abraham had begun to tell his story to Chaim, weeks during which he had not mentioned the subject. Once in the butcher shop Chaim had mentioned it, but Abraham had waved it away with an odd expression on his face. "Not now, Chaim; another time."

Now, on another Friday evening as they sat on the bench outside the synagogue and watched the children playing across the street, he continued as though he had not been interrupted by the passage of time.

"I lost my mind, my eyes that could see ahead of me. I did not merely desert Him, I became insolent. I spoke to Him, to say rudely is correct, but not merely rudely—with storm, with hatred.

"We fled blindly. We stole across the border to Poland. Everywhere I thought I saw how He had turned His hand against me—not merely against me, against all of Jewry.

"We were met at the border by Polish Jews who helped us to escape—helped us! Pious Jews with long sideburns and black frocks —they made a living of it. Big business. They stole the very stockings from the legs of my wife. Everything they saw they took. Of this too I accused Him. How He must despise us, to take my sons and let these grow to make us hated by all the world, to make us even hate ourselves.

"In Warsaw we stopped. Where to next? There was an ocean ahead of us. I wanted to plunge myself into it. Ha! All sorts of things go on in the world, whether you pay attention or not. And when you want to do something, suddenly they're there. Countries want you, countries don't. Who wants a Jew? This is our life, to hammer on doors.

"Here they wanted only farmers. So, I am a farmer. I started to make papers to go with my family as farmers. In the meantime I went to work. Papers cost money, and what I had left that I had saved from the various thieves was needed for papers and for the journey.

"The man I went to work for knew well that I was in need. He put me to work as though I were under the whip. I am not such a young man as I once was, when I was strong as a bull and could carry half a carcass as nothing. Sometimes of late I have begun to feel pains in my arms when I must lift a heavy section, and when I go from the warmth to the refrigerator. But for him I worked. And I didn't care. I was glad that the sweat ran from me in the icebox. I was glad that when I came home to the room with the roaches and the bedbugs at night I lay down and could not move. There are times when all the work that you have done and all the suffering that you have lived through lay themselves down on you. Then you cannot move, you cannot breathe.

"Still inside of me I raged. I do not know what went on between us those few months. We lived together, we moved about, as shadows cast upon the same wall, meeting, touching, unseeing, unfeeling."

Abraham listened for a moment while a mother called to her children from the house across the street. He sighed—a long sigh—without knowing that he had done so.

"I scarcely realized that they two had been left to me. I was selfish, wrapped up in my own storms.

"In Poland there was a typhus epidemic. Just as our papers had come through and they were already making out our ship's cards, Isaac caught the typhus."

Abraham stopped talking again. How could it sound so commonplace? Inside of him an excitement was forming, and pain, like the scar of an old wound, throbbed in his voice when he spoke.

"Do you know the typhus?" Abraham looked about him. How could he describe it? "A fire was kindled inside of him. He lay there and the fever steamed from him." In his mind he could see it, the dingy room, Isaac tossing on the bed—yes, steaming. "For days I watched him lying there, helpless against the tortures that scalded him. I felt the hot drenched sheets. I looked on his suffering face. It seemed as though I saw him now for the first time. I had not known the way his underlip curved outward. I had not realized that his jaw was so thin. This was my son!

"Gradually the fever built itself up in him. One night he could contain it no longer. He ran screaming from the bed. I caught him in my arms and fought with him. I clenched his body, drenched and squirming against me. It was as though he were swimming in a fiery bath. It was scalding to hold him. He looked at me with hatred. His fingers tore at my beard. He cursed me!

"It was then that I knew, my God, that You had left me one son. And he was leaving me. You were tearing him from me! How fiercely I loved him, I who had almost forgotten him in my selfishness! I fought with You that night. I clung to him. I breathed on him. I carried his kicking, screaming body to the bed, and I held him. I laid my head against his heart and heard the tumult within him, and I prayed. I prayed that You should forgive my great error. I wept! I cried that You should not take from me the gift that I had seen too late.

"All night I held him, I poured my strength into him, I prayed—all the prayers that I knew and prayers that came of themselves. Beside me my wife sat, a frozen prayer.

"Toward morning there was a miracle. He opened his eyes and called me 'Father.' We, Sarah and I, we could do nothing but weep."

Chaim Knopp wiped his eyes with the back of his hand. "A miracle," he said.

Abraham resumed a little while later. "By the time the boy was well enough to travel, our papers were no longer any good. Now the Canadian government wanted something else. We had to make new papers. We waited for months. Now I wanted to hurry because I was impatient to begin again, to send down our roots, somewhere. I was worried about the boy, you know. It left him with a touch of the heart—all he'd gone through. Every time I looked at him I thought: A miracle. I knew I had to bring them someplace soon. My wife could not bear much more. The boy's illness had sucked what was left of her spirit from her.

"Somehow, at last, we were on the ship. Then we were on the train. We had been running, moving, for so long, I no longer knew how to stop. It was as though the wheels below had taken control of our lives. On and on we rode. It's strange how we came to this city. All of a sudden I knew, as though I had received a message, that it was time to stop. And so I gathered them up, my own ones, and we came away. The wheels moved off without us."

Abraham looked about him. It was late. He had not noticed when the street lights had gone on.

"What do you think, Chaim, a wristwatch is a nice thing to buy a boy for his birthday? Not a boy any more, really—a young man. Sarah and I were thinking of a wristwatch. His friends all seem to have watches, and he should not go without, hard-working boy that he is."

"A wristwatch would be a fine thing," said Chaim. "I remember how happy Ralph was when we bought him his first watch."

When Abraham came home he found that they had waited supper for him. The boy, bless him, was reading from an English book.

Chapter Five

————◄●►————

When Chaim Knopp's youngest daughter finally married her boy friend, who was not a doctor and not a rich man's son, but a good hard-working boy, Chaim saw to it that Abraham and his wife were invited to the wedding supper and that Isaac was invited to the dance afterward. His wife, whose heart was not in the marriage, and who had put many obstacles in the way of the young couple, did not object very strenuously. There were people whose presence she considered more valuable, but as she had worked herself into an attitude of martyred acceptance of the whole affair, it was a small thing to accept also the presence of a family who, although they'd been five years in the country, she still considered immigrants, insofar as they still really hadn't arrived anywhere.

They still lived in the little low-lying house with a bootlegger for a landlord. The husband was still the hired hand of a butcher about whom not much could be said that was elevating except that he knew how to make money. Chaim sometimes said something about a partnership with this Avrom, but Chaim was not one to carry a business through, she had discovered long ago. And their son was an ordinary worker in a factory. It was true that this son was a bit of a *malomed* on the side, but the few pupils that he had did not really make him a member of the teaching profession. What good did it do him to be clever, as Chaim said he was, if he could not raise himself to be anything more than a laborer in a factory?

Not that Chaim's wife was in reality such an ill-natured person. She was, as everybody knew because she told them so in her definite way, clear-headed and far-sighted, unlike Chaim. In the bad times she had taken her full share of work and had, when the family was floundering because of Chaim's total inability to calculate and look

73

ahead, done more than her share in helping to steer it off the rocks.

When her children grew up and were successful, she wanted to share fully in their success. She insisted on being invited to all of the social functions her daughters and daughter-in-law held, until they finally managed to steer her to the older women's branches of the charitable organizations to which they belonged. Here she found herself a natural leader. She threw herself into charitable work. Indeed, since her children were rich, she could afford to feel more than charitable; she could feel philanthropic, and she brought with her an aura of philanthropy that lesser women couldn't quite muster. Presiding over a charitable society was really very much like presiding over a household that one's husband couldn't manage properly. One organized teas, one made decisions about benefits, one voiced opinions loudly enough to make the inadequacy of feebler opinions felt. Above all, one worked. No one could deny that Mrs. Knopp was a worker.

It was not at all because of snobbery that she could not interest herself in forming a friendship with the butcher's wife. Really, if the woman were truly interested in getting to know people she could always join one of the societies. She'd even sponsor her herself. But no, this did not seem to satisfy Chaim. What did satisfy Chaim, ever? He wanted her to come and sit and talk to this butcher's wife. But she didn't have time to hold the hand of every immigrant who had a story to tell. What Jew hasn't a story? She had her own troubles too, and who would sit and listen to her if she put on a piteous face? No, she wasn't a sitter and talker. She was a doer. Let Chaim sit and talk. He hadn't done much more all his life. Thank goodness Ralph was like her, a doer. When you came right down to it, it was selfish to sit on your own sorrows when there was so much to be done in the world.

Isaac brought a girl to the dance and introduced her to his parents. He danced all the modern dances with her, but when there was a waltz he surrendered her to his father and took his mother onto the floor. Abraham danced with the long movements of the old-fashioned waltz, and the girl, whose name was Ruth, had a hard time fitting her steps to his. But she learned quickly and was not ungraceful. And she was healthy. When he took her as his partner for a *shair*, while Isaac stayed out with Sarah, she romped through the long measures and was not nearly so tired as he when they finally collapsed, laughing, onto the chairs at the side of the hall.

Chaim brought his children over at different times during the evening to introduce them to Abraham. They were all polite and spoke pleasantly. Chaim was very happy about the marriage because, to tell the truth, he liked his new son-in-law.

"You see," said Abraham to his wife, "he is not ashamed to introduce his elevated children to his friend Avrom the butcher. We stand somewhere in this world yet." He had been very tempted, when Chaim had introduced him to his son-in-law the doctor, to talk to the doctor about medical matters. He had thought that perhaps he might mention to him that he himself had two arms that sometimes he could not think what to do with. True, he rubbed them every night with oil of wintergreen. But what good this did, beyond making the room smell pleasant, he did not know. He would have liked to know, in a friendly way, what the doctors thought of such an ailment as his nowadays. But the doctor did not appear to be a young man who would invite a friendly discussion. After a few polite words he was silent and stood off a way, overlooking the people, with a look on his face as though his mind was elsewhere, as though he really did not think he had an equal among the crowd.

Abraham's eyes sought Isaac's figure among the dancers. The boy was enjoying himself. He executed the figures of the modern dance as though he had been born dancing them. An attractive little girl. It was good to see them laughing and dancing. The boy was at home altogether too much with his books, some of which, from the things he had come out with lately, were downright irreligious. This was the first time that he had introduced a girl to his parents. Of course it didn't mean anything, and he, Avrom, was not going to be an old woman. But from the way she talked she was an educated girl—a native, too. It was not often that the native girls paid much attention to an immigrant boy—as though their parents hadn't been immigrants themselves. But Isaac didn't have to be ashamed in any company. He was such a man with this girl. Well, naturally, he was a man already. Look, the way he took her by the arm and led her to the refreshment stand! Sarah was laughing with pleasure. Abraham took her by the arm and led her to the refreshment stand.

"I had a feeling," Ruth told Isaac, "that I'd like your parents. I always get feelings about things."

"Really?" asked Isaac. He looked down at her head of short black curls. She really was a remarkable girl.

Polsky was not a malicious man, but he was unable to resist telling Abraham that he too had met Chaim Knopp's son Ralph, the manufacturer, socially. At the home of a friend, he said, they had spent a very pleasant evening, playing cards and having a friendly drink. "He's certainly a shark at the cards," Polsky said with honest admiration, "and quite an all-round boy at that."

Abraham did not have to guess the name of Polsky's friend. Ever since her husband had been arrested and put away in prison Laiah's apartment had come to be known as a place of mixed delights. It was a place where men with money could come together, drink and play poker all night, and where a willing hostess and her friends would help them to relax in any other manner that they might desire.

Polsky's relationship with Laiah had cooled into what was partly a business arrangement. Polsky was not averse to turning an extra dollar, and, with liquor at a premium, he had undertaken to supply her soirées from secret channels of his own.

Laiah's husband was serving a sentence in the provincial prison. He was a craftsman in a respectable trade, but he had also stood watch, in the middle of the night, for a gang of thieves. When they were discovered, he had signaled the others in time for them to escape, but had himself been caught. In prison he would say nothing, though it was well known that there were certain higher-ups who were interested in the business. People who knew everything—and Mrs. Plopler was one of them—said that it was really a terrible shame. He was a good-natured, harmless young man who had been driven into crime by the ambitions of his wife. Not that he wouldn't be well paid afterward for keeping his mouth shut. Thieves look after their own. Unless, of course, he was a greater fool than even Mrs. Plopler imagined.

That was as it might be; Abraham did not know the young man. But the shame was for Chaim. So this was his son the manufacturer. It was a thing that might well bow his friend's head closer to the ground in his old age. Better that his Isaac should never become rich, never become a manufacturer and develop such tastes. A man with a family, too! But there did not seem to be much to fear from Isaac in this direction. It was the ideas he picked up, the books he read. And so stubborn about them! Who was the older, anyway, himself or his son? To call his father old-fashioned because he refused to believe that he was descended from a monkey! Abraham had heard that there were races in the world who worshiped animals. But to have his own son turn into a monkey-worshiper in God's eyes was too much. And to have his own son tell him, furthermore, that he, Abraham, didn't understand what he was trying to say, that he was narrow-minded, had been the crowning insult. He had threatened, heaven forbid, to throw Isaac and his atheistical books out of the house together.

He had flown into such a rage—he was ashamed of it now, but a man comes home from a hard day at work to be told over the supper table that his grandfather was a monkey, Laib Moishe, a monkey! How can he help being angry? Poor Sarah had begun to cry because they were arguing so violently. For her sake he had decided to hear the boy out. Calmly and dispassionately he would point out to him all the flaws in his argument. A young man, even if he is a thinker, is entitled to make a few mistakes when he is still young and overenthusiastic.

So he had heard the boy out, and it turned out that the whole thing was not so serious as he had at first made it out to be. Isaac— and this was probably the fault of the books—had not explained it properly. Of course we are all the creatures of God. Now the ape is the creature that, in his outward aspect, most resembles man. It was something that he himself had not thought much about before. But when he came to consider it, it was true. Accordingly, in this sense, he was man's closest relative—not really his ancestor, but this was, so to speak, an expression. What was there to make a fuss about? He had been happy that he had been able to straighten the whole thing out.

This was the way to deal with him—not with an exhibition of temper, because, after all, he was a man already ·in his own right, but with patience and the. thoughtful consideration of the things he said. He might perhaps let himself be carried away by some ridiculous ideas out of his youthful enthusiasm sometimes, but he was, nevertheless, an equal, and in many ways far more educated than his father.

Avrom had afterward had an interesting conversation with Chaim Knopp on the subject of man's relationship to animals. And together they had discovered many similarities not only between man and the apes, but between man and many other creatures of God's world. Truly the world was filled with many wonders. And what a thing was an education that helped you to see these wonders! Sometimes the things that Isaac said made him long to throw himself into the books, to find the things the boy talked about. It was not enough to argue from. what he himself as a religious man knew to be true. He wanted to be able to examine for himself these odd facts and theories that Isaac hinted at. How could the boy call him narrow-minded when he would have liked so much to know?

"I should have known better," said Isaac, "than to mention it to him." He sat with Ruth on her veranda steps and brooded over his latest argument with his father. "The whole world could be descended from anthropoid apes, but my dad would still come straight from Adam."

Ruth didn't answer. She was looking at Mad Mountain. The hill, rising above the houses across the way, had already thrown off its day cloak and was wrapping itself in evening blue. Just such a dress

Ruth wanted to sew for herself, that exact color. Contemplating it, she lost track for a moment of what Isaac was saying.

"And he'd be right, too. I suddenly realized, talking to him, how silly I am. What did I want to get out of him? Why do I want to belittle his world? Did I think I could make myself feel more like a man by making my dad feel more like an ape?"

Ruth caught the last part. "You are a man," she said, dropping her head for a moment on his shoulder and then raising it quickly again, shaking her short dark curls.

"You think so?" Isaac interrupted his train of thought for a moment to smile at her. He slipped his arm around her and pulled her down so that her head fell back on his shoulder. Ruth relaxed contentedly. Then he was off again. "I may think that he's stubborn and narrow-minded and old-fashioned. I may feel that he's living in a world that's not the real world, but I don't know. Do I really see things he doesn't see, or does he just see them in a different perspective?"

How long had she known him? She knew to the day. It was almost a year now since they had caught sight of each other at the party, somebody's birthday party. The thin boy had been standing with his arm around another girl, looking down at her and talking. He had glanced up at her when her escort spoke to him. For a moment he hadn't closed his mouth from talking. Then with a nervous movement he had jerked his arm away from the other girl. She knew with a feeling that bordered on smugness that he hadn't put his arm around another girl since.

He was so clever, so sweet, with his funny accent. Even though she'd been born here, she didn't know as many long words in English as he did. He read so much. He was interested in everything. And yet— He talked about the real world. Did he know about the real world? Here was the real world beside him, and what did he do? He lived in the real world. The real world was something close to him. It was something today and tomorrow; it was now. She knew the real world. She could feel things about it. It had been strange the way she had felt something about that party even before she had gone to it, a way that she hadn't felt about any other party. And there he'd been. And the way she'd known that she would like his parents and they'd like her, before they'd gone to the wedding a few months ago. She'd just known. It hadn't stopped her from being nervous about meeting them or anything; she'd just had that feeling over and above her nervousness. And the way he'd talked to her beforehand and explained things about them, it had been enough to make her nervous. Still, she'd known. He was so funny sometimes, with his real world.

"It's innocence," Isaac was saying. "It's just as though a man were to build himself a grass hut at the North Pole and run around without any clothes on. But nothing would happen to that man, because he didn't know he was at the North Pole. Now if I came up to the North Pole in my polar-bear skins and told him where he was he wouldn't believe me, and nothing would happen to him. But what if he did believe me? He'd die of the cold. That would be awful. But no one can live naked at the North Pole, even the innocent ones. He'd die anyway, without knowing what he had died of. And, looking at him, even though I was wearing my polar-bear skins, I'd die too, I think." Isaac was silent, not knowing where he'd led himself.

Innocence, thought Ruth, turning her head slightly and breathing deliberately down his neck. That was just the word for it.

In the house everything was disarranged. Isaac had got the sudden impulse that the whole place should be painted. The ceilings, he complained, seemed very low and gray. The house was old, it was true, but give it a bit of paint, new curtains, and a few other touches, and it would acquire an altogether new atmosphere.

Sarah and Abraham exchanged quizzical glances during Isaac's tirade. They agreed solemnly: A freshly painted ceiling gave a room at least a foot in height. Abraham approached the landlord. The landlord thought it was a good idea but expensive, and, considering the rent they were paying— Well, he didn't think he could manage it.

This did not stop Isaac. He set to work on the ceilings himself. Abraham painted the woodwork that he didn't have to strain his arms too much to reach. Together they repainted the kitchen and whitewashed the summer kitchen. Abraham painted the icebox and the old kitchen table. Sarah bought new curtains and a new bath mat. Isaac painted, if not the whole outside of the house, at least the window frames and the little wooden front fence. By the time they were finished the house glowed. Even Isaac was satisfied. Abraham and Sarah sat back and waited.

At his machine in the shop, Isaac tried mentally to evaluate his role in life. It was passed to him from the cutter's table. He stitched it together rapidly. Speed, that's what counts in piecework. He was quick. The scraps fed into his machine and came out stitched, formed, ready for the next operation at the next machine. Every piece was a few cents. Zip zip—five cents—zip—seven cents—zip zip zip—another dollar. Another bundle. Was this what he was made for? Why should his father think that he was made for something better? Why did he feel that way sometimes himself? Because he wanted to do something, he didn't know what, to work at something that would lead him somewhere, to discover, to create—not just pockets and facings day after day. To read, to teach . . . The boys that he prepared for Bar Mitzvah—there was something in that; to watch their minds work, to discover suddenly something about a boy that would win him over—like fat Shmillig, who had been given up by three *malomeds*. Accidentally, almost by instinct, Isaac had hit upon a way to handle him.

While his enormous mother listed her complaints about him the child had sat stubbornly looking at the floor, his head resting on his double chin. Then Isaac had taken him into the living room. "Well, Sam, let's forget what's past and begin again. There's a lot to learn." And that was it, nothing more. From then on the boy had learned, and he was not stupid either. Shmillig. What could lock him more securely in his cage of fat, to be laughed at as though everything about him was funny, than a name like that in a land where it was a meaningless, comical sound? To Isaac the incident had been a revelation. With one word he had given a small human being back his sense of dignity. Now he could not help approaching each new pupil with a curiosity, a delicacy, almost an excitement at what he might discover.

All right, so he would like to teach, but what chance was there? As a full-time private teacher he could never support himself, let alone ever think of raising a family. As a teacher in the Hebrew and Yiddish school—well, he could live, but what chance had he of ever getting a job like that? Not much; they wanted somebody with bells on, somebody who would be recommended by someone noisy, not just a plain immigrant boy who worked in a factory and studied by himself at night.

Would he end up like old Rusen, then, who sat across from him, glued to the machine, his hands trembling when the foreman shouted for more speed and he tried to hurry? He imagined himself an old man, bent over the machine, afraid to steal a moment to pause and crack a joke, resented by the other workers because he sometimes worked through his lunch hour and they thought he was trying to get ahead of them, picked on by the foreman because he was too slow. The foreman had it in for Rusen in particular because, though the boss was always yammering at him for more production, he wouldn't let him fire the old man. Every time he brought a prospective buyer to the factory the boss pointed out that this was no ordinary sweat shop that worked on the principle of mass production at the price of good workmanship. Here, for example, was Rusen, one of the best old-style craftsmen left in the city, at one of his machines —and not just turning out samples to fool buyers; turning out the actual goods. In his shop it was quality first, speed second. Whenever the boss said that within hearing of some of the boys they gave him the old ha-ha, roaring their machines in rhythmic unison. Two years ago, when they had struck for a return from piecework to a regular salary, he had closed down the shop until they had to give in. Quality first, but survival of the fleetest, Isaac had told his father.

He had gone on strike with the rest of them and had stood as a picket outside the shut-down shop. The boss had gone to California on a holiday until the workers came to their senses. The strike had a bad effect on his nerves. And when his nerves were bad he got carbuncles or something. Isaac had greatly admired the way Ned Strom had spoken to the workers, had urged them to hold fast. What would he himself not have given to have had a golden voice, a dauntless courage then? When the workers finally filed back into the shop again Ned had not been with them. He was in jail for uttering threats. He himself had been a coward, Isaac knew, to feel secretly relieved that he hadn't uttered his threats loudly enough. The thought of his own cowardice filled him even now with shame.

Screaming voices jerked Isaac out of his thoughts. They were fighting over the bundles again. When you finished a bundle you went to the foreman's table and he gave you another. If he liked you he gave you a bundle that you could make a few more cents on, one that required less complicated stitching, and you rushed with it back to your machine. Two girls had wanted to grab the same bundle, to run back and sew more belts. They were tugging at it and arguing shrilly. Jenny shouted that she had got there first. Bella screamed that Jenny already had three bundles hidden in her machine. Jenny yelled that Bella always got the better bundles because, as everybody knew, she was willing to do any filth with anybody to get them. The foreman shouted at both of them. The girls pulled at the bundle. It came apart, and the pieces scattered all over the floor. Jenny swooped after them. Bella turned and rushed over to Jenny's machine and from under the box that Jenny kept beside her pulled out two bundles.

"Aha!" she shouted dramatically, waving the bundles for all to see. Jenny threw the pieces of the first bundle down on her machine and grabbed Bella by the hair. Bella screamed. The women began to take sides and shouted across to them. The men sat and laughed. The foreman tried to get between the girls. What if the boss came in?

Some of the workers, who remembered that time was money, regretfully started up their machines again, so that the variety of noises clashing together in the shop was deafening. Only Rusen had not stopped the steady pace of his work to look up. He continued to stitch, a tight expression of distaste on his face.

The foreman had finally separated the two girls. He stood in a semi-crouch between them and hissed at them to get back to their machines. They would pay, he promised them, they would pay.

"What's all this?" The boss's tenor voice shrilled across the room. The machines roared suddenly louder. The boss advanced slowly into Isaac's vision. "So I have a foreman a ballet dancer?"

The foreman straightened his knees and dropped his arms under the boss's sarcastic glare. "What's the matter?" the shrill tenor barked again. "Is it tea time that you're all sitting around doing nothing?" Isaac, with the others, urged his machine to a more frantic tempo. "Thieves!" The tenor rose, trying to soar above the machines. "When it's slow season you rush through your work and cry because I don't give you enough work to do!" Isaac pressed hard against the pedal of the power machine. Others did the same. The boss's voice was momentarily drowned out. Odd words penetrated. ". . . busy season . . . my few cents . . . you play . . ." Every time his voice made a fresh attempt to climb the noise the machines roared more loudly. Jenny and Bella were back at their respective machines, and the cloth was flying from under their needles.

"Saboteurs!" The boss was sure they were doing it deliberately. He would like to make them stop and force them to listen to him. But the money he'd lose! He pitted himself once more against the machines. "I lost my hair over you! I worked my head off and you're out to ruin me!" The machines raced on. "Pretend you don't hear me! Moscovitch!"

The machines slowed slightly because everyone wanted to hear what he said to the foreman. "I'm telling you if anyone so much as pauses to go to the toilet to smoke a cigarette—oh, yes, I know why you go to the toilet—" He had worked in a shop himself long ago, before piecework came in. "I want them thrown out, fired! We'll see if they find another boss like me to tolerate thieves and cripples."

The boss stormed out. Moscovitch started to prowl furiously around the shop. The machines settled into a steadier tempo. Finally Moscovitch stationed himself behind old Rusen. The old man's hands trembled as he guided the material into the machine. He did not stop working when the foreman spoke to him, but his furrowed, anxious face began to sweat.

Leave him alone, thought Isaac. Leave him alone. For a moment he saw himself in Rusen's place, his back misshapen by the years of bending over the machine; slow—even now he was sometimes tired—unable to feed the machine quickly enough to fill the bellies of his family, and not even a master craftsman to be kept on by a whim of the boss.

The foreman continued to stand over the old man. "All right, all right," Isaac said out loud. "Leave him alone." The neighboring machines paused suddenly. Isaac felt his body begin to shake as though with a chill. His heart thudded irregularly. He stopped his machine. "Leave him alone," he repeated, noticing, to his amazement, that he was almost shouting.

When he left the shop he was without a job. His heart still beat too quickly, so that he had to pause, leaning for a few moments against the wall of the building. But the fresh air smelled good. Only now he realized how he had hated the shop. Perhaps he might be able to get work doing something else. As his spirits calmed somewhat, on the way home, he realized that there was not much chance, not in times like these. But it was a thought. He hoped his appearance wouldn't frighten his mother. He'd have to tell her right away that he wasn't ill, not really, he'd only been fired. He would have to get work quickly, though. It was a good thing that it was the busy season in tailoring. He would be taken on elsewhere. He did not bother to consider, for the moment, what he had really accomplished in throwing away his job. It was something he had wanted to do. He had wanted to stop the foreman. He had wanted to change things. He was young; he was quick. He wanted to bring a girl home to his parents.

" 'Take your job, take your miserable pay.' " Abraham made up the words as he went along. " 'Do you think we're your slaves here, that you can bully a man who's nearly old enough to be your father?' "

"Ah," said Chaim. "Aha, that was telling him. Right into his gall-stones."

"To look at the boy you'd think that he wouldn't utter a contrary word. But just you step on his toes, just try to offend his sense of justice. Ha! Then you'll hear from him. And can you imagine the sheep, not one of the other workers to lift a finger, not one to take his part. That gross barbarian could have flayed the old man alive, and none of the workers would have stopped sewing. That's the world we live in. No wonder it took forty years to get across the desert. But wait, wait, just rely on my sons."

"Has he got another job yet?"

"And that's another thing. He wanted to get on as a full-time teacher in the Hebrew school. He went to Reb Slotnik. You know Reb Slotnik, how he gargles with joy when he talks about the way Isaac prepares his pupils for the Bar Mitzvah? And well he might! I've never missed one of Isaac's Bar Mitzvahs yet, if I could help it. I don't have to tell you, you've seen them yourself—how the words come out clearly, and the little speech afterward, how cleverly it's turned, and never the same thing twice. One can see that Isaac teaches them not only the words and the mechanical things, but shows them how to feel what an important thing it is that they are coming into their manhood, into their responsibilities as Jews. And the mothers praise him. Only last week that Mrs. Katz, who has the little barrel Shmillig for a son, spread herself over one of the kitchen chairs and started to sing his praises; her voice still rings in my ears. She wanted to kiss him on both cheeks; she wanted to marry him to at least three different girls that she knew. But this I told her not to worry her head about.

"Reb Slotnik? To praise the boy is one thing, it doesn't cost him anything. But to give him a job is a different story. The school is poor, it doesn't pay much, they already have their quota of teachers and not enough pupils, giving jobs is not really up to him—every possible excuse. But he promised Isaac that he would keep him in mind. So, in the meantime he has a job in another shop. He won't stay idle. And especially now that he has his mind on a girl already."

"So?" said Chaim.

"So," said Abraham. "On Friday night we will have a guest for supper."

On Friday evening, with Ruth clinging nervously to his arm, Isaac tried to approach the house as though for the first time. How would she see it? Would she be disappointed? It was true that her sister's house, where she lived, was not much better. Still— Isaac had explained to her that it was not very modern and that it was rather small. Wishing to be completely frank, he had told her, further, about the landlord's being a bootlegger—not really a bootlegger, but a sort of contact man, from what they could gather. Sometimes strange things went on around the back-yard garage at night. Trucks drove up, trucks drove away. But all this they tried to pay no attention to. It was, after all, the landlord's own business if he wanted to risk his neck in dishonest affairs. Isaac noticed the newly painted fence and window ledges gleaming under the late setting sun. Attractive, he thought hopefully. He stopped outside the yard. "This is it."

"I think I've passed it before," said Ruth, unwilling to admit that she had slipped past this house many times. "It's been painted?"

"Oh, just freshened up a bit," said Isaac. "My father and I did it ourselves. Don't like it to get too shabby."

They lingered outside for a little while.

Inside, Abraham helped Sarah to lay the dining-room table. He did not usually help with the knives and forks, but today he felt active. "Poor child is an orphan," he told Sarah. "We must do our best to make her feel at home right away. It cannot be too happy for her to have no real home, to have to live with a married sister. We must make her feel that we're her own."

Sarah agreed. The time had come. She didn't know whether she was happy that it had come or not. It was the first time that any other woman had shared her table with her men.

"There is only one thing that is worse than to be left without your parents," Abraham was saying. "And that is to be left without your children. And who should know better than we, who have had a taste of both?"

When Isaac and Ruth arrived Abraham set about making the girl feel at home. He monopolized the conversation for the greater part of the evening. If there was a pause he rushed in to fill the breach. He joked and he told stories, and he felt that the evening was a tremendous success.

"Did I have a time in the shop today! A butcher has to be made of iron." Abraham turned to Sarah. "Do you remember the Slutskys from the old country? Sure you do. He used to speculate. 'Slutsky the foolish thief,' they used to call him. Couldn't read a page of Hebrew. They used to say he had to get someone else to count the money he stole. His father was a fine old man. I remember him. How he could have such a son! And his mother, with one brown eye and one blue—they called her 'the speckled hen.' Well, in Canada he's not such a fool. He's got a big family. His wife is dressed in honey and in butter—a big feather in her hat, paint on her lips so that she looks as though she's got something bitter in her mouth.

"This Mrs. Slutsky, she comes in, and I'm making an order for Jack Lazar—you know, with the short foot. He watches the scale like his life depends on it. It always gets busy like this when Polsky is away at the slaughterhouse.

" 'It's all right,' she calls out. 'It's all right. I'll slice my own corned beef. You're busy, I'll make myself at home.'

"So she gets herself paper, and she starts to slice. But I know her already, so while Lazar has his face pushed in the scale—he's worried maybe I'll give him a drop less—I've got my eye on her. One slice she cuts on the paper, the other slice she slips in her mouth; one slice on the paper, another one in the mouth. And she's so dainty! Fat little fingers with points like a fork, red like blood. Born to pick up the corned beef. One finger in the air—throws back her big feather, like a rooster, and into the mouth. And thinks yet that I don't see her.

"Meanwhile I'm trying to hurry and wrap the meat for Lazar, but he's not in such a hurry. He scrapes off a little bone from the scale, puts on another piece of meat instead, craning around right from the other side of the counter. It weighs too much. He takes it off, looks at me, makes like he doesn't know anything, puts it on again.

"And she slices, slices, eats, slices.

"At last Lazar lets me wrap up the meat, not until he's pulled out the paper so it has to lie naked on the scale—thinks maybe the needle will go down a little. And with Lazar it's funny; he always tries to do all this and yet make like he doesn't care about it. Stands with his face in the scale and pretends he's looking at himself in the little glass. Dances on his long foot, dances on his short foot. Pulls the paper out from under the meat like his hand got in with it by accident.

"When he goes out, thank God, I come over to Mrs. Slutsky, take the slicer from her hand. 'You'll tire yourself,' I say to her. 'How much do you want?'

" 'Oh,' she says, 'that's about enough. Just for my family, you know; I don't eat so much of that kind of stuff. But they like it, so I take.' And she gives the meat such a look that it almost gets up and crawls into her mouth.

" 'I hope your family enjoys the meat,' I say when I give her the little parcel. 'It's freshly made.' So she burps, if you'll excuse me, in my face—but not common, no, the red nails in front of the mouth.

" 'Excuse me,' she says. 'Gas.'

" 'No,' I say. 'That's too bad. Is it your diet maybe?'

" 'I don't think so,' she says. 'I'm very careful.' "

They all laughed at Abraham's description. "Why do you take it?" asked Ruth. "Why don't you tell her off? Believe me, I'd tell her."

"No, you have to be nice to a customer. So much you consider is overhead. Besides, God's got His eye on her. Who do you think is going to have gall bladder trouble, she or I?"

"Personally," said Isaac, "I'd weigh her when she comes in and weigh her when she goes out and make her pay for the difference."

"So, clever fellow, Polsky would need a livestock scale too. One thing I know"—Abraham turned to Ruth—"my grandchildren won't be butchers or tailors." Abraham explained to Ruth how he had had a son who would have been a wonder cantor, and how one of his sons had started his studies at three and had put to shame his teachers.

"And do you think that Isaac would have been a tailor? Even now he makes those others at the synagogue who stare blindly at the holy books look silly, in spite of the fact that he sometimes talks like he is a bit of an atheist."

Sarah noticed how tactfully Ruth steered the conversation away from this dangerous point, and she watched the girl with a kind of helpless fascination, knowing that the time had really come.

Isaac's heart seemed to expand in his chest with the pressure of gratitude and love. Fool that he was, he could not resist discussing his ideas with his father, knowing what the result was likely to be, yet feeling at the same time that they were somehow not clean and honest thoughts unless he admitted them to Abraham. It was like a blockade that his ideas had to run to give them the right to exist. But everything went so smoothly with Ruth. How well she fitted in with them. She made herself right at home and insisted on helping with the dishes. His father liked her, he could tell. When she went with Sarah to do the dishes in the kitchen, Abraham decided that he too would help. And there he was, with a towel in his hands, as though he did this every day, talking and joking, telling her about the partnership that he was going someday to form with Chaim Knopp.

It was already some three years since the thought had entered the heads of Chaim and Abraham that they should form a partnership. During that time they had discussed the idea, examined it from every angle and in the light of every development in their respective lives, spent long hours in meeting imaginary obstacles, and repeatedly come to the conclusion that it would be a fine idea. It took some time for Abraham to realize that Chaim, even though he was the elder, would not make the first move. Gradually he began to understand that the shoichet would be content not to make any move at all, just to talk. Having to make a move might even upset Chaim, considering all the real problems that it would present. So he gave up any idea of having the partnership become in reality a fact, although both he and Chaim continued to refer to it as an imminent possibility.

At home it became a sort of joke, and Abraham explained to Ruth how one department of the partnership was devoted to preparing kosher tidbits for the family cats, and how they had expanded the business, just as Polsky always talked of doing, but of course on a grander scale, so that now it was an international affair. Unfortunately they would have to abandon plans for a branch on the moon. How could a good Jew mix meat and cheese?

Abraham was delighted at the sound of this girl's laughter in his house. He was not now unhappy that the partnership was not a fact. It was getting late for the old to conquer the world. Let the young start anew.

"Do you think he really liked me, your father?" Ruth asked as Isaac walked her home.

"Liked you? You're a family concern. Did I get two minutes alone with you?"

"Your mother's very quiet, like you said. It must seem funny to her—I mean, you and a girl. The way she looks at you . . ."

"How—" said Isaac, "I mean what did you think of them, of us?"

"I liked them," said Ruth, "even from before. I feel at home with them. It's so good to be able to feel at home." She pressed against his arm.

"You are," said Isaac fervently. "You are."

Chapter Six

She did not like to gloat over other people's misfortunes, Mrs. Plopler announced as she was struggling out of her winter coat, but she had just heard that the police had raided Laiah's apartment. Somebody's wife, so the story went, had not been able to stand it any longer and had phoned the police and told them that red-headed Laiah was running a gambling and bootlegging and who-knows-whatelse establishment. So the police had paid her a visit and, according to what Mrs. Plopler had been told, several of the town's well-known names had been caught—some said on their knees shooting crap, others said with money on the table, others said with bootleg liquor. Nobody knew for certain, because it was all hush-hush.

Obviously, Mrs. Plopler's nose opined in its significant way, there were too many big names involved. But the redhead had over-reached herself this time. Mrs. Plopler knew definitely that she was looking for a new, for a smaller apartment. But no doubt Avrom knew all this already? She and Polsky had always been thick as thieves.

Abraham took advantage of the pause during which she bent to undo her galoshes to bid her an ironic good evening. It no longer occurred to him to take offense at the fact that she assumed that because Polsky and Laiah were as thick as thieves he was expected to know everything the woman did.

He had already heard, as it happened, that Laiah was looking for a smaller apartment. But if there had been anything about the police mentioned in her conversation with Polsky he had not noticed it. Of course he had not paid much attention. A few words here and there, when they raised their voices, had forced themselves into his consciousness—something about how hard it was to keep up a large apartment nowadays, and how the depression had hit many of Polsky's and Laiah's mutual friends badly. Then, after more conversation that he had ignored, had come Polsky's voice raised in a joke. Laiah's business would never be that bad, he assured her. After all —Polsky chuckled in that way that he had when he was expanding on a joke—she could always peddle it on the streets. But Laiah, who did not like to be spoken to in this way, especially in front of people like Abraham, answered Polsky sharply and called him a *grobion*.

Then Laiah had strolled over to where Abraham was busy cleaning the slicer. Very politely she had asked him whether perhaps he knew of a small flat for her. Abraham was embarrassed for this woman who was so vulnerable to a public insult from such as Polsky. He answered her with equal politeness. A woman like this could find herself very lonely someday. What stake had she in the future? And the future was creeping up on her. He could see that she was maybe in her forties already. Yet she still made those unseasonable movements that reminded him, in a way, of the tentative wag of their landlord's shaggy puppy when he tried to make friends with Knobble and Pompishke. On a little dog it was an attractive thing, but she was a grown-up human being. She could not waggle her hips forever in the face of time.

When Mrs. Plopler had finished temporarily with Laiah she went on to tell them who had died lately, who had lately been operated on, and who had been visited by other misfortunes. Not until she had oiled her tongue with these drops did she go on to the question that she had uppermost in her mind at the moment.

Raising her nose from her cup of tea—"Where's Isaac?" she asked with a little laugh.

"He's gone out somewhere," said Sarah.

"You don't know where?"

Abraham shrugged his shoulders. "I don't ask him where he goes."

"I hear he's got a steady girl friend already," said Mrs. Plopler.

"Steady," said Sarah with a touch of pride. "She's been coming into the house for more than a year."

"Oh," said Mrs. Plopler. "You mean it's still the same one?"

"Isaac's past the age already where he wants to run around from one girl to another." Abraham leaned back in his chair and smiled. "Ruth's like our own child."

"Oh, he's changed, then," murmured Mrs. Plopler, looking with an air of distaste into her empty cup. Sarah rose to fill it. "So he's really settling down?"

"He was never such a wild boy that he needs so much settling down," said Sarah.

"When he wants to settle down he'll settle down," Abraham pointed out.

"And you, you're really pleased with your little daughter-in-law?" Mrs. Plopler pursued in a mock teasing vein.

"She's not my daughter-in-law yet," said Abraham, dipping his square of sugar into his tea before he bit on it, then taking a sip, "but if she were my daughter-in-law I would be pleased with her."

"It's funny how the boys choose girls nowadays," Mrs. Plopler said and cracked the lump of dry sugar between her teeth. "Sometimes I think they go to too many parties and get their heads turned so they hardly know what they're choosing."

"My son"—Abraham's voice was firm with only a slight edge— "knows what he's choosing."

"Yes," added Sarah with unusual asperity, "he's met enough ninnies to be able to stay clear of them."

"Well, Isaac was always a sensible boy." Mrs. Plopler's concession had a deceptive air of defeat about it. "You know, as a matter of fact I think I know who his girl friend is."

"You may have seen her here at the house," said Sarah.

If you didn't know all about her by now, Abraham refrained from adding, I would worry about your health.

"Yes, I've seen the girl herself, but I mean I know the family— what there is of it. Poor thing."

"Poor?" Abraham didn't like the word.

"Well, an orphan, you know." Mrs. Plopler nibbled happily at a piece of Sarah's cheesecake.

"It's a pity"—Abraham's voice took on its rhetorical timbre—"that her parents aren't alive, it's true. They would have rejoiced to see what a fine girl she's become, what a fine boy she's chosen. They are probably even now rejoicing somewhere. But poor she is not. We are all of us orphans sooner or later. Your poorness is a thing of the spirit. Ruth is a brave girl."

Abraham would not accept that anything that was attached to him could be called poor, not by an outsider. It was an expression of defeat, a calling for pity. He might himself, in talking to Sarah, refer to Ruth as a poor child, for it was obvious from the way the girl had attached herself to them that she had never had a real home before. They knew from what Isaac said that when she was still a child herself she had already had to help raise her sister's children. And from what Isaac said about her brother-in-law, he had never allowed the girl to feel that she was more than an encumbrance. Still, that was different. That was between themselves, not for Mrs. Plopler, who was only too happy to cry over you.

"You're right." Mrs. Plopler allowed her teacup to be refilled and appeared amiably to change her tactics. "She must be a brave girl, after all the misfortune she's had to live through, even before she was born. Of course you probably know the story already."

"We know what there is to know." Abraham could tell that Mrs. Plopler wanted to say something; there was something to dredge up from the past. And it would come out. Neither the irritation in his tone nor Sarah's apparent attempt to drown her by giving her too many cups of tea would stop her.

"It was such a shame that her father should die before she was born." Mrs. Plopler sighed. "At least if he had lived her mother wouldn't have had to face the world alone. To tell you the truth, I didn't remember about it. But the other day I was talking to a friend of mine who was their neighbor at the time. I happened to mention your Ruth, so she reminded me. We were just green at the time ourselves." Mrs. Plopler cracked another lump of sugar between her teeth and took a few sips of tea through the piece that she still held in her mouth. Neither Abraham nor Sarah said anything. With Mrs.

Plopler one could only wait. Abraham smoothed his beard under his lip and squinted up at the yellow light bulb.

"She was already in her fifties when he died," said Mrs. Plopler and paused. "Ruth's mother, I mean." She paused again, nibbling at another piece of cheesecake.

"And then soon after he died people saw that she was pregnant." Mrs. Plopler took another bite. "At her age.

"Such an embarrassment for the grown children. She had one married son, I think, and a daughter, the one that brought the girl up. She was already engaged, I believe, at that time. Sure, she has a girl of fifteen or sixteen herself now.

"Of course people laughed. At their age—romancing on his deathbed!" Mrs. Plopler pushed the rest of the sugar into her mouth and looked fastidiously at her fingertips. "As for me, I tell my husband, 'Enough of this foolishness,' if you'll excuse the expression. We're not children any more. And anyway, maybe if he'd saved his energy instead of making like a hero when he was a sick man he might have lived longer. Having a child at her age shortened her life too. The remaining few years she had she was sick most of the time." Mrs. Plopler drained the last of her cup of tea, chewing up a few tea leaves that were left on her lips. "When I think of how ashamed my girls would be if I did anything like that I could die straight away. And then what did she accomplish? She left a small child to be a burden on her daughter."

Abraham was silent. What would happen if he leaned through the round yellow haze the light bulb had left in his eyes and seized the pernicious witch by the nose? It was an old theory of Isaac's that if they held her nose still she would not be able to talk. His fingers itched.

Sarah, who had begun to pack Isaac's lunch for tomorrow, turned to Mrs. Plopler. "It was a sad thing that she had to kill herself to bring Ruth into the world. But we will always bless her."

The very sweetness of his wife dissolved Abraham's anger. He laughed suddenly. "Do you suppose they made fun of Sarah too when she had Isaac at a hundred years? You remember that story?

Her husband's name was Abraham. We call him the father of Jews. That's a fine story. Can you imagine what a joy it would be to have a child when you are a hundred years old? Now I would gladly use up my last bit of energy to achieve such a thing. There was no shame to it then. None of us would be here now if it were not for the late flowering of a certain Sarah." Abraham got up and put his arm around his wife. "What's your name, little one—not Sarah? And mine's Abraham! What a coincidence! So, we may yet have an extraordinary event at a hundred years, eh?" He winked at Mrs. Plopler. "And we will certainly have a distinguished' daughter-in-law." Abraham kissed his wife noisily on the forehead. "You see," he said to Mrs. Plopler, "we are not just anybody. Let the world laugh at such things. It shows how small people have grown. We will have strange events to distinguish our lives."

The tea was beginning to weigh uncomfortably in Mrs. Plopler. She excused herself. Funny people, these. Such odd views on things. Well, people make their own beds. The thought of beds made her wonder. When she returned, Abraham still had his arm around his wife. At their age! That's the way it was. So so so.

Abraham interrupted her musings by offering to walk her part way home. "Come," he said gallantly, "we will walk in the snow, and the moon will shine down and show us that we are young yet, for our hundred years. The moon is the sun of the young-old ones. Let the young have the sun to illuminate them. We will have the moon to transform us."

Well! thought Mrs. Plopler and hurriedly thrust her feet into her galoshes. "Well," she said to Abraham with a little laugh, "you must have been quite a young man once."

Abraham didn't answer but smiled down at his wife. Sarah smiled back and then turned again to the sandwiches. When they had left, the tired, slightly vacant look settled gradually over her face again.

A crisis had come into the life of Chaim Knopp. This was not, he assured Abraham, the only crisis that had ever come into his life. But this one was certainly attended by more misfortunes than any before. And it was not, as others had been, the kind of crisis that he could pass through simply by shutting his eyes tight and praying. His wife was not at his elbow this time to guide him while he had his eyes shut. His wife—ah, the greatest of the misfortunes.

What can you do with a wife who will take care of everyone in the world but herself? This society, that society, she was always up and running to help. But her own stomach trouble she had no time for. So comes the time when he, Chaim, gets up in the morning, and there's his wife, groaning in the bed beside him.

"What's the matter, Bassieh?"

"Oi oi oi!"

"Bassieh, something hurts?"

"Oiyoiyoiyoi!"

He, Chaim, runs to and fro, wringing his hands and suffering. Still Bassieh writhes on the bed and says, "Oiyoiyoi."

"God, what shall I do?" Chaim pleads out loud.

"Fool," God answers in Bassieh's voice from the bed, "get a doctor!"

Praise God! He, Chaim, runs out, and a neighbor calls a doctor. The doctor comes, an ambulance comes, and Bassieh is rushed off to the hospital. In the ambulance all Bassieh can say is "Oiyoiyoi."

And Chaim, sitting beside her, can only wring his hands and tear his beard. "Oi Bassieh, oi Bassieh, oi Bassieh!"

In the hospital right away they open her up. Who knows what they found there? You know how the doctors are, secretive. Even his son-in-law George, the doctor, will only polish up some long words for him.

"George, tell me, what does it mean?"

"It's all right. She's recovering nicely from the operation. We don't think she'll need another. Of course she'll have to be careful."

"But what was it? Why did they have to use the knife?"

"You don't have to worry, Father. A little something inside. Just take good care of her. See that she gets checked up regularly. We'll keep her in the hospital awhile until she gets her strength up. She has to be kept quiet."

"A little something. That's all he tells me. But I'm not an entire fool in my old age. So I understand she had a growth. You grow older, little things start to go wrong. As long as she'll be all right." Chaim shrugged his shoulders. "Keeping her quiet in the hospital is a problem, though. My wife was always a nervous type. They give her a nice room, semi-private; so she doesn't like her neighbor. The room is filled with flowers; but one society didn't send flowers till almost a week after the operation, so my Bassieh was so aggravated she almost had a relapse."

These, however, were minor complaints. More important: an operation, a semi-private room, the doctors—all of these cost money. Where would the money come from, now that business was so bad? Who could afford to buy chickens nowadays? They talked about crashes, about depressions. All it boiled down to was that people couldn't afford to buy chickens any more. And if hardly anybody bought chickens, hardly anybody could bring them to Chaim to slaughter. But this was his livelihood. He had a sick wife to take care of. They and their depressions!

It was plain that here was a time when Chaim's children could help out their father if they wanted to. Well, if they wanted to help he couldn't stop them. But ask them? Not he. Abraham could understand this. It is a different thing when children do not offer to help and when they refuse to help. If he asked them they would have the opportunity to refuse, and a refusal, no matter what the excuse, is still a refusal. Whereas if he did not ask them and they did not offer —well, perhaps there were good reasons. As Chaim himself said, they had their problems too. His youngest daughter was married to a working man. They had a baby to look after and were having a hard enough time as it was. They were even thinking of trying to move down to America to see if things weren't easier there. As for the son-in-law who was a doctor, he had helped out at the hospital. Chaim had seen for himself how he'd had long conferences with the other doctors and how he had put his mother-in-law into semi-private, regardless of expense, because it was better for her to be there. Beyond that, he had three children of his own to feed. Chaim didn't like to ask any more help from him. The daughter who was married to a rich man's son lived in another city. And from what he had heard, business wasn't going so well for this son-in-law. Nevertheless his daughter had left her family and come east to see her mother. It was an expensive trip. What more could he ask of her? And from Ralph, especially now, he wouldn't ask a thing.

This, too, Abraham could understand very well. Once, when he could keep it to himself no longer, Chaim had told him that Ralph had left his wife. For the last three months he had been living in one of the big hotels. His wife remained alone, with their little girl, in their home.

"A home like a palace." Chaim's eyes shut and his chin raised, pointing his beard directly in front of him, as he visualized it. "The goyim didn't want, but my Ralph said, 'Let them try and stop me,' and he moved into the heights anyway. I asked him, 'Why do you want to go where they don't want you?' And he said, 'Because I'm a man, Father, and I can walk where any man walks on this earth.' That shows that he's not all what—what people say. But it is not only money that buys a man the right to say that he is a man. He must be a man in other ways. A little girl like an angel, pretty, sweet; a wife like other wives, a good housekeeper, a good mother—and where is he? What good does his money do him? The whole world has to know about his quarrels."

Certainly if Ralph could afford to live in a big hotel he could afford to help out his parents. But for weeks now he hadn't even been by their place to see how they were. Chaim had tried to get in touch with him to tell him that his mother was ill. He had found out from Ralph's wife that he was still living away from home. She was not a bad daughter-in-law. She had come right away to the hospital. Then Chaim had tried to phone Ralph at the hotel. But he was so nervous with that instrument. And he couldn't understand the man at the hotel who had answered, and the man couldn't understand him, so that the man had finally hung up, and Chaim had found his shouts answered by nothing but click-click-click. He had flung down the receiver. Let the other children tell Ralph. He was certainly not going to go to any big hotel to seek out his son.

That was why Chaim had to engage himself finally to one of the local packing plants, where they also slaughtered a certain number of beasts for kosher consumption. Twice a week he went down to the abattoir. The things he had to tell Abraham about that abattoir! Poor Chaim, who was anyway so sensitive to smells. There were not only the smells; there was the big hammer that they brought down on the heads of the non-kosher cows to stun them before they were killed; there were the pools of blood and the entrails; and there were the rebellious beasts who just didn't want to climb forward to die, who had to be coaxed and pushed and shoved. Chickens Chaim was so used to that they no longer made any impression on him, hardly. He just tried to kill them before they could squawk, although he had often wondered whether it wouldn't be more humane at least to let them have one last good squawk before he shut them up forever. But the abattoir . . .

About the abattoir and its horrors people knew nothing, the people who came into the clean butcher shop with the sawdust-strewn floor. Even to Abraham himself these cuts of meat were thoroughly dead and didn't matter any more. The abattoir was out of sight. It was part of the dark underside of life. Abraham knew something of this side. He too had once stood on the brink of life. He had created death. A whole world heaves over and dies in a moment like that. He himself could never have been a shoichet, bringing the knife down again and again, rejecting life after life. Of course you had to be educated to do a job like that. The education must make a difference in your attitude. Luckily Chaim was educated to his task. Still, it was not nice work for him. He was getting to be an elderly man.

Chaim's son Ralph after a while came forward of his own accord to help with his mother's hospital bill. It turned out that he had been out of town on a business trip for several weeks and had not known of his mother's illness. Chaim could not hide his grudging satisfaction. "As a son," he admitted, "he isn't all bad." And he could not help smiling when he said this. "But we had an argument," Chaim continued soberly. "He told me I should stop going to the abattoir. It doesn't behoove him to have a father who has to work in an abattoir. Well, it doesn't behoove me to have a son who . . ." Chaim mumbled something and let his hand finish the sentence. "I said to him, 'When you stop living in a hotel and go back to your family I'll stop working in the slaughterhouse.' "

Chaim stroked his beard and seemed surprised at himself. He had never been so firm with any of his children before. That sort of thing he had usually left to his wife. It took a crisis to bring out the lion in a man. "That's not all I told him. I didn't give him a chance to cheek me before I got my word in. I said to him, 'All right, you go and live in hotels, leave your wife to bring up your child, let your reputation be chewed over by a million mouths. You go your way, and I'll go mine. Remember, me you haven't given anything. You paid your mother's bill—all right, your mother thanks you. You don't care what you do to your father's name, so you don't care about your father!' That's what I told him."

Chaim sighed. "You can understand he was very angry. I really didn't want to drive him away from me altogether."

"Don't worry," Abraham reassured him. "He can see what you've lived through these past few weeks. And he'll see that his old father was right yet. You won't drive him away."

"You think so, eh? Of course. Maybe I should have started to be firm with him long ago. It's a little late now that he's a man with a family himself."

"You can't tell," said Abraham. "Afterward it's hard to tell. I've often thought that if I had been a little firmer with my sons when they were young they wouldn't have been so anxious to come home and see us in the holy days. Just a little bit harsher, perhaps, and they would have been content to stay where they were instead of rushing home. But the truth is that afterward what might have been doesn't matter, except as a dream. The wheel will turn again, your Ralph will go home to his wife, your wife will get well. You'll dance with her yet at my Isaac's wedding."

"God willing," said Chaim.

The wedding was closer than Abraham had thought. What was the use, Isaac was thinking, of waiting any longer? Ruth was as good as his wife already. If they tried to outwait this slump they would both be old before they married. In the meantime he was just avoiding his responsibility by not taking Ruth to be his wife, into his home where she belonged. She didn't belong with the married sister and her husband, who didn't really want her or need her as he did. She had always known, in that way she had of feeling things, that they had taken her and brought her up because it was a duty. They had their own children to love. Ruth could remember a lifetime of trying to edge into the warmth of this love by taking care of these children. He had told her that she didn't have to earn his love, or his parents'. It was there for her, only for her. She would never have to stand in the shadows again. And that was true. He needed her. A depression can't dictate to a man what his needs are, not when his need is Ruth. Ever since he had met her he had wanted to take her away from her sister, to bring her home.

Why didn't he? Isaac admitted to himself that he was afraid, afraid that he wouldn't be able to support her, to do for her all those things that he wanted to do but didn't know how, afraid that he would disappoint her, afraid, he didn't know of what, as he so often was when it came to making a decision, unless he made it quickly, without thinking. Would she even want him if she knew of all his fears? She thought she knew him, and he tried to tell her about himself, but she really didn't, because she didn't feel his fears as he felt them. Well, in a way that was good. It was enough that he knew. She must know only the man he would like to be. It was not that he wanted to fool her, but rather to become the person she thought she knew. The man he wanted to be was not afraid of a depression or of a responsibility.

"Ruth," he brought out one day when they were sitting in the living room. Sarah had tactfully closed the door between them and the kitchen. "Ruth," he repeated, licking his lips, which had gone dry. "Don't you think we should get married soon? If you want, I mean." This last had not even occurred to him before. Did she want? He looked anxiously into her face. What he saw there reassured him. He felt a great relief, a sudden delight with himself, with Ruth, with the idea. He had not thought that she was as anxious as he—Isaac smudged the tears on her face awkwardly with his hand—the way she had talked, so practically, about jobs and money.

"Of course we must," began Isaac after a long interval during which they rediscovered that they really must. "We must"—Isaac liked to try his hand at fancy English phrases—"legalize this debauchery." As always, Ruth laughed, this time almost hysterically.

"I had a feeling when I got up today. I had a feeling; it made me so nervous all day."

Giggling a little, they began to tidy themselves up and prepared to burst open the kitchen door and make their announcement. There would have to be much discussion yet, about arrangements and dates. When they were tidy they paused to look at each other. Later in the evening they made their announcement.

The months melted away like the snow on the ground. Lingering bits of muddy ice still lay about in shady spots, but in the sunny places green was sprouting from the earth. The wedding was an affair, both Abraham and Chaim considered, to be remembered. Not that it was such a big wedding, for they did not know so many people in the city, but it was a wedding!

"Aha!" said Chaim Knopp when he talked of it. "Aha aha aha!" Because Ruth was an orphan and the married sister with whom she lived was not a rich woman and had as well a family to look after, and because Ruth in the past year or so had become as a child in his own house, Abraham considered that he should treat the affair not only as though he was marrying off his son but also as though he were marrying off his daughter at the same time. This was one of the excuses that he gave for ordering twice as much of everything as was considered necessary by anyone else. It would be months, he told himself happily, before he could finish paying off the expenses of this wedding. Well, it would happen only once. Let it at least try to make up for three.

At the wedding feast he presided like a king. His forked beard, which was generously threaded with silver, shone against the navy blue of his new serge suit. He was not ashamed to admit afterward that he too partook of the drink that he urged upon his guests. When Isaac took his bride onto the floor for the first waltz Abraham sang loudly against the music of the three-piece band. With a gesture he claimed Ruth for the second dance, while Isaac took his mother onto the floor.

Abraham was everywhere at once that evening. With his wife on his arm he moved among the guests, urging people to eat and drink, not tolerating refusal. Chaim remembered fondly that his stomach had been like lead for a week afterward. He, Chaim, had spent the entire evening trying to avoid his wife, who was better, although she could not yet dance any but the very slow numbers. He had had to avoid her because when Chaim was drunk he got a little foolish— not much; he just giggled a little and grinned about him. When his wife saw him that way she did not scruple to tell him how foolish he was. And on an occasion like this he didn't want to be told. At a celebration he could be as foolish as anyone else. So he left his wife close to a few other heavy ladies who didn't dance much, and wandered about, nodding and grinning at people foolishly but contentedly.

Even Sonya Plopler, when she saw that her daughters were having such a good time dancing with Isaac's friends, that her husband was so happy with too much to drink, and that she herself had so many good things to taste and recipes to collect, forgot to spread the rumor that the bride was older than the groom.

When Abraham got up from the supper table to make a speech he opened his heart and spoke so stirringly that even the woman who had been hired to help with the catering, who understood not a word of Yiddish, wept like a child. Chaim swore to it.

Chapter Seven

Young people are good for a house. With young ones there is no lack
of entertainment. There is a freshness; the walls light up; the whole
house seems to come alive. And when the young ones are a young
married couple, such as Isaac and Ruth, it is as when a man has a
cherry tree in his garden. There had been such a cherry tree in
Abraham's childhood. It was a pity that cherry trees didn't grow in
this climate. But who could complain? Weren't Ruth and Isaac like a
cherry tree that a man could sit and watch in the springtime? The
young buds swell and strain and puff themselves out in the sunshine.
A man wakes up in the morning, and suddenly the blossoms leap
into his eyes, waving their new-released petals so that the whole tree
sways with happiness and freedom. So the two of them in their excitement, they too broke forth in his eyes as the cherry tree that
blew its blossoms in the sun. And where the blossom is, the fruit
will follow. This was a thought to smile over, one of the few that
could win a little smile from the lips of his wife. Often he had to remind her of this fact when she was in one of her dark, silent moods.
It was a point in favor of life.

Such a little housewife Ruth had become. When Sarah fell ill in
the winter, who else would have been able to look after her so capa-
bly? He hadn't reckoned that such a young girl would have such a
talent for nursing. Everything had to be done just so. And who else
could have prevailed upon Isaac to go see the doctor and ask why
his heart beat uncomfortably at times? At least now they had a modern doctor's explanation for it, although with these doctors it was
hard to know one word from another.

"What did the doctor say to you, Isaac?"

"He said that I could live to be ninety."

"Well, did you thank him for this blessing?"

"But he said that I should try not to overwork or get excited. It makes the heart run—something like that."

"Nowadays they have to go to the doctor to find this out."

"He said that if it ever got worse I should come in to see him again."

"If it gets worse he knows you'll have to come in to see him again. You went to him so it shouldn't get worse. What about the colds? Did you ask him why you get the colds?"

"Yes. He said it's because I get run down, I work too hard, I don't get enough fresh vegetables to eat, and I'm not enough in the open air. He gave me some pills."

"Not enough in the open air—well, that's understandable; that the shop is an unhealthy place is a thing the doctor doesn't have to tell you. You will have to have a child soon so that you can play with him outside after work. That will give you fresh air. Vegetables? So, it could be. The doctor knows best, after all. If he says vegetables, it must be vegetables. But he would pick vegetables, just because fresh vegetables are hard to get in the winter, and expensive. He couldn't pick meat—that we get at a discount. Pills—well, that's more like a doctor. And you work too hard? It needs a doctor to tell us that you work too hard? If it's not the shop, then it's the children you teach. When it's not the children it's the books. How many things can a man do at once? One would think that you married your wife just so that you would have someone to send to the library. How many times have I myself told Chaim Knopp that you work too hard?"

And now he had the doctor's own words to prove it. Isaac simply worked too hard. What could one do when one had a son who had to know everything, to read everything? Good books, foolish books, all of them he read. Well, there was something in him, that was all, something that drove him to learning. Who would wish him to stop? Just not so much, that was all. As the doctor said, not too much. Someday, yes, someday people would see what a teacher Isaac would make. Then there would be no more shop. Then they would take him into the Hebrew school and then they would hear; then they would find him worth listening to.

If anything, Ruth was a little bit too fussy, especially about doctors. What could a doctor tell him about his arms that he didn't know already? To rub them with oil of wintergreen, as the first doctor had told him years ago? When Chaim Knopp asked his son-in-law why a man should get terrible aches in his arms when he lifted something heavy or when he went from a warm room into a refrigerator, Chaim's son-in-law the doctor had said that the man who got such aches should stop going to the refrigerator from the warm room and should stop lifting heavy things.

Chaim had said, "Well, then, how is a butcher to live if he does not do these things?" And his son-in-law, the elevated doctor, had laughed and told him that he was a doctor, not an economist. This was your doctor. If that was all the help he could give you, then it was wiser to keep your three dollars in your pocket.

Even if she thought too much of the doctors, it still showed that she wanted it for their own good. Another daughter-in-law wouldn't care, would say, Let them look after themselves. But she—the way she fussed over Sarah and wouldn't let her do anything, especially now that she wasn't working any more. Poor Ruth, she was not the first one to lose her job these days. What was there to cry about? They had never had to rely on the earnings of their wives before, and with God's help they wouldn't have to now either. There was plenty for her to do in the house. And what a little cook she was. All the new recipes, so that you didn't know what to expect on your plate any more and could hardly recognize what you found there. Good, yes, undoubtedly. And then Sarah must teach her all the old recipes so that Ruth could make them without Sarah's having to strain herself. That was a daughter-in-law!

Of course sitting and resting, good though it was for her, was hard for Sarah, who was used to working and cleaning and doing and making. Sometimes she even complained to him a little—well, not really complained; his wife had never been a complainer. But now occasionally there was a moment of something like irritation in her. It was nothing—it passed quickly—a word. "I sit all day and look at my hands," she had said once after her illness, when she was not allowed to move about much. She did not have to tell him what she thought about when she sat and looked at her hands. The thing to do then was to remind her of the future, of Isaac's future, of Isaac's children, who would take the names of their uncles. That was the fine thing about the future. It contained all the unknown good that God had planned, if only a person had the patience and the strength to wait.

"What burden, when burden?" he had said to Ruth when she cried after she lost her job. "You couldn't be a burden; wait, wait, you will bear the burden yet, eh? The only burden a woman should bear. We don't talk about burdens. We talk about life!"

Of course he could not say more than this at one time. He was not going to be vulgar, though he could not help wanting to urge a little sometimes. Usually what he wanted done he did for himself. Now it was a matter of waiting for Isaac and Ruth. Isaac was perhaps a little too cautious. A man shouldn't have to consult his pocketbook before he makes his wife pregnant. Did the wind consult the weather bureau before it picked up the seeds or blew the pollen to the waiting flowers? These things have to happen. It was not just for himself that he was impatient, but for Sarah.

Abraham did not like to think too much of the changes that seemed to have taken place in Sarah. She had not really changed, he told himself. Perhaps she had withered and twisted about a little, as a delicate tree will when its branches have been torn off. And something in her still surged and beat against the dry wounds, seeking its outlet. It was not for him, who understood so well, to find fault when he could find no aid. But that was where a grandchild would help. A woman can't always look to the future. She needs the present, the immediate satisfactions of life. These things a man wants too, but he looks beyond them. He sees the present stretching out toward the future. A woman claps her hands and is happy because a child is learning to walk. A man is happy too, but in his mind is the question, In what direction will the child's steps take him? A man could be compared to the wind, which must riffle through life, turning over the leaves of time with a restlessness, trying to see everything at once, always seeking. A woman waits, rooted in the earth, like a tree, like a flower. Patiently she lifts her face to receive the gift of the wind. Suddenly he sweeps across the earth and stoops to blow the dust. Then she comes to life; she seizes it, clasps it, and works with it the miracle of creation. Now it is his turn to wait. He hovers over her, trying to see, to understand.

What a fine idea! Sometimes the thoughts that grew in his head were a surprise even to himself. "Blessed is God, who has made me a thinking man. Blessed is God for the singing thoughts." Chaim must hear of this. He would appreciate the philosophy in it. And Isaac. He and Isaac would have a good discussion. Isaac could take the strangest meanings out of a beautiful idea. He was never content to examine merely the beauty of the flower. He had to find its very roots. You could tell him your idea, for instance, about the flower and the wind. And Isaac would say, "Yes, but you seem to put man and woman on different levels, as though the man were somehow the more important of the two, the master. They have different physical functions, it's true, but nowadays we recognize that women can think just as men do."

"Isaac, in the first place I didn't say anything about masters. Have I ever given you any indication that I am one of those old-fashioned Jews who thinks he is his wife's master? And I didn't say women can't think. My wife can think just like anybody else, even though she herself prefers to trust to my judgment. It's just that, like the flower and the wind, she is different because she is a flower, he is different because he is the wind. She stays home and cooks and cleans and waits for him, and he goes out and seeks a living, and—"

"Let's forget about the flower and the wind for a minute, Papa. That much is true, but the difference is not that great. Nowadays a woman can think about the same things that a man thinks about. She can go out and make a living too. We don't think about women

as our inferiors any more. Marriage is a partnership. Each one gives
what he can."

"Just so, just so, precisely so. And a man can't have children. And
yet a man is physically stronger than a woman, and because he can't
concentrate on having a child he must put his strength and his
thoughts to something else—isn't it true? Who talks of inferiority?
It is a wonderful thing to be able to have a child. You will see. The
woman becomes busy, her womb fills out. Her breasts become milky,
and on her face there is a look—you'll see, you'll see. What is he
to do then? What feeling fills him when he looks on this, when he sees
life working in her? Something must work in him too. So you read
and you work even harder. Always you want to do a little more. You
try to reach into all four corners of the earth at once. Like the wind,
you would shake down the stars. Don't tell me no, my son. I know
what's in you."

And they would go on with their discussion, sometimes not understanding each other very well at first, so that one of them would
maybe shout a little—not so much Isaac. Well, it was because Isaac
was never satisfied to take a statement in the way it was meant that
Avrom sometimes lost his temper. It was infuriating to find himself
arguing about something that he had not even had in mind at all at
the beginning. He started out with a beautiful thought like that about
the wind and the flowers, and before he had fully explained himself
Isaac was brushing away the wind and the flowers and was telling
him something else altogether. Of course after all the shouting he
would end up by seeing the truth in much of what Isaac said. And
Isaac would as often as not end up by admitting that Avrom's idea
was a very fine one, really. It went to show what a scrupulously careful thinker Isaac was, how fair he tried to be, even though, as in this
case, he was not even a woman himself.

Abraham would have to remember, when he told Chaim of his
idea, to mention that he meant to imply no insult to women. They
were certainly not inferior to men. Who knows but Chaim might
disagree? In some ways he was a bit old-fashioned in his ideas, hav-

ing been educated in an old-country Yeshiva. A man must keep up with the ideas of the times. He himself was lucky that he had a son like Isaac to discuss them with.

It was only natural, Abraham felt, that he should expect a grandchild soon. All about him he could see the visible proofs of the movement of time. Look at Chaim, who was surrounded by grandchildren. Seven grandchildren he had already. What a wealth of story they made. Of course each one was a prodigy. Every day there was a new proof of it. Today it was the doctor's boy—five years old, and there was distinctly another doctor in the making. Hadn't he been found by the kindergarten teacher behind the shed in the back of the kindergarten, playing doctors and patients with two little girls? Of course they had had to punish him, as children can't be allowed to play together in such a manner, but still, in spite of the child's mistaken idea of what doctors and patients do together, it was obvious that he had the urge in him to be a doctor.

And then there was the marriage of Sonya Plopler's eldest daughter. She had been married for scarcely two months, and here she was, carrying what looked like a five-month child in her belly. And Sonya Plopler running about from house to house, denying everything and telling everyone that she too had grown very big very quickly, so that everyone, even those who didn't normally go around counting months, expected a premature birth.

Even Polsky's children seemed to have shot up suddenly. After school Polsky's eldest son came in to help around the place and to do deliveries. Hymie, who was getting to be a strapping lad, like his father, was not even out of grade school yet, and he was already beginning to talk about quitting school. And Polsky didn't seem to mind, although in front of people like Abraham and Chaim Knopp he liked to make a little show as though he cared.

"I don't care what kind of old bats your teachers are," he would shout at Hymie. "You'll damn well keep on going till you finish your grade eleven if it takes you ten years!" But at the same time he would encourage Abraham to teach Hymie how to be a butcher in the old style, how to pickle meat, how to cut it. The other children, if they wanted to, might go on to study more, but this oldest son would come into the business with him someday.

Abraham could not help trying to encourage Hymie to stay in school. Polsky had money. He had more than one source of income; this he did not hesitate to boast about. Why shouldn't the boy at least continue to go to school and try to make something of himself? But it was impossible to talk to him seriously about anything. He was still a child in his mind. Try to speak to him reasonably. "Why do you want to stop going to school? Do you think you will ever have another chance to learn?"

And Hymie would shrug his shoulders—"Ahh-h-h-h"—and talk about his teachers, or tell about how he got out of doing his homework. Well, it takes a kind of mind to be able to get out of doing homework, too—crafty. He would make a good partner for his father someday.

It was an interesting question. Had he, Abraham, carried on the kind of business that Polsky boasted about, business in the shade, then he too would have been able to send his son to study. There were many thieves who sent their sons to the universities, and these sons became honorable men sometimes. Was it worth it, then, to become a thief? And how did one go about it? One needed a stomach for everything. God should forgive him for even thinking about such questions.

An uncouth boy, that son of Polsky's, full of smut and back-talk, too, when he thought he could get away with it. Still, he was not on the whole ill-natured. Just mention Isaac to him, and Hymie was all amiability. Ever since Isaac had coached him for his Bar Mitzvah—which had involved getting right up there with him when the time came, because Hymie could not remember his lessons, and whispering the words from behind a prayerbook when Hymie forgot them—Hymie had been Isaac's big friend.

This was something that he might point out to Chaim Knopp, who had taken such a dislike to the boy. He might be a ruffian, but he was a good-natured ruffian. A good-natured ruffian is better than an ill-natured gentleman. This was a true thought.

Chaim Knopp had his own opinion of the kind of man Hymie Polsky would grow up to be. "A no-good," he told Abraham. "Feh!" And when the boy came into the shop when Chaim was present you could see that Chaim could scarcely bear to look at him. What kind of madness is it when an old man wishes to carry on a feud against a young boy? True, Hymie was not as clean as he might be. Dirtiness was something that Chaim could not stomach. When he had to slaughter fowl he wrapped himself in a huge apron and afterward scrubbed himself thoroughly. In spite of his precautions he often complained that he smelled chicken everywhere he went. And here was Hymie. How many times had Abraham himself told him that the customers would not have any confidence in a butcher who kept his fingers in his nose? A filthy habit.

It was true, too, that the boy was disrespectful sometimes. But this disrespect was not directed solely at Chaim. Didn't he talk about "my old man" in front of the customers? Who had taught him better? And if his mind was already tainted with vulgarities—well, whose mind was it had given him the example? This was no reason for Chaim to speak the way he did, especially on that day when he had caught Hymie up in front of customers and told him what a no-good he would be someday.

Even a young ruffian can have his feelings hurt. Abraham had seen this by the way the boy stood there with his mouth hanging open and his jaw hanging down. But Chaim had been blind to it. The boy's slack face, in which his eyes shifted sideways from Chaim to the customers, who were laughing and nodding at what Chaim said, and finally to the floor, had only seemed to irritate the shoichet further.

"A Jewish son," he had continued angrily, "a young *shneck* like you, running around in the poolhalls already. And what are you hanging your head for with your mouth open, eh?"

This was no way to do things, to make fun of him in front of people like this, somebody else's son. It actually hurt Abraham to see Chaim behaving in this way—Chaim, who was such a philosophic man, who had really such a kind heart, who was a man full of goodness. It was as though Chaim had in his heart a boil of bitterness that had pussed up suddenly and had to be let out somewhere. Why on Polsky's son? God only knew. It would pass; Abraham was sure of it.

Things did not go well with Chaim at home. His wife, ever since her long ailment, was not so strong as she used to be. Although she herself tried to ignore this fact, there it was. She had to stay at home and rest more. Other women took her place in the societies—women who, she was now sure, had always been her enemies. Every few months she had to go to the hospital to be checked up. She was restless and cranky. It was lonely for her, Chaim admitted, to have to stay home so much, crossing off her list of friends those society women who now no longer came to visit her as often as before. So she got notions into her head.

Bassieh's big notion was that they should give up their home and move in with Ralph and his wife. Ralph had returned to his wife, and for a while all had run smoothly. Then again the troubles had started. Bassieh had the theory that her daughter-in-law deliberately refused to have any more children, just to spite Ralph because she knew he wanted a son and heir. She was convinced that her own presence would straighten out the marriage.

At first she did not even bother to pay any attention to Chaim's refusal to consider the idea. He had tried a tentative "No" before. It was when Chaim for the first time in their life together said, "No," and said it continually that Bassieh sharpened her arguments.

What was he afraid of? Didn't Ralph have enough room for them? If he had enough room in the house to entertain Her parents for weeks on end. when they came in from the country, then he had enough for his own. In fact, Ralph would be happy to take them in, just to show his wife, whose parents were so dear to her, that his parents were just as dear to him. Of course they need not stay with Ralph permanently, unless he really wanted them to—just for a little while. Hadn't Ralph held his father to his promise and made him stop working in the abattoir when he returned to his wife? Weren't they finding things harder now that that money wasn't coming in? So they would give up their house, which was too big for them anyway now that all the children were married. They would move in with Ralph until they could find a smaller suite.

Chaim continued to refuse. Her arguments became recriminations. All of Chaim's shortcomings as a husband, father, and provider were dragged out and reviewed. It got so that, when he was through with his work in the shack where he slaughtered the chickens, Chaim took to wandering about instead of going home. Sometimes he dropped into the synagogue to have a conference with the shamus. Or else he would come to the butcher shop and sit on the barrel that Abraham kept especially for him. At other times he would get an impulse to visit one or the other of his children, to see the grandchildren. But these surprise visits were not always successful. Children are children. When they see you so often they do not notice you so much. As he explained to Abraham, grandchildren are wonderful to think about and talk about and play with sometimes. But you can't follow them out on the street when they want to play with their friends.

"I wish I had a grandchild already," said Abraham, "that I could see playing with his friends someday. That would be *naches*."

"Yes, it's a pleasure to have them," Chaim agreed with a sigh.

Abraham went on to talk about his future grandchildren, conceiving prodigies. When he noticed that Chaim looked sad and far away, as though he were thinking of his troubles, he, for the sake of *naches*, invented for Chaim, too, a special grandchild, a boy, who would be the late-born of Chaim's son Ralph. This Abraham knew was Chaim's secret woe. But it could still happen. It was not an uncommon thing for ten or even fifteen years to pass between the birth of two children. Why shouldn't it happen? Abraham, whose heart was heated with the thought of his own grandchildren to come, talked in such a way that he soon had Chaim, too, relaxed and chuckling over the very thought. They would be close friends, those boys whose birth meant so much. They would walk the surface of the earth together, the rich man's son—the rich man who still honored his father, Abraham amended—and the poor man's son—the gifted, scholarly poor man, Chaim amended. Yes, it was entirely possible, Chaim agreed. Indeed it had a good sound to it. Time, Chaim agreed, the future.

"They won't like it." Sarah followed Ruth to the open door of the summer kitchen.

"Close the door, Mother," Ruth called back, her words billowing frostily out of her mouth. "Do you want to be laid up again? Close the door; you're not dressed. It's cold out here."

Neither was Ruth dressed, Sarah noted, but it did not occur to her to take up this fact in argument. She swung the door gently without closing it, so that Ruth could push through a moment later, her arms full of wood for the stove.

Sarah coughed. "You see," said Ruth, brushing herself off beside the stove, "one little draft will start you coughing again. You mustn't go near the summer kitchen. It's no good for you."

"They've never liked that kind of food," Sarah repeated. "They won't eat it."

"They'll have to eat it." Ruth began to explain again, wondering how many times she had already explained this. "The doctor told Isaac that he needs more of this kind of food. Besides, the way I've dressed it they'll like it. They didn't like fish either, but they've eaten it every time I've cooked it." Ruth laughed. She enjoyed housekeeping, and she rather enjoyed disproving all those odd little notions that her mother-in-law clung to about the tastes of the men. Not that it helped. No matter how often Abraham ate fish that Ruth had prepared, no matter how obviously he enjoyed what he was eating, when Ruth suggested fish again her mother-in-law would object that the men didn't like it. But Ruth had found a way around Sarah's objections that involved very little fuss. Since the time of Sarah's illness Ruth had done much of the household shopping. She merely went ahead and bought the fish, or the vegetables that Sarah regarded so suspiciously, and then they had to be used. Sometimes there was a moment of irritation on the part of her mother-in-law. But from irritation she could easily be diverted. Ruth felt a sentimental tenderness for Sarah when she thought of her ways about the house—so gentle, so absent-minded, so absolutely sure that it was not she who had left the saltshaker in the linen cupboard, so gently indignant when Ruth suggested that she might yet recall what had happened to the eggbeater. Of course it could be irritating, too.

In a way it was a good thing that she had lost her job. Sarah was still not strong enough to do all of the housekeeping. Leave her alone and she would be wandering in and out of the summer kitchen, inviting the bronchitis back.

Ruth began to sing as she busied herself about the woodstove. She had the sort of pleasant, somewhat resonant contralto voice that sounds especially good to the singer himself, resounding melodiously in his head and giving him a gratifying sense of dramatic power as he builds up to the particularly forceful notes. Abraham liked to hear her sing. This song he had taught her himself. It was good to be able to sing whenever you liked, in your own home. At her sister's it had always been a question of waking the children or bothering her brother-in-law. Ruth felt her voice swelling within her. The kitchen was just small enough to bring out the roundness in her tones. She gestured with the arm that held the soup ladle.

The notes vibrated in Sarah's head. There was a shrill, childish screaming as though someone were calling her. Her heart started, and she stood, grasping the edge of the table, looking anxiously toward the door. Wild-eyed and frightened, Jacob came clattering into the room. What had the child got himself into? A mother needs eyes in the back of her head! From top to bottom he was stained with berries. His face was smeared with purple, etched with rivulets of tears. From his chest dripped the juice of squashed berries that he had stuffed into his shirt front.

"The Wolf!" he screamed. "He's got Moishe!"

The Wolf! She dropped her work. What's he done to my child? She seized the baby in her arms. She ran, leaving the house, leaving everything. With Jacob running and wailing behind her, she flew to the butcher shop. Avrom!

Together, Avrom stalking grimly ahead, to the home of the Wolf, to the high-walled orchard. Why? Why? Had they wanted berries she would have given them the kopek to buy at the market. Was this the wall? Had they climbed this wall? Her heart stood still to look at it. And the dogs—those baying hungry dogs that were chained to the trees inside. Sometimes at night, when they set up a howling, the whole town could hear them. And he beat them, too, the children, sometimes when he caught them stealing from his orchard. God, what's that black monster doing to my child?

From the gate they heard him. Abraham's expression as he turned to her was as a mirror of her own astonishment. They paused for a moment outside the gate to listen. Then the clear soprano, like a silver thread, wound them through the gate and into the orchard. Fat little Moishe, his whole face stained with blackberries and dry tears, singing in the orchard. With his knees dirty in front of the great landlord! And the Wolf sat with his wife and his dogs, ears so drawn to the child's open mouth that he didn't even hear them approach. Even the dogs, as Abraham told about it later, had sat as though they were entranced.

"You have a singer here," the Wolf, Phillip Gregor Molinikov, said with admiration. "A real singer."

Ruth interrupted her singing and turned around to say something to her mother-in-law. Sarah stood, gripping the side of the table, an attentive, distant smile on her face. What was she thinking about? At first, even though she had been warned by Isaac and knew what there was to know of their former life, Ruth had been a little frightened by the length and intensity of Sarah's silences. With her face either frighteningly blank or paralyzed in the expression of some emotion, she went about almost mechanically, doing her chores. At such moments only Avrom had the courage to interrupt her. He did this with a gentleness that was to Ruth surprising in a man so forceful in his outward manner as Avrom. If the moment occurred, as it did sometimes, when they were all assembled together, then it seemed to her as though they were suddenly suspended, the three of them, in a thought from which she was excluded. She would look from Abraham and Sarah to Isaac, her husband, and he would be sitting quietly, not looking at anything. If she went up to him and touched him, then he would look at her and smile with something, an oddness, in his look.

Sometimes she was ashamed of herself for wanting to belong even to these moments. Isaac's face, brightening when he looked at her, was enough to reassure her that she belonged at least to his present and his future. They had proved it to her. That day when she had discovered that she had lost her job, when she had spent the morning going miserably from one dress shop to another, asking for work, and when she had come home to cry all afternoon, hadn't Isaac scolded her for her foolishness? And Abraham had laughed at her. Why was she apologizing? She no longer had to pay board and room to her brother-in-law. She was needed at home. Hadn't she been fired because she had taken those three weeks off to stay at home and look after Sarah? Even Sarah had spent the afternoon hovering over her solicitously, comforting her. The feeling of warmth expanded in Ruth. She began to sing again.

Who was singing? Sarah experienced a sense of irritation. Avrom could make as though he liked that voice. But it was shrill, too loud and shrill for her. It pierced through her head. There were no singers nowadays.

It was time, Sarah knew instinctively, although Ruth stood in front of the clock, to set the table. Sarah shook her head. "Avrom won't eat any of it," she complained, but her voice was so soft that Ruth did not hear it through her song.

At the supper table Isaac told about something that had happened in his shop that day. This Laiah woman, who was quite well known to some of the other workers in the shop, had come in to ask about a job. But she did not want a full-time job, just half-days, in the afternoons. She explained to the foreman that it was boring for her to sit around all day, so she wanted to occupy herself a bit and earn some money at the same time. The foreman had had to turn her down, although, as Beraleh, the shop joker, had said, you could see that it made his glands sweat to have to turn away such a broad pinching territory.

The other workers had had a good laugh over it. How many people came in every day to beg for work to keep themselves and their families alive? And this one wanted work because her afternoons were slack. Not that she cared much when the foreman said no. She said she thought maybe she'd take a little trip if she didn't get a job. From what they said, she made enough money. According to Beraleh, this husband of hers, who had been in jail for a while, had not returned to her when he was released. Instead he had left the city altogether. They might even be divorced by now, but he was probably paying her money to help support her. There were laws about that sort of thing. Anyway, she didn't look as though she were starving.

"That one doesn't starve," commented Abraham. "She eats with both cheeks. I know; she's an old customer."

"Well, she's luckier than a lot of people. I met Hersh Gottleib the other day. They've been on relief for six months already."

"God preserve us from relief," said Abraham. "God preserve everyone from relief."

"He has a lot of preserving to catch up on, then," was Isaac's comment.

Chapter Eight

————— ◄►◆►◄ —————

At last Ruth was pregnant. And it would be a boy; there was no doubt of it. Even before there had been much swelling Sarah had seen, by that species of abdominal phrenology that is traditional among the women, that it was pointed in front, rather than rounded, which surely meant that a son would be born. Abraham, lest Chaim should think that he gloated too much over his good fortune, promised him even more positively than before that he too would have a grandson by his son Ralph. Glowing with his own happy event, he did not find it hard to make the prophecy. And so he was scarcely surprised when, two short months after Ruth had revealed her condition, Chaim bustled into the shop with his news.

"She's pregnant, my daughter-in-law!" Chaim didn't seem to realize that it was young Hymie Polsky's hand that he had seized and was pumping wildly up and down. Hymie's body jerked loosely to and fro with Chaim's energetic movement; his mouth was half open in an astonished grin. Chaim let his hand go as suddenly as he had seized it, and rushed forward to embrace Abraham. Hymie, grinning with fatuous delight, watched the old man dance across the sawdust floor, spilling out his news anew to Polsky. In his excitement Chaim tripped over, and then apologized profusely to, the ever pregnant "Poosy." They all laughed. It was spring, and everyone was pregnant.

"A miracle!" Abraham boomed above the congratulations of Polsky. Of course it was. It was a sign. He had been ready for it—oh, from the moment his own Ruth had announced her condition, some sign, some overabundance to show the hand of God.

"A miracle?" Chaim marveled, scarcely able to believe it.

122

"Of course, a miracle," Abraham assured him and was hugely contented, for he felt at home with miracles.

"You think it could be a boy?" Chaim's grin was anxious.

"What else?" Abraham was not one to skimp his miracles.

Hymie Polsky, whose hand still tingled warmly from Chaim's handclasp, felt a chill recollection move slowly through his mind. Gradually his mouth gathered itself shut and the astonished grin disappeared from his face. Memory of an old resentment spread itself over his heavy features. Looking around him, Hymie saw that all eyes were on Chaim. With a sudden furtive movement he made an ugly face and an obscene gesture at the old man's back. "I hope it's a girl," he muttered fiercely, but not quite loudly enough for anyone to hear. Then slowly, in spite of the fact that he tried to maintain a sneer, his mouth, of its own will, relaxed open again, and his lips twitched helplessly back into their comfortable grin.

The grandfathers-in-waiting met regularly to compare notes and discuss progress. It was a harrowing experience in some ways, Abraham discovered, this becoming a grandfather for the first time. Truly he did not remember such agitation as this when he was about to become a father. Actually, when he tried to think back on it, he could scarcely remember what he had felt at those times. He had been a father so intensely and so long that the sense of fatherhood had grown into him. But of one thing he was certain. His wife had never during her pregnancies been inclined to get such notions as Ruth. What perfectly healthy woman would want to have her baby in a hospital? When he went with the news to Chaim he received small comfort. The little shoichet was all bitterness and resignation. It was just as he had expected. He had lived through it all before. His own was to be born in a hospital bed as well. Didn't Abraham know that that was how it was done nowadays? The mothers were fed unclean meat. A crowd of young interns made indecent and unnecessary examinations at will. And of course the mothers were separated from their babies. Who knew for a fact whether they ever returned the right babies to the right mothers? And there were no wise Solomons nowadays to judge.

Abraham was determined to convince Ruth of her folly. She was a spirited girl, right enough, and he was inclined to be proud of her because of this. In a house where he and Isaac often teased each other, she could stand up to them both, never at a loss for words. But to be so willful, and to lead Isaac with her, and their grandson, no.

"It's just such notions that make for unhealthy births, God forbid," Abraham remonstrated over the supper table. "I remember a second cousin of my wife's went mad and became a Christian." Abraham paused to let them appreciate the full enormity of his statement.

"So?" said Ruth.

"That's just the point. Who knows if he was a Jew in the first place? Some said the gypsies changed him soon after he was born. That's why you have to watch these things. Can you watch your baby when the nurses are shuffling them all around?"

"That can't happen, Pa," said Isaac. "They mark each baby so they know which is which."

"Yeh, yeh," said Abraham. "We had services for him when he became an apostate, just as though he had died. I remember how his mother cried herself to death." He shook his head several times and murmured audibly, "Oiyoiyoi, children, children"—but throughout the rest of the meal maintained a gloomy silence.

Ruth and Isaac exchanged glances but kept hopefully silent on the subject. Isaac tried to tell an amusing anecdote about something that had happened at work that day, but with little success. Finally Abraham, over his tea, burst out indignantly, "I don't want them to mark my grandson."

Isaac tried to explain that the procedure, whatever it was, for identifying the children—and he wasn't quite sure of what it was himself—was a perfectly harmless one. At any rate, he pointed out, they had several months to go yet. Nothing was really decided. They didn't even have a bed in the hospital yet. There was no need to argue about it. With these assurances Isaac and Ruth escaped from the house for a little while, to walk and plan in the warm summer evening.

They left Abraham pleased with himself, almost convinced that he had won Isaac over.

"He wasn't my cousin; he was yours." His wife's voice broke softly across his thoughts. He looked up, startled, but her face was averted, her troubled gaze on her hands in front of her.

Abraham felt shame sweeping over him, covering him with self-disgust. It was true.

"Sarah," he said, taking her hand and turning her to face him. Still she looked down, as though ashamed of what she had let slip.

"Sarah," he repeated pleadingly. The Christian cousin was a disgrace that had long been a useful member of his store of object lessons. It had been one of the shames of his childhood. He could not remember when he had transferred him to his wife's side of the family. It just seemed, somehow, when he was telling about it, to slip out that way. She had never complained before, but how it must have hurt her! What had he taken on himself? He was horrified now, thinking of it.

"Forgive me; of course he was mine. My Aunt Tanya's son. I am a liar," he said with self-loathing. "God should only punish me."

"No," she said. She let him pull her toward him and lean his face in her hair. Her hair, he noticed, was whiter than the gray streaks in his beard.

"Sarah," he mumbled into her hair, "what will I do without you? What will I do without you?" He realized while he spoke the implication of what he was saying, and gripped her tighter in the terror of a sudden spasm of foreknowledge. She was silent in his arms, as though already distant. What will I do without you? He closed his eyes tightly and choked back the words.

Ruth allowed herself to relax more heavily on Isaac's arm. She felt him brace himself slightly to hold her weight and felt, rather than saw, the pleased smile that lit his face as he did so.

"You want to turn back?" he asked.

"No, not yet." Neither did he, she knew. The thought amused her a little. There was really much of his father in him. Or did she only imagine that since her condition had become more obvious he smiled more frequently at the people they passed?

She sighed. Isaac bent over her anxiously. She heard herself saying, "All of a sudden I have a longing for an ice-cream cone." While she waited for him to fetch it she wondered why she had said that. She had not been aware of any longing for an ice-cream cone until he had bent over her so anxiously. They expected her to want things. Sometimes—was it to satisfy them or herself?—she play-acted a little. She could remember a time when she had wanted things desperately, many things. Once, for instance, she had wanted boy friends, and she had fought for them. When she had won, that had seemed to prove something to herself, and when she had lost, that had also proved something. What? Those times seemed so vague and distant now that she could not at the moment remember any specific occasion. She could really be aware now, for any length of time, only of the sureness inside of herself, of the ease with which she could reach out for the ice-cream cone, surprised that it was just what she had wanted after all.

"At least he didn't harp on the atheist business this time," said Isaac. Never, he told himself, would he be able to follow his father's reasoning processes. There was no one, of this he was convinced, not anyone in the whole world who could start with two totally unrelated points and end by welding them as securely together as his father could.

Suddenly, the other night, when they had been sitting out on the front porch, out of a clear blue sky—an evening sky in which even the stars seemed suddenly to blink in a startled way—Abraham made a hopeless gesture, turned his eyes to the sky, and declaimed loudly, "O God O God O God, that my only remaining son should become an atheist!"

"What's brought that into your head?" asked Isaac hastily.

"A father can tell." Abraham sighed. "A father's heart feels."

"What can you feel?" protested Isaac.

"What can you feel," countered Abraham, "when you go to work on Saturdays?"

"But I've told you before, Pa, in this country you can't keep a job in my trade unless you work on Saturdays. The bosses are no longer very sensitive to the feelings of religious immigrants. Either you work when they tell you or there are plenty of others who are only too willing to work on Saturdays, if they could only find the work."

Abraham smiled with a certain ironic satisfaction. "And I suppose," he said with elaborate sarcasm, "that in this country the women can't have babies any more outside of hospitals either?"

Having made his point, Abraham allowed the silence to lengthen while Isaac found himself blinking back at the stars. In a way, though, he was relieved that his father's argument had taken this turn. . . .

"I wonder," Isaac mused out loud, "whether they had funerals for those who became atheists as well."

Ruth felt a movement within her that seemed to indicate perfect satisfaction with the ice cream. "Funerals?" she said vaguely.

When they got back to the house Abraham still waited up for them in the kitchen. He stood up to face them grimly, cutting through Ruth's greeting with a gesture of his hand. Ruth and Isaac exchanged dismayed glances.

"It was my cousin, the apostate, not your mother's," he stated firmly. "You should know." After waiting for a moment to give them a chance to reply, he nodded seriously and bade them a dignified good night.

Abraham continued to agitate against a hospital birth. Time and again both Ruth and Isaac countered his arguments by enumerating the advantages of the hospital. As was his way, the more he felt himself being gradually convinced that they might perhaps be right, the further afield he went in his attempts to prove them wrong. But inwardly he was already pulling in his last defenses. The baby was the important thing. One could outwit the doctors. He himself would go to the hospital. He would be there from the moment the child was born. He would not let it out of his sight. Wherever they took it, he would follow. If Ruth thought that she would have better care in the hospital, then far be it from him to deny her. But he would be there, alert, watching.

When the time came it was Abraham who urged Ruth, somewhat incoherently, to hold on until they could reach the hospital.

"We will call him Moishe Jacob," Abraham stated to the anteroom at large when they heard the news, "for my eldest sons who were killed in the pogrom. You see," he explained to the others who waited, most of whom did not understand him but smiled with a sort of nervous sympathy, "new grapes on the vines." He laughed and spread out his arms. "Who can be my equal now?"

When the nurse brought the child out to them Abraham led Sarah forward so that, after Isaac, she should be the first to hold him. Holding the child, she wept bitterly, partly for joy and partly because she had a fear of church bells and always when there was a movement toward happiness inside of her she thought she heard a carillon ringing.

Chaim performed the operation. A few friends of the family—the Polskys, Mrs. Plopler, Ruth's relatives, and one or two young couples who were acquaintances of Ruth and Isaac—came to the hospital for the ceremony. Chaim, his eyes bright with awareness of the dignity of his office, did not mingle with the guests before the operation but stood, slightly aloof, behind the little table that had been prepared for him. His little beard, freshly manicured, nodded politely now and again as he caught the eye of one or another of the guests. He draped the long white satin talus over his shoulders.

The nurse brought the child in and laid it in Sarah's arms. Sarah lifted it up to Abraham. Abraham strode with it to where Ruth's brother-in-law waited. Mrs. Plopler's nose moved rapidly in expressive disapproval. She had expected her husband to be given the honor of taking the child from Abraham. In fact, she had turned up at the house the day after the child was born and in a remarkable duet with herself had contrived to invite her husband, express agreeable surprise, and accept the invitation, all before she was well within the door. There had been a few difficult moments spent in trying to appease her when she discovered that the honor had already been promised to Ruth's brother-in-law. Even now Mrs. Plopler wasn't sure whether the insult wasn't big enough to warrant her staying away from the affair altogether. But she had not been able to bring herself to stay away. Her husband, however—he, certainly, had refused to come. Mrs. Plopler felt a disagreeable sensation inside of her now as she recalled that she herself had invited her husband, in Abraham's name, to help in the ceremony. And then when she had come home to him with the news that he would not be able to take part! Mrs. Plopler closed her eyes for a moment, and her nose positively shuddered.

Ruth's brother-in-law carried the child to where Chaim waited.

Chaim with conscious eloquence intoned the circumcision prayer of the first Abraham. When the baby uttered its cry the watchers nodded solemnly.

"Yes," said Abraham softly to his grandson, "it's hard to be a Jew."

"Harder still," said Isaac as softly, "to be a human being."

Abraham looked around at his son with a puzzled expression, and then his eyes lit up and he nodded his head up and down vigorously. "It's true," he said out loud. "You're absolutely right, my son. It's hard to be a Jew, as we all know. But it's still harder"—and Abraham emphasized his words with a gesture of his hand, glancing over to see that Chaim caught what his son had said—"to be a human being."

Chaim, whom Abraham addressed politely as "Reverend" for that whole day, handed the child back to Ruth's brother-in-law, who returned it again to Abraham. Abraham laid it ceremoniously in Sarah's arms, and Sarah returned it, at last, to the nurse.

The serious part of the ceremony was over. Food and liquor were unpacked, and the little celebration began. Isaac found himself in a

corner, trying to think of nice things to say to a much aggrieved
Mrs. Plopler. Abraham sought Chaim out among a group of guests
who were plying him with liquor. "Well, what do you think of him,
Reverend?" He beamed, his face flushed.

"I was just saying"—the Reverend Chaim chuckled, his face
equally flushed, "that he is a smallish Jew, but perfect!"

"Perfect!" echoed Abraham.

"Absolutely perfect!" Chaim said with a chuckle some two months
later. "A perfect little rascal,"

"Well, what did I tell you?" Abraham laughed.

"You were right, thank God." Chaim was secretly annoyed with
himself because he had all along been afraid to believe that it really
would be a boy. A lot of good your education does you, he told himself afterward, when you are afraid to believe simply because you
might be wrong. And what if it had been a girl? You would have had
those nine months of joy to look back on instead of nine months of
secret worry. That would have been a little miracle in itself.

But now the time for worry had passed. As Chaim explained to
Abraham, the baby had already brought about a species of truce
between his wife and his daughter-in-law.

"My Bassieh came and sat with her, and she talked to her, and
she told her how it's the woman that always suffers, and how the
men don't understand anything about it. It was a pleasure to see
them talking together so nicely," said Chaim. "We're even planning
to give up the house and move into a flat," he added with satisfaction.

It was strange, and he and Chaim often discussed it, how all had
happened almost as though they had planned it. It was meant to be,
there was no doubt about it. Looking at the child, Abraham could
not recall a time when his grandson had not been there, implicit in
his life.

"Whom would you say he looks like, Isaac?"

"You."

"Don't joke with your father. Look at him. Whose side of the family? It's important to know these things so we should have some idea of his character. The first thing your mother and I used to ask, as with one thought, 'Is it normal?' And when we knew that it was physically normal, this would satisfy your mother, but I would always look for a sign of its character. You, for instance, I knew right away were a stubborn one. I would not be surprised if, when Gabriel tapped your mouth to make you forget the Torah before you came into the world, you bit his finger. Hah! I wouldn't be surprised. With this one, now, it's different. Just look at him."

"I can see your character written all over him," said Isaac. "Look at that chin, that nose—not as large yet, perhaps, but one can see it has ambitions. That forehead—"

"Laugh, laugh; a few people can remember your father as a handsome man yet."

"I know, and haven't you a handsome son to prove it?" Isaac's pale face had assumed a surer look since he had become responsible for the bearing of a son, as though the feat had somehow won him a greater right to be.

"And a handsome grandson, and you'll have superb great-grandchildren, and if you ever run out of breath your wives will continue to tell the world all about you." Ruth had come in and busied herself about the red little body in the basket.

"I was just telling your husband," said Abraham, who was not above a gallant lie, "that it would be well if the child showed some of your characteristics."

"Oh, I don't need a full dedication; a footnote will do."

Abraham laughed with his son appreciatively, although he could not be sure that the joke wasn't partly on him. An educated girl. She could hold her own.

Ruth picked up the baby and pushed through the curtain into the bedroom. Sarah, who had followed her into the living room, followed her aimlessly into the bedroom, trying to tuck the covers more closely under her arm.

Ruth hugged the child to herself. There was something so personal about holding her baby. Sometimes she wished they could go off somewhere, just herself and Isaac and their baby, for a little while, away from everybody. Lying down across the bed, she cradled her child in her arms and began to croon as she fed him, forgetting her mother-in-law's presence entirely. Sarah watched her for a moment, then turned and slipped through the curtain.

"I cannot help wondering"—Abraham was musing—"when a child is born, what will be its destiny? What secret message is it that God has written on its forehead?" He let his eyes rove slowly over the features of his son, who sat, his eyes clouded with thought. "What sign will he bring to his people, to the world?" He was handsome, Abraham thought with pride, sitting so deeply in thought.

Isaac stirred uncomfortably. "Why should he bring any sign, and to us in particular?"

"I don't know," said Abraham. "I just feel. You must have this feeling too sometimes, in spite of the fact that you like to argue with your father. You in particular . . ." Abraham let his sentence trail vaguely, suggestively, leaving Isaac with a sense of discomfort, almost of fear.

To break away from it, Isaac began again. "But how can we be a glorious race when we are as sinful as those about us?" he threw out challengingly.

"Why"—Abraham was surprised—"I have never denied that there are villains amongst us, although I do not know whether I would agree with you that we have as many as they have." He answered sweetly, for some reason unwilling to be provoked.

"We have as many thieves as they," Isaac went on with some irritation. "Aren't our exploiters, sinners, and hypocrites as bad as theirs? And to be a villain amongst us is an even worse thing than to be one amongst any other nation, for the eye of the world is magnified upon us."

"Let them look," said Abraham comfortably. "You know how well a Jew can do a thing when he sets his mind to it. Why else are we hated? It may seem to them that we have more villains than they simply because one gifted Jewish villain can outshine any three of theirs." Abraham waved his hand in deprecating acknowledgment of this excess of talent. Then he leaned forward, no longer smiling. "But as the villainies of a few may stand out, so will our faith, our grand desire. It is for this that we are chosen." He noticed again, leaning forward, the curve of his son's jaw, the restlessness in his eyes. Remembering that Isaac probably wished to argue, he gave a little half-smile from behind his beard and cocked an inquiring eye. But Isaac, for once, was silent.

As Moses began to grow perceptibly from day to day, and every day brought its new story about him, its new anecdote, to be repeated and discussed at the butcher shop and the factory, Sarah began, almost imperceptibly at first, but in Abraham's eyes at least more clearly, to fade away. It was as though a long tiredness was creeping over her, wrapping her up in its filminess, drawing her in. There were still times when she swept into action, when she swept all before her in a pleasurable frenzy of doing. But these times were sporadic and left her puzzled and tired. Her life had become like a long conversation in which she had somehow said all that she had to say, and to which she was now even forgetting to listen.

Abraham could not remember when it was that he had first developed that feeling about his wife. It was not a feeling that could be put into words. It came upon him at odd times, unexpectedly. When, for instance, he and Chaim, in that long interchange of formal questions with which they greeted each other, had dealt with each other's health and the health of Mrs. Knopp, and Chaim asked in his turn, "And how is your wife?"—then the feeling came over him. It was as though the strings of his spirit that bound him to Sarah twanged suddenly, spreading through him vibration upon vibration of a feeling that was a confused mixture of fear and sadness and certainty. He would answer merely that she was well, or that she had a cold or a constriction in her chest. Chaim would offer a few words, either of advice or of general good will, while the vibrations rippled down gradually. In the surge of his feeling, while he tried at the same time to listen to Chaim's words, Abraham would promise himself again that he would cherish her. It was the only protection that he knew against the feeling. If he promised to cherish her fervently enough he could forestall the knowledge that was in him and drive it back.

Chaim's voice would cease, and Abraham would become aware that he was waiting. It was Abraham's turn to ask after Chaim's children. By the time Chaim had come to his counter-question about Isaac the ripples had faded, soothed by the fervent promise. As he gave a detailed description of what Isaac had accomplished lately his spirit would gradually recover, so that by the time his turn came to ask about Chaim's grandchildren the feeling was a faint discomfort only, in his heart.

And in fact he did cherish her. It was a byword among the people who knew them well, a byword first composed by Mrs. Plopler, that Avrom carried his wife around like on a silver platter. Even Mr. Plopler, when his wife mentioned it to him in her injured way, replied only, in a tone that in any other man might have sounded a trifle wistful, "Well, she's such a quiet one."

Ruth, who had gradually come to consider her mother-in-law more as a dependent than as a co-worker in household affairs, looked with a certain sentimental pleasure on the relationship between Abraham and Sarah. Someday perhaps, she supposed, time might add its embroidery of quirks to her own nature as well. Then Isaac might treat her, too, as though she were made of glass. The idea pleased her. It was like a pleasant fantasy, for she could not really imagine herself as a very fragile type. Still, from what they said, Sarah had not always been as she was now either.

It was not easy to be always as patient as she wanted to be with her mother-in-law. Ruth was of a direct and practical turn of mind. She could not help being irritated sometimes. Over the business of the cats, for instance, she had often had to bite her tongue.

"Ruth," Sarah would call suddenly, apprehensively, "where are the cats?"

"I don't know," Ruth would call back, perhaps a little impatiently, for she was used to the question. "I think they're outside."

"Are you sure," Sarah's voice would resume a moment later a little querulously, "they're not by the child?" And Sarah would make a room-by-room inspection of the house, peering into the bedroom where the child slept several times on the way.

"Don't wake him, Ma; the cats aren't there."

Shaking her head, Sarah would return to her chair. Cats had been known to strangle children. Ruth was altogether too indifferent.

One day, thinking to put Sarah's mind at ease, Ruth suggested that Knobble the Second and Pompishke should not be allowed into the house. "Isaac can make a little house for them outside, and we can feed them. They won't come to harm; animals are tough. And then you won't have to worry about them harming the child."

"They're our cats," said Sarah slowly. "How can we drive them from the house?"

"It won't hurt them to sleep outside. Why should you have to worry about them?"

But Sarah would not hear of it. "They're ours," she repeated. "We don't want them to have a grudge against him. Animals understand these things."

"Well—" Ruth began, a little exasperated.

Feeling for a moment as though all her powers were being called upon, Sarah interrupted her. "Don't worry. I will watch the child," she promised.

Chapter Nine

——◆◆◆——

Sucking his thumb reflectively, Moses paused for a moment outside the bedroom where his mother and the lady had disappeared. The door was open a trifle, but not enough for him to be able to see. He sniffed close to the crack in the door. A slightly acrid smell made him wrinkle his nose. Pressing himself against the door, he pushed it farther ajar and slipped part way around it. From here he could watch what they were doing to his grandmother.

The yellow blind was pulled more than halfway down the window, cutting the blue light of the winter afternoon and making the room yellowish and shadowy. His grandmother lay, face down, close to the edge of the big bed that was hers and Grandfather's. Her face was pressed down so that he could see only the gray hair straggling along the pillow. The bedclothes were pulled down to her waist, and her back and arms were bare. His mother and the lady—whom Moses, had he been pressed, would have identified as Mrs. Pyopyo —hovered about the bed, their attitudes intent. Mrs. Pyopyo muttered quietly, words he could not understand, her nose working as though she were getting ready to sneeze. His own nose worked sympathetically.

On a chair beside the bed were laid out on a white cloth several rows of odd little glass cups, smaller than those he drank from, and with curled-back edges. Beside them a white cup stood.

As he watched, the lady took a little stick from the chair and wrapped some white fluff around it. Then she dipped it into the white cup. In the dim light his mother leaned forward and struck a match against something in her hand. The match flared up, and as she cupped it the smell drifted across the room into his nostrils. His mother held the match against the lady's fluff-wrapped stick. The stick flared more brightly than the match, and for an instant the faces of both his mother and the lady leaped into light with dancing shadows playing across them as the lady moved the stick, so that for a moment they were two grotesque-faced strangers.

The lady seized one of the glass cups from the chair, inverted it, and thrust the taper into it. The taper puffed out immediately. With almost the same movement the lady withdrew the taper and clapped the inverted glass to his grandmother's back. Moses stifled an exclamation of fright. The odd, sweetish smell of the taper followed the acrid match-smell into his nostrils.

On the bed his grandmother moaned slightly. Moses reached up to the doorhandle and, holding on to it, pulled himself up on his toes, craning his neck to see his grandmother better. He could see that there were several other cups stuck grotesquely onto her flesh. As he watched, the match flared again, and then the taper, lighting up his mother's eyes, which, because they did not seem to be intent on what was familiar to him, seemed to him to be the eyes of a stranger. Again the taper puffed out in the glass cup, and another cup was clapped onto his grandmother's back.

Disturbed, Moses forgot that he was not supposed to enter this room. He pushed the door farther open and came forward to his mother's side. She had just lit the taper again when she felt his hand tugging at her skirt. Ruth looked down into the child's pleading eyes and uttered a startled "Oh!" Mrs. Plopler, who was about to thrust the taper deftly into the center of the glass, looked up. The taper wavered before it went out, and Mrs. Plopler, automatically completing her movement, clapped the glass down on Sarah's back.

Sarah cried out in pain. The taper had heated the curled edge of the glass. Louder than Sarah's cry was Mrs. Plopler's exclamation. She wrenched away the cup. A red welt formed where the cup had touched the skin. Mrs. Plopler began to wail and wring her hands. Distracted, Ruth pulled away from the child and bent over the bed. Moses, confused, sensing that somehow something had happened that was his fault, began to cry loudly.

"Why is the child crying?" Sarah raised herself suddenly so that

the glasses with their great gobs of discolored flesh stared at him from
her back. Her voice sounded hoarse and unfamiliar to him. She
twisted about; the side of her face which had pressed against the pillow was red and ridged. "What's wrong with the child?" Sarah's eyes
glared past him. Her head fell forward and she moaned again. Moses
bawled louder still. Ruth seized him up in her arms and carried him
from the room, trying to comfort him and calling back instructions to
Mrs. Plopler at the same time. A moment later Mrs. Plopler came
rushing past them, muttering loudly, to look for some butter to put
on the burn. Her distraught appearance, the sounds she was making,
the stabbing of her nose, brought forth another frightened howl from
the child and helped to imprint on his memory as the first indelible
recollection of his childhood the strange, yellow-shadowed scene at
his grandmother's bedside.

"I admit," Mrs. Plopler often said, "that there are few people who
can set the cups as well as I." Mrs. Plopler would go on to enumer-
ate compliments she had received on her setting of the cups. It was
true that she was an expert with many cures to her credit. In their
family alone she had several times drawn a cold from Isaac and the
threat of bronchitis from Sarah. Once she had even effected a partial
cure on one of Abraham's arms when the pains had become particularly strong.

"What can you see with pills?" Mrs. Plopler was fond of asking.
"Do you know what the doctor's giving you? He stuffs your mouth
with a pill or a bitter medicine and tells you you're cured. With the
cups you can at least see what's being done. The cold and the poi-
sons are being pulled out of your body, drawn out straight through
the flesh. That's medicine."

And those who had been cured by Mrs. Plopler were usually inclined to agree with her. Certainly she never finished her work without leaving dark red and blue welts to prove that something had
really been done to draw out the ailment.

It very soon became evident, however, that this time the cups
were not enough. Sarah's ailment grew worse. When the doctor was

called in, another ritual took the place of the cups, and Ruth was busy all day boiling pots of water, and Sarah lay all day inhaling the steam.

Gradually it dawned upon Abraham that what he had feared for so long without naming it, lest the naming should bring it closer, hovered dangerously near, and Sarah's every painful, rasping breath was as a loud acknowledgment of its presence. "A while longer," he begged in his prayers. He pointed out that Sarah had received so little joy in life. Did she not deserve a few more years at least to see the child grow up, to see whatever it was that He, the Lord—and Abraham did not presume to prognosticate—at least to catch a glimpse of what He had in store for their house? Sometimes, when he prayed, it occurred to him that she would probably be happier where she was going, with her two other sons. But he reminded himself that beyond life there is the mystery that none must seek before his time. It is life's miracles that the living must find. And he would be filled with a strange bitterness that now his wife, too, would leave him to seek them alone.

Isaac, trying not to think of what the doctor had hinted, trudged, as was usual for him on a Wednesday evening, straight from work to the home of a pupil. He paused in his upward climb through the snow and stood waiting for the streetcar to overtake and pass him on its way to the heights. He breathed quickly, holding his gloved hand against his mouth to prevent the sharp air from burning his lungs. His damp breath lay unpleasantly around the side of his mouth. He wiped it away with the back of his glove. The moisture formed beads of ice on the wool. He stood and rested until the streetcar was only a tail light wiggling in the distance. Another carfare saved. Isaac hunched back down into the collar of his coat, and, breathing through his clenched teeth, continued his climb.

The wind that blew down from the northeast past Mad Mountain and whipped across his shoulder blades seemed, in its way, to be trying to help him along. Every now and then a strong gust lifted and carried him a few steps upward. But Isaac's mood was not a grateful one. He would have liked to sit in the streetcar, on the first seat of the bench, closest to the little coal stove that stood behind the conductor. Thinking of it, he could almost feel the pins and needles melting inside of him.

He dwelt on the thought of the streetcar deliberately, conscious that he was doing so in order to prevent himself from thinking of something else. But in spite of himself his mind slipped back to the moment when he had come home the other day and had gone in to see his mother. He had looked at her as she lay frail on the bed, her breath rasping and sawing through her body, as though for the first time in many years. The mother he had looked at yesterday had not been like this. What yesterday was he thinking of?

Nothing, Isaac told himself with a sense of injury, seems to meet a man face to face. Things creep up from behind while you keep your eyes ahead of you, trying to edge your way safely through life. All of a sudden you're shoved from the last remembered point in time to the present. As though to prove this, he turned quickly and caught the mountain in the act of creeping forward in the dusk. Always there was something that followed, something that waited to fall on a man.

Why not face to face? What if something should come suddenly face to face with him, some demand, some choice that would require from him a pure response, some terrifying decision? And what if something were to occur that would demand from him nothing, only fortitude, only the acceptance of fact? What would he do then? The answer was spontaneous in his mind. Grown man though he was, his first impulse was to turn his back, run. Isaac stopped in his tracks and laughed. The cold air burned his lungs— Serves me right. He breathed again and again through his mouth until his lungs seemed on fire. This was how his mother's lungs must feel. He closed his mouth abruptly, fighting panic.

But she was alive. He had seen her alive just this morning. She was. Alive. It was absolutely necessary to be convinced-of her aliveness. He wasn't satisfied with just the word. He needed more than the word; he needed the feeling of it. Alive, alive. Alive. The word began to lose itself in its repetition. Again he felt panic. He looked around him for something to grasp at, for something to bring back the meaning of life. He became aware that the frost was nibbling at him, the snow crunched noisily beneath his feet, and the wind breathed lustily across his shoulders. He began to experience such a feeling of aliveness himself that everything about him seemed to come alive.

That was it! To be alive now, really alive, was the secret. For a moment he felt that if a man ever came really alive he could never die. How could death touch the living? Something tried to tell him that this was an odd thought, but it was blithely overruled. Nothing could force its way through the purely sensuous pleasure of his aliveness. It seemed as though he had never been actually aware of every part of himself as he was now. His mother lived, surely. And who could be more alive than his father?—and his wife, and his son, and even the cats. He himself would keep them alive, feed them from his inexhaustible store of life-energy.

Another streetcar was approaching. Isaac paused to listen. If he ran he might still make the streetcar stop. The pins and needles in his toes, alive like the rest of him, urged him onward. He started to run through the snow, freely, like an athlete, the pleasure running through his body as his feet flew of themselves over the white earth. The wind blew him forward, and he flapped his arms as though in flight, as though he were about to take off from the ground. It came fleetingly into his mind that the conductor of the streetcar must think him an odd apparition, but instead of feeling embarrassed he tried to speed even more quickly.

He could hear the streetcar gaining on him. As he ran along the sidewalk parallel to the tracks he turned his head to see the streetcar almost up to him. The mountain, too, seemed to jog along with him. He pushed forward with another burst of speed. For a moment there was a sensation of pure freedom. Then the streetcar roared in his ears. Something tumbled violently inside of him, and he seemed to tumble with it, sideways, collapsing suddenly and staggering to a stop against a tree. For a long moment he struggled to release his breath, which was impaled on a series of sharp, shaftlike pains. A sensation of nausea spread through him, and his chest contracted as though trying to force him to vomit. The sensation of misery, as pure and unadulterated as the unreasoning joy that had seized him a few moments ago, doubled him over. Trembling and sweating all over, he heard, as though remotely, streetcar after streetcar sweeping by him.

For a long time Isaac remained there against the tree, so that in the end he knew that it was too late to visit his pupil. By the time he had started on his way home, placing one foot uncertainly in front of the other, he knew too, without even thinking about it, that his mother was going to die.

As though each in his own way had already struggled with Sarah's death and lost, when the time came Abraham and his son, at least partially forewarned against the inevitable surprise, lent themselves passively to the actions of mourning. Only Moses wandered about, detached, a little frightened what with all the strange things that were happening and everyone's being so preoccupied, trying to find a place for himself. He had a notion that it actually was his grandmother who lay on the floor, covered over with a heavy dark cloth and surrounded by candles that burned and threw flickering and terrible shadows on the wall. But he could not bring himself to walk right up to the thing and lift up the edge of the cloth. What if it was she?

Some of the women who came, and Mrs. Pyopyo was prominent among them, cried and wailed and made funny gestures. Fascinated, he watched them, and when they noticed that he watched them admiringly they were annoyed and chased him out of the house and into the yard, where they said he would not be underfoot. But he was not under anybody's foot anyway.

On the day of the funeral there were even more people in and out of the house. Moses played on the green box that had been put on the front porch. He managed to pry the lid up and, after climbing in, crouched, peering out through a slit in the lid that he could make

larger or smaller by pressing back or ducking down his head. When
Mrs. Pyopyo came up the steps he popped the lid open and said
hello to her. She clapped her hand to her breast and began to scream,
so that Moses, frightened, dropped back into the box again and tried
to hide. Mrs. Pyopyo ran into the house, and the next thing Moses
knew the lid was wrenched open and his father had lifted him out,
while Mrs. Pyopyo wrung her hands and continued to wail and make
dreadful faces at him behind his father's back. Moses buried his face
in the safety of his father's shoulder but a moment later raised it
cautiously to wiggle his nose experimentally.

His grandmother's death did not seem to have made much of an
impression on the child. Thank goodness, Isaac pointed out, he was
too young to understand. Only months later, when the landlord's
shaggy old dog died and Moses found her behind the garage in the
lane, he covered her partially with a piece of old cardboard, took his
shoes off, and, sitting beside her in the mud, watched the flies buzz-
ing around the still carcass, and so his mother found him, sitting
solemnly.

"Chaim," said Abraham to his friend as they sat outside the synagogue on a Friday evening that spring. "I have a thought that keeps
coming into my head. I wonder what you, as an educated man,
would say about it."

"You make too much of my education, my friend," replied Chaim
modestly. "Life is the only teacher."

"Still," said Abraham, "you cannot deny that, having studied
many great thoughts, you have gleaned something more than just an
ordinary man like myself, for instance, could do."

"Well, perhaps."

"Well, then"—Abraham hesitated—"supposing I were to tell you
that I have come to the conclusion that death is not such a sudden
thing." Abraham looked at his friend, but Chaim continued to re-
gard him wordlessly with his face screwed up seriously in his listening attitude.

"I mean that I think that death is a seed that is sown, like life, inside of a person, and comes to fruition from within." Abraham spoke these words in a stubborn, resolute tone, as though voicing an opinion which he felt sure would be opposed.

"Ah," said Chaim in a slightly trapped tone. His mind riffled half-heartedly through its file on death, and a few words from the prayer for the dead and other odds and ends on death flitted through his head, but nothing that seemed to bear any direct relation to Abraham's words. He nodded his head seriously, for Abraham was talking again.

"You may think I am mad, but I could see it growing in her, like a weed, like a fungus."

"Death?" Chaim asked timidly. He had come to an age when the word was beginning to make him uncomfortable.

"Yes." Abraham jerked his finger to his eyes. "Here, in her eyes, from behind. We think it's a sudden thing, and it is, in a way, in its moment of triumph, when it has drawn the last bit of life into itself and flowers into its own world of stillness. And yet, try though he may, a man can't choke it off. I think that death is sown in all of us when we are conceived, and grows within the womb of life, feeding on it, until one day it bursts out. We say then that life is dead. But really death is born."

"Well," said Chaim, somewhat relieved. "Perhaps you are right. But it all seems to come to the same thing, doesn't it?"

"I don't know," said Abraham. "When it occurred to me I said to myself, What of my sons, then? I did not see death growing in their faces. Only life and the promise of life bloomed there."

"That's right," Chaim was even more relieved. "How could one account for that?"

"I don't know. But I say to myself, life and death are opposed to each other. Life is good, isn't that right? We can feel that, or else why do we strive to stay alive? Why do we weep for our dead ones? So then death must be evil, a kind of evil. Every man carries his own death in him, but in some men death is so strong, so evil, that it must feed itself on the conquest of other lives besides its own. That might explain what happened to my sons."

"Well, it might," said Chaim uncomfortably. "But I would not take such thoughts too seriously. You yourself say that you cannot work it out too clearly. And to tell you the truth, I can't recall having seen it written anywhere."

"Still," said Abraham, "if one could only seize it and hold it back and stop it somehow. Or if one could know why, how— It's foolishness I'm talking, and I know it. A man hates to lose something, just like that, that's precious to him. He would at least like to think that some gesture is possible to him. But that's for God Himself, isn't it, Chaim?"

"We must all die." Chaim was happy to be able to point this out. It was a concrete fact. "If God will have it so, then we must accept it, although, of course, we are right to put it off as long as possible."

"You're right, you're right. A man can mull it over in his own head until he is entirely lost. Then he must go to someone who can appraise his thoughts with a clear head and a knowledge of the ancient wisdom. It's up to the One Above, as you say."

"We all seek the truth," said Chaim, rather pleased.

One hot summer day Polsky brought a bottle of schnapps to the shop to celebrate the fact that he had just bought the whole building. Hymie Polsky, who during the summer holidays was supposed to be helping out in the shop but really spent most of his time in the poolroom across the street, turned up shortly after his father arrived with the liquor. The barber from next door came in to toast his new landlord, but the jeweler who had the other side of the premises didn't come in. He and Polsky had never been on good terms. This was what, for Polsky, added zest to the celebration. This was putting it over on his enemy. The jeweler was probably sitting there now in his back room, which Polsky knew was an unlicensed pawnshop, waiting for the ax to fall.

He could have him out tomorrow, Polsky reflected as he raised his glass to his lips while the barber made a toast. But let him wait. Polsky could afford to be big about it. Oh, he had plans for that part of the building all right. Only it was too soon. The boy wasn't old enough yet.

Hymie wanted a drink of schnapps too. Polsky put a bit in the bottom of his glass. "Ahh," whined Hymie, "not even a taste."

"Never mind, never mind," said Polsky. "See if you can get that down."

Hymie flung back his head as the others had done and gulped his bit down. A sour look spread from his mouth over his whole face. His face worked, trying to adjust itself into an indifferent smile. He held out his glass again. Polsky was rather pleased with him. "Look at the young punk," he said to the barber. "Thinks he can take it. Shall I give him a real slug and let him get good and sick?"

"Just try," said Hymie.

Polsky reached forward with the bottle but, on catching Abraham's glance, instead of filling the glass he put another bit in the bottom.

"Is that all?" whined Hymie. "Huh!" With an elaborately careless gesture he threw his head back and flung the liquor into his mouth. This time it plashed all around the inside of his mouth, giving him the full taste and filling him chokingly full of alcohol fumes. He gasped and coughed, his face suffused with color. Abraham, muttering to himself, rushed over and pounded him on the back. Polsky and the barber laughed uproariously.

"All in one gulp he wants to become a man," said Polsky.

Hymie, the tears still standing in his eyes, sat down on Chaim Knopp's little barrel.

Polsky pressed another glass on the barber and refilled his own. Abraham declined another glass. "I'll bring you some water in a minute, to wash the taste away," he told Hymie.

"I don't want any," said the boy sullenly.

Abraham went into the back room. Hymie watched his father and the barber resentfully. They were leaning against one of the counters, talking and drinking. Every now and then his father took a handkerchief from his pocket and wiped his sweating forehead. The barber followed suit. Hymie's eyes sought the bottle, but his father had put it down behind the counter in case a policeman should happen by and look in at the window. Everybody ignored him now that they thought they had shown him up. The feeling that he had been hard done by rose in Hymie's breast. He stared at the spot on the counter behind which the bottle stood. A look of sly purpose crept slowly into his eyes. Casting a glance around him, he slipped quickly off the barrel and ducked behind the counter.

A moment later the bell on the butcher shop door tinkled. "Well, look who's here!" shouted Polsky. Laughing her throaty laugh, Laiah held out her hands and swept forward.

"A million dollars," said Polsky, setting down his glass and taking her hands. "A million dollars with small change," he amended as she turned around before them in the manner of a mannequin, her bright cotton print swirling about her legs. "What brings you back here? I thought you'd left us altogether."

"There's no place like home," said Laiah, pursing her full lips and brushing her tinted auburn hair back from her face.

Her figure, Polsky noted through his pleasant, sweaty alcoholic haze, though a good many sizes larger than it had been once—and she had never been exactly a stick—still stacked up like a good evening's entertainment. "A million dollars," he said again. The barber nodded his head and continued to nod it, smiling vaguely.

Behind the counter, Abraham wrested the bottle from Hymie's lax fingers. In his eagerness to drink as much and as quickly as possible, Hymie had slobbered the liquor all over himself. The stench of schnapps and sweat made Abraham hold his breath. Hymie put one finger against his lips and with a somewhat glazed look of pleading uttered, "Psssh."

Abraham, his arms groaning inside him with the strain, heaved the boy up off his knees and leaned him against the counter where he was partly hidden behind the cash register.

"You'll have a drink with us to celebrate, eh? Two drinks, in fact," said Polsky. "One for my new building, and one for your return to the city. You can be sure we won't let you go again so easily."

"It's nice to be with friends again." Laiah laughed. "Out East it just wasn't the same. Hello!" Laiah, catching sight of Abraham, flowed toward the counter, extending her hand. "You haven't changed," she said. "Of course I've not been gone that long, have I? You people probably didn't even notice."

"How could I help noticing?" Polsky winked. "The best poker partner I ever had." He reached under the counter for the bottle and poured while Laiah's laugh crooned out huskily.

"Lachaim," said the barber.

"Good times," said Laiah as her red lips closed over the glass. Polsky looked into her eyes, enjoying the game. I like a flashy looking woman, he told himself.

Abraham looked with some wonder at Laiah. The make-up, which seemed to be trying to bolster up the sagging cheeks, ended, he noted, right under her chin. There was a mass of blue-green stuff around her eyes. Her red lips had left a stain on the glass. The whole face could be wiped off. What would be left underneath?

Laiah flashed him a smile. She was telling about the apartment that she had been lucky enough to find in the district, inviting them all up for a drink sometime. She noticed Hymie standing, head down, behind the counter. "Who's this?" She looked incredulous, opening her eyes wide. "It can't be! Not Hymie!" She gave a little laugh of disbelief.

"Who then?" asked Polsky, laughing.

"I can't believe it!" Laiah batted her eyelashes. "The last time I saw him he scarcely reached the top of the counter."

She moved toward him. Hymie looked up and giggled, keeping his mouth shut, and looked quickly down again.

"What a fine strapping fellow!" said Laiah. "You don't have to be shy of me. I've known you for a long time." She laughed disarmingly. "Why, your father and I were young together." She glanced sideways at Polsky, who laughed.

Hymie giggled again, as though with a full mouth, and tried to draw back behind the cash register.

"How big you've grown," said Laiah again. "Let's look at you; you look just like your father."

From Hymie's throat there issued a sound as of a sewer backing up. He ducked behind the counter. Abraham sighed, glanced at the startled Polsky, and went in search of a rag. He came back a moment later and, pressing the cold, wet rag against the forehead of the wretched boy, led him into the back room.

The barber turned to Polsky and Laiah and with the spontaneity of drunkenness clapped his hand to his stomach and, puffing his cheeks out bigger and bigger, ran his hand from his stomach up his chest to the front of his mouth, forcing at the same time a very loud, variegated burp that was a convincing imitation of Hymie's eruption. Then, stepping daintily over the boy's puddle, he wove toward the back room, muttering that he would offer his help.

In the back room Abraham heard peal on peal of laughter from the front of the shop. The barber entered, glanced at Hymie, stepped over to the sink, dipped his handkerchief under the tap, and began to bathe his own forehead.

Polsky stopped laughing suddenly. "Maybe we shouldn't laugh so loud," he said.

"Why not?" Laiah had laughed so hard that the tears had run rivulets of mascara down her cheeks. She was busily trying to repair the damage, between fits of laughter. "It's so funny. He'll see it himself someday."

"It's not that." Polsky motioned toward the back room. "His wife just died a few months ago, you know."

"Whose, the barber's?"

"No."

"Ah," said Laiah slowly, "that's too bad."

"Yes." Polsky wanted to pour himself a little more but decided against it. "He's still in mourning, naturally. So—"

"Of course," said Laiah. "Naturally."

A moment later Polsky chuckled. "The little son of a so and so!" He began to laugh again. Laiah laid her finger to her lips and Polsky, nodding, chuckled quietly, his belly shaking.

"She couldn't have been such an old woman, was she?" Laiah asked, nodding in the direction of the back room.

Polsky shrugged. "I don't suppose so. But getting on. He's no youngster."

"He took it badly?" Laiah kept her voice down to a near-whisper.

Polsky shrugged again. "His wife, after all."

"He's still a good-looking man," Laiah mused.

"What, on the scent again?" Polsky raised his voice.

"*Grobion.*" Laiah glanced around. "Can't I even have an opinion?"

"Of course." Polsky grinned and rolled slightly against the showcase. "Can't I?"

"Oh, talk through your mouth," muttered Laiah a little testily.

Polsky laughed. "The kid's growing up."

"Let's see how he's getting along," said Laiah.

Hymie was flopped in a chair, his arms and legs loosely sprawled, his head lolling back. Abraham took the rag from his head and turned around to find Laiah beside him. "I'll help you." She smiled, taking the rag from him. She went to the sink, poured fresh cold water on the rag, and, still smiling, came and laid it gingerly on the boy's forehead. The water dripped down Hymie's face. Polsky had also come in and was standing looking down at his son and shaking his head. Abraham took another rag from the pipe under the sink and went to clean up the mess in the shop.

Chapter Ten

No one who knew Chaim Knopp could fail to recognize him on the street. Even strangers took notice of him. For Chaim, in his long black coat and ancient derby, had a way of bobbing along that was individual and unmistakable. And yet one early winter morning as Chaim was on the way to his slaughtering shed, hugging two chickens under his arms for warmth, his son Ralph drove by him in his big car, without stopping.

That was a heavy day for Chaim. Each one of his sixty-nine and a half years came to him individually, so that for the first time in his life, even though he had often talked of age, he knew what it was to be an old man. Strange thoughts kept coming into his head. If it had been his mother he would have stopped, he found himself thinking. A little ashamed, he corrected himself— At least he would have stopped for his mother. And then: Thank goodness he would have stopped for his mother, he amended still further, righteously, while his heart swelled with aching self-pity.

Was it Ralph, after all? he asked himself at another moment. And if it was, how could he be blamed for not stopping? I would have absolutely refused to get into the car, Chaim told his chickens at one point. I can just see myself climbing into the big car with the chickens smelling and dropping their fleas and feathers and God knows what else all over Ralph's rich friends.

All day long Chaim avoided people that he might have to talk to, and put off even his visit to Polsky's butcher shop, although it was a day when he usually collected several orders. He closed up the shack early and walked home by another route altogether than that which he usually took. I won't tell Bassieh, he decided for the tenth time. Bassieh would see that there was something wrong, and she would ask him, but he would not tell her. He would bear it himself. Bassieh would be likely to point out some reason why Ralph had not stopped, and bawl him out into the bargain, making it all his fault. She might even mention it to Ralph, and then they would both turn on him. Maybe he had been on his way to a big business conference, so how could he be blamed for not wanting to stop? What would he have said to his friends—"Excuse me, the business must wait, I want to stop and give my father and his chickens a lift to the slaughtering shed"? Chaim himself had to smile a little at this.

He let himself quietly into the front hall and stood there for a moment in the darkness. Through the door he could hear voices in the living room. It dawned on him that one of them was Ralph's voice, loud and angry-sounding. Flustered, Chaim had difficulty in unwrapping the long black woolen scarf in which he trussed himself up in the wintertime—like what Polsky called an Egyptian mamma. Hastily he took off his overcoat, galoshes, and the ancient derby, under which his skullcap sat firmly. He stood for a moment, rubbing his hands together and listening. Certainly Ralph did not sound apologetic. Chaim was overcome with embarrassment. How should he face his son?

"Here he is," said Bassieh as he entered the room, still rubbing his hands self-consciously. "Speak to him for yourself."

"Pa"—Ralph wasted no time—"I've been waiting for you. When are we going to have enough of this chicken business? It's time you quit." Ralph had obviously been talking long and vigorously. His face was slightly flushed. Instead of looking directly at his father when he spoke, he looked at his clothes.

Chaim seated himself on the edge of a chair, at the same time plucking a feather from his vest.

Ralph did not give him time to consider answering. "And how long have you been planning to get rid of this house?" Chaim sensed a boundless contempt in his son's voice. "Four years, five years, ten years?"

"God knows how long," Bassieh broke in. "Only God knows how long."

Ralph paced the floor with the restless tread of a man who has many important things on his mind, and has been forced to pause over some irritating detail. "And what's been stopping you?" Ralph faced his father. In his green tweed suit, which fitted him loosely to cover up the fact that he was spreading out, he looked the picture of a successful man. Even now Chaim couldn't resist a feeling of admiration, of awe. Ralph stood, spread-legged and stocky, in front of him, but commanding, at his ease. Chaim raised his eyes to his son's face. Ralph's features were sharp and straight, cast from his mother's mold. But good living and advancing middle age were adding a softening background of flesh. Ralph did not meet his eyes, but stared severely at his father's sleeve cuff. Chaim cast a furtive glance at his linen.

"Well?" asked Ralph with modified sarcasm.

"Well," repeated Chaim timidly, trying to think of something.

"I can see it's no use relying on you to do anything. I can have this house rented in two days, if not sooner. I can get you a little flat that will cost you practically nothing. The rent from the house will cover the flat rent and then some. As for an allowance, I'll arrange it with the others. You'll have everything you need." Ralph paused to draw a dreath, expanding his chest.

"Oh Ralph, my son." Bassieh's eyes shone and spilled over.

Ralph glanced at his father, who was tucking his underwear under his shirt sleeve. "You understand, Pa? No more work. From now on you're retired."

Chaim nodded his head, without looking up. "My practice, my shack?" He waved his hand vaguely, questioningly.

Ralph gave a loud, patient sigh and exchanged glances with his mother. "You want me to deal with that too? Well, we'll get rid of it right away." He glanced at his watch. "Do you know anyone who'd want to take it over?"

Chaim shrugged vaguely. "Maybe young Lachter—or Kalinsky the Litvak."

"Come on, then. We'll drive down right now and see about getting rid of it."

"Now?" Chaim blinked at his son incredulously. The idea that his whole life's work could be disposed of so quickly was hard to grasp. He laughed a little, nervously.

"Now," cried Bassieh with excited impatience. And to Ralph: "You hear him? 'Now?' he asks. If you had learned what 'Now' meant fifty years ago you might be someone today, instead of dragging yourself to and from your shack every day."

"Pa," said Ralph, "once you've decided what you want to do, you do it right away. That's how to get on in this world."

"Go then, go then, get your coat on," said Bassieh. "You see, that's what sons are for. We worked hard to bring them up, and now—" Bassieh didn't finish her sentence but smiled fondly at her son, who returned her smile. Bassieh's eyes filled with tears again. "For your old father," she said, "your old father." She choked slightly and turned away to wipe her eyes.

Chaim felt his own eyes filling with tears. He nodded his head up and down quickly several times. "We've lived to see it." He spoke hesitantly, still a little confused.

Ralph, in spite of himself, felt the tears come to his eyes as well, and at the same time he was conscious of an overmastering sense of his own virtue. He laid his hand on his father's shoulder. "You think you have such an entirely bad son, eh?"

Chaim shook his head wordlessly, and Bassieh sobbed openly.

"Well," said Ralph, "we can't stand here crying all day. We've got work to do."

Ralph drove his car masterfully, starting it up with a *broomph!* that sent the snow flying from under the wheels. "You don't have to worry, Pa; I can afford it. I don't like to have my father still walking about the streets with chickens under his arms. And especially at your age. You're not a young cockerel any longer, you know." Ralph laughed.

"Why else do we work," said Chaim hesitantly, "if not to hear our sons say this?"

Ralph laughed again pleasantly and turned his eyes to the road. This was the precise spot, that they were passing now, where Ralph had this morning passed his father. Ralph accelerated, throwing Chaim suddenly backward. But the picture had already sprung into his father's mind.

Had it been Ralph after all? Already it was dimming in his memory; the judgments he had been tempted to make seemed monstrous. You would think from the way Ralph had attacked him when he came into the room that Ralph had reason to be angry with him. Chaim smiled vaguely. That was his son, always brusque when he did something, to avoid gratitude. One of the men in the back of the car had looked back, Chaim remembered, and Chaim had looked quickly down, pretending he hadn't seen. He shook his head to clear it of contradictory thoughts. Ralph was like his mother. Everything had to be done swiftly, loudly, sweepingly. But it would be done. He would take care of everything.

Abraham put down the chopper, leaned his arm on the counter, first putting down a piece of paper so as not to stain his underwear, over which his sleeves were rolled, and scrutinized his friend. Chaim was not in his working clothes. His black suit hung about him with an air of festive unfamiliarity. His shoes, from which he was carefully removing his galoshes, gleamed.

Abraham, who could not fail to see that this was an occasion, began with suitable formality. "Good afternoon, Reverend Chaim."

Chaim smiled. "Where's Polsky?"

"At the wholesale." Abraham came around the counter and took Chaim's coat from him. Chaim nodded questioningly toward the back room, and Abraham shrugged his shoulders. "As usual," he murmured. He took Chaim's overclothes and went into the back room to hang them up. Hymie sat reading a magazine. On the days when he played truant from high school and had no change with which to entertain himself in other ways, he spent his time in the back room, reading picture books.

When Abraham returned, Chaim was sitting on his barrel, smiling to himself and fingering his beard. Abraham leaned on the counter again.

"Time flies," Chaim began, measuring his words with enjoyment. "Do you know, my friend, that I am a man of seventy years?"

"Up to a hundred and twenty," said Abraham. "You certainly don't look like a man of seventy."

"Thank God, I'm alive. A man of seventy"—the grin widened on Chaim's face, and his pointed beard stood horizontal—"is old enough to retire."

"To retire from work?"

"Absolutely." Chaim watched his toe execute designs on the sawdust. "You see, my children absolutely don't want me to work any more. So I've retired."

"Already?" asked Abraham admiringly.

"Already. I have turned over my practice to young Lachter, the shoichet from Poland. He knows his business. He'll get along with my customers. It's done." Chaim spread out his arms and, looking down, noticed and brushed a speck of dust from one of his sleeves. "I am a free man."

"Mazeltov, mazel mazeltov." Abraham came around the counter with extended hand. Hymie Polsky came out of the back room and stood listening, magazine in hand. "And your children saw that it was time for you to quit and they made you quit," said Abraham enthusiastically. "Enough, just like that." Abraham laughed. How fine it was.

"Of course"—Chaim was ruminating dreamily—"I might occasionally be persuaded to do a circumcision still. I can't resist a celebration. But otherwise, nothing."

"You mean you won't be coming here any more?" Hymie's voice, grown strangely like his father's in timbre, broke heavily in on them.

"Well," said Chaim a little haughtily, "I'll drop in to visit occasionally."

"Your place will always be here for you," said Abraham courteously.

Hymie grunted. Chaim turned back to Abraham. "I will go about like a ladies' man. Years will pass"—Chaim closed his eyes ecstatically—"and I will never smell another chicken."

Abraham was as happy for his friend as though it had happened to himself. All of a sudden new possibilities had opened out. He had never tried to visualize before what would happen beyond the time when he could lift his arms to the meat no longer. And yet he knew that it was a time not too far off. Now he knew. Isaac would say to him, "Papa, you must absolutely retire. You have done enough." And he would say, "There comes a time when the old must obey the young." And he too would take off his working clothes and put on his blue serge suit.

"You understand," said Chaim confidentially, "it embarrasses them when their friends see me in the street, still with a chicken under my arm."

"Because they know it's not right, at your age, when you could be resting. So they say, 'Enough!' That's the way to deal with stubborn fathers."

"Yes, yes," Chaim agreed. When you look at it that way— A sweet Jew, this Abraham. Chaim nodded his head vigorously. He comes straight to the point, the important thing.

Hymie scrutinized Chaim Knopp carefully, pulling back the curtain to the back room, in which he had reseated himself, in such a way as to prevent Chaim from noticing that he was being watched. It's about time, he told himself. He tried to find in Chaim the censor from the adult world who had once frightened him so. Instead here was this bent old man, who sat like a gnome in his sabbath best on the herring barrel. The place was full of old men, and Hymie was a child no longer.

Hymie dropped the curtain and thought about it. The place needed new blood. New blood—Hymie liked that term. He saw himself with the visionary eye of the inveterate reader of comic books. He would enter the business. He would make money. He would come into his own.

When Abraham came home that evening he was full of Chaim's retirement. The child met him at the corner, for Moishe knew on which days his father had lessons to give, so that on those days his grandfather came home from work before him. On the days when his father came home earlier the child waited on the other corner, the one closer to the synagogue. Abraham pretended to race him home through the snow. Every mock running step that Abraham took reminded him that he was no longer young, and the thought of this pleased him because it reminded him of how his son would some-day say to him that it was time he should retire. He would devote his time to study. All day he would sit with Chaim in the synagogue, and they would discuss the ancient wisdom, and he would watch his sons and his grandsons grow. The child was waiting for him at the gate, laughing at the way he ran.

Once they were inside the house and had removed their outdoor things—"Well, have you been a good boy?" Without waiting for an answer, Abraham hoisted Moishe onto his knee. "Let's sing a little."

It was a song that Moses had learned before he could properly lisp the words.

" 'What will we eat when the Messiah comes'—sing!—'at the cele-bration?' "

" 'Leviathan and Shorabor we will eat.' " Moses opened his arms wide to indicate the size of the fish and the ox. His mouth stretched round, open and tight at the corners. " 'Leviathan and Shorabor we will eat.' " Moses rolled his eyes and rubbed his belly—"Ay ay"—as they sang in chorus.

" 'What will we drink when the Messiah comes, at the celebra-tion?' "

" 'Wine from the holy vines!' " Moses made his hands into a goblet and gulped from them greedily.

" 'Leviathan and Shorabor we will eat, wine from the holy vines we will drink, at the celebration.' "

" 'Who will teach us Torah when the Messiah comes, at the cele-bration?' " sang Abraham.

" 'Moses the Rabbi will teach us Torah!' "

"That's right." Abraham laughed. "Not wild!" he cautioned, for Ruth sometimes complained that he made the child wild when they romped together. Moses nodded and remembered for one chorus.

" 'Who will teach us dancing when the Messiah comes?' " Abraham waved his hands in imitation of a harem dancer.

Moses followed suit. " 'Miriam the Prophetess will teach us to dance!' "

" 'Who will teach us to play, then, at the celebration?' " Abraham pretended to strum some musical instrument.

Moses strummed the air vigorously. " 'David the King will teach us to play.' " Moses rushed ahead of his grandfather. " 'Who will teach us wisdom at the celebration?' " he shouted.

"Who then?" Abraham winked, trying to hold him still on his knee.

" 'Solomon the King will teach us wisdom' "—Moses laughed— " 'at the celebration.' "

" 'Leviathan and Shorabor we will eat,' " they bellowed together, " 'wine from the holy vines we will drink' "—Moses cupped his hands and made gulping sounds—" 'Moses the Rabbi will teach us Torah' "—the two of them frowned and looked studious—" 'Miriam the Prophetess will teach us dancing, David the King will teach us to play, Solomon the King will teach us wisdom' "—they nodded wisely at each other—" 'at the celebration!' "

For a second there was silence, and grandfather and grandson looked about them mysteriously. " 'And who,' " Abraham half whispered, half sang, holding up one finger in the air, " 'will bless us when the Messiah comes, at the celebration?' "

Moses held up a finger too. " 'The Holy God will bless us, at the celebration!' "

Together they went down the list, making the appropriate gestures as they sang, with Moses trying to get slightly ahead of his grandfather all the time, so that Abraham was forced to race too. By the time they sang out simultaneously, " 'The Holy God will bless us!' " Moses' voice, together with the voice of his grandfather, produced a great thundering.

"Enough!" His mother ran in from the kitchen, clutching her ears. "Enough enough! Heroes both of you, my cake just collapsed in fear of you."

"Of course it's enough," Abraham pointed out, still gasping a little.

"What more could your cake want than the blessing of the Holy God?" They both laughed at Grandfather's wit.

"Enough," Moses repeated, and they doubled up with laughter again. They followed Ruth into the kitchen and demanded of her whether the Shorabor and the Leviathan were not yet ready for two hungry Jews. Ruth began to bewail the fact that she had now not only one child but two to put up with, and as soon as Isaac came home she would probably have three. They danced around the kitchen and mimicked her, wailing, "Oiyoiyoi," until Ruth broke down and laughed with them.

When Isaac came home and they sat down around the supper table Abraham broke the news to them of Chaim's retirement. In highly dramatic terms he described how Chaim's children had come to him and had said that he had worked hard enough. It was time for him to rest.

"Would you like to retire already, Pa?" Isaac asked, laughing a little, for there was to him a tinge of unreality about the very question. At the same time a feeling very like fear tugged at his heart. Someday it would happen, of course; it was only right that it should. Strong though his father was, someday the reins would fall to him. Isaac could not visualize it except in terms of a multiplication of the fatigue that he felt now after his double labors.

Abraham was laughing. "Retire? Now? Do you understand what you're talking about? I knew if I mentioned it you'd right away tell me to retire too. I know you already. You'd offer me the money you haven't got in your pocket, just to show me that you want to give me everything. In the first place I'm not quite as old as Chaim yet. A few more years, let's say, and in that time a lot can happen. In the second place all the money that both of us bring in is just enough for us to live on, and maybe hope a little for the child. In the third place—"Abraham was warming to his topic, and when he warmed to his topic his voice grew loud and rhetorical.

."In the third place," Isaac interrupted, "you don't have a house to draw rent from, and your children have empty pockets from which to draw your allowance."

"Oiyoiyoi," sang Abraham. "Oiyoiyoi," sang Moses. "Oiyoiyoi," they all wailed together.

"But aside from that," said Isaac, "it's a sssp-l-en-did idea!"

"Sssp-l-en-did!" they agreed.

"And besides," Abraham continued when they had stopped laughing, "what would Polsky do without me? Can you imagine, he has asked me to keep an eye on the cash register when his own son's around. His own son. I can just imagine what will happen when he takes the boy into the business. I will have to watch the father for the son and the son for the father, and the business for both of them when they're busy watching each other."

And yet, though they had turned the whole topic into a joke, it did not remain so in Isaac's mind. It knotted itself in with the other problems that made his brain feel like a lumpy mattress at night and would not let him sleep until his mind was tired and bruised. This at least he should be able to offer someday, of all the things that had been expected of him. But then the child must have an education too. And what of more children? They had determined, Ruth and he, that they would have only as many children as they could afford to bring up and educate properly. It had seemed a logical idea, had given them a feeling of control over things. They had not thought that this might, when it came down to it, mean only one child. Why, in terms of such thinking, even that child might seem at times like an extravagance. The more he thought of it, the more of an affront the idea seemed—one child. Living in pinches and snippets. But did he dare to take the responsibility of more? His father had hinted frequently of late that it was time a child arrived to take the name of Sarah. It was true. But then his father should retire, too, someday. What was all their logic and their control and their planning but an enforced yielding to a necessity that would not give quarter but would keep pressing in and in? Isaac tried to imagine the time when his own son—sons—would say to him too that it was time he should retire. What would he be like then? He could not visualize it, though old age was so often in his mind.

It's because I don't feel well that I get depressed. It's when I'm tired. For a long time Isaac had known that he was not a well man. No doctor had ever completely explained to him the nature of his ailment. His father was inclined to the opinion that it was beyond the understanding of mere doctors. It had to do with the heart; that much he knew. And except for the times when he was taken with what he called an attack, he did not think of it particularly. It was another scar, concrete, physical, that the past had left him, another weakness to become aware of when strength was needed.

But his son would be strong and whole, without fear, without blemish. That was why he had felt so bitterly disappointed when Ruth, in her anxiety to check up over every little thing that she suspected, took the child to an eye doctor, who said that he would need glasses.

"Doctor says it's nothing serious. He won't have to wear them always," she had explained. "I had a feeling it would be something."

"Glasses at his age. I don't like it."

"It's all right," Abraham had insisted. "He'll shine, in spite of them, right through them he'll shine."

"We don't have to get them right away. We can wait a little," Ruth had suggested.

"He's just a baby yet. Why should he need glasses?" Even now, as he fell asleep, thinking about it, he was conscious of a terrible personal affront.

"Isaac, Isaac!" He was jerked suddenly out of his dream.

"Wha—what?" his voice croaked, apart from himself. The dream stayed with him an instant longer so that he could remember vaguely. And then he was left with only the physical sensations, painful fatigue, the feeling of having run a long way, the difficulty in drawing his breath. Gradually he realized that it was his wife's hand that gripped him by the arm, her dark, familiar eyes that he made out dimly above him.

Her voice, as from a distance, seemed to fight its way through to him, frightened, slightly shrill in the darkness. "Isaac, what's the matter? You were breathing funny!"

There was a pushing still inside of him, and his limbs quivered slightly as though after a great strain. "I was dreaming."

"How do you feel?"—her voice, still anxious, from beside him.

"Tired. Oi, what a dream."

"Can you remember this time? What do you dream?"

He tried to recapture the peculiar, wild intensity of the dream. "I don't know. I'm stretching, pushing. Something's pushing me. I don't even want to remember."

"If you remember it, maybe it won't come again. Try."   •

"It'll come."

"It's when you're tired. You work too hard."

"I can see my face. Somehow I'm naked. The tendons in my neck are bulging. My veins are ready to burst. But where am I? What am I doing?"

"You must see a doctor— No, don't argue. A specialist."

"So you see doctors about dreams now too? You're right. I've read about it, but maybe I should wait till I have a dream that's worth more money. Those dream doctors are expensive."

"Don't laugh. Look at you. I can feel your heart pounding even now. You're sweating. It's not just the dream."

"Maybe." Isaac's voice was beginning to recede. "Let's sleep."

"But will you go to a specialist?" She leaned over him.

Isaac could feel his body relaxing, lifting, drifting away. He was so achingly tired. From a distance his voice murmured something unintelligible.

Ruth turned over, and then over again, and listened for the sound of his breathing.

Late in the spring the jeweler's lease ran out, and Polsky began to make preparations for the renovation of the business. A trail of contractors made their way through the building, and Polsky explained, described, listened to suggestions, and haggled. Every day Abraham came home with new items concerning the future of the butcher shop. One evening he explained, "The butcher shop itself will have

very little done to it. Only he's going to have the floor fixed up so
that we won't need to use any more sawdust, and they'll take the
stove out and put a furnace in the cellar. They're going to knock out
the wall between the butcher shop and the jeweler's old place, and
from the jeweler's half they're going to make a delicatessen with
booths. Polsky says this was Hymie's idea."

"Congratulations," said Isaac. "If Hymie has had an idea then it is
time he was taken into the business."

On another day Abraham brought home· more news. "Do you
know what else we're going to have? He's enlarging the jeweler's
back room. He'll knock out the wall between and just leave a small
kitchen behind the butcher shop, and we're going to have a
kibitzarnia too."

"A kibitzarnia," said Ruth. "He's ambitious, that Polsky."

"All day and all night they'll play cards. He'll charge them rent
from every pot. Sandwiches they'll eat from the delicatessen. If I
know Polsky there'll even be a drink to be found."

"What about dancing girls?" said Isaac. "You wouldn't think that
place could hold so many businesses."

"The kibitzarnia will be a private affair," Abraham explained.
"He is calling it a club, and only members of the club can come into
the back room. Hymie's friends will give their business to the delicatessen."

At last the carpenters came and the work began. Business in the
butcher shop continued as usual while the walls were being knocked
away and the changes being made. Chaim Knopp, who found that
time dragged for him now that he was a retired man, although he
would not yet admit it, came every day to ·watch the work. As he explained to Abraham. he could not wear his good clothes now that the
shop was in such a mess, so he arrived and ·wandered about in his
old working clothes, offering suggestions to the carpenters or sitting
and discussing the progress of the work with Abraham. Gradually
the place was being transformed; its old contours were torn away,
and a new shape began to·emerge.

Isaac, who dropped in one evening with the child after work to see how things were going, remarked on it. "It's strange how the old shop is gone now. The new place isn't even finished yet, and it's hard to remember how the other looked. And it existed for so long."

"It's true." Abraham looked about him. "It's not like it was. But then the future always brings something new." Abraham ruminated this thought cheerfully.

"And there's always something gone that was," said Isaac. Since his mother's death Isaac had thought a good deal about this. It seemed to him that, between that mysterious point in time when he had last really seen his mother and the time when he had suddenly discovered that she was dying, a whole period had been lost to him, a long stretch of time in which his relationship to her had been dimmed by his inattention. He did not want to lose another lifetime so. He determined that he would pay attention, watch, catch every fleeting moment. It was a hard task he set himself, for although it seemed to him that he was so much more alive now that he had forced himself into an increased awareness, the very acts of living became more fatiguing, more difficult, more crowded. The more alert he grew, the denser grew the life about him that drew his attention, so that at times he had simply to force his mind to stop for a little while its incessant grinding.

The alteration of the butcher shop took time. It was already early summer, and the painters were still there, putting the final touches on the place. Polsky was busy running around and arranging things, so that the work in the shop was left to Abraham, who came home more than usually tired in the evenings.

One Saturday, after they had eaten lunch, Abraham and Isaac took the child to the park. Abraham lay down with a paper over his face and immediately went to sleep. Isaac lay on the grass with his son. He stretched out his hand. "Hold my hand, we'll go for a ride. Look at that cloud—that one over there, the puffy one. Keep your eyes on it."

The child, stretched out in the same attitude as his father, one hand firmly clenched in the larger one, squinted up at the sky. The cloud was round and puffy and soft.

"Can you see it move?" His father's voice was soft too, and a little excited.

"Wait," said Moses, concentrating. "I'm not sure. Yes, it's going. It's moving!"

"Well, listen," said Isaac quickly. "It's not really the cloud that's moving. It's us."

"Us?" Moses could see clearly that it was the cloud that moved, sailing trimly, fatly across the sky. "Us?" He tried to conceive it.

"Yes." Isaac was laughing a little. "Can't you feel it? Lie very still, and you can feel the whole earth moving. See the trees moving away from that cloud?"

The tops of the trees in the distance did actually seem to be moving away from the cloud. He clutched his father's hand more tightly. "Yes, yes, we're moving," he shouted excitedly.

"Keep looking at it, keep looking—fast fast!" Isaac laughed.

"Fast fast," shouted Moses. The whole earth was speeding quickly past the clouds. Moses felt a little dizzy. They were rushing along, and he couldn't stop. With a sudden little scream he wrenched his eyes away from the cloud and twisted his body around so that he toppled right on top of his father. "I jumped off!" He adjusted his eyes to his father, blinking a little. His father, close and solid in his vision, laughed too.

"The earth goes round and round," said Isaac, "fast fast fast."

"That's true." Abraham pushed the paper away from his face and smiled at the two of them. He had not been asleep after all. "You can't jump off." He shook his finger at his grandson.

"Yes I can." Moses jumped from Isaac and attacked his grandfather. They tussled noisily.

Isaac's eye sought the cloud again. Its position had changed. Strange how a child will skip from a thought into an action, afraid neither that he will lose the thought nor spoil the action. It didn't matter to Moishe that in the time he had taken to tussle with them the cloud had changed position a fraction. At that moment it had been more important to tussle. The warmth of the afternoon began to seep into Isaac's bones and scramble his thoughts. He closed his eyes, and the cloud remained, orange on the inside of his eyelids, then purple, then faded into other shapes and colors. In the confusion of pre-sleep it seemed to him that his son had committed an act of courage, jumping off that way, and as he fell asleep he was pointing this out with a swell of pride to the figures that crossed his eyelids.

His mother opened the door for him, and Moses stepped onto the front porch. "Be careful," she cautioned.

Moses looked around him experimentally. The outlines of things sprang sharply into his eyes. He blinked once or twice. On his nose perched the spectacles, round, black-rimmed. They seemed to be all over his face. He swiveled his eyes round and round, trying to see the entire circuit of the rims. Experimentally he took a step or two forward to find out if the world would remain steady about him. He stretched out his arms and stepped cautiously, at the same time peering through the glasses as though he were afraid that they would fall off suddenly and he would lose his balance. Carefully he seated himself on the top step, unnaturally owlish, a thin-faced little boy, wriggling his nose uncomfortably.

While he was preoccupied with the sensation of wearing the glasses, taking them off, putting them on again, Dmitri appeared suddenly, sturdy legs on the rungs of the fence, his gang ranged sturdily beside him. His body leaning far over the fence, he bawled in his rough, child's voice, "Yah Moses, the freak, has to wear goggles because he can't see the pot he pees in!"

Moses looked up, heart beating, acknowledged the greeting with elaborate sarcasm. "Dmitri Biblbiblbibl"—finger on lip.

Laughter from Dmitri's gang.

Angry, the voice of the enemy—"Come on out and fight if you're so smart."

"Your gang will jump me."

"Okay, we'll let my sister Junie fight on your side. Junie Jewlover."

Laughter from the gang.

Moses didn't answer. Instead he made a face and laughed out loud, convinced that the joke was between himself and the glasses, that though he could see his enemies they could not see the face he made behind the glasses.

"Hey ya, blind! Goggle-eyes!" The voices of the gang now assailed him in chorus. He made a face again, then looked past them with pretended indifference toward Mad Mountain in the distance. Pretend it's the loonies howling.

The words separated and detached themselves from one another, and gradually from their meanings. Moses listened to them almost with pleasure. "Dirdyjoo, dirdyjoo"—until a rock shattered his little pose.

They didn't dare come near him at other times, though, not when he marched to the synagogue, all dressed up in his Säbbath clothes, with his grandfather striding along beside him. His day to go to the synagogue came before their day to go to church. They knew nothing of meeting Reb Chaim Knopp, and of the eversame amiable question. "You like to go to the synagogue with grandpapa?" And of the eversame delight in blaring up at him, "Yoh!" in that loud trumpeting voice that everyone seemed to wear for his grandfather, a shouting that was something fine and joyous.

What could Dmitri and his gang know, standing around bedraggled and dirty, of the discovery he had made about the skullcap of the Reverend Chaim Knopp? When he was a baby Moses had always thought that because the Reverend Knopp was such a holy man— almost as holy as his grandfather, although his voice was not quite so loud—God had sewn on the little black skullcap Himself. His grandfather's skullcap, his father's skullcap, everybody else's skullcap could be taken off. The Reverend Knopp's skullcap was irremovable, fastened to his head by the invisible stitches of God Amen. Even when he wore his other black serious outdoor hat, the skullcap remained underneath it. This Moses had seen.

And then one day at the synagogue Moses, because he was a baby no longer—they even gave him snuff for sneezing sometimes—had realized that the skullcap of the Reverend Knopp could be removed

like anyone else's if he chose to do so. No one had had to tell him.
He had understood for himself. Dmitri wouldn't know this. He was
too dumb. Dmitri was—you mustn't say—a prick.

"Well," said Abraham, "we will have Hymie Polsky with us from
now on." It was late in the evening. Ruth had made a glass of tea,
and Abraham, Ruth, and Isaac sat around the kitchen table, drinking tea and nibbling pieces of rock-hard honey cake, one of Ruth's
specialties that was a particular favorite of Abraham's. "He will be
the big doer at the opening of the business on Saturday evening."

"Oho," said Isaac. "So he's finally passed his exams?"

"Passed his exams!" Abraham pushed his glass away from him.
"I don't know how he isn't ashamed to show his face. You should
only know."

Ruth and Isaac exchanged glances. All evening they had seen that
Abraham was upset. Gradually now Isaac drew the story from him.
Through either mischief or laziness, or through an impulse of vanity,
or all three, Hymie Polsky had decided to do well in his final exams.
Accordingly he had managed to bribe one of the poorer boys, a bril-
liant student who was already beginning to save money to enter the
university, to write his final exams for him. All had gone well until
the third test, when one of the invigilators happened to be a teacher
from their own high school.

"So they threw them both out of school," concluded Abraham.
"And it served them right."

"Whom did it serve right—Hymie Polsky?" queried Isaac ironically. "What kind of a punishment was it for him? Graduating and
being expelled, they are one and the same thing for him. At worst
he'll get a beating from his father for getting caught, if his father isn't
afraid to lay a hand on him now that he's grown into such a strapping
hulk."

"Yes," added Ruth, "the punishment fell on the other one's head."

"It's he who's had his chances ruined. He must have needed the
money pretty badly to risk so much to get it," continued Isaac.

"Hymie says he had started to save money to go to the university," repeated Abraham, "but was this a way to save money to go to the university? To cheat?"

From his couch in the living room Moses watched the hazy long streak of light from the open crack of the kitchen door play on a strip of wallpaper in front of him. His mother left the door slightly open almost as though she knew that he was still sometimes afraid of the darkness.

"But how far could it really be called cheating?" He heard his father's voice respond thoughtfully to his grandfather's rumbling. "He knew it made no difference to the Polsky boy, and those few dollars might mean the difference between saving enough for college and never getting there."

"Was that"—his grandfather's voice was raised somewhat, sternly —"the kind of money to use to build himself a career? Money he sinned for?"

His mother's voice sounded a little sharp, as though it were cutting into the smooth pudding and deep chocolate sounds of his father and grandfather. "All right, so it was a sin, but how much of a sin was it?" she said. "Polsky had the money the other one should have had to go to college, so when it was offered to him he took the chance. What opportunity does a poor child have? It's a pity that he was caught."

"Cheating?" Abraham's voice rose. "What kind of a start was this for a career in the university? What would someone like that study? There are enough lawyers in the world already. Tell me, my son, would you have done it?"

"It doesn't matter whether I would have done it. I don't know whether I would have done it. But I can understand how someone might be driven to it. How can we condemn him?"

"And do you think they'd give a Jewish child another chance?" Moses cringed in bed at his grandfather's sudden shout. "His father went to the school and begged them! He came to the shop today to find out if Hymie knew where his son had disappeared to. You should have seen it. Hymie stood there with that oafish smile on his face and told the crying father that he'd seen him climbing onto the freight train!"

It was as though he could hear the sudden silence rush into the vacuum left by his grandfather's voice. He strained his ears to hear a noise, a reassuring sound from the kitchen. But all noise was frozen except for the scudding sounds his heart was making. They did terrible things to Jewish boys. They had done something terrible to his uncles, he knew. Was his mother still there, in the kitchen? "Mama!" called Moishe in a frightened voice.

A sudden, reassuring rasping of chairs. The light streak widened on the wall. His mother's pleasant, sharp voice beside him.

"A drink of water?" whispered Moses.

In the kitchen Isaac took the question up again in a lowered voice. "We can't say it's because he's Jewish. There are rules, after all." And then again, after a moment's silence: "It's as much because he's poor." Isaac shook his head. There were so many reasons. "One could almost just as easily say it's because he is alive."

The new butcher shop-delicatessen-kibitzarnia was opened on a Saturday evening, after the Sabbath was officially over. Saturday evening had always been a busy time. Now, in addition to the regular customers and the old friends who came to see how the business was going, the pool-hall boys swept over en masse for corned-beef sandwiches, and an inaugural game had been started by some of Polsky's old cronies in the back room. Here Laiah presided, and her hoarse, throaty laughter often rang out from behind the curtain.

The place had never been so busy or so noisy. Every now and then someone would sweep back the curtain to the kibitzarnia and shout out an order for drinks and sándwiches. The poolroom crowd lounged around, talking loudly. Polsky ran about, large and jovial. Hymie, like his father, excited, sweating, important, repeated the story of his expulsion from school as though it were some heroic exploit, to each new friend that came in. Chaim, who had dropped in for the opening, found that his barrel was occupied, and the noise was so deafening that he left after a few shouted words to Abraham. The din at last seemed to come from within Abraham's head rather than from the room.

When finally he swept out the butcher shop and turned off the lights he felt as tired as though he had just completed a whole week of steady work. The kibitzarnia and the delicatessen were still going strong. Abraham locked up the butcher shop, for Polsky, on the theory that two front doors give a place a classy look, had kept the two separate entrances. As he was leaving, Hymie, sweating in the face and swelled out with importance, called out to him with a new-found familiarity.

"Avrom, I forgot—would you do us a favor? Deliver a parcel on your way home, eh? She wants it for tomorrow morning. I've written down the address."

The silence of the outside was like a sudden blow. It was a pleasure to walk through the darkened streets, enjoying the stillness, the freshness of the air, the knowledge that he was nearly home. Almost he forgot about Hymie's parcel. When he remembered he had to turn around again and walk back. So Hymie really was a boss in the business now. Well, all right, but Polsky was still his employer. As long as Hymie didn't try to interfere with his work or make a habit of sending him, like this, blocks out of his way, let him be a boss. He thought of his own business and of his partner Isaac, of how their percentages would increase and their dividends multiply. There was Moishe Jacob, there would be Sarah, there would be even more children, perhaps, someday. They would not be idle in the world. In spite of his fatigue, his legs moved more quickly to the rhythm of his thoughts.

Chapter Eleven

————— ◄◄◄❂►► —————

Abraham waited until Ruth had filled the basin with soapsuds and water, so that there should be no splashing noises to distract them. The child sat with his elbows on the table, his mouth slightly open, waiting— He doesn't take his eyes from my face. He listens, he wonders, like a grown-up human being.

Isaac too sat at the table, leaning back in his chair, his mouth pursed slightly while his fingernail idly scratched through some breadcrumbs on the tablecloth. He listens too, thought Abraham, as I listen. No matter how often one has heard it and even told it, one always listens. Always there is a moment of happiness before the beginning, a rising up, a reaching. This is ours.

Abraham spoke slowly, savoring his words, reflecting. "In those days the people were still wild. Instead of worshiping God they worshiped idols of clay. And to these images they prayed and made sacrifices. They laid their children on the altars. They sacrificed human beings to their wild gods."

"Did they kill them when they sacrificed them?" asked Moses in his clear, earnest treble.

"Yes."

Human children. Ruth pulled a chair up to the sink quietly and dropped into it. Barbaric. She laid down the dishrag carefully and listened.

"Abraham's father was Terach, a rich man, a maker of idols. People came from all over to buy his idols. He offered them many gods. And the people bought them and worshiped them.

"Now this was something that Abraham, even when he was a little boy, could not understand. He could see that these gods that his father made were only things of wood and clay, things of the

173

earth. He himself had often watched them being hacked out of blocks of wood, molded out of wet blobs of clay. Could these be gods of earth and sky?

"He was curious. Often he went to the place where his father and the workmen were. One day when he was still a child he waited until all the workmen were gone from the place. And he went in and looked around. All about him were the idols, standing quietly in the shadows. Now another child might have been frightened, standing there in the still, dim light, surrounded by all of those mighty gods. But Abraham, instead of running away, went quickly up to one of the gods, almost before he knew what he was doing, and tweaked his nose! Well!"

Moses laughed. Abraham had tweaked his nose unexpectedly.

"He waited. Nothing happened. There was no sudden thunderbolt of revenge. The gods stood dumbly as before. So Abraham went from one to the other of the images. And one of them he scratched on the arm, and from another he chipped a little bit of clay. And still nothing happened. And Abraham, who was still very young, thought that this was very strange.

"Still, as he grew older, the question perplexed him. Gradually he began to feel that it was a terrible thing that human beings should be sacrificed. This idea grew on him until one day a few years later he found himself again in the factory with the gods. This time he had to be sure! He seized a strong wooden club and with it he laid about him, shattering the gods, breaking them into little pieces. When he was finished, one image remained standing. He left his club in the arms of this remaining god.

"In the morning there was great excitement. Abraham was dragged out of bed and brought to where his father stood amid the broken gods. His father said to him, 'O Avrom, my son, last night you were seen entering the factory. What have you done to the gods?'

" 'I have done nothing, Father,' answered Avrom. 'You can see for yourself that this god has beaten all the others.' "

Moses laughed and wriggled in his chair. Ruth nodded in appreciation.

" 'How can he have beaten all the others,' cried Terach, 'when he himself is but a block of wood?'

" 'Aha!' cried Abraham. 'If he is but a block of wood, then why do you fall down and worship him, and why do you sacrifice your children to him?' And Abraham said to the people, 'I do not believe in these gods. I believe that there is only one God!'

"But his father said to him, 'And what does your God look like? How may we depict Him?'

" 'It is impossible to depict my God,' said Abraham. 'For He is the God of Heaven and Earth. We cannot conceive of Him in wood and clay.'

"But the people demanded that Abraham should be punished as an unbeliever who had destroyed their idols. So his father had him cast into a flaming furnace, and all the people believed that here was the end of this heretic who dared to believe in one God.

"But Abraham walked through the flaming furnace and was not destroyed. And when the people saw this they knew that the man was a prophet. And his father ceased to build idols and would worship them no more."

Ruth had resumed work with her dishrag, scrubbing vigorously in water that was now cool. But she could not help holding up one ear to listen.

"But throughout the lands most of the people still worshiped idols and destroyed children. Avrom knew that he must preach against this and teach them that there is only one God, and that God did not want them to destroy their own. All his life he went about and talked to the people and tried to make them understand. But people are hard to change. As he grew older he saw that there was no one to carry on his work when he died. So at first he tried to persuade Eliezar, who was the manager of his estates, to follow in his steps. But Eliezar was a businessman. He wasn't interested in such things. One God, many gods—why should he bother his head to go out and preach and get laughed at, yet? He was making a living.

"Abraham grew very old. But he and his wife Sarah did not have any children. And Abraham longed for a son. He thought that if he had a son his son would carry on his work. So Sarah, when she saw that her husband was sad, told him to get a child from her servant Hagar."

Abraham hurried delicately through this part, for the child need not yet be bothered with the whys and wherefores of having wives and children.

"He named the child Ishmael, and he thought that his son would go in his steps. But he was disappointed again. For Ishmael grew up to be a hunter, and the words of his father went in one of his ears and out the other. He was interested only in roaming through the fields.

"So finally Abraham prayed to God and asked Him what he should do.

"And God said to him, 'Do not worry, for Sarah will yet have a child, and you will name him Itzhok, and he will go in your steps.'

"And it was so. At ninety and nine years Sarah bore a child, and they named him Itzhok."

"I knew," said Moses.

Abraham smiled. "And his father loved him very much, for he grew just as Abraham had wished him to grow."

There was a momentary silence, and Ruth seized the opportunity to empty her basin and splash fresh rinsing water into it.

"But that's not the end," said Moses.

"No." Isaac stirred slightly.

Abraham waited till the tap was turned off again.

"For a while they were happy together. But God had decided that He would test Abraham, to see if he was really as faithful as he should be. So He said to him, 'Go up into the hills; I wish you to make a sacrifice.'

"And Abraham asked Him, 'What shall I sacrifice?'

"And He replied, 'Take with you your son Isaac.'

"When Abraham heard this he said, 'Very well.' "

His grandfather's voice had slowed to a pause again, and Moses leaned forward, his mouth rounded as though to catch the words from his grandfather's lips.

"So he took the boy and went with him to the top of the hills. When they reached the top of the highest hill Isaac said to him, 'What will be your sacrifice, Father?'

"And Abraham said, 'You will, my son.'

"So Isaac looked about him at the blue sky and at the hills and the fields, and at the sun which shone down on him, and he said to Abraham, 'Then bind me tightly lest I struggle and spoil your sacrifice.'

"Then Abraham bound him and laid him down and prepared to do as he had been commanded. And just as he had raised his hand to strike, God called out to him, 'Abraham, look behind you.'

"He looked behind him, and there was a young ram with his horns caught in the bushes.

" 'Sacrifice the ram,' God commanded.

"So he sacrificed the ram, and Isaac was saved."

Moses let out his breath slowly. His grandfather was frowning, nodding his head over the words that he had just finished speaking.

"And so," said Isaac, "as a proof of his faith his one God asks him to do the one thing that all his life has seemed most dreadful to him. What had turned him from idol worship? What had he fought against all his life? He finds himself near the end of the circle of his days with his own God asking him if he is willing to make even this surrender. And was he aware of the irony when he said, 'Very well'?"

"What was he not aware of?" said Abraham. "Can you imagine what he felt, with his hand raised to strike? What they all felt? In that moment lay the future of our people, and even more than that. In that moment lay the secrets of life and death, in that closed circle with just the three of them, with Abraham offering the whole of the past and the future, and Isaac lying very still, so as not to spoil the sacrifice, and the glint of the knife and the glare of the sun and the terror of the moment burning into his eyes so that when the time comes many years later when he must in turn bless his sons he is too blind to see that Jacob has again stolen the march on Esau. And God himself is bound at that moment, for it is the point of mutual surrender, the one thing He cannot resist, a faith so absolute. You are right when you say that it is like a circle—the completed circle, when the maker of the sacrifice and the sacrifice himself and the Demander who is the Receiver of the sacrifice are poised together, and life flows into eternity, and for a moment all three are as one.

"That was the moment that even God could not resist, and so He gave us the future."

Isaac shook his head.

"Well, isn't that right?" Abraham laughed, excited, aggressive, as when he was satisfied with the sound and the feel of his words. "He said, 'Kill the ram and let your son live. In him is your future!'"

"Yes." Isaac smiled. "I suppose it's as right as anything else I know."

"What about Ishmael?" Moses interrupted. "You forgot to tell about Ishmael."

"You've heard enough for tonight," said Ruth. "And you've got your bath to take yet."

"But it's not finished." Moses turned to his grandfather pleadingly.

Abraham held up his hand to Ruth. "I'll tell him about Ishmael. It'll only take me a minute, and then I'll throw him into his bath myself. All right?

"Ishmael"—Abraham turned to Moses quickly before she could answer, and Ruth glanced at Isaac, who shrugged—"was a man of the fields, more used to action than to speech. When Abraham and Isaac were coming home from the hills Ishmael, who had heard of all that had happened, rode ahead of them to bring home the news. When he arrived home he ran straight to Sarah. And instead of saying, as a sensible man might have done, 'Abraham has almost killed Isaac,' he cried out to her, 'Abraham has killed Isaac.' And Sarah dropped dead before he could say 'almost.'"

The old man and the little boy stared at each other, shaking their heads at the stupidity of it. "That just goes to show," said Abraham. "That just goes to show."

"What?" asked Moses hopefully.

There was a sound from Ruth.

"That it's time you had your bath," sang Abraham. He seized the child's hand, and the two of them made a hasty exit.

"But who's to say," Isaac began when he and Ruth were alone and they could hear sounds of water splashing in the bathroom, "that it's not just an excitement of the imagination? Killing children is a brutal and wasteful habit, as Abraham realized, just as any killing is. So, being a clever man, he evolved a method of convincing his credulous people in terms that would excite their imaginations and make them take notice. And, earlier on, maybe Terach wasn't so anxious to kill his son; maybe he wanted Abraham to win the respect of the people and become their leader—provided, that is, that all this actually happened, which is questionable. Maybe the furnace was not stoked as properly as it might have been, so that a brisk run through could be arranged that was not at all fatal. And in the end humanity is served, animal sacrifice takes the place of human sacrifice, and eventually all sacrifice ceases except for the ritual killing of creatures for food. Abraham has plotted well. How's that?"

"He must have been a clever man," said Ruth. With one ear she was listening to the splashing and the hectic noises from the bathroom—I'll have a whole lake to clean up. I should go in and take a look.

"And yet," Isaac went on, speaking musingly, a little ruefully, "it's strange how, whether or not you believe it, there's something in the idea itself. You try to imagine a scene like that, in spite of yourself, with the three of them bound together in their awful moment, and the knife poised between them, its blade flashing in the sun. . . ."

"Hey, that's no way to hold a knife!" In his haste to get off the high stool behind the cash register, which now occupied a small desk of its own in the archway between the delicatessen and the butcher shop, Hymie almost brought the stool down with him. "You could goose somebody that way." Hymie took the knife from Laiah's hand. Laiah surrendered it with a surprised little gesture that gave Hymie complete mastery of the situation.

"A knife's a dangerous thing," said Hymie, holding the bread knife by its handle and making an illustrative thrust forward. "That's why when you hand it to someone you hand it like this." He handed the knife to Abraham, pointing the blade away from both of them.

Laiah shuddered expressively and ran her hand through her thick auburn hair, from which gleamed exotic orange highlights, the result of the rinse she used to touch up the graying parts. "I don't like knives," she drawled in her pleasantly husky voice. "Only this one hardly cuts anyway." She addressed herself to Abraham. "The other day I noticed you were sharpening knives on a whetstone in there. I thought perhaps . . ." She let her voice trail off in delicate uncertainty.

"Oh sure," Hymie broke in cockily, "anything for a good customer. But it'll be sharp now; you'll have to be careful."

Laiah smiled slightly, moving her full lips. "Don't worry, I'll be sure I won't"—she hesitated for a fraction of a second—"prick anyone."

Hymie caught the pause in her words and the playful rebuke that seemed to imply a bond between them. He tried to catch her liquid eyes again, but she had already turned in response to Abraham's question.

"Do you need it right away?" asked Abraham.

"Well, Avrom"—Laiah made a little helpless fluttering gesture with her hands and smiled—"before supper. I'm sorry to be such a nuisance."

"It's all right." Abraham took the knife and was about to turn away with it. It disturbed him to watch a grown woman, filled out with middle years, trying still to move to the rhythms of spring. Behind it there was something frightening.

"Oh, and Abraham"—Laiah called him back—"while you're at it would you get me two chops and a half-pound of salami sliced? I'll pick them up on my way out. And Avrom—" Abraham turned again. Laiah smiled. "Thank you."

Hymie climbed back on the high stool, where with a turn of his head in either direction he could survey both sides of the business. Laiah paused beside the register. "Anything going on in back?"

"Pa's in there with Mandelknaidel and somebody else. Go ahead." Hymie flushed slightly as he spoke and watched her slantwise. It was said that she was living part-time with a lawyer and part-time with this Mandelknaidel, though both were married men with families. Laiah merely nodded and pulled out a package of cigarettes. Cool one, thought Hymie. The things she probably knows.

Laiah offered him a cigarette. Hymie fumbled clumsily in his pants pockets for a match. Laiah waited. Finally he lit their cigarettes. Laiah thanked him with a glance from her wet eyes that gave him a feeling of moist places and warmth. She turned then and undulated lazily toward the back room. Hymie remembered to blow out the match.

It was a pastime with the older guys to boast that they had slept with her. Mandelknaidel claimed that he was now her one and only. But she didn't act like it. There was no percentage, as his father said, in making a one and only out of a shlemiel like Mandelknaidel. He probably hadn't got past the front door.

Hymie watched her, craning his neck till her figure disappeared sideways behind the curtain. Had any of the boys been present there would have been giggles at her exit. Someone would have made a crack about antiquated red-hot mammas, and Hymie would have joined in their laughter. But alone he allowed himself the luxury of certain speculations. He was, after all, a young man of the world, having long since acquired a certain number of addresses that he had tucked away, because his mother liked to go through his things, in a secret compartment in his wallet, with cryptic comments attached to each address.

Oldish she was, if you looked at her face, and dressed to play up too much figure. But you didn't have to be seen in the street with her. And the things she could probably do— The more he thought about it the more pleasantly certain did he become that Laiah had really been acting very friendly toward him under cover of the semi-motherly manner she adopted in public. Take, now, this cigarette, for instance, and the glance from the auburn eyes with their secret amusements. Hymie saw himself already stealing the march on Mandelknaidel and the other old boys. "Always the killer," his friends would say with admiration.

Someday, Hymie promised himself, he would find out. She would betray herself, what she really wanted and was willing to do. What if he actually did something? He could put out his hand accidentally. What would she do? He would know by the way she responded. Hymie shifted about restlessly on the high stool.

His speculations were interrupted temporarily by the entry of several people into the delicatessen. For the next little while he was busy making sandwiches and serving the customers. Still, within him there was a certain excitement.

Chaim Knopp pushed open the door of the butcher shop and held it open for a moment, looking about him while the bell flew back and forth overhead. He let the door fall to again, and the bell set up a clamoring anew. Nowadays he liked to look in first, to make sure the place was not too busy before he came forward to make his visit. Sometimes the place was so full of people wandering back and forth from the delicatessen and making so much noise that there was no chance of catching Abraham for a few moments of conversation. Abraham would be busy then, taking orders in the butcher shop, and, if Hymie or Polsky didn't happen to be around, making sandwiches and serving drinks in the delicatessen as well.

They're turning him into a waiter in his old age, Chaim would tell himself sadly and try to think of someone else he might visit.

For Chaim's life in retirement had become a routine of visits. In the mornings he got up early through force of habit. He dressed carefully and quickly so as to be out of the apartment before Bassieh awoke. After he had said his prayers and drunk some tea, he slipped out to inspect the world.

At the synagogue he discussed the latest news about the newest Haman, name of Hitler. For Chaim, being a thinking man, had lately become interested in politics. It was an interest which could give him little pleasure. As he complained to Abraham, "Between Hitler and my Bassieh I find it hard to get a good night's sleep." This was something of an exaggeration, however, for Chaim was so saturated with fresh air from walking about and visiting all day that he was tired enough to be able to ignore his wife's complaints and fall asleep soon after the evening meal.

He found Abraham in the small kitchen partitioned off from the *kibitzarnia,* sharpening a knife on the whetstone attached to the table. When he was finished, they came back into the shop and Abraham wrapped the knife carefully in paper and tied it about with string. Chaim sat himself down fastidiously on his barrel.

Abraham could not help noticing, as they talked, how well Chaim looked in his glossy black clothes and carefully shined shoes. Old age had used its most delicate tints on him. There were none of the harsh, grim changes that add themselves, layer on layer, year by year until in the end an entirely new person appears and is greeted with surprise by those who knew him once, who exclaim internally, How he's aged! Time had used another technique on Chaim, softening and rounding, printing in the little wrinkles and stretching them gradually longer, tinting in the pink cheeks with a loving delicacy, with little coursing veins of the color of ripe plums. His beard, white and soft as cashmere, was clipped and combed neatly around to a point. Retirement must be a very fine thing.

Hymie, his customers disposed of, was about to climb onto his high stool when he realized that a vague irritation that he felt was traceable to the voice of Chaim Knopp. He glanced around toward where Chaim was earnestly engaged in conversation with Abraham and grimaced. With noisy, irritated movements he banged on the cash register.

"Abraham," he called out authoritatively, "you won't forget to put up those chops and that salami, will you?"

Abraham glanced up and Chaim turned to look at Hymie, who

swung on his heel and, moving as though he were being driven from his natural haunts by an unpleasant presence, made his way to the curtain that concealed the kibitzarnia. But the sullen expression slipped from his face as he listened for a moment before pushing aside the curtain.

Inside, Hymie saw that Laiah was already seated at a table with his father and the other two. Hymie hitched up his trousers, came over to the table, stationed himself behind Laiah, and pretended to look over her hand in the manner of a kibitzer. Laiah threw him a tolerant smile and continued to play her hand. Hymie leaned forward and brought his face close to her ear to whisper some advice. Laiah nodded and laughed, and Hymie drew slowly back, his nostrils charged with the heavy scent of her perfume. He shifted slightly closer, planting his large hands on the back of her chair so that when she leaned back he could feel the softness of her back. Though she appeared only casually aware of his presence, Hymie was sure that he could feel the bond of a stronger awareness tightening between them. He looked over her shoulder and down to where her rather extravagant bosom heaved gently as she breathed. Hymie's heavy lower lip had parted company with its mate. The back of his neck had begun to sweat, and a curious impulse began to tingle in his right hand. All he had to do was lean over and point out something about the cards. Instead, with a great effort of resistance, he raised his hand and scratched the back of his neck. He shifted his feet again uncomfortably, but could not bring himself to move away from her chair.

In the butcher shop Abraham was telling Chaim about the child. "You know, lately I have gotten into the habit of lying down for a little while when I get home, before supper. It gets so busy here nowadays, like a ship without wheels, everybody running around. So the other day Moishele asks me, 'Grampa, why do you lie down now when you come home?' You understand he likes it better that I should play with him, instead of lying down.

"So I said to him, 'I like to lie down for a few minutes to wash the shop from my head.'

"Well, yesterday afternoon he comes into the house and goes straight to his couch and lies down. What can be the matter with the child? Ruth comes in to him. 'What's the matter, Moishe?'

" 'Nothing,' he says to her. 'I'm washing Dmitri from my head.' "

Chaim laughed and clapped his knee delightedly.

"Every word he catches." Abraham chuckled. "Nothing escapes him. Jacob was like that."

There was a sudden commotion from the kibitzarnia. Laiah, her voice almost mannish in its indignation, swept out into the delicatessen, through the archway, and into the butcher shop, all the while calling back over her shoulder.

"Vulgarians! The father's a *grobion* and the son's a *grobion*. The next time he'll lose his hands! Just like that!" Her hair was slightly disheveled, and as she spoke she blew a strand away from her mouth. She brushed her hands angrily across her bosom, smoothing her dress. Her face betraying in her indignation a certain fleshy looseness of age, she whirled around at the door of the butcher shop, her eyes flashing past Abraham and Chaim and coming to rest on the little group of hapless men who had followed her out of the kibitzarnia. "What do you think"—she addressed Polsky—"that I'm your family nanna that you should all try to cut your teeth on me? Since when has he the right to paw me about in public?"

Polsky spread his arms in a gesture of appeasement, but she had already whirled about, wrenched the door open, and slammed it shut behind her, leaving the bell to echo her indignation.

Hymie emerged from the kibitzarnia, his arms hanging down sheepishly. "What does she think she is?" he muttered sullenly, his face confused, not meeting their eyes.

The men turned on him. "What did you do? What did you do?" asked Mandelknaidel excitedly. "I was looking at the cards. I didn't even see." He almost moaned his disappointment.

"For a one and only you're not very watchful over your girl friend," the other man said, laughing.

"Well, you can see she doesn't need watching," said Mandelknaidel, sliding quickly out of the trap. Then: "But what did you do?"

Hymie's face was still a dull red. "Nothing. I just leaned over her." His voice rose. "What did she make such a fuss for?" He particularly avoided his father's eye.

"For a minute," said the other man slyly, "it looked as though you were trying to shuffle her cards. And she keeps them pretty close to her chest."

Mandelknaidel laughed with the other man enthusiastically.

Hymie's face ripened visibly. "So I just leaned over her. She's old enough to be my grandmother. Who's she kidding?"

Polsky himself stood undecided as to whether he should laugh out loud, as he felt like doing, or bawl the boy out. He was aware that Chaim Knopp and Abraham were in the butcher shop, both of them trying to appear as though they were elsewhere. Best not to laugh. He felt a certain pity, not unmixed with contempt, for his son. Apparently to give him money and tell him to go and learn about girls had not been enough. He had noticed that there was something oddly restless about the way Hymie had hovered over Laiah. And then the clumsy swoop—and in full view. Could he have hoped to pass it off as a casual gesture? Or had he nerved himself for something and come loose like an ill-controlled spring? And Polsky was surprised that, with all the fresh little things around that his own eye sought yearningly, Hymie should pick Laiah for his sloppy assault. Just went to show that the old girl had something in her still. But he would give Hymie a talking to. He did not, inside of himself, feel quite right about Hymie trying it on Laiah. Her remark had hit home. In Polsky's ill-defined morality there was something vaguely incestuous about the idea.

Hymie was blusteringly trying to fend off the teasing of the older men. They don't build them the same nowadays, Polsky told himself. He could not remember a time when he had been so callow.

Suddenly Hymie changed his tack. "So I copped a feel." He turned on Mandelknaidel, practically bellowing. "Bet it's more than you ever got!" Hymie was taller than Mandelknaidel, and the little man stepped back quickly.

Polsky's loyalty was aroused. At least this was no jellyfish. "Listen," he said loudly. "What's it to make a fuss about? If you ask me it's her change of life. She never used to be so touchy. They get capricious at a time like that. But it'll blow over. She'll be back. You'd just better stay out of her way for a while." He turned to Hymie. "Women don't like to be felt around in public unless they're drunk."

Polsky had by this time steered them all back into the kibitzarnia, and here he felt free to laugh with them over his last remark. He laughed heartily, the laughter he had suppressed outside. Hymie looked as though he were getting ready to run out of the place. "It's quiet out there." Polsky addressed him after he had stopped laughing. "Abraham can handle things for a while," he continued, not unkindly. "Maybe you want to take her place for the rest of the game?"

Hymie glared at the others. In Mandelknaidel's eyes he thought he detected a certain respect. "Sure," he said, "if you can stop killing yourselves." Dimly he began to recognize that it might make a pretty good story to tell his friends, one in which he needn't necessarily look as foolish as he had felt at all.

Chaim left the shop soon after. It was not right that he should stay around now, after what had happened. Some gesture on his part must be made to show that he was the Reverend Chaim Knopp, albeit retired, in front of whom all this had happened, even if there was no one left but Abraham to appreciate the gesture. He said nothing about this, but Abraham understood. Chaim took his leave ceremoniously, steadfastly refusing even to glance in the direction of the delicatessen, through which the four men had disappeared into the kibitzarnia.

It was not until Abraham was ready to close up the butcher shop that he remembered Laiah's parcels, left behind when she had flounced out of the shop. He mentioned them to Polsky.

"A knife too, you say." Polsky scratched his head. "Well, I can't send Hymie, and the boy won't be in till after supper. She said she wanted it before, eh? And if she doesn't get it—mmmm! Look, Abraham"—Polsky had an inspiration—"she likes you. She isn't liable to throw anything at you. How about taking it up to her, eh? I'll close up the shop. I'd go myself, only, to tell you the truth, I'm afraid. She's a mighty temperamental woman." Polsky shook his head admiringly. "And of course," he added hastily, "the kid's a young fool."

By the time Abraham had reached the third-floor landing, and stood there resting for a moment he had repeated Polsky's last words to himself half a dozen times. "Young fool," it had been every time he paused for breath. "Young fool," he muttered to himself vehemently for the last time as he punched the doorbell, for he was embarrassed and ill at ease. He was prepared to thrust the parcels at her and rush off without meeting her eyes, but he couldn't do that. He must show that he was a more civil man than the Polskys. Still, he held the parcels out in his arms so as to be the more quickly relieved of them.

He waited for a while, but there seemed to be no sound from within the apartment that his ears could catch. He bent over and was about to deposit the parcels on the door stoop when the door was wrenched open. He started back. Laiah stood looking at him as though she didn't recognize him.

"I was just going to leave." Abraham held out the parcels again. "Polsky," he added.

Laiah's face brightened; her full, mobile lips moved caressingly back over strong, predatory teeth. "Avrom! I wasn't expecting you! But come in." She ignored the parcels and stepped back into her hallway. "Come in." She turned and walked through the short hallway and another room that was in semi-darkness, and finally into the kitchen, where the light was burning. He followed her, still holding the two packages awkwardly in front of him.

"Oh, you didn't close the door. Never mind, I'll get it." She brushed by him, and for a moment he was alone in the kitchen. He put the parcels down on the kitchen table and turned to go back. Laiah swept into the kitchen again. "Sit down a minute, will you? I've just put the tea on. It tires you out climbing those stairs, doesn't it? You'll have a glass of tea with me." And when Abraham remained standing: "Sit down, sit down." She directed him, her hand on his arm, to a chair. It was as though nothing had happened. She showed no trace of her earlier mood, only delight at the unexpected visit of an old friend. But he was not an old friend.

"You will have a glass of tea with me, won't you? I was getting ready to have one all by myself. It's lonely, drinking tea all by yourself in a dark house." She made a gesture with her arm. "And I've been in such a mood all day."

Abraham wondered uneasily whether she was going to say more about the incident at the butcher shop. He half arose from his chair. "Well, I must get home for supper."

"Ah, I suppose you have your big meal in the evening." Laiah had come around to lay a place at his corner of the table, so he was forced to fall back into his chair again. "I have mine in the afternoon. Then I just have a cup of tea and a bite in the evening. It's different," Laiah continued warmly, "when you have a family. Then your big meal is in the evening, and you all sit around the table together." She laughed. "I haven't had much family life. Still, I promise you I won't press anything but a glass of tea on you so you can go home and eat. But you must at least be the first to use my bread knife, since you have renewed it for me. Will you cut me a few slices of bread while I pour the tea?" Laiah put the parcel of meat into her icebox, brought out butter, cheese, honey, and cookies, and began to pour the tea.

Abraham, a little ashamed, conscious of his good fortune in having a family so that he need never ask a stranger in to tea for sheer loneliness, unwrapped her bread knife and cut the bread.

"You're very domesticated, aren't you?" Laiah laughed as she brought him his tea. "You cut such nice thin slices." She sat down then, at right angles to him. The folds of her housecoat brushed carelessly against his leg, and he moved away slightly.

"A butcher learns to cut anything," he replied.

For a moment they drank in silence. Laiah watched him curiously. Abraham, unable to think of anything to say, kept his face bent down to his glass of tea. It occurred to her that she had once, a long time ago, said to Polsky jokingly, "Send me our friend Abraham sometime and we'll see what can be done with him." And Polsky had often teased her about the interest that she showed, when the fit was on her, in his butcher. Was this Polsky's way of suing for peace, a joking reminder of an old joke? Her luminous eyes reflected her amusement at the idea. But it was doubtful. The Polskys, she reminded herself, were not a very subtle family.

This Abraham must be at least twenty years older than herself. No, fifteen. Almost old enough to be her father, anyway—or so she would have thought once. When she traced it down, it was the beard that she liked. The first man she had ever known, a long time ago in the old country, when she had been a child almost, had worn a beard. She could recall even now the curious commingling of sensations in which the feel of his beard had played no small part. And he too had been fifteen—no, twenty—years older, probably more. Laiah shuddered slightly, not with displeasure. Abraham was studiously eating a piece of buttered bread. She noticed the crumbs on his beard. Crumbs must be a hazard for bearded men.

Abraham's eyes met her own reluctantly. "I haven't had an easy life," she burst out suddenly, a little surprised at herself. But after his first startled look Abraham's eyes were not unsympathetic. "I know, I know"—Laiah brushed her hair back from her shoulder—"that it's not nice, my telling such things to someone who's practically a stranger to me. But somehow I feel as if we've really known each other, as if I can talk to you."

Abraham lowered his eyes and nodded. He didn't want confidences. He wanted—he cast a furtive glance toward the hallway—to go home. What was he doing in the strange woman's apartment, he who should be lying down right now for his pre-supper nap? But how could he just cut her off like that—someone, a woman like this, whom he had seen insulted, who suddenly wanted him to share her confidences? He didn't know which way to look, particularly since the low-cut, loose bodice of her housecoat prevented him from looking directly at her. So he continued to nod his head into his glass of tea. She rose and refilled it, and he cast a sideways glance of thanks in her direction.

But her next words seemed to awaken a memory in him, so that, forgetting her bodice, he could not help searching her face, as though for some clue.

"My mother died when I was very young," Laiah was saying, her voice deep and rather resonant, so that she did not have to raise it for him to hear her clearly. "I was left, the oldest, to bring up two others, a sister and a brother. My father was a worker without a trade. You know what that meant in the old country. He went about from town to town, trying to earn enough bread for all four of us."

Abraham nodded again.

"At last he decided that maybe if he went to the new lands even he, the luckless, might be able to scrape together some of the gold off the streets. So he went. And we were left. For two years we didn't hear from him at all. We dragged about, going from one aunt to another uncle to another aunt again. I went into service as a maid when I was twelve. Sometimes I had some luck; my master was kind to me and I was able to bring something home. At other times . . ." Laiah shrugged.

Abraham nodded. His nodding distracted her somewhat, as though he were pacing out her words in a rhythm of his own. But his words reassured her. "So it was," he murmured.

"But that was not all. I wish that had been all of it." She was surprised at her own eagerness to tell him. "I went as a maid to a rich family on a neighboring estate over the winter. When I came back in the spring I found that my brother had been used for rifle practice by soldiers passing through the town. He was nine."

"Ah," said Abraham. "The same book."

Laiah smiled at him. "We have something in common, then?" she asked gently. He nodded. "Well," she continued, "finally my father sent for us, all three of us. He didn't know. He didn't find out until we landed and came here, my sister and I." She shrugged again. "And we found the New World. My father didn't live long after we arrived. We went to work. My sister and I separated. She married and went East. I stayed here." Laiah paused to drain her glass and remained pensive, a distant, somewhat ironic smile on her face. "Still, family ties call you," she went on after a moment. "You want to know what has happened to people, especially as time passes and you are more alone. So I went East, two years ago. I found that my sister and I had not much in common. She had her family. She wasn't interested in me. And I"—Laiah laughed and got up from her chair —"I somehow felt more at home here, even though I'm all alone, and it's hard to be alone."

Abraham got up from his chair too. "I'm sorry, Avrom." Laiah took his hand in hers and held it for a moment. "I've aroused bitter memories in you too, I can see it. We have both suffered. Someday perhaps you'll tell me."

Abraham nodded vaguely.

"Maybe sometime you'll come in and have tea with me again," she said. "But maybe you won't want to come. What a hostess I've been, talking about myself all the time! Forgive me." Laiah smiled her full-lipped smile at him over her shoulder as she preceded him to the door.

At the door he remembered to thank her for the tea.

"Thank me? It's I who should thank you. It's nice to know that you can talk to someone as to a friend sometimes."

Laiah closed the door on her guest. What had come over her? A discreet little tea party, a sad little tale. She did not usually remember those things. But it was so. Life had not dealt squarely with her. Her past woes, and the incident of the afternoon, which she was aware that she had handled badly, both combined to bear out this truth. Nothing had ever gone right for her from the very start. Laiah found her way to the couch in her bed-living-room and gave herself up to a storm of weeping, calling up again and again memories that would prolong the fit as it threatened to peter out. Finally, when she could weep no longer and merely lay sniveling comfortably, assorted memories of less tragic content flitted through her mind.

She remembered again her first master and the sensation of his

beard against her naked breasts, which had been large with her premature adolescence and so tender that his movements had traced
themselves in fire. She had realized then, when she had pushed his
head away and then pressed it down again with her hands, that she
was as much his master now as he was hers. Laiah stretched herself
on the couch and placed her hands on her breasts. There had been
a pair of shoes for her out of that, and the next time a gown. And
then a hat with a big green feather. And then—Laiah sighed—her
mistress had sent her home. Never had there been a beard like that
again. Rubbing her breasts gently, she wondered idly if another
beard, even now, could reawaken that first delight.

Then the scene of the afternoon, in the kibitzarnia, came into her
mind, with the sensation of Hymie's big, sweating body bent over
her, and his hamlike hands. And suddenly she was laughing helplessly, and the tears were rolling down her cheeks again, and she was
hanging tightly onto her breasts again for lack of anything else to
hang onto. The stupid, clumsy fool! The animal uncontrol of his
strong young paws. What else could she have done? In public, after
all. And she had been carried away by the drama of the moment.
Still, she was a little sorry now over the fuss.

Still hugging herself, Laiah dropped off to sleep. She awoke feeling relaxed and contented, though a little weak. Her body felt as
though it had been completely washed through. She was surprised
to find that her legs were slightly shaky as she attempted to get up.
But she was hungry again.

While she ate she realized that the evening was young, and that
she didn't want to spend it alone. What if she turned up now at the
kibitzarnia? Actually, where else could she go at this time of the
evening? She would have to make up again to cover her swollen
eyes, of course. But it would be amusing to see the look on Polsky's
face if she breezed in again this very evening. And Hymie's face!
Come to think of it, it was better to go back now. The sooner she
went, the easier it would be. And this way they would probably be
more embarrassed than she. She could let Polsky know that she
thought it was very clever of him to send, of all people, Abraham as

his peace emissary. Whether he had done it with the old joke in mind or not, he would pretend he had, once she mentioned it to him, to show his cleverness. And a Polsky flattered was a pleasant Polsky.

Laiah made her entry into the delicatessen and had the satisfaction of seeing Hymie's mouth open and drop even wider open when she greeted him with ironic cordiality. Polsky himself welcomed her with brief extravagance. Altogether, however, the reconciliation wasn't as satisfactory as she had expected. She did not hold the stage for long, for the place was already humming with the news of the old synagogue.

When Abraham left Laiah her story was still sounding within him. Remote though the comparison between them might actually be in many ways, the fact remained: they had had similar beginnings, had been scarred by much the same fires. There were so many strange coincidences in life, so many secret sorrows that people shared without knowing it, people who were otherwise as strange to each other as—well, as he was to this Laiah, who had been the scandal of the town for as long as he could remember. It was something that he would like to discuss with Isaac.

Abraham crossed the street and rounded the corner of his block. As he approached he could see that the child was leaning over the fence, shouting something. Suddenly Ruth appeared, hurrying out the gate. Moses caught sight of him.

"Grampa," shouted the child. "The synagogue!"

There was a certain amount of pleasure to be got from the autumn evening, Isaac found, from walking home with the knowledge that both the factory and an hour and a half with a particularly obtuse student were over with, and that what awaited him was at last his own part of the day. Not that there was much day left, since already it had grown dusky and the sky above him had deepened its blue. Still, just ahead of him were a few hours with his family. This was a fact, and simple anticipation served to dispel some of the habitual melancholy of his thoughts. Three minutes, he calculated—past the synagogue, around the block, and halfway down across the street. Home.

The frame boards of the synagogue were a dirty gray. The sunset, Isaac noticed, was still casting its glow in the synagogue windows. But that was curious; the sun was already down. The glow came from within. It took him a few puzzled seconds to realize that the synagogue was on fire. Isaac whirled about. On the corner was a fire-alarm box.

In a few moments two arms of flame had shot up from the synagogue, as though in supplication, leaping up crimson against the royal-blue sky. A crowd gathered as from nowhere as the cry went up that the synagogue was on fire and as the streets were filled with the howl of sirens. Moses and Abraham and Ruth ran with the others, down and across the street and around the corner. A great woeful wail assailed Moses' ears as the men and women watched the firemen vainly trying to quell the blaze that had shot up its two enveloping arms. The president of the synagogue rushed to and fro, wringing his hands, and was almost hysterical when he remembered the thousand-dollar chandelier. Chaim Knopp, who had appeared as from nowhere, stood beside Ruth, moaning out loud that the Sepher Torahs, the Holy Scrolls, would be destroyed.

Hot black clouds of smoke rolled upward, and now the flames licked out from the roof of the building, reaching not only upward but down along its side, while in the windows flickered a dance of flame and shadow.

A woman began to scream hysterically that it was a pogrom. Moses had heard that word. He stood trembling with excitement and fear at the screaming, for the woman's cry had been answered by a renewed wailing of those who watched. His face flushed hot as the flames seemed to reach out and scorch him. He remembered his grandfather's stories and crowded toward his mother, looking about him fearfully and telling himself that he would protect her as he sought shelter between her skirts.

Suddenly there was a shout, and Abraham looked up and gasped. His heart filled his mouth. Leaping out of the inferno, like a revelation bursting from the flaming heavens, ran Isaac, his hair and the arms of his shirt on fire. Clutched against his shirt were the Scroll and the Crown. The great wail hung for a moment in breathless incredulity, and then miraculously it changed in mid air to a deafening roar of triumph, a tremendous "Hurrah!" which lifted Moses' insides and whirled him up into a vast ecstasy. His father! Never-to-be-equaled sight, bursting out of the synagogue, all in flames of crimson, with his head up, and wild-eyed.

"Like a prophet," whispered Abraham.

Then Isaac fell to the ground, and Moses screamed as he saw the firemen leap upon him. He rushed forward to save him, and was flung down amongst the pressing crowd. Abraham, beside himself, picked up the boy. Carrying him, he pushed his way through to where they were trying to revive his son.

Chapter Twelve

Isaac was frightened. He was imprisoned in a transparent bubble of some plastic material. It pressed inward with a constant contracting pressure, forcing him to brace his feet and hands against its inner surface to prevent himself from being crushed. As long as he pushed outward with all his strength it maintained its size. If he relaxed slightly it shrank in on him, so that it was the action of his own body that determined the size of his prison.

Sometimes, in a burst of energy and desire, he pushed out and outward, expanding his sphere, stretching his limbs beyond any length that they had ever achieved, so that the tips of his toes and fingers alone touched its surface, and he poised in the ecstasy of effort, certain that one final burst of strength and will would stretch the bubble to its limits and he would break through.

But he could stretch no farther. At the tips of his body it waited, firm and resilient, cruelly patient, ready to spring in upon him and crush him the moment he could hold it back no longer. The pain in his arms and legs was unbearable. His body was torn and exhausted. Slowly he had to relax his pressure, and slowly the inexorable sphere closed in. Now was his greatest danger. If he relaxed his arms and legs beyond a certain point they would collapse entirely and he would be lost.

But in spite of the pain and the fear and the danger there was always the feeling that someday, perhaps, a superhuman movement would release him, and he endured, waiting for that moment. Gradually, as he strained his eyes to see what lay beyond his sphere, he began to realize that although it was transparent, he could make out only his own face grimacing at him in reflection, the tendons of his neck bulging, and his own body stretched out in agony before him.

Ruth's eyes snapped open in the darkness, and she lay for a moment, trying to identify the sound that came from beside her. He was strangling. For a long instant she was paralyzed. In that moment her ears identified a curious note in the sounds, a sort of gasping—no— Confused now, she raised herself up on her elbow. "Isaac, what's the matter?" She could feel the movement of his head. "Isaac!"

"It's nothing," he said finally.

"Are you laughing? You frightened me. Why suddenly laughing in the middle of the night?" Her voice became reproachful.

"It was a dream," said Isaac.

"Well." Ruth dropped back on her side. "It's nice to know that you're having good dreams for a change."

"It was the same dream, the old dream I could never remember. Only this time I caught it. I was laughing because it's just the dream for me, a problem dream for a man who has much time to think of problems."

"Don't talk like that," she said. "You're not supposed to worry your head about anything. What is the dream?"

Isaac's hand searched along her side and found her own. The palm of his hand was damp. "If it's a bad dream I don't want to hear it," she added quickly. "I don't like the funny way you were laughing."

"So you don't want it to be a bad dream and you don't want it to be a funny dream." He tried to tease her. But her fingers tightened in his. He rubbed her hand soothingly. "I don't even know if it's bad or good. Nothing happens in it. And yet here I am. Picture it to yourself. I am totally naked, of all things—and a fine figure of a man, too. Does that arouse your curiosity?"

"You're joking. It's not my curiosity you want to arouse."

Isaac laughed weakly, and they lay for some moments in silence.

"I was in a sort of prison," he murmured.

"I don't like it." She roused herself. "You'll get sick again."

"Sicker, you mean. The horizontal hero."

"If only you wouldn't worry so, you'd get better. The doctor said rest. It won't be so long," she said.

"You're not talking to Pa now," said Isaac quietly. "I know what indefinitely means."

"No you don't. Nobody does, not even the doctor. That's what it means, that nobody knows how long or how short a time. It's not definite."

"All right, all right. It's God's will, as Pa would say. God wants me to contemplate His infinite goodness in return for saving His Torah. So He is keeping me on my back. This way I can gaze at the ceiling all day and think heavenly thoughts, and at night sweet dreams."

Ruth had raised herself up on her elbow again and passed her hand over his forehead. "You must try not to dream. You become excited and it brings on an attack."

"I don't dream on purpose. And besides, what if it's the other way around? Maybe when I get an attack my brain doesn't know what to do with the feelings in my body so it makes a story out of them, if you can call it a story."

"What were you doing in this prison place?" asked Ruth.

"Trying to get out. Don't ask me why. I didn't know what I'd find when I got out, if I got out. I don't know why I longed so for it. I could have stayed as I was, maybe, husbanding my strength, keeping a sort of balance, at least for a little while. But that I couldn't bear."

"What couldn't you—" Ruth had lost track.

But Isaac was talking to himself. "Or else just give up entirely, let it crush me. If I broke through I'd no longer have the sphere as my boundary, but I'd lose its protection too. The bubble bursts, and I burst with it, into the unknown. On the other hand, if I give way I collapse, I am crushed, again into the unknown. Aren't the two things in the end the same, my victory and my defeat both illusory?"

"What are you talking about?" said Ruth drowsily.

Isaac chuckled. "I don't know. That's why I was laughing. I'll never know."

"Then go to sleep. And tell yourself that you are not going to dream."

"Absolutely," said Isaac.

At first the fact that Isaac was so ill after he had saved the Torah seemed in a way to heighten the value of what he had done. When the doctors insisted on keeping him for so long in the hospital Abraham, half believing that they kept him not only because of his heart but because they wanted to observe for themselves what manner of man this was who would rush, heedless of danger, into the flames to save the Word of God, used to say to Chaim, "They'll not find out by listening with a machine to his heart. It's deeper than that they'll have to search for the secret soul of a man that only God can know. To them it's all a great mystery. The doctor told me himself that he thought it was a miracle that Isaac lived through that attack outside the synagogue."

Chaim chuckled. "Wasn't it all a miracle? I can remember it as though it were taking place this very moment." Chaim shut his eyes, jutted his beard forward, and rocked slightly sideways on the barrel. "Shout?" he recalled. "I shouted myself hoarse. 'The Messiah will come!' I shouted."·

Chaim's voice rose, and he waved his arm and nearly knocked himself off the barrel. " 'The Messiah will come!' It was the only thing that came into my head, the only thing worthy of shouting at such a moment. And when I saw you run after them and jump into the ambulance I was shouting it still, after you. I don't know if you heard me, but old Dreiman the shamus says he had to hold one ear while he was cheering because I was yelling so loud. He said to me that he wouldn't have believed that I could make so much noise. So I told him that God gives us voice for praise."

Abraham could not remember whether he had heard Chaim's particular voice shouting. There was such a shouting in his own head at the time. He had been so frightened. There was Isaac at one moment, leaping out of the flames with the smoke gushing out after him, and the next moment lying so still in the ambulance. Ah, but what a thing to be able to look back on in joy! "It's true, Chaim, isn't it?" Abraham leaned forward to ask his friend so that he could hear it once again reiterated. "Wasn't it—inexpressibly fine?"

"Inexpressibly," Chaim agreed. "In-ex-pressibly."

So many people knew them for that first little while after the rescue of the Torah. Strangers stopped Abraham on the street to ask about Isaac. Even the papers, the English dailies as well as the Yiddish weekly, wrote about his heroism so the whole city should know. Such a thing spreads.

"That son of mine?" Abraham would tell people when they asked him. "They say it's a wonder he's still alive. Not just the burns, you know; they were minor. He'd tell you himself they're nothing, although of course what to him is nothing would be much more than nothing to anyone else. It's his heart. He's had a heart condition since the old country. What he lived through there you may well ask. Time and again the doctors have warned him not to exert himself, to avoid excitement. But when the time came did he stop to think of that? No!" Abraham laughed his contempt for the doctors and their warnings. "He ran. Without thinking about himself or the doctors he ran, into the fire, into the blazing oven."

When they brought Isaac home at last and installed him for what the doctor called an indefinite period in his own bed, Abraham was surprised at first that, at least on the surface, he had scarcely changed at all. For every question he had his own entirely irrelevant answer. He would even contradict you on something you had seen with your own eyes, and when you tried to reason with him he would say, "Look, who saved this Torah anyway?" and make a joke of the whole thing. But Abraham himself could joke a little too. And when it came to argument who stood on ground as solid as he? While Ruth washed the supper dishes and the child practiced on the violin that Abraham had bought for him to surprise Isaac with when he came home, Abraham fled with the cats to the comparative quiet of Isaac's room.

"Tell me, my son, if you're such a heretic, why did you save the Torah?"

Isaac rolled his head on the pillow. "So we're back there again, are we? How many times have I tried to tell you? But you're still not satisfied, eh? So I'm forced to confess the real reason." Isaac winked and added in a confidential, exaggerated stage whisper, "Because it's expensive, that's why."

"Is that so?" Abraham laughed. "Every day he has a different answer, and every day the answer gets better." Abraham's voice became naïve, with a heavy overtone of mockery. "Then why didn't you save the chandelier? It's much more expensive. That's what the president would have saved, the chandelier. The president and the monkeys would have swung from the rafters to save the chandelier. And if you were a monkey like the president, you too would have saved the chandelier. God should only forgive me for calling a fellow human being a monkey, but then God himself knows what's in that man's blood, the way he was weeping and wailing over that chandelier. You tried to tell me once that we come from the monkeys. If that's the case there is at least one man in the congregation who hasn't come far enough."

Into Abraham's mind had sprung a vision of the president, a much-respected pants manufacturer, clinging desperately to the chandelier and swinging back and forth among the tinkling crystals, wild-eyed and paunchy. He couldn't restrain his laughter. He laughed until the tears came to his eyes, until his breath came in short gasps. Isaac couldn't help laughing too at the sight of his father's enjoyment.

"Tell me," said Abraham cajolingly after he had recovered from his laughing fit and saw that Isaac was smiling at him tolerantly from the bed, "can't you think of any better reason than that? Why don't you give your old father the pleasure of admitting to him what is obvious?"

"I freely admit to you what is obvious," said Isaac promptly, and they both laughed again, although Abraham shook his beard and waggled his forefinger.

"You may think you're twisting me around again, but you've caught yourself there."

"What is it that you want me to admit to you, then?" Isaac was suddenly serious. "What I don't know? I've been asking it of myself ever since I woke up to find myself not quite dead yet. You may be right. But it's not so simple at all. What does it prove? I've figured out at least a dozen reasons. You're welcome to any one of them, although you've already picked the one that suits you best. I wish I could. But while you and the One Above are busy congratulating each other, ask Him what I'm doing here. How long will this last? What will happen next?" Isaac's voice had quickened as he spoke.

"Don't excite yourself." Abraham was leaning over him, frightened at the sudden change in his mood. "Rest. I've bothered you too much. You need lots of rest, the doctor says. And the other things you needn't worry about. Now that the One Above has found someone to go through fire for Him, He'll know what to do. But you must have plenty of rest to get better."

"I have gathered," Isaac could not resist the sardonic comment, "that I must have plenty of rest so as not to get worse."

"Why should you get worse? You don't have to get worse. Let our enemies get worse. You get better."

"Yes, *mon capitaine.*" Isaac made a mock salute. "After all, my next mission may be to take this Hitler singlehanded."

"You may laugh," said Abraham, "but stranger things have happened."

"Do you want to hear?" Moses had appeared at the curtain, holding his violin.

They listened while the child played, a serious frown on his face as he found the notes painstakingly. Isaac flexed his arms under the covers. It was this feeling of being out of control, of being at the mercy of every chemical shift in his body, that was so frightening. Rest rest rest, he told himself again. And beyond?

Abraham looked from the child to Isaac and back again, his face glowing. He nodded his head vigorously when Moses had finished. "Now play the other little song that you played yesterday." He relaxed in his chair and continued to nod his head as he listened, now and again peering attentively at the child's fingers. A wonder instrument. How a person could draw such music out of such a small machine! He fancied that his own hands might have been suited to such a task had they not been roughened and hardened to the butcher's trade. My father never meant for me to be a butcher, he reminded himself sadly. But his grandson would make music. His grandchildren would do all those things about which a man like himself could only dream. Isaac would see to that.

When Moses had finished playing and they had praised him he went up to his father to say good night. Isaac turned over on his side to take the boy in his arms. He saw that the child's eyes were fixed on the scar that remained on his temple, and was pleased at the wonder in his son's eyes. He pulled him close and kissed his cheek. "Good night, my son," he said softly, and again he felt himself flooded over with a poignant excitement, as though there were something permanent in this good night. "Come and say good-by to me before you go to school in the morning," he whispered. The little boy nodded. Isaac felt suddenly greatly relieved, as though tomorrow had been insured in the child's nod, in the feel of his soft young body.

On their way home from school the children often stopped to play in the pit where the synagogue had stood. Now the earth had cooled and dirt had sifted over and softened the bare emptiness with shoots of tough wild grass and yellow dandelion. Moses could sometimes stand there in the emptiness, though, and think hard enough to bring it back, the moment as it still existed in him, and feel the various emotions tingle through him and see with the back of his eyes everything that he remembered most about the dirty frame building, inside and out, burning and whole.

On one such good day, as he paused with his books under his arm and an absent smile on his lips, Dmitri, in friendly mood, trailing his gang and miscellaneous dogs, came barking and shouting past.

"Hey, Moishe, let's go play in the pit!"

Junie too: "Come on, Moses."

Gladly he threw his books on the grass. After a little while Tony suggested, "Let's play bows and arrows!"

The boys yelled assent.

"Across the pit!" shouted Donald Gregory McNeill. He spread out his arms, arched his narrow chest, and, making the noise of a diving plane, ran headlong into the pit. Still yelling and slapping his buttocks enthusiastically, he clambered out again on the other side.

"Sitting!" commanded Dmitri.

"Sitting," they assented.

The boys unbuttoned their flies. Donald Gregory zipped his neatly but cautiously open. Dmitri, two buttons missing, gave a dexterous wriggle without using his hands. Blue-eyed Tony grinned at Junie, who stood watching around the curve of the pit, and pretended to take aim at her. Moses watched them without moving, happy, waiting for a sign.

"I bet I can pee farther than any of you," he said suddenly, boldly.

"Oh yeah!" Dmitri sneered.

"Yeah"—Moses, bold, confident of his sign. He undid his fly. "See"—proudly—"mine's different."

The boys crowded round. Junie couldn't see from where she stood. She came up closer. "Is it bigger?"

"Nah." Dmitri snorted contemptuously. "It hasn't got a frill. Well, if you're so sure, come and sit down already. Scram out of the way, you dame," said Dmitri, arrogant with his sister.

"Ya," chimed in grinning Tony, "if you don't want to get wet!"

They sat down on the edge of the pit, their feet dangling under them, and adjusted themselves seriously in their places. Donald Gregory removed a sharp cinder from under his thigh. Fat Michael wriggled and rubbed his behind and thighs in the dust for a moment. The ground was warm.

"All right," said Michael excitedly, leaning forward and straining his eyes intently toward a spot at a distance which indicated that he had no mean estimate of his abilities.

Tony leaned casually with one hand on the ground. He glanced at Junie to see the effect of his pose.

"Just a minute," said Donald Gregory. "I can't get started."

"Okay?"

"Okay."

A passer-by laughed out loud as the sun-streaked arrows streamed into the air.

The warm sun leaned out of the sky and dazzled Junie's eyes. She couldn't see exactly whose went farthest. The boys were down in the pit, arguing about it.

"I didn't aim right," said Donald Gregory.

"I could hardly get anything out," said Michael. "Sometimes I can pee farther than all of you."

"I didn't even try," said Tony, elaborately casual.

Moses and Dmitri were still arguing, although the sun was already drying their evidence.

"You know yourself that mine went farther," said Moses indignantly, feeling, for the moment, no fear of the brawny Dmitri.

"Whaddaya mean, ya liar!" Dmitri clambered out of the pit and noticed Junie, who was standing with her legs crossed. "Ha! Look at that dame! She can only pee downwards."

Mortified, Junie stared at her brother. Suddenly she turned and began to run out of the empty lot. When she had safely crossed the street she whirled and yelled with all her might, "Moses peed farther! Moses peed farther!" Then she ran.

Pausing only to pick up his books, with Dmitri, the dogs, the gang in full gallop behind him, Moses ran too, but not really fearful— triumphant, knowing that this time they wouldn't catch him; ran exultantly all the way home. Only then did he stop, remembering to turn the doorknob quietly and tiptoe softly into the house.

Abraham did not approach Polsky for a loan until he had examined the question from every angle and at last had to admit to himself that there was no other way. Still he put it off as long as he could. Finally he called Polsky into the tiny kitchen behind the butcher shop and explained to him the difficulties, feeling as he did so inexplicably ashamed, as though these money problems were somehow his own fault. Polsky had no money problems, except in the sense that he was occupied with the problem of making more and more money. But this was not a question of profits; it was a question of living itself in the present circumstances, with Isaac unable to work and all the bills that had accumulated in the past year.

Polsky listened very reasonably with the slightly frozen frown on his jovial face that money matters always brought on. Distaste for having to reveal his difficulties, for having to ask for money, for finding himself in a situation in which he was helpless, made it very hard for Abraham to find the words with which to speak, so that it seemed to him that his voice had in it more servility than he meant. He finished up his explanation in almost angry tones.

But Polsky was sympathetic. The old man was having a very bad run of luck. Here his son had done something that took a lot of guts. Polsky had not lived a very religious life, but still he had respect for certain things, and the Torah was the Torah after all. So what did the guy get for it? A big pain, Polsky could tell you where. He was beginning to wonder about the nature of this long-drawn-out illness of Isaac's, and where it was likely to lead. But that was not something that could be mentioned to the old guy.

So Polsky agreed to lend Abraham the money. Before closing time he would have it. Abraham was not to worry. Polsky knew he could trust him. Hadn't their long association proved it? As he suggested, Abraham could pay it back gradually out of his wages. He would not be rushed.

Abraham was greatly relieved. It was true, thank heaven, that all his life he had lived honorably, so that now no man need fear to trust him. The money would be paid back. Isaac and he would see to that. Still, the thought of having to borrow made him uncomfortable. Perhaps that was why, when Chaim burst, beaming, into the shop later on in the afternoon, he felt a brief, wild hope.

"What do you think?" Chaim began, without pausing for the customary greeting. "I have been talking to my son Ralph about your Isaac. You know what a big doer Ralph has become in the community. And when I reminded him, he too thought that it is a shame that the community has not done anything to show its appreciation of what Isaac has done." Chaim's rosy smile as he paused for breath indicated that there was something delightful forthcoming. Abraham's imagination raced ahead, inspired. "Do you know what he is going to do?" Chaim continued. "When they build the new Chaider for the children on the heights he is going to propose that Isaac be made a teacher. Ralph is going to be a big shot on the board of the school, and you know my son Ralph. Once he says a thing it is as good as done." Chaim beamed on his friend.

Abraham's disappointment was only momentary, and he was a little ashamed of it. They certainly did not want charity, after all. Best that they should deal with their own financial problems. This was a very fine gesture on the part of Ralph. It would surely inspire Isaac to get well more quickly, and once he was better what need to worry? He was touched by Chaim's enthusiasm. Here was a true friend.

"Do you know," said Chaim, "what has pleased me most in Ralph's promise? It is that another wish of ours will be fulfilled. When Isaac comes to teach in the school he will bring your Moishele with him. And our Arnie will also come to the school. It will be just as we have always said."

Ever since the miracle of his grandson's birth this had been a favorite topic with Chaim. Abraham had of late begun to doubt whether it could possibly come about, for no matter how obviously it was meant to be, half of a miracle is its acceptance by those for whom it is intended. And Abraham knew that the heights would not willingly come down to the flats, even for miracles. If at all, the friendship might come about later on, when the boys were grown and one man forced from the other instinctively the respect of manhood. But now it seemed that it all might come about even as they had planned once.

"There's only one thing," Abraham reminded himself suddenly. "The doctor said that Isaac is to be kept in bed indefinitely. This might mean quite a while yet."

Chaim thought seriously for a moment. "But the plans for the school are indefinite, too," he remembered. "Ralph said that it would take a while to get things going. They are not sure whether they should be affiliated with the Hebraists or the Yiddishists, or should remain neutral; whether they should be Zionists or not, and if they are Zionists what kind of Zionists they should be. You know these politics. It makes me feel as though I'm back at work again, the way they talk about right wing and left wing. It could even take them a year yet before they start building."

Just before closing time Polsky brought the money in to Abraham. He did not give him a check but counted the money, in cash bills of small denomination, into Abraham's hand. A grave, almost ritualistic tone crept into Polsky's voice as he counted off the five-dollar bills. The sight of the money moving from Polsky's large hand to his own, the way Polsky wetted his thumb and felt every bill, made Abraham nervous. It was as though Polsky were trying to make sure that he, Abraham, felt the full weight of the debt. His hand began to tremble slightly. It will be paid back, he told himself. He needn't worry.

Glancing past Polsky's shoulder, Abraham saw that Hymie was moving about in the delicatessen, apparently innocent of what was happening.

"Well, ha ha." Polsky's short laugh broke the tension that the handing over of the money had created. "That's that, eh? Be careful on your way home."

"Thank you," said Abraham. "You don't have to worry. You'll be repaid."

"I know, I know." Polsky's hand descended on Abraham's shoulder. "By this time we should know each other."

Hymie approached them. From the look on his face Abraham could tell that he knew. He folded the money quickly into his pocket and turned aside to fasten the pocket with a large safety pin. Polsky was talking loudly to his son, proving by his manner to his own satisfaction that he could part with such a sum of money without turning a hair. But then, it wasn't even a gamble.

Abraham was relieved that it was closing time and he did not have to stop for a long exchange of politenesses. When he was out in the fresh air, hurrying along the darkening streets homeward, he reminded himself that it was for Isaac, after all. There was nothing to be ashamed of. It was a temporary thing. It was funny that at a time like this they should find themselves apparently much worse off than before, what with Isaac and his illness and the problems with money. And people, too, were funny that way. Nowadays he was not stopped so often to be asked about Isaac or to discuss that unforgettable day. As often as not it was he who had to bring it up. The weeds of everyday life sprout up quickly around the rare flower and seem to choke it off and hide it away. But push aside the weeds and the flower is there. There are some things that remain because they remind people of what is greater than themselves. No wonder Polsky had loaned him the money. Even Polsky's soul, overrun with weeds though it was, could cherish the flower.

And then there was Ralph's promise. And Ralph scarcely knew them personally. That was something to tell Isaac about. Things might look difficult now, but just look where they were tending. On the strength of it Abraham stopped at the grocery and bought a cake, not with the money that was pinned up in his right-hand pants pocket, but from the change purse in his left one. The other money must be dropped into Ruth's hand intact.

Ruth met him at the door. With a swift gesture to her lips she indicated that all was not well. The curtain to Isaac's room was drawn closed. They tiptoed past into the kitchen.

"What has happened?"

"He's all right now," said Ruth.

"So?"

"He had an attack," she said. "I got frightened and called the doctor. The doctor said he'll be all right now. I just didn't want you to disturb him." She sat down. The child was already seated quietly, listening.

"Oh." Abraham seated himself a little unsteadily. "How did it happen? You didn't let him run around out of bed?"

"What kind of a question? Of course not," said Ruth sharply. Then, more gently: "But can I stop him from worrying? You know him. He has to think, think. At night he dreams. The doctor says it is not just movement that can disturb him. He mustn't worry."

Abraham nodded his head. "He's always been that way. How can we change the nature of a man? Confine an active man to bed, and he'll still be active. Inside, what drives him will still drive him."

"But where 'will it drive—" Ruth caught herself. What was the use? She leaned forward, covering her face with her hands. Almost immediately, remembering that the child was watching, she straightened again.

"But I have news," said Abraham. "When he wakes up I'll tell him something that will make him concentrate on getting well. And I have a surprise for you too." Abraham unpinned his pants pocket and pulled out the roll of money. He explained to them about the money and about how in the outside world they counted for something yet. Looking at Ruth, he was startled at how she had aged in the past year, how her pretty face, plumper now, had rearranged itself around the lines in her forehead and beside her mouth. And it was harder to make her laugh now. Even with the money in her hand and the good news about Isaac's future job, her face had that new uncertain look. It bothered Abraham, that look. It made him anxious to go and see for himself. He got up from his chair and moved quietly toward the bedroom.

"Don't wake him!" Ruth's voice was edgy, worried.

Abraham pushed aside the curtain. Isaac lay quietly, his eyes closed, his face so pale that the red fire scar stood out sharply on his temple. Abraham stood there until he was sure that the bedcovers moved up and down to Isaac's breathing. Then he let the curtain drop again and with a sigh turned back into the kitchen.

Isaac's eyes opened slowly as he heard his father's steps receding. He wanted to call out, to bring his father back, but allowed the moment to pass while he tried to summon up the energy to do so. Some perversity had prompted him to feign sleep, to take a certain hide-and-seek pleasure in the feel of his father's eyes fluttering softly over his face. He had intended to open his eyes suddenly, surprising his father as children do, but somehow had allowed the moment to pass, almost afraid to move. Now he was sorry. He wanted to talk to Abraham, to feel his living presence. He wanted to release all his uncertainties and watch them disappear in the vast area of his father's confidence. Somewhere, there, was safety.

He was tired in every part of him of the fingering of motives, of staining them with the sweat of afterthought. What was it all about?

At least let me understand. Was it worth it? Was it after all so important? Anyone else in that position, at that moment, would probably have done the same thing. An impulse—an accident. Did I even realize the danger of the moment? I don't know. And suddenly I'm a hero, I have committed an act of faith. They crowd around me, flattering, confusing. I let myself believe, well, maybe it was as they say. I demur, I shrug my shoulders, I am indifferent, I deny, change the subject, act as a hero should act. And I begin to feel like an actor who has lost all sense of reality and continues to act on both sides of the curtain. Somewhere in the wings a part of him is trying to recover, to evaluate. What is it that I really did? And what has been done to me? If it is as they say, should I not be a different man from the one I was before? I am not a better man, not with this vanity throbbing inside of me and this humility parading outside.

If there was a moment, a moment of absolute truth when I was driven into the fire, as my father claims, should not this feeling have remained with me, a new purity, a change in me? It seems to me that only others have the enjoyment of it, the false lift. What really happened is that I provided a momentary jolt for the imaginations of a handful of people. For a moment I stimulated them beyond themselves. Fine, but what about me? Why didn't I die then, before I had time to wake again, to be afraid, to realize that I don't want to die? That was not for me. I must be given the chance to regret, to wish that it had never been, and to lie here waiting. . . .

"Ruth, Ruth!" His sudden, urgent call brought them all in one bunch, hurtling together through the curtain.

"What's the matter? Why are you so excited?" Isaac demanded. "Did you think I was dying?" Instantly he regretted his words.

"Don't look like that; I was only joking," he pleaded with his father's stricken face.

"Who talks of dying?" whispered Abraham finally.

So he too is afraid. "I do." Isaac could not control the instant of perversity, though he tried to say it jokingly. "Does it surprise you that I want to live?"

"Surprise me?" Abraham's voice was uncertain. "You're still joking?"

"Of course." Isaac felt his face flush up again, felt the moisture at the corner of his left eye. "Why should the mention of death startle you so? We should all be familiar with the idea. You see it doesn't bother me." But the look in his father's eyes was acting on him, unnerving him. "I'm sorry, Pa, forget I said anything. You know the crazy things that come into your head sometimes. I called you because I was lonely in here. I wanted you to come and sit with me. Jump on the bed, Moishe. Tell me how was Chaider. Sit down on this side, Ruth. Pa, pull up the chair closer. You see what an ill-natured, selfish invalid you have here?"

Isaac's arm sought the body of his son. With the other arm he pulled Ruth down beside him on the bed. There was a river of warmth creeping down his left eye, and he was blinking down another pool that had gathered in the hollow between his nose and his right eye. He held the child's arm gently, squeezing it slightly. Ruth's body lay warm and pulsating beside him. He absorbed the contact, the vitality. He felt a desperate need to touch, to feel the reassurance of physical contact.

"Pa," he said, reaching up his hand blindly, not wanting to turn around for fear of disturbing the precarious balance of moisture in his eyes. "When I was small I used to touch your beard. I've almost forgotten what it feels like." The curly, wiry soft hair came in contact with his hand, tingled between his fingers. He ran his hand down both prongs of his father's well-kept beard and then slipped his fingers upward till they touched the softness of the cheek above.

"Well, what's everybody so quiet for?" With a movement of his hand he smeared the tears from his eyes. He knew that in the crook of his arm Ruth, her face hidden, was weeping. He desperately wanted them to talk, to drown the voice of contempt within himself — Scared them, didn't you? "Tell me something," he pleaded with his father.

"When you were a little boy you used to say that," said Abraham slowly.

"So I haven't changed much," said Isaac. "What happened at work today? It's so annoying to have to lie here. It puts you into such a black mood you don't know what you're saying. Did you see Chaim Knopp?"

"I almost forgot." Abraham remembered his news. "I have news for you that will make you forget your black moods." Abraham was gradually beginning to recover his normal tone and manner, but his eyes still searched his son's face in a disturbed way as he spoke. "Chaim Knopp's son is going to keep a place open for you in the new Chaider they're building in the heights. Chaim says it'll be a while yet before it's built and ready—you know them and their politics—so that you will have plenty of time to get better if you'll stop worrying your head about nonsense."

Isaac laughed at the commanding tone. "That's fine. All I have to do now is to get well, eh?" It had such a simple, straightforward sound to it.

"That's right." Abraham went on to describe the sort of school it was likely to be. He pointed out that Isaac could take the child up with him and he went on to describe all the other aspects of the job that he and Chaim had discussed. There were great future possibilities in it. They would be able to move into a house closer to the heights—not that they had any ambitions to wag their tails after the rich, but at least into a better district so that the child could have nice friends. Isaac would at last have the chance to teach, to study and develop his ideas. And he would have an audience who would listen. After all, people knew who he was. In describing it, Abraham grew heated and persuasive. Wasn't this more in the line of things as they should be?

Isaac, still writhing inwardly with self-contempt, began to wonder if, at least to some extent, it might not possibly be so. He was still alive, and while he remained alive there was still the future. Granted he might never be a completely healthy man again, still it was quite possible that he would recover to the point where he could take on these duties. He felt a certain buoyancy, a certain optimism beginning to grow in him, magically remodeling his perspective. Life was a reality too. His arm tightened around Ruth, who had wiped her eyes and was now merely resting against him, listening to Abraham.

"It was nice of Chaim to talk to his son about me," said Isaac. "Thank him for me, will you?"

"You will thank him yourself. But in the meantime I have already thanked him for all of us," said Abraham.

"You know, I should have started saving Torahs a lot earlier in life," said Isaac, letting himself be carried along. "I'd be a successful man by now. What do you say?"

"So it was you who saved the Torah, was it?" Abraham recognized the playfulness and all too gladly joined in. "I thought it was some other fellow who valued God's Word."

Something in Isaac would not let him leave well enough alone. "Talk about valuing God's Word, here's a little problem of values for you. According to our friend Mrs. Plopler, that Torah that I brought out was the one that our first millionaire here in the city, our big what's-his-name, donated as his conscience money. You know who I mean, that mortgageer, that real-estatenik who first elbowed his way onto the heights; that champion of ethnic rights, except where they concerned the real-estate developments that he was promoting."

"So what are you trying to tell me?" Abraham looked at his son with an expression on his face that showed that this was not an argument that was worthy of him. "It wasn't Schwarzgeist you saved, it was the Torah. What does it matter who donated it?"

"Yes, but when they build the new synagogue this Torah will have the place of honor. People will say, 'There is the Torah that was miraculously saved'—because of course to everyone but me it was a miracle and not an accident. And they will examine it and want to know its history. And someone will say, 'Yes, it was donated by one of the first Jews of the city, Schwarzgeist.' And someone else will say, 'Schwarzgeist—aha, he must have been a fine man if God saw fit that his Torah should be saved.' And so the name of your son will go down on a scroll of honor beside the name of this other sterling citizen, and both these names will be preserved in the annals of time. Old men will bless us." Isaac's voice was mock-lyrical, faintly sardonic.

"Pooh-pooh!" Abraham interrupted at last. "What nonsense you're talking." But his voice betrayed his concern.

Isaac was silent a moment. "It may very well happen," he said slowly, "but I wonder if it really matters? Few things really matter in the way we think they do. There is always another way of seeing them. I even think now that if things could happen over again I would not change them." Knowing that he could not communicate all of it in words, Isaac tried by holding his father's eyes to make him understand. "And if we can't seem to see the same thing in the same way at different times, how can we tell what is the true way of seeing it? So we will not worry about Schwarzgeist."

"I have never worried about Schwarzgeist," Abraham said positively, yet smiled at the same time in a way that struck Isaac as being so naïvely delighted that it pierced through him. "Do you know what?" continued Abraham after a moment's pause. "I can hardly wait for you to get better. It seems to me that you give in too easily when you are sick."

There was a sort of harmony between them for the rest of the evening. The child told how his day had been spent, and after supper he played the violin for them while Ruth lay beside Isaac and he hugged her shamelessly. When the child had finished practicing, Abraham told the story of Iloig the giant king who had sent his spies to find out exactly how much room Moses and the approaching Israelite people took up and then lifted up a mountain big enough to crush them all. But by the time the Israelites had come close enough he had grown so tired with carrying his mountain that it rested around his forehead, and a giant tooth had grown from his jaw to help hold it up. And Moses, who was himself a very tall man, as can be judged by the fact that his ax was four ells long, approached Iloig and jumped up and swung with all his might, and the ax was to Iloig as a fly tickling his shin. But by now Iloig was so tired and his tooth was so deeply embedded in the mountain that he could no longer lift it off. So gradually Iloig disappeared beneath his mountain, and Moses and his people passed onward.

Still they bothered him, Isaac's words. What did he mean by this talk of dying? Later, when both Isaac and the child were asleep, Abraham spoke to Ruth. "Is there something you're not telling me about Isaac? I see how you and the doctor always whisper quiet-quiet. And Isaac acts and sometimes talks so— What did he mean when he talked of dying?"

"There's nothing we're keeping from you, Pa," said Ruth tiredly. "The doctor's told you the same thing. He's sick. His heart is hanging on a thread. They don't know so much about the heart but they know he's sick," she repeated, "sick."

"Yes, I know," said Abraham. "He's sick," he repeated after her automatically. Somehow he'd got used to these words so that there was something almost undisturbing about them. "He's very sick." But this he'd known all along. He stood there, looking down at Ruth, noticing automatically that a few gray hairs were sprinkled among her disheveled black curls. "But it's nothing, he's young yet," he said half aloud, almost argumentatively. "He's much too young." He looked to Ruth for confirmation, bending forward a little. But she remained seated, her forehead downbent, resting on the palm of her hand.

Abraham felt suddenly very tired, as though he could scarcely stand on his feet. "It's late," he murmured apologetically at Ruth's bent head. "I'm so tired." He moved, feeling as though he were already asleep, in the direction of his bedroom. "I'm so tired," he repeated to himself mumblingly. With difficulty he groped his way through the living room, where the child slept, and down the hall to his own bedroom. It was almost too much effort to fumble out of his clothes. "I'm tired," he told himself plaintively and dropped suddenly into a deep, terrifying well of sleep.

Chaim was the only one he could talk to, and he didn't come that day until very late in the afternoon. When Chaim did come finally, he was surprised that yesterday Abraham had been so full of optimism and plans for the future and now his manner was distracted, his words sometimes confused, sometimes almost wild-sounding. Personally Chaim didn't like it, this rushing of the imagination toward possible foes. What good did it do a man to stand there at bay, surrounded by thoughts that could not possibly help anyone? He, Chaim, even in his worst moments, had always shut his eyes and prayed. Something, through God's help, had always come along, one way or another.

"Ever since it happened"—Abraham, his hands gripping the counter, leaned forward toward him—"there have been two voices in me. One of them sings all day. Every other moment it reminds itself of what he did, of how he ran forward. When people stop me to ask about him it takes the words of praise from their mouths and weaves them into a song. The newspapers—you read them with me yourself, Chaim. Remember how Mrs. Plopler told—oh, I have heard it from at least a dozen people that she went about telling them how she took us in first when we were homeless immigrants. Of course she didn't mention that it wasn't charity, that we paid for that room of hers that no one else would rent. And she tells people that Isaac was crazy about her daughters and would have married one of them had he not been afraid of hurting the other. I can tell you for a fact that she winds it all out of her imagination. Isaac was afraid of her girls, if such a man can be afraid of anything.

"Take even the child's friends. That Dmitri that hits him all the time asked him if they were going to cut off Isaac's arms because of the burns. He came crying home. Children with their imaginations.

"But all the time while one voice rejoices the other one is whispering. What is wrong, then? Why is he still in bed? Why did he have an attack yesterday? The things he talked of made the whispering grow to a thundering in my head. When I looked into his eyes, and after, when I spoke to Ruth—I don't know what it was, I can scarcely remember now, except that when I woke up this morning I knew that somehow something was trying to turn the one glorious moment of my life into ashes. Chaim," said Abraham, leaning far over the counter in his urgency, "my son is the heart in me; he is my arms. He must get well, isn't that so? What will happen to us? Didn't he save the Torah?"

"Of course," said Chaim a little awkwardly, a little frightened by it all. "He is a hero. But we cannot do anything—that is, God will help us. Don't worry. He saved the Torah," Chaim finished lamely.

Hymie Polsky had heard Abraham's voice raised as he stood kibitzing behind his father in the back room. Chewing gum with noisy, circular movements of his jaws, he moved into the delicatessen and around to the cash register in time to hear Abraham repeating for the millionth time that his son had saved the Torah.

So he got his balls singed, thought Hymie impatiently, just to save a piece of paper telling him to save them for his wife. That was a good one for the boys. It occurred to Hymie that he could add a few original thoughts to this discussion of the saving of the Torah.

"You know what?" he said out loud to the two of them. "I was just figuring it out the other day, when my dad lent you that money." It was rather clever, his idea. "I just want to prove something to you." He lifted his buttock over the stool and searched about for a pencil and a piece of paper in the drawer by the cash register. "How long is it since Isaac saved the Torah? About a year now, I should say, last Octo— September, toward the end of September. All right." Hymie leaned forward over the table, pencil in hand, his pants straining over his heavy buttocks. Chaim looked questioningly at Abraham, who glared at Hymie in angry shame that he had mentioned the loan.

"Let's say"—Hymie looked at them over his shoulder—"thirteen months at fifteen, at most twenty dollars a week for wages, maybe even less, probably. Twenty times four times thirteen." Hymie figured noisily. "Well, we can take a rough guess. Now what about doctor bills and hospital bills? At least half as much again, if not more. Now, how much would a new Torah cost, eh?" Hymie looked around him triumphantly. "Don't you see? If he hadn't saved the Torah, by now he'd have enough money to donate a new Torah and some to spare, and you wouldn't have had to borrow any money, and he wouldn't be lying around in bed either, probably. That's pretty funny."

Chaim cast a frightened glance at Abraham, whose eyes were fixed on Hymie, his face curiously gray. "Everything you think you can count on your fingers," Chaim began angrily.

"Look." Hymie was looking at Abraham, realizing that something was wrong. "Look, I'm not saying that it isn't a brave thing, what he did. All I said was— Well, look, figure it out for yourself."

Hymie didn't have time to say any more. The telephone rang beside him, and he picked it up gratefully and turned away.

"What?" Hymie's voice rang out heavily in the silence. "Who? Oh, okay." He turned around, a slightly puzzled look beginning to gather about his eyes. "It's for you," he said to Abraham, and his voice faltered. "They want you to come home right away."

Abraham turned the corner. Sunset was ingathering the daylight and softening the colors of things. In the west the colors had their last fling of red and purple across the sky. The little knot of people that was gathered in front of the house was all black in the early evening contrast. Abraham moved toward them, his eyebrows drawn together in concentration. A head was raised in his direction, and there was a sudden silence in the group. Now Abraham's feet seemed to take a long time to reach the ground. Instead of air he walked through some heavily resistant material to which the ground was not very firmly anchored.

This was something that he had lived through before; the red and purple clouds, the dark figures waiting for him, had waited for a long time. It was as though he were walking into a picture that had hung

on his own wall all his life, waiting for him. He passed through the
still-standing, faceless figures.

Through the open door of the living room he saw the child sitting
quietly at the kitchen table with his back bent like a little old man.
Someone stood beside him. Behind Abraham, Chaim Knopp joined
the group of silent figures.

Abraham raised his eyes, avoiding the bed, to the figure in the
chair. Had Ruth been able to help him, she would have rushed forward. But she was still filled with the fear and the shock of it, of coming in and finding him so, just so, irrevocably. Now in the old man's
eyes she read, almost like an accusation, the fact that she was still
alive. Abraham moved toward the bed where Isaac lay.

Chapter Thirteen

From the living-room floor, where she and Abraham sat on pieces of sacking, Ruth heard her sister talking to Mrs. Knopp and Mrs. Plopler. "Poor child"—her sister's voice was placid, pitying—"never had any luck."

"Death," Mrs. Plopler enlarged eagerly, "before and after, and now. Oh!" Mrs. Plopler wept.

Ruth's mind functioned independently of her will. With a dreary clarity it recorded Mrs. Plopler's oft-repeated satisfaction, expressed to Mrs. Knopp, that there had been a good turnout at the funeral. It did not fail to register the fact that Mrs. Knopp's presence in the house indicated that Isaac's death, as nothing else had been able to do, had convinced her of their social eligibility. And it caught also Mrs. Plopler's shrill-voiced opinion that the reason Mrs. Polsky had not come to help make meals for the family during the mourning period was because she was afraid to visit a house of death.

Even when the old men of the synagogue brought, on Monday and on Thursday, the very Torah that Isaac had saved, to be read, she was aware that some of them watched eagerly, with a sort of ardency, for signs of heightened grief. But she felt none of her customary tongue-sharpening woman's anger. Perhaps later, when the shock of the greater grief had worn away, she would be indignant over lesser evils. Now she resented only her sister's words. It was not true. I have had luck, I have. Isaac, she thought. Isaac Isaac Isaac.

In the kitchen Mrs. Plopler and Mrs. Knopp talked about their gastric troubles. Mrs. Plopler discovered to her relief that the older woman had had symptoms much like hers before her second operation, although they had not occurred in quite the same part of the stomach, nor in quite the same way. Still, they had been severe pains.

222

Mrs. Knopp was eager to convince Mrs. Plopler that what she needed was an operation. Mrs. Plopler was not so easily convinced.

"I don't like the knife," she said again and again. But Mrs. Knopp spoke with authority. And finally Mrs. Plopler had to admit that it was worth it to let them use the knife for the sake of a complete cure. Here was Mrs. Knopp, a very old lady already, and she had come out alive. Mrs. Plopler became enthusiastic.

Mrs. Knopp began to reconsider. Mrs. Plopler should not be too optimistic about these things. She herself had almost died during her operations. And furthermore she had never been the same afterward. How can you be the same when you have whole pieces of you cut out? And besides, an operation is an expensive thing. It should only be used as a last resort. Hers had been cheaper because, after all, her son-in-law was a doctor and in the profession these things can be arranged. An ordinary person, however, had to think twice about such things. What, for instance, did Mrs. Plopler's sons-in-law do?

Mrs. Plopler, for the moment even more convinced by the very exclusive sound of it that an operation must be the thing for her, countered sweetly that of course an operation, like everything else, was in God's hands. But she had the advantage of being young enough so the risk would be lessened.

"Lessened?" Mrs. Knopp could not contain her short derisive laugh. She waved her hand in the direction of the living room. "There," she said almost triumphantly, "is your lessened risk. Even the young can die." Mrs. Knopp smiled with a certain bitter satisfaction.

Mrs. Plopler turned her eyes reluctantly toward the living room. The child appeared in the doorway. "Oi!" Mrs. Plopler stretched out her arms and bore down on him. Before he could more than half turn to escape she had seized him in her arms. "My poor little orphan, oi!" Mrs. Plopler wailed energetically. "An orphan!" Mrs. Plopler drew out the word so that it keened through the house, shrilling up and down Abraham's nerves. The child, frightened as he was by all that had happened, stifled by her breath and the grip of her arms and helpless against the nibbling wetness of her nose, parried her shriek with a terrified wail of his own and struggled to free himself.

In Abraham's head the word echoed and re-echoed. Back it dragged him to the years of his childhood, to all that being an orphan had meant. Everything that had been since then, the gradual building up, the rich, fine growth of his sons, stretching out like the arms of some fine tree, the reaching upward—all this swept away. His mind was like a churning ocean on which bobbed the bits of wreckage that had once been his life. Again and again he broke the surface, staring about him with salt-washed eyes, caught sight of some fragment, and because it was only a fragment and the salt had burned his eyes clean saw it with a ruthless, useless clarity before he sank to the massed confusion below. And now there remained only this frail sprout, again on the brink of life, unprotected, as though all his prayers and his efforts had never been, no further ahead. Was this it?

Something in him cried out then in protest. He wanted to rush forward and drive from the house this woman with her wailing and her empty cries. A real fury overcame him. He heaved himself up from the floor and rushed to her and seized her by the arm. He wanted to shout. He wrenched her away from the child, who stood there smearing the cold wetness of his cheeks where her nose had touched. Mrs. Plopler whimpered and turned her eyes up to him. He opened his mouth to speak, but in her eyes there was such misery and such fear, and something else too, a sort of pleading. It was as though she weren't looking at him at all, as though when she had hugged the child and wailed her shrill cries over him it had not been the child that she had addressed at all. The fury went out of him. "You don't look well." He scarcely heard himself say it.

"I don't feel well," she said quickly, and her nose started and jerked slightly after she had ceased speaking, as though to add something more. For a moment even Mrs. Plopler felt as though she had lost her footing, and she grasped in vain for some platitude that would assure her that whatever it was was bearable. She began to snivel and murmur to herself.

"That dame," sobbed Moses to his mother. "That—dame!"

"Shh, it's all right, never mind, it's nothing." Ruth crooned words of comfort to her son.

Abraham turned away from them. No words of comfort for him, only shattered sounds in his head, fragments of a life. Wait, he told himself. What he had to hold back were those feelings that threatened him. Almost something had broken out when he had rushed at Mrs. Plopler. Wait, wait, it isn't final. There's something to be said yet, something, perhaps, to be done. Once before he had rushed to the extreme conclusion, and what had happened? Well, what had happened?

He sat down again on his sackcloth and covered his face so that he could see only the space where Isaac had lain. The day his mother had died came to him and washed over him; the death of two of his sisters from the cholera; the whole of the lives of Moses and Jacob telescoped in the memory of the moment when he had found them dead; the passing of his wife, Sarah, clutching the relative happiness of having seen her grandson born and not having had to see the last of her sons die. Only Isaac he could not recall in death but as he had been alive, touching with wistful fingers and caressing his father's beard, clinging to it as though to life itself. The beard burned against Abraham's skin as though it were afire. He pressed his hands over his face. He tried to shut it all out, to hold it back. He tried to concentrate his mind on the prayers. But it waited there for the moment when he relaxed his grip, when a kind of sleep slipped, unrecognized and unacknowledged, past his defences.

All of them merged together now in his memory, a series of long, narrow boxes, lying horizontally side by side in the bareness of an empty room. And he, in a sort of dream, rushed in and out among them, from one to the other, trying to pry open the tops, trying to find something. But the lids had been closed very tightly. He tore at them with his fingers, hammered on them, cried out to them, one after the other, unintelligible things. Now he called to them, each one, begging them. He pleaded with his wife. Intimate things that he had long since forgotten came to his lips to make his voice sweet and persuasive. But the coffins remained still. And he didn't even know who was in which one, and this suddenly became of enormous importance, and he was asking tentatively, on all fours, beside each coffin. Like some four-footed creature he scuttled from one to the other, calling out their names. "Let me in," he was begging them finally, and it seemed to him that all he wanted now was just this, for one of the lids to lift itself so that he could fling himself in too and lie silent with the rest of them, without having to see or hear or know or care.

In the kitchen the women looked at each other and leaned forward to listen to the sounds that came from the living room. Mrs. Plopler shuddered. Ruth, who sat across from her father-in-law on the living-room floor, peered anxiously at where he sat, cross-legged with his face hidden in his hands and bent over so that his hands almost touched the floor. Suddenly, as though awakening, he jerked himself upwards. His hands fell momentarily away from his face. His reddened eyes descended on Ruth and went through her.

Could they really be shut away there separately in their boxes? Or were they all together now somewhere? Did they weep for what had happened? Or did they sit now, all of them, at a table from which only he was missing? At the thought he felt again the great longing that he had felt in his dream. Never in his life had he wanted to think too much about such things. It was a sin against life for a man to pry into the ways of death. But his thoughts kept slipping back longingly. He would sink deep, deep down. He would no longer grasp after the bits and pieces of his life. He would forget. He would leave the surface noises. A deeper current would carry him swiftly, noiselessly, indifferently.

On the ninth night, when the period of mourning prayers was officially over, Ruth got up late in the night from the bed in which she was sleeping for the first time since her husband's death. The last of the mourners had left after the evening prayers. Mrs. Knopp had filled their glasses with schnapps, and they had drunk to the soul of the departed. Ruth had helped Abraham to his feet and had taken the two sacks out of the living room. Finally they were physically alone, the three of them, almost for the first time. But the impact of being physically alone together at last did not, as yet, seem able to break through their individual aloneness. Ruth put the child to bed in Abraham's room and chased the cats from Abraham's side of the bed. Unable in her exhaustion, as well as unwilling, to try now to think, although she knew that she would have to think soon of what was to be done, she said good night to Abraham and walked automatically around the place where Isaac had been laid, pushed back the curtain into what was now her room, undressed in the darkness, and dropped into bed.

Now, partially asleep, she did not bother to turn on the lights but groped her way with hesitant familiarity to the curtain that separated the bedroom from the living room. By the time she reached the curtain her eyes had begun to make out the familiar shapes of objects. She slipped through the curtain and made for the opposite door, which led to the hallway and the bathroom. Not until she had taken a step forward did Ruth see the figure on the floor.

In the first moment of shock her sleep-fuddled brain grasped only that her dead husband lay before her. She stepped back automatically and felt something give, like a live thing, behind her. She whirled round with a wailing intake of breath. Only the fact that her hands struck out and grasped the curtain prevented her from slipping to the floor. A thousand stories that she had never believed sprang to her mind. For an instant she was convinced, though she knew of no reason why, that it was all due to the fact that she had not changed the sheets on their bed since Isaac had died. But this was her husband! She whirled again toward the apparition. It lay still, a dark mound in the middle of the living-room floor.

"Isaac," Ruth whispered.

For answer, in the darkness came a soft, chilling, sibilant sound, as though he were struggling to speak with queer sounds brought back from the grave. Ruth shuddered. But as she listened, paralyzed, the noises resolved themselves into a regular rhythm. Standing there, she listened for its recurrence above her heartbeat. Often in the last few months she had awakened and listened for reassurance to Isaac's breathing beside her. She released her own breath in a series of gasping whimpers. A part of her mind was beginning to function clearly. Slowly she edged along the wall to the light switch.

Even with the light full on his face Abraham did not awaken, but lay there, stretched out, an effigy of death, marring the illusion only by the persistent regularity of his breath. Ruth switched off the light and closed her eyes in the same instant as she heard the soft, explosive spluttering of her own giggles. Forgetful of her earlier errand, avoiding another glance at the figure on the floor, Ruth found her way back into her empty bed and collapsed, unable to control either the quivering, or the raking sobs that tore through her. Her fingers grasped and twisted the sheets that warmed to her body. For the first time she lost herself utterly in the realization of her grief.

After the first violent reaction had worn itself away Ruth tried to consider what she had seen and what she should do. She tried to think of some reasonable explanation. He had forgotten that the time of mourning was already past. He had walked in his sleep. Worse, it was some madness of grief. She could believe anything now. Should she wake him? Maybe he would get up by himself and go quietly back to bed. She pressed herself, face down, into the sheets and waited hopefully. No.

The more she thought of it while the tears dried, tightening the skin on her face, the more she realized that it was wrong for Abraham to be lying there, stretched out in the middle of the living-room floor as Isaac had lain—fantastic. She prodded herself. Bizarre. She must find out. She pushed herself out of bed finally. The blue light of an early dawn was already filtering through the living-room curtains. It gave his face an eerie, unearthly tinge and highlighted his beard, which was now almost completely gray. There was a frailness about him as he lay there that she had never noticed before. It occurred to her now that, no matter what it was that was wrong, she alone would have to cope with it. It was something that she had not before given a thought to. There were the two of them to care for. The knowledge brought a certain order to her thoughts.

Abraham heard a familiar voice calling him. He listened with a lazy pleasure, trying to identify it. Who had come to meet him? Soon he would have them about him. How they would laugh together with relief and gratitude after he had told them how he had been made to believe that Isaac had died, how he had begged for his own death as well, not knowing all this time that it was he who lay dead and not his son. And God, seeing how he suffered, had realized that he had been punished enough. The voice was closer, more urgent. He would tell them first about the child, or perhaps about the saving of the Torah. No doubt they already knew. But they would want to hear again, at first hand. Sarah no doubt worried about this ailment of Isaac's. When a man died he lost his deafness, Abraham noted clearly, for the calling voice rang clear in his head. "I'm coming I'm coming," he said a little teasingly. Smiling a little, he opened his eyes.

Ruth saw his face change and wrinkle up, as though he were a child who has just discovered some terrible truth about the hidden adult world and is about to oppose it with his only weapon, tears. But the expression passed almost immediately. Without a word, Abraham got up from the floor. Without looking at Ruth, he went out of the living room and quietly into his own bedroom.

Ruth wanted to call out, to ask a question. But she didn't, too weary to cope with a possible answer. Best to leave him alone.

In everything else that he might have talked about, Chaim would have been forced to remind Abraham, willingly or not, that he. himself had four children, all of them still alive. This fact would not be softened, no matter how often he mentioned that his wife, however, was doing poorly. So he talked instead of Hitler, of the world situation, of how everything seemed to be going wrong nowadays. He talked because he could not bear the long silences, because he was afraid of what lurked behind them. Abraham had never been a man of silences. It made Chaim nervous.

"If Bassieh, my wife, dies—God should prevent it," he blurted suddenly, "but the doctor says we should be prepared for everything; after all she's no spring chicken. If she dies you know what will happen? The children won't want me to live by myself. They'll want me taken care of. They'll all want to take me to live with them. But then each one will want the honor to have me first. They will argue, and the end will be that to keep the peace they will send me to the Old Folks' Home."

Chaim looked at his shoes and laughed nervously. Why had he said it? In one mouthful he had mentioned death and his children and had thrown in some of his own troubles. There was such a contrariness in him. No matter how much he tried to control himself, if he met a man who limped all he could think to talk about was cripples; if he was with someone who stuttered all he could remember were stories about people with speech impediments. What would his friend think of him?

Chaim gazed mournfully out the window, where blue shadow figures hurried through the descending snow, beyond the frosty tracings on the glass. "They say," he was surprised to hear his own voice resume, "that Mrs. Plopler is a sick woman." Chaim seized his tongue between his teeth and glanced quickly to where Abraham stood, feeding little bits of meat into the grinder. Perversely he remembered a story that Polsky had once told them about Mrs. Plopler. Polsky had been walking down the street one day and passed a funeral procession. It was a long funeral with cars and people following behind. Chaim glanced again quickly at Abraham and lifted his hand to his mouth to make sure he wasn't saying it out loud. At the end of the procession there was Sonya Plopler, following. And she was crying, and she was wailing, and she was beating her chest. Polsky thought to himself, Maybe I know this person; it must be somebody if poor Mrs. Plopler is so upset. So he ran up to her and took her by the arm. "Mrs. Plopler, Mrs. Plopler, who's dead? Who passed away?" And Sonya Plopler looked up at him, sniveling and swallowing. "I should know?"

In spite of himself Chaim felt his lips twist into a smile. He quickly turned his face away from his friend and forced himself to frown severely at the window. "You're going into your second childhood," his wife's voice reminded him. Second childhood, Chaim repeated to himself, knowing that if he repeated it often enough it would frighten away all traces of unnatural levity from his mind.

Nowadays it was easier, Chaim found, to talk about his friend than to talk with him. "I have just come from my friend Avrom the butcher," Chaim would say when he got to the green synagogue, where the miracle Torah was held temporarily till they collected enough money to build the new synagogue. His friend Dreiman the shamus, who was helping the caretaker of the green synagogue till their own should be rebuilt, would shake his head understandingly. "And how is he?"

The caretaker of the green synagogue would come and sit down with them for a little while, and anyone else who happened to be around would drift over. Chaim would sigh. "How should he be?" It was not for them to question the will of God. Still, it did not seem, somehow, quite fair. Such a young person, still in his early thirties, younger even than Chaim's youngest. So talented, so good to his father. He had rushed like a martyr into the flames. Hadn't he and Dreiman seen it with their own eyes? And then to be taken suddenly like that. But what could one say? God knew best.

God knew best, they agreed. And someone who was particularly intrepid in his thoughts would finally mention, "We all must die sometime." And the old men would nod their heads and murmur over this fact. It was an unbelievable truth that had superseded all others. Loyally, however, Chaim would have the last word. "But we don't all have to be preceded by our sons," he would remind them.

"God prevent it," they would exclaim in horror, and each one would return to his prayers.

Chaim sighed heavily and glanced up at Abraham, who was weighing out the ground meat.

"Did you say something?" said Abraham.

"No, I don't think so," said Chaim. Lately Abraham had developed this disconcerting habit of asking a person suddenly if he had spoken, when, as far as he could make out, he had been merely thinking. Sometimes it gave Chaim the queer feeling that Avrom was somehow listening for something—perhaps he was even just on the edge of reading his thoughts. On the other hand, how could he be sure that he had not spoken? His wife had assured him several times that he had taken to talking aloud to himself. It was part of her campaign to convince him that he was going into his second childhood.

"What?" said Abraham.

"Nothing," said Chaim, "nothing. It's just my Bassieh." Chaim sighed.

Hymie Polsky came in from outdoors and stood for a moment, stamping and blowing in the butcher-shop doorway. He nodded and walked past them into the kitchen and stood making loud noises in front of the hot-air vent before he took off his overcoat.

"There will be a war," said Chaim. He shivered under the blast of cold air that had followed Hymie into the shop. He did not want to leave the shop just yet, to head into the cold wind, but it was so hard to find things to say. "A terrible war. They won't be allowed to go on tormenting us. The world won't let them. The people will rise up."

"There'll be a war all right," said Hymie, rubbing his hands and blowing on them as he emerged from the kitchen. "But not because anybody gives a damn about us." There was authority in Hymie's voice. He enjoyed letting the old man know. As he spoke he glanced sideways at Abraham, who busied himself behind the counter.

"God will help us," said Chaim.

Hymie laughed patronizingly. "Yeah." He went into the delicatessen, glanced at the empty booths, and moved toward the kibitzarnia. Chaim watched him with an expression of distaste on his face.

"It is said"—Abraham spoke suddenly—"that thousands are being murdered."

"Thousands? Millions," said Chaim. "They say that they want to wipe out all the Jews in the world." Chaim snorted. "Can you imagine that?"

"Where is God, then, Chaim?"

Chaim's eyes rolled instinctively upward.

"Where is God when all this is going on?" Abraham repeated.

"God knows," said Chaim. "He knows what He's doing."

"Is He doing it, then?" Abraham persisted.

"Ah, well, no I wouldn't say He was doing it exactly Himself." Chaim squirmed on his honorary barrel. "It's being done, it's true, by our enemies, by His enemies. He won't be quiet for long. They say it's getting worse day by day. The refugees tell such stories they make the skin shudder on your body. But there is action. They are making campaigns for other countries to let in the refugees, to save their lives."

"But they don't want to," said Abraham slowly. "God sees. He sees this too. And everything He writes down in His book. Isn't that so, Chaim?"

"Yes," said Chaim.

"And yet everything that happens seems to be trying to say something else. Do you hear it, Chaim, like a whispering around you?"

Chaim looked around him. "No," he said reluctantly. "But I talk," he confessed eagerly, "to myself sometimes, my Bassieh says. Maybe you hear me too?"

"What does it matter who hears if He will not hear? Does He hear, Chaim?"

"It is written that He hears everything," said Chaim. "Even my Bassieh." Chaim sighed. "Even God is to be pitied sometimes."

"It's not," said Abraham, "that I don't believe. I made the mistake once of throwing myself about like a wild man. But the strangest thoughts take hold of a man sometimes. Before, just like that, it came to me all of a sudden— But does He believe? And then I think, But He knows. He doesn't have to believe. And then I ask myself, What is it that He knows?"

Chaim turned Abraham's thoughts over in his head and could do nothing with them. Strange thoughts can be forgiven a man who has lived through so much. Who knew what thoughts he himself would have had if— Chaim shuddered inwardly.

The door of the delicatessen opened and slammed shut. Hymie Polsky came out of the kibitzarnia to serve his customers.

To listen. To listen with concentrated attention and to try painstäkingly to piece together everything that went on in the world about him; that was the only way, Abraham knew. It was clear that it was intended for him to go on living yet awhile. But pray though he might, he could not come close to what it was that he lived for now. The child? Yes. But that too was in God's hands. What plans could he make that could be assured for the child? What could he, who had not even been able to keep his sons alive, do, now that he was an old man, for the child? Try to insure the moment, yes, and that was hard enough with Polsky's eye upon him and Hymie muttering in Polsky's ear. Oh, yes, he had seen it. He had not let on, but he had seen. And the way Hymie only half looked at him when he spoke to him.

Only the other day Polsky had overheard him groan as he hoisted a section of meat into the refrigerator. "Your arms aren't what they used to be, eh, Avrom?" he had remarked. "Don't strain yourself." It had been kindly enough said, but Abraham, straining, had caught an undertone of hidden meaning. And it had caused a sweat to break out all over his body so that now when he thought that Hymie or Polsky was about he found himself trying to work more quickly and watching them with a feeling of anxiety that was new to him, out of the corner of his eye. He should be afraid of Hymie? What had happened to him? What had happened to the whole world?

Polsky yawned and stretched, scratched his belly under his pants, listened for a moment as Hymie banged the cash register, and then, alone in the kibitzarnia, picked up a deck of cards from the table and began to shuffle through them absent-mindedly.

Why should she come here to make scenes anyway? Did she make them with those "gentile" friends she talked so much about? What did he owe her, when it came to that? Whatever you said to her nowadays, you got from her like from the horse's rear. It hadn't been that way once—a temper, yes, Laiahle the red, but not such airs, such demands, like the Queen of Sheba. And if you happened to say something she didn't like, hoo-ha! Right away she was tossing her ass to the empty air. And with Hymie? At knife's edge. So if she found those "gentiles" of hers, whoever they were, so satisfactory, let her keep them and not expect everybody around here to— But Hymie could really squeeze her gall bladder over those new friends of hers. Every time she mentioned her "Christian" or her "gentile" friends, he made like he didn't know from nothing. "Your what? Your who? Oh, you mean your friends the goyim!" Scenes then! With Hymie and Laiah swearing at each other in the kibitzarnia and Avrom in the butcher shop, he didn't know whether he had a whorehouse here or a synagogue.

Not that it was up to Avrom to judge what went on in his own business. But who said he was judging? There he himself didn't agree with Hymie. The old man had enough of his own troubles to worry about.

That was the trouble with Hymie—Polsky ran his hand thoughtfully over the smooth skin at the top of his head—with the whole younger generation. The old dog can't work any more, throw him out, have him shot. "We can't cry for everyone." Those had been Hymie's words. True enough, in their own way. Polsky had never in his life wasted many tears over anyone else. But that was not the point now.

It had been a long time, a long time when it hadn't been just a question of paying a man a salary. There had been a time when Abraham had virtually run the shop when he had busied himself elsewhere. And even now Hymie couldn't claim that the old man didn't pay his way. Who could pickle meat like him? There were still customers from the heights who came to Polsky's and nowhere else for their briskets. It was all right to talk about streamlining the business, all very fancy. But it was still what you gave the customer for his money that counted.

Polsky dealt himself a hand of solitaire. Avrom had got it up the wrong end, and it hurt, naturally. But what the hell? And what would people say if he threw him out now, after all that had happened? When it came down to it, Polsky was after all a religious man.

The thing about Hymie—Polsky didn't bother to fight the temptation to cheat—the thing about Hymie was that he liked the idea of being boss. Sometimes he even liked to let himself forget that his father was still around. Polsky listened for a moment. The door to the delicatessen had closed but he had not heard the cash register ring. Polsky frowned. The register banged belatedly. Polsky cheated again, and the game moved smoothly.

In a way he felt a certain kinship with Abraham. He himself was no old man yet, but a man in his fifties is no longer a youngster either. Someday the time would come for him too. But he would be smart about it. There are ways an old dog can make sure of having his warm bed to die in, even when he's useless. And there are ways of keeping your sons clucking love all over you. Polsky triumphantly collected the cards. Just keep the property in your name, and they'll love every senile part of you.

Still—Polsky scrupulously reshuffled the cards—there was something in what Hymie said. It might do to give Morton a bit more experience in the place. Someday, when they expanded and Hymie had a shop of his own to manage, Morton would have the run of this one. It might not be a bad idea, for a while anyway, while Avrom was still in mourning, to let him go home earlier and let him deliver the afternoon parcels on his way to or even back from the synagogue. He had to leave early anyway to say Kaddish.

That was an idea. Polsky dealt again. It was sound business and at the same time generous to old Avrom too, like a gesture of sympathy. A man was always better off to sit himself down and figure out all the angles. He always ended up more right that way. The butcher-shop bell tinkled and the cash register banged simultaneously. Polsky sneaked a look at the next card.

Abraham paused at the foot of the stairs, startled by the frivolity of his thought. He had been just about to mount the stairs when it had occurred to him that surely Laiah could not now be what people claimed she was. It was not practical. A few years ago, perhaps, yes. For a young man these stairs would be nothing, a brisk run before a heavy meal. But what could a man of her own age aspire to after climbing three steep flights of stairs? It was the sort of thing that

Isaac might have said to him; it was almost as though Isaac had said it to him laughingly just now. And he would have answered reprovingly, for how could he go up to her now and hand her her parcel and look her straight in the eye with such a thought in the back of his mind?

Oh, Isaac. Abraham shook his head as he started up the stairs. You would have said it right out, just like that, in front of Ruth, in front of Sarah, even in front of Sonya Plopler. And the next thing, Sonya Plopler would be asking you questions with a funny look in her eye. "Hm," she would say, "I didn't know she went after young men too." It would be all over town in no time that Laiah was having business with men half her age, and my son, yet, would be given as the authority. How many times have I told you, in front of that woman bite your tongue. Abraham stopped and gripped the banister, staring down at the stairs. Then he looked around him sharply, from the brown stairs to the brown walls to the dim gray ceiling. With one hand on the banister he pulled himself upward again.

Every afternoon now, afternoons that were dark with the premature winter evening, Abraham stood in doorway after doorway and smelled the smell of supper being prepared by plump, busy women, and saw their children running about the kitchens. Often he had to step aside to let a husband, returning from work, into a house that was warm and noisy with the shouts of children and their scolding mother. He could not help remembering how—wasn't it only yesterday?—his life too had been full of the cries of children. Sometimes his heart seemed to cry out in him with pain and a sort of hunger. And it seemed to him that there must be something more for him, something that would bring him hope, that would help him to understand.

All around him everyone but he had settled back willingly, easily into life. Only he stood, alone seeing how everything had gone wrong. What could the child know?—so small, so distant from him, so unaware that something lurked around every corner. Ruth had her work now, in a dress shop somewhere on the heights. He could see that each new day brought her entirely new things to think about, things that had nothing to do with them, with what had happened. The gap where Isaac had been was still there. But all the ragged underbrush was beginning to creep up, to cover the wounded earth, to try to hide the spot where something fine had stood.

Even in himself he found sometimes that he could relax into a sort of— No, it was not happiness but a sort of acceptance, almost of pleasure, over certain things, like trudging through the snow with nothing to fight against for the moment but the wind and nothing to contemplate but the sparkling crispness of the ground. At such times his mind would wander away into his memories, and he would relive for a few moments happier times and rediscover scenes that he had almost forgotten. Or else things that had never really even happened would come to him, as though they were actually happening, and they would extend the bounds of his actual life, until he remembered.

Laiah's door was opened by a strange woman who stared at him with large, rather vacant eyes.

"Butcher," said Abraham.

"Laiah, it's your butcher," the woman called over her shoulder in English, then turned back to stare at Abraham, who was fishing a parcel out of his canvas sack.

"Tell the boy to come in, Jenny." Laiah's husky voice caroled from within.

Jenny smiled and gestured to Abraham to follow her. "It's no boy," she said as she entered the kitchen. "It's Father Christmas." Her eyes widened in startled pleasure at her own witticism.

"Avrom!" said Laiah, brushing past her friend. "But you look frozen! How come you're delivering? Is Morton sick, or is Polsky trying to make an errand boy out of you?" Laiah could not resist this dig. Of late she had not been feeling very kindly toward the Polskys. "Walking around in the cold, and then having to climb three flights of stairs so that you get all sweated up inside—what kind of business for a man like you? Look how it's dripping from your beard. Jenny"—Laiah turned to her friend—"set the teacups now, will you?

You can do my nails afterward. Avrom will have tea with us." And in Yiddish, to Abraham: "I'll hang up your coat. No, no, it's absolutely no use to argue with me. You should know that by now. Remember the other time you had tea with me? After tea Jenny will read our cups. But you drink from a glass, don't you? I've become assimilated. I like to have my cup read. My friend Jenny," Laiah explained, "is a gentile, but a very fine one. Jenny," she called, "will you set a glass for my friend?"

Laiah felt the afternoon's boredom slipping away from her. She was a little annoyed with herself for sounding so eager. It was his deafness and having to yell up at him that made it sound so, she told herself. "Your coat," she said, laughing. "No one will steal it here. I'll just hang it up a minute."

Jenny busied herself delightedly in the kitchen. In her heart she positively thrilled with the strangeness of this exotic Jewess who was her friend. They did things differently. Here was this bearded old man. What could she call him? Distinguished. He certainly didn't look like a butcher. Could it merely have been a code word? Jenny felt the parcel on the table. It could be meat.

Ever since she had moved into this district, into the attic room across the hall, and had made the acquaintance of Laiah because they shared the same toilet on the landing, she had really learned; it had been an education. At first she had been just a little wary of this woman with her peculiar accent. But Laiah had been so friendly and really so interesting. When they had got to talking about personal things that first time, and Laiah had asked her with such an incredulous voice, "You mean you really haven't, not ever?"—why, she hadn't known where to look. Of course Laiah had been married. But Laiah knew very well that she was single. It wasn't marriage that Laiah was talking about. She could still see Laiah's unbelieving fulllipped face leaning toward her, her moist eyes, and feel the delicious horror of realization that, even without marriage, Laiah had. What would her mother think if she were still alive? Jenny cast a shy, darting glance at the back of the bearded man.

"You must be frozen," said Laiah. "I'm absolutely chilled from holding your coat." Laiah caught Jenny's eye. That one was getting a real thrill. In her most gracious English manner Laiah introduced her guests to each other.

"You look tired," said Jenny daringly.

"Yes," said Abraham. He felt his tiredness and was grateful for the chair and the warmth.

Jenny looked at Laiah delightedly. "It's a long way up." She addressed Abraham. "Fifty-eight steps. I've counted them. That's not counting the front steps. They make it sixty-three." Jenny blushed.

Laiah explained that Jenny was her neighbor and that they had become very good friends, and while Jenny was recovering from her blushes Laiah moved on to other subjects. With a certain delicacy, partly because she was not sure exactly what to say about such a subject, Laiah ignored Abraham's recent bereavement. Still her questions worked around the subject. Abraham answered briefly questions about Ruth and the child. Again she asked him how he came to be doing deliveries and Abraham explained.

"A Polsky good turn," said Laiah. She started to tell, in English, of the Polskys and their business. She spoke in a lively and acid manner which titillated her friend Jenny into an endless fit of giggles.

There was something unreal to Abraham, and yet at the same time very real and simple, about the fact that he was sitting here now— These people are alive too. He turned the thought over, trying to find its hidden significance.

Laiah's anecdotes about the Polskys grew more pointed and even less complimentary as she continued. Abraham's mind wandered as the English phrases skipped by. Suddenly he remembered his own thought about her that had come to him on the stairs. Vexed with himself that he should have indulged such thoughts at her expense and now sat accepting bits of her buttered coffee cake and drinking her tea, he grunted out loud and made a gesture of annoyance.

Laiah stopped talking abruptly. "I've bored you," she said. "Men don't like women's gossip. It's your fault, Jenny. You let me go on and on."

"No," said Abraham. "It was something else."

"You don't like, maybe, the way I talk about— Never mind." Laiah sighed. "Someday perhaps I'll tell you. It's funny how"— Laiah leaned forward and looked sympathetically into his face— "you're the kind of person one can talk to. I've felt it before. There are some people who aren't like others." Laiah made a vague, general gesture, noticed Jenny's eyes quizzically on her, and said in English, "Cups." After quickly draining her own, she handed it to Jenny.

Abraham glanced through the doorway to where his coat was hung. It was time for him to go. But his eye was caught now by Jenny's ritual movements with the cup and Laiah's air of vivacious interest.

Jenny, after a moment of serious study, which involved much movement of the head and widening and narrowing of the eyes, fluttered her fingers to her chest and glanced coyly at Abraham. "I see a man," she said.

"So do I," said Laiah a little sternly, trying to hint with a glance that Jenny was not to take too much liberty along that line right now.

Abraham remembered the gypsies of his childhood. Was that what it was? They were making passes into the unknown.

"He's—well, a very distinguished-looking man," Jenny pressed on, ignoring Laiah's hint. "And he'll come to see you." Her imagination soared. "It looks as if he might"—Jenny interrupted herself to giggle—"there might even be a long trip. And you seem to be—tied to him, somehow."

"Foolishness." Laiah, who tended to believe her cups implicitly, laughed. "I occasionally have a friend visit me, but it's been a long time since anyone took me on a trip." The truth of this statement struck her as she spoke, and she continued a little irritably. "Stop making it up and read from the cup."

"But I am reading from the cup." Jenny's voice rose to falsetto injured. "Look."

"Well, what are those leaves over there?"

Jenny began to giggle nervously again. "Well, I'm not sure; that's why I say you're attached. But I think they might mean—well, they look like— That means marriage, of course," Jenny ended hastily and, blushing, couldn't raise her eyes even sideways to glance at Abraham.

Laiah smiled at Abraham. "That's enough for me now," she said. "Shall she read your glass, Avrom? Of course she only knows how to read cups, not glasses, but I'm sure if we ask her nicely she'd be willing to try."

"My glass?" said Abraham.

"Your future," Laiah went on in Yiddish. "She'll look into your tea glass and tell you your future."

"I can't guarantee that I'm always right," said Jenny eagerly, "but people are always coming back to me and asking me how I knew it would happen.

"Jenny's practically a professional," said Laiah. She reached for Abraham's glass.

"No!" said Abraham with sudden violence. "More future? God will tell." He looked with a sort of horror into his glass and quickly turned it over in his saucer so that the remaining tea and bits of leaves ran out. At the same time he got up from his place.

"What did he say?" asked Jenny, a little frightened. Laiah didn't answer. "What did he say?" Jenny repeated.

"He said that only God can tell him his future," Laiah snapped.

Jenny was a little disturbed. Alone in the kitchen as Laiah helped Abraham on with his coat, she surreptitiously upturned his tea glass. He had made a mess of it, shaking it so. What did he mean by bringing God into it? There was something sinister about it all.

"We hardly got a chance to talk," said Laiah. "Well, another time. There's always a glass of tea. Now that he's got you harnessed to the delivery bag you'll need it occasionally. I don't usually like to order things because it's so much trouble delivering them, but they aggravate me so much sometimes that I don't even like going in there."

After she had let Abraham out Laiah leaned against the door for a moment and listened to his footsteps receding down the stairs. Funny. Who could tell what he thought? Behind her she heard Jenny moving about in the kitchen. Her smile curled itself downward on her face. She went back into the kitchen and picked up a dishtowel. "Next time," she mused out loud, "I'll give him the bread knife to sharpen."

"Who?" said Jenny.

"Him—who else?" said Laiah irritably.

"I thought you said he was a butcher," came Jenny's voice, insistent and vaguely suspicious.

"So?"

"Now you say he sharpens knives." Jenny was keen.

Laiah sighed patiently. "He has a whetstone in the shop. They have to keep their knives sharp."

"He doesn't look like just a butcher, somehow. You know, I really like a beard on a man, even though it is old-fashioned."

Laiah didn't answer. She was thinking irritatedly that she didn't care what Jenny liked on a man. How did she know what there was to like on a man?

"Will they send an order to someone they don't know? I mean a new customer?" Jenny asked.

"Why not?"

"Maybe I'll make an order one of these days. I seem to like this kosher meat, though it's so expensive," said Jenny.

"If you like I'll have him send up what you want when I order again," Laiah offered politely.

"Oh," said Jenny a little archly, "I can phone myself."

Laiah looked at her for a moment. Then she gave a low chuckle. "He's really made an impression on you, eh, my bearded Avrom?" She put just enough malice into her words to scorch Jenny's cheeks.

"Whatever are you talking about?" Jenny shrilled, her face red and offended.

"I'm only joking." Laiah smiled placatingly, though not with enthusiasm. "I really mean that it would save Avrom the trouble of having to climb the stairs twice if we made our order together."

"Well, if you're so anxious you can have Santa Claus all to yourself," snapped Jenny. "I wouldn't think of tiring your poor old man."

"Look how she's blushing! I believe you, I believe you. Can't I tease you a little bit? You know you're not so innocent as you pretend. And besides, between you and me, he's not so poor and not so old as all that, is he? He has had a great tragedy happen in his family lately. Sometime I'll tell you all about it. You haven't even done my nails yet."

Jenny let herself be reconciled. All the same, as she sat expertly buffing Laiah's fingernails she alternately rankled and preened inside herself, remembering bits and pieces of their little tiff. She was certainly quick to warn you off her territory, this one. That she should even think! Well, it showed what some people had in mind. But she had told her, all right. Some people assumed that because you were nice to them you were like them. Wasn't there a certain note of jealousy in what she had said, the way she had sprung in with it? Well, perhaps she, Jenny, could do some teasing herself.

Laiah caught the changing expressions on the face of the one whom, for the sake of the gang of schleppers at Polsky's, she had expanded into a "whole new crowd, some of them gentile." Let them know that the kibitzarnia was by her not such a necessary thing.

"Maybe"—Jenny looked up suddenly with a roguish smile on her prim, rather vacant face, which made her eyes glare out suddenly. "Maybe"—she went off into one of her long giggles—"I will order meat from your friend Avrom after all."

Laiah, who had had to change the expression on her face very quickly, smiled in an accentuated way. "You do that," she said.

Jenny went off into another trill of laughter. "Aren't you finished yet?" Laiah interrupted her restlessly. "You're taking a long time today."

Jenny smirked and went back to work. Laiah sucked her under lip. Tired, she told herself, of you and your silly face. But she kept her hands very still. Gradually, her mind drifted into a voluptuous consideration of the promises of the tea leaves.

Once he was out in the open, Abraham could scarcely believe it had happened. Of course they were not serious. It was some game they played. His future. What kind of witchcraft was this? What could she know about his future? Almost from the first moment when they had, as though by command, come to this city, this Laiah had been there, moving always in a direction that was exactly opposite to his path in life. And now she spoke casually of his future, as though at her bidding her friend could look into his glass of tea and reveal to him God's secret intentions—as though the Almighty would choose to reveal His secrets in such a manner. And who were these women, that they should play so triflingly with such things when he had offered up his whole life and had it struck away from him? Here, Abraham, is your life. Trace it out in the dregs of your empty glass. See, here's my cup. It's empty too. Laiah's lips twisted themselves into a smile in front of his face. He rubbed the back of his mitt across his face and shook his head. What kind of foolishness!

She had not paid him. Abraham stood still. What would Hymie say about it tomorrow morning when he turned in the money? For a few moments he worried about it. "Never mind," he burst out suddenly, half shouting aloud with vexation. "I'll tell him to collect it himself." Startled at the sound of his own voice, he looked about him. But the street was dark and empty of people. Only the yellow lights in the windows glowed with an inward warmth up and down the street, making him long for the child, for Ruth, a longing that drove him more quickly forward, that distracted him because it would not stay within the bounds of the possible, would not stop with Ruth and the child.

It seemed like a long time ago, in another life altogether—when he had been a baby, was the way Moses put it to himself—that his grandfather used to tell him stories about all the wonders that had happened in the world. Those wonders, like his grandfather's booming laugh, were things that did not happen so often now, since his father had died and he had become an orphan and grown up. He knew other things now that he hadn't known then, especially all about Hell and the Devil. They belonged mostly to Donald Gregory and the other goyim, but Donald Gregory said they were all over too. Time and again he had wanted to ask his grandfather about Hell and the Devil—if they were really true, and why his grandfather had never told him about them. But he was afraid to ask. If Grampa said that they really were true, then he knew he would have to be punished. They would come after him and they would throw him into the fire, and he would not be able to come running out as his father had, carrying the Torah, because the devil would hold him down for his sins, and he would burn all over.

He was afraid of his father's ghost, that was why. Not always; sometimes, in daylight when he was with other people, he would silently beg his father's forgiveness because he had been afraid last night that his father would haunt him. Donald Gregory knew all about haunting. His church had a Holy Ghost. But Moses didn't want to be haunted. How would his father feel, up there, if he knew that his own son wished and prayed never to hear from him again? He would think that he didn't love him. And that wasn't true. It was just the dark he was afraid of, and suddenly hearing and-feeling someone in the room with him that he couldn't touch. How did he even know it would be his father? They might change him and send down someone else instead, pretending to be his father, for some dreadful purpose. Sometimes, when he was alone in the house, without even wanting to, he would think about it, and he would become so frightened that he couldn't move his head or even his eyes, because a presence was there, somewhere.

Every day on the way home from Chaider, where he went straight from school, he prayed earnestly, as hard as he could pray, that either his mother or his grandfather should be home already so that he wouldn't have to try the door and find it locked, and so when they came home and found him waiting outside they shouldn't ask him why he hadn't opened it with his own key and gone into the house. That key. When his mother had given it to him and told him what a big boy he was now and that she trusted him enough to give him a key to the house, warning him that he must never lose it or give it to anybody, he had felt like a grown-up somebody. He carried it tied to a string around his neck, inside his shirt. When he had shown it to the other boys who ate lunch at school they had all crowded around him. Tony's mother worked too, but he never got a key to the house. After four he went to Dmitri's till his mother came home, because his mother was afraid that one of the customers might come into the house and drink the booze without paying for it, and Tony would be too small to stop him. Moses was certain that if there were booze in their house his mother would still give him the key, because he could make anybody pay. But of course they weren't bootleggers.

Only what good was it to have the key when he was afraid to go into the house by himself, afraid to sit in the kitchen because then he might start thinking and listening for sounds in the house? Usually God was on his side, and by the time he came home from Yiddish school his mother was already home. And when she wasn't he played in the yard by himself or with the cats, telling himself that he'd go in when he wanted to, waiting for her, and praying for his father to forgive him at the same time, so that his feelings were all mixed up in him and he played his game fiercely, trying to forget who and what he was.

When she was late, when Madame Claire had kept her, Ruth liked most the moment when she recognized the child coming toward her through the snow. He had waited for her. And though she would scold him for it because he was cold and wet from playing so long in the snow, she was glad. Together, while she asked him questions about his day, they turned in at the gate. Then she took out her key, or if her arms were full of parcels she asked him to unlock the door. But he usually gave her the key and held some of the parcels while she opened the door. And she liked this childlike gesture too.

Perhaps it had been too much to expect, she sometimes told herself, to be perfectly happy. It was no use even to think about that. She still had this much, the child waiting for her, their supper to get, a hundred other needs to fill. So much at least he had left her. The supper that she had prepared last night was warm and ready long before Abraham opened the door.

Chapter Fourteen

After the argument they sat there at the kitchen table, surprised and a little ashamed, for during the quarreling each one had gradually managed to make clear to the other, in spite of the raised voices and the injured tones, that at the bottom of it all was a misunderstanding.

Abraham turned at last to the boy, who had sat still, the tears drying on his cheeks, looking from one to the other all this time. "Why didn't you tell me that your mother had already said no?"

The boy fidgeted with his hands. He was still shocked that they had shouted so, even for a few moments. There had been quarrels before in the house. But there was something about the way they used to argue long ago, when his father was alive, that had been different. There had not been the feeling then, hanging in the air, that they were somehow implacably, hatefully, opposed to each other, that each was somehow sure that the other was trying to do him vital harm. He hadn't meant any harm.

"I thought that if you said yes, Ma would let me go," he said lamely. But what of the funny excitement he had felt, as well as the fear, when they had started to quarrel? "I didn't mean it! I didn't mean it!" He began to cry again.

"Never mind," said his mother. "Never mind, it's all right. Go and practice now. Maybe tomorrow if you're good you can stay out longer."

The boy accepted his dismissal, but he still hesitated, wanting to tell them that he was sorry, that it was his fault, but that all he had wanted was— "Go, go," said his grandfather gently, "make a little music."

"I'm sorry, Pa," said Ruth when the boy had left the room. "I didn't mean to jump down your throat that way. I'm so nervous lately."

"It's nothing," said Abraham. It was nothing, a mistake. As if he would do a thing like that. How was he to know that the child had already asked her? But was that any reason for her to jump on him that way, to tell him that she did not want him to interfere with her upbringing of her own child? And in front of the boy, too. What was he, then, a stranger, that he must not say anything to his own grandson without her permission? He was Isaac's child too, his child. And how could she think that he would deliberately do anything to spite her? Was that how little they knew each other? He looked over to where she sat across the table from him, her elbow on the table and her head against her hand. A few moments ago they had been like two strangers facing each other, antagonistic, misunderstanding.

He still had that feeling now as he watched her, that she was a stranger to him, capable of hidden things, of different thoughts and actions. And was only she a stranger? When he had heard himself shouting a few moments ago, when he had realized the bitterness in himself at what she had said—and not only at what she had said, a general bitterness, bubbling up inside of himself—he had felt for a moment capable of God alone knew what. The sense of strangeness grew upon him now as from the bedroom the first few hesitant notes of the child's violin broke in his ears.

Unnoticed, the dusk of an early spring evening had crept in through the kitchen window, muting the clear distinctions between one object and another. The notes of the violin laced through the dim-lit air. There was a fuzzy blueness about Ruth, close though she was to him. He did not even know what he himself really looked like any more. He had only a feeling of face. Here his arm lay in front of him loosely on the table, his fingers drumming, a thing apart from him. He had only a feeling of arm, a throbbing feeling of two aching arms. The threaded violin pierced in and out, tied him to the table, bound him to Ruth, looped through the room. Where was the knowledge that had given form to his existence once? Where was the whole man, Abraham? What is man without meaning, without purpose? Best to die like this, merging gradually with everything about you, with only your spirit singing its last frail notes in your ears.

It was with an effort, with the deliberate movement of all his body, that he restored the feeling of the whole outline of his physical self. He dragged himself up from the chair and went to turn on the kitchen light. Ruth shifted slightly as he came back to his chair. What was she thinking? What did she plan in her mind when she was alone? They talked so little nowadays to each other—a question, an answer. What was she, this young woman whom he had taken for a daughter because his son had taken her for a wife, whom he thought he knew once and who now told him so shrilly not to interfere? "I didn't even know that he'd spoken to you," said Abraham again.

"I know, Pa." Ruth lifted her face from her hand, and he saw that her cheeks were damp. "I don't know how it happened. I worry so much that he'll go wild. He's alone so much. I don't see him from morning till night. I don't know what kind of children he plays with all day, where he wanders around. At lunch time I worry, is he running around on the streets? What does he do until it's time for Chaider? What are they teaching him, those friends of his? It's not the district for a child to grow up in, alone all day. And when he asks to go out again after supper, when I've hardly seen him— I'm sorry, Pa. He's growing so quickly; sometimes it seems as though he's slipping through my hands altogether."

"Long ago," said Abraham slowly, not looking at her, "when my Sarah and I were just married and had started to raise a family, we decided that no matter what happened, no matter what should come about and how angry we should be with each other, we would not quarrel in front of the children. We were angry sometimes, not very often. You know what an appeasing angel Sarah was. I found myself anyway doing her will, though it always appeared to me that she was giving in to me. But never in front of the children; never did the children see one of us speak rudely to the other. It was the way my mother had taught me. And it was the same with you and Isaac. I said to Isaac, 'Don't let me hear of anything that goes on between you and your wife. Don't call on your mother and me if you have an argument.' So it was, and it was well!"

Ruth felt a mixture of shame and irritation at the rebuke. She tried; God only knew that she tried. Why did he have to throw up to her how she fell short of them, of his family? And yet he was right. The child should be shielded. The child should not see them quarreling. If only there were someone to talk to, to discuss things with. It was all very well for him to criticize. But when she tried to talk to him about something constructive, about opening a dry-goods shop as the salesman had suggested, what help had he been? He had scarcely listened. He had seemed almost unwilling to understand that it might be necessary for them to move out of here, to take some steps toward reordering their lives more satisfactorily.

"If only," she began, "we could plan things out so that I could have him home for lunch, maybe even both of you. We could have a small place, maybe with living quarters in the back. As long as I'm near him, so I won't have to worry about him all the time. You understand, Pa?"

"About me you don't have to worry," said Abraham. "You can be sure that no one will ever say that I have been a bad influence on my grandson, even though maybe once I did accidentally tell him that he could do something his mother had forbidden."

"I know, Pa, I know. And if he grew up to be like you I'd have nothing to complain about."

Abraham frowned. "I don't want him to grow up to be a butcher."

"That's why we must plan," said Ruth quickly. "Pa, we could start afresh. We could start to plan for him. This is no way for him to be brought up, wandering about in the streets."

How did she mean to start afresh? One started afresh when one knew where the start was, and when one thought one knew where the end was. And it seemed to him that her starting afresh involved, somehow, her demand that he should not interfere. Not interfere? How could he not interfere? What about the child? What about the future?

Ruth waited for him to answer her, but he seemed to have forgotten her words. Perhaps if she tried again another time, when he was not so upset, he might understand. She would find out more about it from Harry. The salesman really thought it was a good idea, and he had offered to help. Maybe if she planned it all out carefully herself and then came to him when it was all ready to be put into action, he might realize that it could be done.

. . . She deals with the child. What can I say? She treats me as though I too were a child. She won't even argue with me properly, to hear my full opinion. When Isaac lived it was not like this. When she speaks to me gently, with consideration, with tact, I can see that she is choosing her words for tact, for gentleness, not so as to come to grips with me as a human being, as though I were really someone to consult, to listen to. She evades; decisions are already made; the child has already been told before I have been consulted, and I am told not to interfere. . . .

Ruth had risen and stood by him, putting her hand on his shoulder. "Why do you still frown like that? Won't you forgive me for what I said? You can see that we will have to plan to move for the boy's sake, can't you, Pa?"

At the touch of her hand Abraham felt a warmth stirring in him, mingled with an obscure sense of shame. For a moment he didn't look at her but mumbled guiltily into his beard.

"You look tired, Pa," said Ruth gently. "And Moishe must be, too. Listen, he hasn't stopped playing. Maybe we should thank him for the concert."

Because he was ashamed he allowed her to help him up from his chair, although at the same time he told himself that he was no cripple. "I am tired." He straightened up and removed her hand from his arm, taking her instead firmly under the arm. "Forgive me too," he said. "I too think of the future. But a man's life moves in a circle. Though he thinks he's moving upward he finds he's back where he started, not knowing, not understanding, waiting for a word. Only now he's old," he added wryly, "and maybe too deaf to hear, eh? But not too old to escort a lady." Abraham laughed, and the child paused in his playing, startled to hear the once familiar sound. With a flourish, and feeling immensely better, Abraham led Ruth to her son.

Chaim waited while Abraham came down the steps and along the short walk, readjusting the shoulder strap of his delivery sack. In silence Abraham turned out of the gate and they walked on down the street. Chaim glanced up at his friend, who was fidgeting still with the shoulder strap. There had been a time, when Polsky had first set Abraham to doing deliveries, that Chaim had shaken his head over the fact that his friend should end up so. "What does a man foresee?" he had said to the others at the synagogue. But now the sight of Abraham trudging through the streets with the delivery sack over his shoulder had become a familiar thing. Neither did it bother Chaim any more that very often, when they were together, he had to make most of the conversation. He had become used to chattering into the sympathetic silences of his friend.

"Did you speak to Dreiman at the synagogue today?" Chaim hurried to keep up.

"No." Abraham slowed down slightly as he felt Chaim's hand restrainingly on his arm. "No time. I still had these to do. With Dreiman you have to stand awhile."

"Poor Dreiman," said Chaim, "he's so bewildered with the news and the rumors; they're driving him crazy."

"Is it true," said Abraham, "that they're not going to rebuild on the old site?"

"Well"—Chaim sighed—"since Schwarzgeist's son is taking a money interest for the sake of his father's Sepher Torah, it's practically certain they won't. This district is too low-class. In fact, they're talking of a site on the heights, near some big church—only it should be bigger."

Abraham said nothing. He was thinking of how Isaac had foreseen this. They would build far out. How would he reach the synagogue on the Holy Days when riding was forbidden? And they would have an expensive membership, too, in their rich man's synagogue, so that even if he could walk those miles he would not be able to afford to pray before the Torah that his son had saved.

"Dreiman doesn't know what to do with himself," said Chaim. "Yesterday he phoned all the big ones on the committee and told each one of them that he knows they've heard rumors about him, that it was through his negligence that the fire started, but that it's not true. All along he's been afraid they'd blame him. But since no one said anything to him he just stayed on at the green synagogue, keeping watch over the Sepher Torah, helping out Pleschikov there, and doing odd jobs around that he has been doing for years. Now that they're starting to plan he's gotten wind that they might not appoint him shamus of the new synagogue."

"He's not good enough for them?" asked Abraham.

"Who knows? None of them gave him a straight answer. Nothing's for sure yet. They're still making plans. He shouldn't upset himself. Pleschikov says he almost burst out crying when he was talking to Schwarzgeist on the phone—how he wasn't so old as they thought, maybe; how Manishin, if they were thinking of Manishin for the job, as he had heard, was half blind; how hard he worked, all the time; how it wasn't true that he had left the synagogue unattended to run an errand for somebody else, how it was anti-semites who had set the fire. You know how when Dreiman gets ahold of you he doesn't let go so easily."

"Meanwhile they're keeping him dangling?"

"Who knows what they intend to do? He's maybe exciting himself for nothing. He made me promise that I'd ask Ralph, because Ralph is tied up with these big shots. Everything they think Ralph can do. Well, I'll ask him if I see him. Of course he's very busy. I told Dreiman, 'Wait,' I said, 'you're expecting the worst; it means the best will happen.' If Ralph gives me a chance I'll ask him. I'll maybe even see him today. He may be even at the suite later on when I get home." Chaim sighed and bobbed along in silence for a moment.

"A man comes to a time in life," Chaim resumed, pressing forward a little breathlessly to keep pace with Abraham, "when he should be able to sit back. His last few years he should be able to enjoy in peace. But instead?" Chaim spread out his arms in front of him, threw back his head on which his derby sat glued, and took a deep breath of spring air, as though it were a heavy chore. His eye, caught by the rich blue of the sky, squinted upward a moment, and he breathed again with less difficulty.

"But instead will she let you?" Chaim went on. "Not my Bassieh. If I'm not an old no-good who runs around all day like a young dandy then I'm a doddering fool in my second childhood. I say to her, 'Bassieh, for the past three years already now you've been pounding it in my head that I'm in my second childhood. All my life I've only been a year and a half older than you. Isn't it right that for the last year and a half you've been in your second childhood too?'

"So she says, 'Oh, because you're crazy you want me to be crazy too?'

"So I say, 'No, I don't want you to be crazy and I don't want to be crazy myself. But you have no more reason to call me crazy than I have to call you crazy.' You can see I talk to her reasonably.

" 'I have had two operations,' she says to me. 'Is this the way you talk to me?'

" 'What has this got to do with it?' I say to her. 'Did you have the operations in your head?'

"So she gives me one poisoned look; she gets her hat, and she's gone. At noontime she is still not home, and there is no lunch for me. I begin to worry about her. After all, no matter what she's like, she's still my wife. She has never left me without lunch before. Then she comes flinging into the house, and she says to me, 'It's all right; you'll hear what Ralph has to say; you'll hear what he thinks about his father telling his mother she needs an operation in her head.'

" 'But Bassieh, I didn't say—'

" 'It's all right, wait wait, you'll see,' she says. So I'll tell him if he comes, not that he's likely to rush over so fast, I'll tell him it's nice to see him occasionally. And I'll tell him that he has no right to criticize; a golden home, golden children, and where does he spend his time?

"I know what she's after, too," Chaim resumed after a moment. "She's decided that the suite is too much for her to take care of. She complains. She is a sick woman. 'A room,' she says, 'is enough for us at our age.' She still wants that Ralph should sweep us up and have us in a room in his house. That's what she wants. I know. Many years have taught me.

"And he doesn't want us. And I don't want it either. Why should I sit at the bottom of his table when for my few remaining years I can still sit at the head of my own? But no. What will happen is that she will convince Ralph that I am getting a little childish, and that the suite and me are too much for her to take care of, and that it will be a good idea for us to move into a room where we can be taken care of. Then she will get the shock of her life; she will find out where they send old people, even with rich children, when they're not wanted." Chaim couldn't keep the grievance from his voice. "You shouldn't think I mind so much the Old Folks' Home," he went on quickly with a heroic shrug. "I have friends there. I know the superintendent personally. He's no youngster himself, when it comes to that. But why should she push so? Why should mother-love be so blind that she will rush to dig her own grave?"

Abraham stopped, and Chaim pulled up short beside him, eying him with damp, inquiring eyes. "We've walked past." Abraham gestured, and they turned and walked back a few houses and then stopped again. "Well," said Abraham and pointed upward to the top story of the house. "A long climb."

"Ah, aha." Chaim scrutinized upwards. "My two feet would never carry me."

"Bit by bit"—Abraham adjusted the sack—"I pull myself upward."

"Well—" Chaim hesitated.

"She keeps me, too." Abraham waved his hand apologetically. "Talks. Doesn't let me go. Customers." Abraham shrugged and squinted fiercely upward.

"Well," said Chaim, "I won't wait, then. I promised Dreiman anyway I'd drop in again before I go home."

"Not to worry, Chaim," said Abraham. "Sholom aleichem."

Chaim smiled. "Aleichem sholom, my friend."

"Not to worry" was an easy thing to say, a gentle way when you had to cut off to go about your business. But who could so easily forget all that it covered over? What comfort could his words be to Chaim, when stirring in Chaim's eyes there was a deeper apprehension? There are more ways than one to lose a son. Was this how it always ended? Did all a man's finer expectations wither like dry twigs in his hands? Oh, there must be something else!

"Often," he was telling Laiah a little while later, "how often it used to happen that my Isaac used to teach me things. He would uproot an old idea and plant in its stead a fresh new thought that would grow in my mind until I knew that this was a truth. I would show it to my friends and say, 'Here, here is an example that the young can teach the old.' I myself am a man who has looked always to the new, who is always willing to learn."

Laiah nodded sympathetically. "Of course. I know."

"Sometimes they upset me, though, Isaac's ideas. It was because they were so grimly anchored to the ground. It was as though a man who could fly deliberately descended to the earth and declared that he could not really fly, and to prove it henceforth he would walk. And then he would go on to explain things, step by step, as seen through the eyes of a man who has clipped his own wings. But surely what he sees now are only the pores on the earth's surface, and not the deep breathings and gentle swellings of her breast." Abraham stared into his glass of tea.

Laiah fingered the bodice of her low-cut housecoat. "You express yourself so poetically," she said gently.

He didn't hear. "Yet I admired his courage, misguided though it was, and his young man's determination. Surely God knew, God understood. I tried to explain to Him sometimes in my prayers, when I knew that something Isaac had said might offend, that he did not mean it exactly so. And wasn't I right? Didn't he save the Torah? No matter what he says, a man like Isaac, when the testing time comes, will lift up his wings."

"Of course," said Laiah. "Of course." Laiah moved quickly and refilled his glass with tea.

"I don't know why I say all this to you," said Abraham vaguely.

"But I want to hear," said Laiah. "You know I have always felt that you and I could—understand each other somehow." She leaned forward, her moist brown eyes on his sympathetically.

"Everybody knows. Everybody thinks he understands. How can I talk to them? Wings? My arms are like lead weights. I can scarcely raise them. And my thoughts turn, like thorns, in my mind that tries to grasp them. Even then Isaac continued to probe. What did he learn? Did he learn why he had to die, or did he learn merely how to die, making his own peace with his own knowledge, his own loneliness?" Abraham remembered that he hadn't helped him then, though Isaac had tried to ask help with his hand clinging to his father's beard.

Laiah had opened her lips to speak, but he roused himself, without noticing. "What did he learn, then? Does he know why his father stands now like the tiller of the soil who worked only so the earth should bloom and finds instead that everywhere where he has passed the earth is seared, as though an invisible destroyer has followed, malignant, in his path?" Abraham stared through her accusingly. When he came at last to this thought there was nothing for him but to sink himself in prayer to escape the ideas that of their own accord began to jump and scrabble in his head. The facts of his life always waited at the back of his mind, and if he let them they would string themselves together in fantastic patterns to form a frightening cat's-cradle of tensions inside him.

Laiah watched a little uncomfortably while his lips moved silently. "I would gladly die," he whispered finally.

Laiah was genuinely shocked. "Oh, no," she said. "Avrom, what are you saying? You mustn't talk like that. You're still a young man. Your life can start all over again. There will be time for dying."

He stared at her, irritated that she had spoken, irritated that she had heard him. How did he come to be sitting here, telling her these things?

"Listen," said Laiah. "Often I've felt the way you do. I've thought to myself, What's the use? It would be better if I were through with all this. But then the very next day, or even the very next hour, something would happen that would make me laugh, an enjoyment would come my way, and I would be happy again, and I would know that this is what I lived for, this joke, that little bit of fun. You see?" Laiah smiled. "That's what life is."

He looked around him, trying to relate her words to reality. What did this joke, that little bit of fun have to do with what was inside of him? What were they, anyway? A joke, a little bit of fun, should come from inside when everything is right.

"I can understand," Laiah was saying, "that you worry about your family. A small child is a burden for a man of your age."

"Not a burden," said Abraham.

"No, I know—a responsibility I meant. But I don't think you have anything really to worry about. I've seen that daughter-in-law of yours. The first time I looked at her I knew she could take care of herself. She's young; she's attractive. She'll find her feet."

"She's a good woman," said Abraham.

"Of course. You can tell by looking at her." Laiah's large teeth bit decisively into a biscuit, and she did not speak for a moment, chewing reflectively. "And she'll try to do what's best. I think that everyone tries to be good in his own way, or at least thinks he is trying, don't you agree?" Laiah paused to chew and swallow again, choosing her words. "But to be honest with yourself, that is the thing." She leaned forward. "Don't you agree?

"I mean she's young," Laiah continued. "She dresses well—neatly, anyway. She's good-looking. Someday she'll find she's lonely. It's hard to bring up a child without a father. Of course," Laiah added, "the child has you, but it is so much to expect of you now, to carry so many burdens when you should be beginning to enjoy the rest that you deserve."

Both Chaim and she talked of rest. But rest comes with completion, with fulfillment. Then you lean back and every muscle unclenches itself as a man unclenches his fist and relaxes his body. For him there could be no rest. "I'll rest when I'm dead," he said.

"Don't talk of dying," said Laiah earnestly. "We shall all taste death soon enough. Let us eat of life for a little while longer. I'm speaking to you now as a friend, Avrom. Perhaps she'll find a fine young man. Whatever she does will be for the good of the child and the future. You too should think of your future, of what can come."

An expression had come into Abraham's face that made her uneasy suddenly. "Of course," she said hastily, "it's not likely. No, it can't be. Your Isaac was such a— No, who could take his place? But think of yourself, Avrom."

"What cannot be?" She was startled at the harshness of his tone. "Who can tell what cannot be? Are you one who can tell what will and will not be?" He glared challengingly into her eyes.

"I?" Laiah was somewhat nonplused. "Why, no, I don't know—I mean I don't think so. But I know"—she was beginning to recover her initiative—"what I would like to happen sometimes." Laiah laid her hand impulsively on his own and squeezed it gently, smiling.

"And it happens because you want it to, just like that?"

"Sometimes." Laiah laughed and removed her hand as Abraham began to withdraw his. "I hope so."

"And what of things you don't want to happen?"

"I don't know." Bemused, Laiah shook her head, and, laughing a little: "I only concentrate on what I want to happen."

Always there was something left unsaid. Always what was said left an apprehension in his mind, about himself, about his family. What did she know? Had she ever borne children? Had she ever reached beyond herself to the future she talked about? No. All her life from the time when he had first heard of her she had used the means and denied the end. She was like a great overripe fruit without seed, which hung now, long past its season, on the bough. How many generations had been denied in her womb? What festered there instead? She had denied creation, and to deny is to annihilate. How was it that he found himself, then, eating at her table, accepting her food? Was he any different from her? It was as though she had said to him, So you had sons, so they're dead, and I have never had sons, never wanted children; they are dead in my womb. Where are we both now? Both empty, both interchangeable from the beginning. Who are you to say that your way is the real way and mine just an illusion of living?

But the difference is in the choosing, he argued. I chose life.

And here we are together, she seemed to say, and smiled her slow, heavy-lipped, enigmatic smile.

The question bothered him still even after he had left her. Her large, loose body with the low-cut bodice of her housecoat, from which he had persistently to avert his eyes, rustled indecently through the passages of his mind. Her lips formed words, ironical— Something will happen that will make Ruth laugh; an enjoyment will come our way. What did she know about them, about Ruth? "What do you want from me?" he muttered irritably aloud, so that a man who had passed him on the street turned back for a moment, startled, and, shaking his head, watched him pass on.

There were possibilities, Laiah mused; there might even be a future in it. She felt a certain stirring in her blood, a certain hostility rising in her against Abraham. He came and he sat—as though she were anyone, as though she were as attractive to him physically as his friend Chaim Knopp. At the thought of a comparison between herself and Chaim Knopp, Laiah had to laugh. What would Chaim think of such a comparison? Funny ideas he had. It would do to get his mind off them. Of course, with these religious ones who didn't crawl all over you the first minute, you had to be shrewd; a lot of finger work with your eyes always on the Bible. But would that be enough? Why not aim higher? He was a widower, wasn't he? It might be amusing to have him, but to hold him would be an accomplishment. To capture this kind of man would still be a conquest. Polsky's eyes would pop. "Well done, little Laiahle," he used to say when he heard of her latest admirer. But this would be better still; his eyes should not only pop but drop right out. She would emerge as the respectable wife of a respected member of the community. Wouldn't there be a commotion when she took her place in the women's section of the synagogue? She might even rejoin, in the company of her husband, one or two societies. A few people who would like to forget her would take another look. Laiah's spirits soared.

Not too far ahead, she reminded herself. What about him? He was considerably older, but that didn't mean anything. She had always sensed something in this man, a certain strength. It was the beard she thought about now, and her fingers in that beard, that other beard that had awakened in her the full sentience of her girlhood and had given an urgent purpose to the movement of her thick young blood. No. Laiah abruptly dismissed the whole thing. It was all non-sense. She would let it drop. There was no point; he was too odd. Maybe she would just tease him a little bit more, but as for the rest — Again she mused on the rest, and when Jenny came in a little while later and looked in a hurt and accusing way from her to the mess on the table that was still left over from her tea with Abraham, Laiah greeted her gaily and with a cordiality which, though it galled Jenny on the one hand, on the other raised her to a fever pitch of curiosity, which Laiah left unsatisfied.

"You'll think," said Mrs. Plopler, wiping the corners of her mouth, "that I just came in because I smelled a glass of tea."

"Of course not," said Ruth, who nevertheless wished that she had not smelled a glass of tea on this particular afternoon.

"You shouldn't have bothered. You'll be eating your supper in a few minutes. I was just passing, so I thought I'd drop in. We see you so seldom. Avrom never comes around, even though I've told him over and over again that he should feel as free in my house as in his own."

"When he comes home he's usually too tired to want to go out again," said Ruth. "He walks around a good deal in the afternoon. The fresh air makes him tired."

"Is he always this late?" Mrs. Plopler glanced at the clock. "In the old days if he came home this late Sarah, bless her, would be out looking for him. But it doesn't worry you much, eh?" Mrs. Plopler sniffed the air casually.

"He's a grown man," Ruth replied dryly. "And from what I can remember, my mother-in-law never spent much time searching the streets."

"Polsky drives him, then, so much?" Mrs. Plopler tried another tack. "At his age?"

"He doesn't get around as quickly as he used to," Ruth explained patiently. "It takes time. Why should he rush? Sometimes maybe he stops to talk with some of his old customers; sometimes he even says he's stopped for a glass of tea somewhere."

"Oh," said Mrs. Plopler, probing the air delicately with her nose. "Most people are busy preparing supper at this time of day. Who would be making tea? Certainly not somebody with a family."

"Can I fill your glass?" asked Ruth pointedly.

"Please," said Mrs. Plopler. "He never tells you? Look how late it's getting." Mrs. Plopler stirred her tea thoughtfully. "Do you know," she asked finally, "has it ever occurred to you"—she looked at Ruth with an air of searching mystery—"that he might think of remarrying?"

Ruth laughed outright. Mrs. Plopler leaned back in her chair. "Don't be so certain. Don't think you can trust them. What man waits till his wife has cooled in her grave? Sometimes I think my own is already picking and choosing. When you don't feel so well and you start thinking about how he'll go out right away when you're gone, to look for someone else, you want to spit in his face and say, 'No sirree, a faithful wife I've been to you all your life, and a faithful wife I'd be after you're gone. About you I'm not so sure, so maybe you should go first.' Of course," Mrs. Plopler hastened to explain, "those are only joking thoughts. God should keep him well. I'd much rather go first." Mrs. Plopler set down her tea glass and stared at it gloomily.

"Better you should stay well and not even think about such

things," said Ruth, glancing at the clock and wishing Mrs. Plopler would leave before Abraham came home.

"Ah." Mrs. Plopler sighed. "How can you help think about such things when you're under doctor's care?" Oddly, she smiled a secret, pensive smile. "You can call them doctors," she said, "but I call them men just the same. That's why I say don't be surprised, don't be surprised at anything a man does."

She'd wait until they were eating, Ruth decided. It would be a matter-of-fact statement, but firm enough so that it could not be brushed aside.

"Just a general checkup," Mrs. Plopler was saying, "because I wasn't feeling good." Mrs. Plopler raised her eyebrows, expanding her nostrils.

. . . a million details, Ruth knew. One couldn't rush into a thing like this without planning.

"So that's why he made me take off my clothes!" Mrs. Plopler expressed shock. Ruth looked at her, puzzled. "Just like that, you can believe me," Mrs. Plopler reiterated, "reaches his hand under the shirt and puts it on my breast." Mrs. Plopler showed how, clutching her unspectacular bosom. "Squeezes one, squeezes the other, pats, feels, takes his time, and all the time he's looking me right in the eye, and he says right out, not even ashamed to look at me"— Mrs. Plopler's voice was incredulous—" 'Lumps?' He calls them, just like that, 'Lumps?' I hardly knew where to look." Mrs. Plopler frowned, and her voice rose indignantly. "I wanted to say to him, 'I'll show you lumps, Doctor, I'll lump you one.' But how can you do that?" Mrs. Plopler's voice softened. "He's after all a doctor, almost a specialist."

"Maybe"—Ruth couldn't hide her smile—"he wanted to see if you had something in your breasts, heaven forbid."

Mrs. Plopler looked knowing. "He saw all right, and he felt too, you can believe me. I know it's hard to believe; I can scarcely believe it myself. 'Lumps.'" She snorted. "But I told him. I told him straight out. 'Ah, Doctor,' I said." Mrs. Plopler smiled a little, sadly, glanced sideways at Ruth, and sighed. "You're right, Doctor. They're not what they used to be."

On her way out Mrs. Plopler encountered Abraham and stopped long enough to tell him that·in the future he could drop in to her place too for a drink of tea, that if he could spend his afternoons drinking tea with people she was an old friend too.

How did she know where and with whom he had just had tea? Abraham had the feeling that the whole world was somehow trying to close in on him. Everybody knew things but himself. Everybody talked, hinted, made suggestions. The feeling grew even stronger that evening when Ruth announced that she had definitely decided to open a small goods shop of her own. Without even stopping to ask him how he felt about it, she outlined her plan. They were enthusiastic, she and the child. The boy was bubbling over with questions. Slower, he wanted to say—a little more slowly. But he did not seem to have the chance to bring out the words. They had already outstripped him, the two of them. Ruth was talking about the need to move quickly if she wanted to be put on the wholesalers' quota list. It had to do with the war. What had not to do with the war? Wholesale death now, a wholesale quota of death. What were these quotas?

". . . all the things I have to figure out," Ruth was saying. "Before I go to sleep I want to write out all the things I want to ask him."

"Ask whom?" said Abraham.

"Ask Harry, of course. Tomorrow I'm meeting him for lunch."

"Who is Harry?"

"Pa! Where have you been for the last hour? I've been talking all evening, and you still ask who's Harry. He's the salesman—I told you, the one who's going to help me." Ruth explained how she had always thought that this Harry was nothing but a big talker. But now he was turning into something altogether different in her mind, not only a keen businessman but a kindly person who was willing to help another along. For instance—and Ruth went on to detail some of Harry's suggestions, repeating how he had offered to let her have goods on credit and to cover for her himself. And she went on to explain the whole idea yet again.

Who was this Harry? It seemed strange to him that she was calling someone he didn't even know by his first name. If she called him Harry, then surely he called her Ruth already. It dawned on him again that she lived a life that was utterly unknown to him when she went off every morning to the heights to work. She dressed, she went away, she met other people. When Isaac had been alive there had been no need to think about the separate thoughts of each one of them. Except for the questions that he and Isaac argued about— and that was different—they had all been together as one whole, one unit, whose purpose was in all important respects the same. But now what did Ruth think about? Could it be true, what Laiah had said, that someday Ruth might start to think not of Isaac but of her own loneliness? Look at her now, all rosy and enthusiastic over some idea that a Harry had put into her head.

"Could I help?" the boy was asking eagerly. "Could I help you sometimes in the shop?"

"Of course." Ruth was laughing. "I'll need your help. I'll need a big man in the place."

Abraham looked from one to the other.

Chapter Fifteen

By early summer Ruth was ready to take a major step. At the supper table she announced her plan of action. Abraham was surprised. He had tried, it seemed to him, to find out what she had in mind, to take part. He had entered into discussions with her, made an occasional suggestion, sometimes even offered a bit of advice. But too often it appeared that what he suggested was not exactly the sort of thing she had in mind, or she was preoccupied and agreed readily with him while her mind was elsewhere. He hadn't realized how far her plans had progressed without him. She and this Harry the salesman had even looked over a location for the dry-goods store, an almost ideal location, she said. During her lunch hour Harry had taken her down in his car, and they had gone through the premises with the landlord. The place was farther up the avenue where Polsky had his business, right close to where the avenue intersected the main street as it worked its way up toward the heights. There were rooms that could be used as living quarters in the back. That meant that she could take care of the shop and the house at the same time. The boy would have to transfer to another school, but he would be able to come home for his noon-hour meal. It would be more convenient for all of them.

Although Ruth noticed that her father-in-law received the news in silence, she was too busy answering the questions of the boy to pay attention to the fact. Her mind was full of problems. After supper, when she had chased the child off to practice his violin lesson, Ruth busied herself, humming over the dishes, while she mentally went over the afternoon's accomplishment.

Abraham sat on at the table, raising his eyes every now and then

to her back. They had decided, she and this Harry. He shifted in
his chair and tried to concentrate on the few moments of pleasure
that he allowed himself every evening, the child's practice. Patiently
he would follow the notes, starting over and over the difficult passages, wincing slightly and tackling again the bits that did not go
right. Working with the boy, he did not have to think of anything else.
But now other things intruded. Who was this Harry with whom she
was on such intimate terms that he went with her to choose their
new home? And where had he, Avrom, been when all this was going on? Had he nothing to say? She had come home, and it was all
done and arranged for. Harry had spoken. Where was Avrom, who
had led his family across the seas, planting in them once more the
idea of life? Not only had his family been stripped from him, but his
word was no longer good enough even to lead his daughter-in-law
from one house to another. A strange Harry had suddenly appeared.
What did they speak of when they were together? How close had
their friendship grown if he now had the right to choose her home?

"*No!*" Abraham banged his fist on the table—not too loudly, for
he was conscious of the child practicing in the bedroom, but loudly
enough for Ruth to turn from the sink. "I'll not live in another man's
house!"

"What do you mean?" Ruth turned back to the sink to turn off the
water, and then turned again to him, picking up a towel at the same
time.

"You know what I mean—you know already." Abraham waved
his hand.

"What do you mean, I know what you mean?" asked Ruth, smiling
a little. "I'm not a mind-reader. What's bothering you, Pa? I know
you don't like to move out of here. But understand we've got to for
Moishe. We've got to think of his future."

"What do you care what I think of his future? What I say matters,
then? With strangers you go out to plan his future."

"Pa," said Ruth.

"Pa, Pa. Why do you still call me Pa?" he interrupted. "He hasn't
got a father, your friend? Better you should practice to call him Pa."

"What are you talking about?" Ruth's voice rose with the sharpness of surprise and incipient anger.

"Shout at me, bring the child in," said Abraham relentlessly. "He'll have to know sooner or later. Why do you have to pretend? Why can't you come right out and tell me? I'd rather be told now than thrown out afterward. Strangers have to tell me these things? You have no obligations to me. But don't try to tell me that this Harry of yours will want your first father-in-law living with you, reminding him of what your true husband was, reminding him that he is a usurper. Because I don't want it. I won't stand for it. A man can be twisted so far. I'll not be a stranger in my own house."

"What has Harry got to do with it?" Ruth was beginning to understand and made ready to explain patiently. "Pa, you're mixed up. Harry is just a friend. He's been very kind. He's not interested in me personally. He knows I want to start a little business of my own, and he's in a position to help me."

"First I'm mixed up, then I'll be a little sick in the head, then I'll be in my second childhood, then I'll be in the Old Folks' Home. It's just the way Chaim says. But you don't have to pretend. I'm not afraid of the Old Folks' Home. Send me now. I don't need any pretenses. Never in my life have I wanted pretenses. If I could just see a thing as it is and know what it is and where it is leading, I am content. But what of the child? Will you not even see how he feels? Do you think you can bribe him with a shop so that he will take just any substitute father?"

"For heaven's sake, shut up!" Ruth flung down the towel. "What are you talking about? Are you really going crazy? No, don't say a word. He's a married man, a man with three children. Do you understand? He's kind to me. Isaac was my husband too, not only your son. I loved him too. I want to do everything I can for our child. So why are you picking on me?" Ruth's voice had sunk to a tearthrottled whisper. From the bedroom the boy's violin continued its tranquil notes. For a few moments there was silence, between them only the vibrating threads of the violin. Ruth had picked up the towel again and had turned her back to him.

Abraham spoke again, his voice subdued, conciliatory. "A father has no choice in the new home, then?"

"I'm sorry, Pa, I didn't know you'd be annoyed. You work so hard; I thought I'd save you the trouble of wandering around with me, looking for places. This one isn't taken yet. That's why I mentioned it, so that you could come down and have a look with me." Ruth felt the tension beginning to seep out of her. Thank God she had held her tongue, had controlled herself at least partially after her first explosion. God knows when he had said those things to her she had wanted to scream at the injustice, at the unreason. How could he accuse her of seeking romance? Why did he twist little things so? She was surprised at the violence of feeling that these little flare-ups could arouse in her. It was as though there were stored-up feelings in both of them that neither had fully acknowledged or explained to himself. Always they managed to cut off the quarrel just in time, before a certain externally imposed control would be lost and feelings and misunderstandings that had never really come to life would be sparked into being. I won't be so nervous, she told herself, when we are finally settled.

"What did I tell you?" Laiah asked Abraham a bit teasingly. "Didn't I tell you she would fall on her feet? You don't really have to worry about her. She can take care of herself. Nowadays the women aren't what they used to be in the old country. They like to go their own way. They don't like to be interfered with. And they get what they want."

"I don't know," said Abraham. "It's all so quick. Why is he in such a rush? Why is he just like that so good to her? He is letting her have so much credit. There was a time once when I would have thought it was a natural thing for one man to hold out his hand to another. Now I wonder. I ask myself, is there something behind it? I ask her too, but she pooh-poohs my questions. All this talk about the war and quotas. He is too sharp. But what is it? Ruth goes ahead, and I must stand on the side and watch."

"She's young," said Laiah. "It is natural for the young to rush.

Sometimes I think that that is what's wrong with us. That's how we grow old. We grow afraid. We slow down. But life rushes on, and suddenly we find it's too late; we have slowed down too much, and life has rushed past us altogether. That's why I say live while you can. Ruth is young; she wants to live. She knows that while you are alive you must take advantage of life. You can't deny her that. And she wouldn't deny you, either." Laiah smiled at him earnestly. "Don't you agree?"

Her words reminded him. That's what he had intended to tell her. In his shame he had searched his memory to find out who had first planted the suspicion in his head that Ruth was planning to remarry. "My daughter-in-law," he said pointedly, almost accusingly, "has no intention of getting married." He wanted to add also that people shouldn't talk when they didn't know, but refrained.

"To whom?" asked Laiah blandly.

Abraham was momentarily disconcerted. Hadn't she herself suggested it? "To anybody," he insisted. "She doesn't even think about it. She looked at me as though I was crazy."

Laiah was pensive a moment. "I'm not surprised," she said finally, nodding. "From all you've told me I've guessed that she was that kind of woman. A woman like that isn't going to think first of herself."

Abraham watched her tongue suspiciously as it moved slowly across her lower lip.

"She will think first and foremost of her responsibilities," Laiah continued feelingly. "I admire that kind of person. You, the child, are first in her mind. You are a lucky man, Avrom."

He felt an unpleasant sensation about his heart. She was too quick. He had told her; it had been a clear and simple fact, and now, with a twist, it was something else. "I am not a responsibility for anyone," he said.

"No, not for someone who loves you." Laiah picked up the teapot and moved to the stove. "Someone who loves doesn't feel it as a responsibility," Laiah continued over her shoulder. "She is glad to cook and sew for you, and wash, and worry about you. I know."

Laiah moved back to the table with the pot refilled, and sat down. "If I had someone, someone that I loved, I would gladly do all those things for him and more. I would be a companion to him. Companionship is a thing that counts—you want to go to the same places and do the same things. Of course"—Laiah smiled and was aware of an irregular movement in her heart as she added—"you have to be closer to the same age for that."

"She thinks of the child. She wants to give him everything," he said. "It's not me. I won't hold her back."

Laiah nodded. "I know you're not selfish. Far from it. You would deny yourself because you would be thinking always of someone else. Ruth is probably that way too. And yet it's funny. People can deny themselves for each other's sakes and end up, with the best of motives, standing in each other's way. Sometimes it's kinder to be selfish. Not that I don't admire her, and you. Perhaps my whole life might have been different if I'd fallen among good people earlier. Now, frankly, it's something I long for. I'm sick of jealous tongues and nothing but insult from people for whom I've done nothing but good."

Was this how the world saw him, as standing in Ruth's way? He didn't want Ruth to deny herself for him. That was not even the question. They would not call him a duty, a responsibility, if they knew how life surged in him still.

"You would think"—he forced himself to attend to Laiah's words—"after you've known a person more than twenty-five years, and have been good friends all that time, that you could really rely on that person as a friend, wouldn't you? Know Polsky?" Laiah snorted. "And how I know Polsky. Where would Polsky be now if I hadn't known him? When others were throwing their money away buying stocks, shares, pieces of paper, I said to him, 'Don't be a fool!' Other ways, too, I helped him. What do you see now—Polsky the big businessman? I could tell you. Do you think a man with a full head himself could have passed on such a coconut to Hymie? And what was it all for, my friendship? Why did I give up— You'll never know what I gave up. Just so that now his pants are tight over his belly button he should remind me when he sees me winning a few cents in a game of cards that I have a bill owing in the butcher shop? In front of everybody, and not just once. Once it's a joke, all right, ha-ha. Once, twice, and then again. Tell me in the butcher shop if you have a complaint. But no, the big sport waits until I'm enjoying myself, until I'm winning, and then he starts to talk. What have the cards to do with the meat? So I said to myself, That's enough! I'm not such a welcome guest as I once was. I can do without them too."

Her bill. It was a good thing that she had reminded him. But how to speak now? He stood up. "Your bill—" he began resolutely.

Laiah flowed to her feet. "Yes," she said, "can you imagine? And you wonder why I'm so bitter against them. *Grobionim*. But I can handle them yet. I can imagine that you've had to swallow plenty too, in the years you've been with them. I'll tell you, if you ever have any trouble with them, just let me know. There are still a few things I can whisper in his ear. And he'll listen, you can believe me. No, no, Avrom, I'm serious. You don't have to be shy with me."

Just pay something on your bill. He wanted to say it but after what she had said the words wouldn't come out, not so bluntly. If she paid him something there would be no whining from Hymie. He didn't want her to whisper anything to Polsky. What was he that he should have to come to her to help him with his job? Laiah was smiling at him quizzically. He gathered up his strength. "You won't pay anything now on your bill?" It was out.

"My bill? Of course," said Laiah. She went to get her purse.

He sighed with relief.

"Tell me, Avrom," said Laiah as he marked her payment on the bill. "You hesitated to ask me, didn't you, after what I said? You mistook my meaning. It's not the paying that I objected to, although I think that for me Polsky can afford to wait a little. It's the time he picked to ask, and the way he did it. You needn't have felt embarrassed. With me you can always speak straight out, as I do with you.

"You see," she continued as he didn't answer, embarrassed, "I know people talk. They say I don't pay my bills. I have suffered from the jealousy of slanderers all my life. But you can see it's not so bad. I'm not so hard to deal with."

It was true. What did they want from her? "I don't listen to slander," he said.

"Avrom." Laiah moved with him toward the door and rested her hand gently on his arm as he stopped in front of it. "We've gotten to be good friends, haven't we, in the last little while? I at least have felt toward you as to a friend. When my heart was full sometimes I've felt I could let it out to you. It's good to know that there is someone to listen, someone I can call on. But then I think, can I really call on you? When do I see you? When you have to deliver an order. Is this our friendship? No. Then I think, Well, perhaps it's just a one-sided thing. I am just imagining that we are getting to know each other! But you too have told me things, have discussed things with me, haven't you?"

Abraham nodded. It was true that they had talked gradually more and more. It surprised him to realize it. In her earnestness Laiah was leaning forward, practically against him. He breathed in deeply, through his nose, of her perfume. His nose twitched slightly at the impact. He could distinguish the grains of powder on her face.

"Then we are friends! Avrom, even if there is no order for you to deliver, couldn't you find time to drop up sometimes for a few minutes? I haven't that many people I can call friends, and you haven't that many friends either, that we should act as though we were strangers, indifferent to each other. Sometimes in an evening you could drop around. We could talk or play a game of casino. We're not so old yet that we can't find ways to enjoy ourselves."

She waited for him to answer, while he, aware of the concrete reality of her presence, a presence he could not quite place in the scheme of his life, tried to weigh her words. "You are not so old," he said finally with a formal politeness that evaded direct recognition of what she had suggested.

Laiah laughed her throaty laugh. "You have never paid me a compliment before. I have always thought that you felt I was too—

well, too bright, too showy even. Perhaps I was. Oh, there are reasons. You dress, you show a happy face sometimes, when inside . . ."

It embarrassed him that she had been aware of his impression of her. He could not help the suspicion which came upon him every now and then that she was more than she pretended.

"I'll tell you what," Laiah said as an afterthought, her hand restrainingly on his arm, for his hand was already on the doorknob. "I don't know if you've noticed what a little scandal-maker my neighbor is across the hall. She thinks that just because we share a toilet she has to know everything else I do. Every time my doorbell rings she's there at her door, spying on me—why, I don't know. Why should you have her snooping around when you come? But we can fix that. Just a minute." Laiah fished in her handbag. "I have an extra key to the apartment. Here, you take it. No, no, take it, take it. Even when you're delivering you can come right in instead of having to wait outside. Sometimes I'm not at home. Why should you have to make two trips up those stairs? And why should she know everybody that comes to see me? Why should all the gossips in the house know? Go go." Laiah slipped the key into his pocket and practically pushed him out the door.

Listening to his steps receding down the stairs, Laiah wondered if with the key she had managed to plant an idea. Well, it didn't matter. He wasn't her very last hope. She could still find one or two who would be only too glad to befriend her. But she could not deny that this was different, though it irritated her that she had begun to take it so seriously. Well, why shouldn't she take it seriously? She would have to invite Jenny for supper again to get rid of some of the meat. It was exasperating to have to make an order at the butcher shop every time she wanted company. Better he should think of a use for the key.

That Laiah. She talked of friendship, like a friend, as though she cared. Why? Thinking about her as he walked down the street, he was momentarily aware of her presence, of the heavy scent, the mo-

bile lips that moved even when she wasn't speaking, of the generous volume of soft live flesh. He remembered the key that she had
slipped into his pocket. . . .

Ha! said Isaac. Chaim should only hear about this!

What should he hear? When should he hear? Avrom protested, feeling himself blush deeply. You think it's nice to tease your father?

I'm teasing you, then? Isaac asked. I can't even make a comment?
My father becomes a keeper of the keys, and I mustn't even con-
gratulate him!

Since when did you find your father an opener of such doors?
That's all I have to think about. And besides, she's making fun.
What could she want from me? I'm no card player, and money she
couldn't squeeze from me.

Maybe—Isaac laughed—it's you she wants to squeeze a little.

So that's what your mother and I slaved for, to bring up our son
to be a *grobion*. That woman— Well, never mind, whatever it is, if
that's what she wants from me, if that's what her door leads to, it
would be a fine way, eh, to agree that her way has been right all
along. What right would I have then to hope for a word, a sign? What
right would I have to mourn my sons? That you don't answer eh?
No, when it comes to that all is silent.

It remained silent. Abraham was sorry. Come, tease me a little
more, he suggested, but he knew that it was no use.

"Hi, Grampa!" Moses came running down the street, limping
slightly. Abraham's heart lifted. He bent forward as though to catch
the boy, and was a little disappointed when Moishe stopped running
just before he reached him. Well, he was a big boy already for such
games. Moses scuffed along beside him in the grass at the edge of
the walk.

"Your ma not home yet?" Abraham asked.

"No," said the boy. Covertly, critically he examined his grandfather's face as they walked along. It wasn't true. His beard was *not*
funny. What did they know about it? His grandfather was somebody,
not just a boozer like Dmitri's pa.

"You gonna grow a dumb beard like your grandfather when you grow up?"—from Dmitri.

"Ya," he countered boldly, because they weren't going to make fun of his grandfather and get away with it. "You better grow one too."

"Who, me? What for? Think I'm a crazy Jew?"

"Raise fleas," suggested Donald Gregory.

"No, I'll grow one because I'm a Jew," Moses said. "You grow one so you can tell your face from your ass." . . .

"Why are you limping?" asked Abraham.

"Nothing," said Moses.

"What do you mean, nothing? Show me," said Abraham. They stopped outside the gate, and the boy rolled up his pants leg. "Where did you get such a bruise? Did you fall?" The boy shook his head. "You were fighting?"

"No."

"That hooligan was hitting you again? I'll go over there and I'll—"

"No, it's okay. He's too dumb. I fixed him." Moses smiled, remembering his gibe.

"If he picks on you, tell me," said Abraham anxiously, letting the boy precede him at the gate. "I'll go over and—"

"Nah." Moses strolled ahead of him, hands in pockets and with more of a limp. "It's okay."

Pride swelled up in Abraham. So grown-up, so self-sufficient! Ordinarily he might not seem like such a wild one, but just touch his honor. With his grandson, as with his sons, that was no light matter.

Moses watched while his grandfather took a key out of his pocket and put it in the lock. It occurred to him that he could do it faster. His grandfather fumbled with the key in the lock, then took it out and examined it in a puzzled way. "Doesn't fit," he said, reached down into his pocket again, and finally fished out another key. The boy moved impatiently from one foot to the other. With his key they would have got in long ago.

Abraham swung the door open, and the boy rushed in ahead of

him. "Tell me what happened to you today," Abraham called after him as he followed him into the house. "What did you learn in Chaider? Tell me while I warm up our supper."

Moses had grabbed a comic book. "About Jacob," he said absently.

"Who?" said his grandfather.

"Jacob," he said a little louder.

"Ah! Our Jacob. Did she tell you how he wanted to be eldest, and when he and his brother Esau were in their mother's stomach and Esau started to be born first, Jacob grabbed his foot and tried to hold him back?"

"No, you told me already. But she told us the whole—"

"And did she tell you how Jacob wrestled with the angel of God for His blessing?" His grandfather went right on, without even hearing him. "He saw God face to face and he wouldn't let Him go until he got His blessing. That is a man."

"She told us that part," said Moses more loudly, "and all the rest," he added.

"Oh," said Abraham.

Moses was sorry. He didn't want to hear the story again now, but he was sorry that he had cut the words from his grandfather's lips so that he now remained silent, nodding his head. Moses pushed away the comic book. He didn't care that his grandfather liked to repeat a story over and over again and that he was different from other people, or that he wore a beard, either. He didn't think it was funny. "That Jacob," said Moses out loud and came close to where his grandfather stood peering into the pot that was warming on the stove. "It sure was a good story."

Abraham looked down at him a moment, then put his hand on his head. The boy pressed against him. "It's not just a story. Can you imagine what it would be to see God face to face? And to win His blessing? My blessing I give you with all of my heart. But to win for you His blessing. Ah!"

The boy moved restlessly.

"You haven't told me what you did today," said Abraham, fondling his hair. "Start from the beginning. I want to know everything."

"Oh." The boy shrugged his shoulders vaguely, and moved out from under his grandfather's hand, back toward the comic book on the table. "Nothing much."

He wouldn't tell her what Hymie had said. Little Ruth cared nowadays what he told her. Maybe, maybe she'd care. But if she cared she'd worry too. And she had enough on her mind to think about. Not that she had cared much when he had told her about Chaim's barrel, about how it had disappeared one day, just like that. Of course she couldn't understand why it should bother him so. Isaac, maybe, would have understood. He couldn't even remember how many years the barrel had sat there in the shop, even from before the renovations. Everybody knew it was Chaim's. Whom did it bother? It wasn't in anybody's way. But one morning, just like that, something was missing, the place wasn't the same. A presence was gone. And Hymie, strutting around with that just-ask-me smirk on his face. Hymie he hadn't asked. Polsky, yes.

"That barrel? What? I don't know." Polsky was very busy all of a sudden. "Ask Hymie. It probably took up space. What was it doing there anyway?"

He hadn't asked Hymie. He had searched, and when he had found nothing he had brought out a chair from the kitchen, where he ate his lunch, and put it in the place where the barrel had been. In case Chaim should drop in, though he dropped in much less frequently now and stayed at the green synagogue more, there should be somewhere for him to sit. And he had just wished silently in his aggravation that Hymie should say something to him, just even a word about it, and he would then be able to tell him; oh, he would tell him. Avrom was still a man who could fight. He could still show his fist. And he looked Hymie right in the eye when Hymie saw the chair, waiting for him to speak. But Hymie still had a little bit of respect for him, at least when they were face to face, and after a moment of silence he moved sullenly onto his seat behind the cash register. Not that the chair could make up for the barrel. It took up too much room. It could not be more than a gesture. He could not help thinking of how the wheel had turned, of how it was turning now still.

In what had happened this morning, for instance. "Avrom, I want you to meet my draft exemption," Hymie had announced in that exaggerated voice he used, as though a man were entirely deaf. A fat little girl. "We're getting married," Hymie boasted amid a good deal of girlish giggling, "right away."

Polsky had brought a bottle. The barber had come in. Hymie had filled up their glasses, and Morton's too. The little girl's he filled up twice in quick succession, and soon the giggling filled the shop with hard, tiny knots of sound that crowded the air. When she had started to make some remark, pointing at Abraham's beard, he had picked up his glass and moved toward the kitchen so as to avoid hearing this child make a fool of herself. It was then that he thought he heard Hymie say something about the highest-paid delivery boy in the city. He had stopped and listened, only to have his ears filled with hoarse laughter and staccato giggles. Was it himself they meant? Who could say that about him? He still did more than his share, and he could tell it right to Hymie's face!

All right, so he wouldn't tell Ruth. She would think he was afraid, maybe, for his job. But talk to her he had to. There were things that he had wanted to say now for days, that he had thought about again and again. His own problems he would keep out of it. She had enough to think about.

"I want you to know," said Abraham a little heavily, for it had taken him moments of struggle to get the words out, and even now he didn't know whether these were the words that he had wanted to speak, "that I will not stand in your way."

"What, Pa?" Ruth's reply was somewhat absent-minded. She sat, figuring, at the kitchen table, going over the initial outlay. She was beginning to be a little frightened about her business plans. Only God knew whether people would want to buy now. Harry assured her that people would buy, that these things would be scarce soon. That was why the wholesalers were beginning to operate on the quota system. He was putting her down for a little more than she would initially be needing, because he could get rid of the stock easily enough, and later on when her business was established she would be glad to get more. There was no real cause to worry. Wasn't he confident enough to advance her credit on this first big order? He made it sound so easy.

She was not listening. Abraham fought back a twinge of annoyance. It was as though nothing that he could say to her would be of any importance. How she had danced around his every word once; but no, it was no use to think of that. He had no right to reproach now. He would let her know that. At least she should listen to this much. He had waited for this moment all evening, had waited till the boy was safely in bed so they should not be disturbed. He had waited impatiently for the time to come when he would sit facing Ruth, and he would break through the silence or the triviality of the words they generally exchanged and talk at last in a way that had meaning to them both. And he would not bother her with trivial things, with his own aggravations. What he wanted was to talk, really, with understanding, with trust, to be able to feel that each knew what was going on inside the other even if he could not understand what was going on in the rest of the world. He wanted her to know, right from the start, that he would not be a responsibility, he who could still feel the sweep of life surging in him. "I want you to know that I will not stand in your way," he said again.

Ruth put down her pencil. "What do you mean, Pa?"

What did he mean? "I mean that you are young." Abraham furrowed his brows together and stared at his hands, which lay on the table. He could almost hear the drilling sound the pains made up and down his arms, through his wrists and down into each separate knuckle. He clenched his fists. "You're young," he repeated.

"You're worried," Ruth said gently, "that I'm taking on too much. You don't have to worry, Pa. It's not so much. It's a risk, I know; we might fail and then we'll end up even more in debt. But Harry says—"

"Why is he in such a hurry?"

"I've told you, Pa, he wants to get me on his customer list. They're starting this quota business at the wholesalers'."

"I don't know," said Abraham. "I don't know, but I won't argue with you. I won't stand in your way. I won't drag you back. What kind of a face would I have if people could say that I tried to rule you? I have no right over you."

"Who says you try to rule me, Pa? You know I'm always willing to take your advice. But we've talked about this before, and you can see for yourself that it's the only thing I can do if I want to better things for us."

Abraham nodded. His fists unclenched, and he drummed his fingers absently on the table. How to tell her that he too wanted to better things for them, but that it was no longer just a question of things? Things came and things went, just as a man could feel that his body grew older. But was this all? That was what he wanted to discuss. He did not want a barrier of polite words between them. All evening he had nourished this feeling that he would talk to Ruth and they would no longer be strangers. He would discover in her an ally; he would lose this feeling of uncertainty and irritation when she spoke of the future and made plans. Try as he might to hold it, the future seemed always to be moving away from him; her plans did not really include him. But why should they? It was true what Laiah said, and what even Sonya Plopler had hinted. She was young; she had a future still.

"Nevertheless," he said, "nevertheless I want you to know that you should not consider yourself tied to me. When you married Isaac you didn't know that you would end up with an old man to look after. I know I'm an old man. I'm not so blind as to think it's a good thing for you to be tied to an old father-in-law. It's not that I feel I am an old man; I feel I could build worlds yet, if I could only make them stand. But that is what shows I am old. A man is young while he thinks he knows. The old"—Abraham waved his hand and could not help the note of bitterness—"can only crouch in their corners and pray."

Ruth made as if to speak, but he held up his hand and went on.

"So I say to myself, Why should I keep her tied to me, invent another duty for her when I know that life will be hard enough? Why should you feel yourself bound? I am not blind. I can see that you pay me a courtesy sometimes, you ask my advice; not maybe because you really want my advice but because you think, you remember, Well, this is Isaac's father. I must acknowledge that he is still alive."

Again he held up his hand to silence Ruth. "No, the plans you make are your own plans; they don't need me. Who knows what plans you would have and what things you would think of—good things, I am not criticizing you—if I were out of the way?" Abraham ceased speaking, turned his hands over, palm upward, and flexed his fingers. Was this what he had wanted to say?

"Why do you talk of being in the way?" Ruth's voice reached out to him through the yellow silence of the kitchen. "Have I ever said that you were in the way? Pa, you should know by now that when I ask your advice it's because I want it. If I do things without asking you sometimes it's because there's so much in my head to think about. It's not because I don't respect your word. Why do you talk of being an old man? I know, I know why you talk this way. I can see that your arms are bothering you. When your arms bother you you get"—Ruth stopped herself just in time from saying "cranky"—"you get depressed. When you're ready for bed I'll bring you a hot-water bottle." Really, it was not fair at a time like this, when she had so much to think about, that he should talk this way. What more did he want from her? Ruth took up her pencil again and began to jot down more calculations on the paper.

Abraham watched her for a few moments. The drilling in his arms seemed to spread into a tingling restlessness in the whole of his body. "I don't want a hot-water bottle," he said finally.

It took a few seconds for his words to penetrate to Ruth. "Well"— she could not disguise the slight edge of impatience in her voice— "what do you want, then?"

"I want that when I talk to you, you should listen to me."

"But I am listening to you. Why are you talking like a child? If you don't want a hot-water bottle I'll make you a hot compress. Whatever you want I'll make for you. What more do you want?"

"Who would have thought once that what I said would be by you childish? There was a time once when you too listened, when my words rang in your ears and brought only sweetness from your lips. Yes, you'll do what I want, you'll stuff my mouth just so that I won't bother you, I won't be a nuisance. I don't want your compresses. I don't want your hot-water bottles." The peevishness fought inside of him with the bewildered feeling that this was not what he really wanted to say.

"I'm not saying that everything you say is childish. Why do you all of a sudden pick on a thing to make a fuss about, and then nothing I say or do is right? First you keep drumming it in my head that the shop will fail, the shop will fail, as if I haven't got enough fears of my own, and now—" Something in Ruth told her that she had said enough, that she should not press the matter further. She tried to be soothing. "We're all unreasonable sometimes. I know I am, and often you're unreasonable too." The truth was the truth. "I know that your arms are hurting now; I can tell already. So I want to do what I can to help you, but all of a sudden you've got a stubborn idea into your head that you don't want this and you don't want that. Well, what more can I say? I can't suffer your pains for you."

"Because it's not my arms, that's why. What do I care if they ache? It's bitter enough for me to be alive when they're dead. When did I say your shop would fail? Why should you suffer my pains? Why should I expect you should suffer my pains? Why should you suffer at all? And your shop won't fail either. I know you can make your way in the world without me, I know already."

"What do you mean, you know?" Something had communicated itself to Ruth, a nervousness. What criticism did he imply? Why should she have to stand for hints like this?

"I mean," he was saying, "what you say, that's what I mean. You can't suffer my woes. Why should you suffer me? Why should I always remind you of something that's dead? Why should you take it as a duty to tie yourself to someone you don't belong to when you might even want to marry another, make another family. I can see that's a thought you'll have in spite of yourself. Well, if it happens I want you just to say so, that's all. You see, now you're annoyed at me. We can't talk for a few minutes without you showing that you're annoyed. I say to myself, Who is she? What are you to her? Yes, she loved your son, and she was a good wife to him. What more can you expect? With me he was the future. You can still find a new tomorrow. Will you want yesterday dragging at your heels?"

"Why do you have to dramatize? Why do you have to feel so sorry for yourself?" said Ruth wearily.

"I dramatize? I feel sorry for myself? The truth by you is to dramatize? When I say to you it's your life, take it and do what you like with it, this is by you to feel sorry for myself?"

"Thank you," said Ruth ironically, "thank you very much for giving me my life, for telling me that I can run around with men in the streets, for telling me that I couldn't have felt the pain you did when my husband died, and for letting me know I don't belong. All of a sudden I don't belong." Ruth's voice was beginning to rise, to sound cracked and ugly in her own ears. Try though she might, she could not stop. "I have this much of a home, of a family left, and you want to take this away from me too. How much does a person have to give to be accepted, to be taken in, and not to have it thrown up to her that she is a stranger? When my child was born and right away you said that he would be named after your sons I said nothing. Did I ever say to you that I too had a dead father and mother whose names I wanted should live in my children? No! I kept still to please you, to please Isaac." Ruth felt the tears rising and dug her knuckles into her eyes, trying to stem the onrush. But it came anyway, overwhelming now that it had broken to the surface. Stupid, stupid, she told herself, to become upset, especially now. What did he want from her? Why didn't he leave her alone?

The sound of her sobs rasped along his nerve ends, quivered through his body to his fingertips. He had come too far. He had come, begging to know, to understand, and suddenly a mirror had been flipped up in his face and he himself stood revealed as he was

to another—a stranger, an enemy, an egoist. "But I didn't mean—"
He grasped wildly. "I didn't think then— What? You've held this
against me all these years, without saying anything?"

"What could I say?" Ruth was sorry that she had spoken. "I let
it go, I forgot about it. Never mind."

"It's not true. Who could forget about it? If you had said anything
— You think I didn't think of your parents? I thought of the boys—
they were so young, their names should be carried first because of
their broken lives. There were to be other children. Where are they?
Did I say you should stop having children, just like that? And if you
had said anything, a word, the child could have had a longer name.
But no, you wanted to have something against me. You enjoyed seeing me trying to be a good human being, and saying to yourself all
the time, Yes, but how he's wronged me."

"No," said Ruth. "That's not true. I didn't want to push myself,
to make a fuss. I knew how much they meant to you. It was your
family, your house. I wanted to belong too."

"My family, my house," Abraham choked out. "As if I didn't try
to do everything for you that you wanted. How many times did I
see you take the child and turn away from Sarah when I knew she
was dying to hold him in her arms? Did I say anything? Yes, once
I mentioned to you that Sarah liked to carry him around sometimes.
And you said, 'But I'm so afraid she'll drop him'—as though she
were a cripple. As though she hadn't raised three such, such godly
sons. And never once did she drop them. But your son she wasn't
fit to hold, when holding him meant renewing her life itself." Something inside of Abraham hammered a counterpoint to his words. Was
this it? Was this the only communication they could make with each
other, tearing like beasts at the raw entrails and the naked heart?

"I know you've blamed me for everything." Ruth's voice was low
but razor-sharp. "When he died, and you came in, I could see by
the way you looked at me that you were thinking, Why wasn't it she?
Why didn't she die instead? And I wish it was!"

"What are you saying?" He tried to interrupt, but she went on.

"It's nice to have someone to blame, isn't it? Not only am I blamed for living, but now I killed Ma. I never let her play with the child. Something new? Sometimes I was selfish, keeping the child to myself, because I loved him, because I had something of my own for the first time in my life and wanted to hold onto it as much as I could. So I killed Ma by you. I killed Ma." Ruth gestured at herself as she spoke. Then she leaned forward, her eyes fixed and her face slightly distorted in his eyes as she leaned closer. "And what about you? Who was it who wouldn't let them take her to the hospital when they might have saved her life? What did we tell you? What did the doctor tell you? But no, you thought she shouldn't go to the hospital and she didn't go to the hospital. You know where she went instead."

"You can say this? You can think this?" He choked on the words. It was as though another vital part had been slashed away from him, and he was all contorted, trying to hold his wounded members in place and at the same time trying to fend off with his own fury the fury that threatened to dismember him entirely. "All this time you have lived in the same house with me, calling me Father, fussing over me, and thinking this of me! I knew; she knew, I tell you. And the doctor knew too. She didn't want to die among strangers. She begged me not to send her away. What could I do? Even the doctor said it wasn't necessary. He sent the tent. He even said once it might be dangerous to move her. Do you think I would have kept her if— if I thought— I could swear by God, by the Almighty—"

"You thought. You and God together are always thinking. Whatever is convenient for you God happens to think. Where do you keep Him, this God of yours, in your coat pocket? What others think doesn't matter. As long as you—"

"Yes, what I— Now I know where the atheistic thoughts came from, that were trying to pervert my son—"

"You know, you know; what do you know?"

He raised his voice to shout her down. "And I can still think a few thoughts yet." She glanced toward the room where the boy slept, and he automatically lowered his voice. "I can still remember a few things yet. You've never had your way, have you? What about when you decided just like that that the child should have spectacles. Nothing would do but for you to take him to a doctor and get him a prescription so he should look like a little—like an old man and all the children should laugh at him. Did Isaac want him to have glasses? No! He needed them like I need the creeping plague. You had to show the neighbors that we could afford to get him glasses. How much does he wear them now? But you said glasses, so it was glasses."

Ruth choked on a semi-hysterical laugh. "Thank you, thank you. I try to look after my child and now you tell me I make a fool of him. It's nice to know how you really thought your own grandson looked. I took him to the eye doctor because I could see there was something wrong. If I hadn't taken him then he might have had to wear the glasses all the time now. But no, don't let me change your mind. It was just vanity. I just wanted to impress the bootleggers all around us that we could afford to throw away money on glasses."

"It's never been good enough for you, this house, has it? The living he made for you was never good enough. You're too good to live with bootleggers. They don't breathe like you, my lady." Somewhere at the back of his mind there was a horrified admiration for the way he could rip her words from his own wounds and with a twist send them, like knives, whistling back at her.

"And when I was pregnant—" Ruth was sobbing continously now, so that her words emerged in choppy, jetlike gasps. " 'A hospital? What does she need a hospital for?' " Her voice rose and fell as she imitated him, her arm extended in one of his characteristic gestures. " 'My wife didn't need a hospital, so why should she go to hospital?' " Ruth buried her face for a moment in her hands. "What did it matter to you that I was frightened? You didn't believe in hospitals, so that was enough. You wanted me to have my child like an animal, in pain. You didn't have to feel the pain."

Her sobbing was like that of a child, and like a child she looked, in a crushed heap across from him. Abraham was beginning to feel the hard shell of anger melting away from him, which had dulled the pain of her attacks. "I didn't know you were frightened," he said hesitantly. "But you went to the hospital," he reminded himself desperately. "I didn't really stop you."

"No," said Ruth. "Isaac wouldn't let you. Over some things he decided he had to be a man and not just a—a figment of your imagination."

"A what, you say?" An ominous fear seemed to pervade him now, an anxiety not to hear any more, and a premonition about what he might yet be made to hear. The tension was building up inside him again as he faltered. "What is this figment?"

Her words toppled over his. "Why did he kill himself working at ten different jobs at once, if not to prove that he was something you thought he was? With a heart like his he had to run around from morning till night? You wanted one son should make up for three. What did you care that God only gave him heart enough for one."

"It wasn't ten," he protested. "He didn't work for me. How can you say he worked for me? He was working for you, for your future and the child's. I didn't make him work—and did you try to stop him?"

Ruth's answer was a short, choppy laugh, disdainful, contemptuous, as it seemed to him. "Stop him? How could I stop him? I knew what it meant to him. You may throw my miserable life up to me. I know I'm nothing to you. But I tried. Every one of your crazy ideas, because you were Isaac's father; I didn't say anything; I didn't mix in. How many times did Isaac come to me, even before we were married, and tell me—" Ruth choked on the words, covered her face.

"What did he tell you?"

The atmosphere in the room was like a live thing pressing down on them. Because of the child, because at the back of her mind was the thought, even in her blind anger, that they must not wake the child, Ruth had not screamed her words, but they had issued from her throat like jets of steam, hissing in his face, scorching him, searing his ears, which strained in spite of him to hear damning words. And somehow this sudden choking off of the flow, this sudden silence on her part was worse to him than anything that she had said. "What did he tell you. *What* did he tell you?"

But Ruth, sobbing, shaking her head violently in the negative, kept her hands pressed tightly to her face. The sudden wash of regret that had cut off her words had shocked her back to reason.

Her unintelligible sobs, her sudden withdrawal that seemed like a deliberate refusal to answer him, left him in a sort of a vacuum. Inside himself forces pressed for an explosion. He sprang up, pushing his chair raspingly back from the table. He began to pace to and fro, like some animal pent up. He pounded one fist into the open palm of the other. "You lie," he whispered hoarsely. "Tell me you lie! What would my son say about me? It's you who tricked him into marrying you with your nice words and pretenses. You think I haven't noticed how, after he was dead, almost on his deathbed, you were painting your lips already and dressing and fussing over yourself? Right away you had to go to work." He scarcely even heard what he said now. His words came rushing and pouring out. "When did you fuss for him, eh? And now that he's dead and you know he can't come forward to show how you lie you want to spoil for me even the little pleasures of memory. But he sees you. I won't curse you for trying to tell me that I killed my own son. He sees you and that's enough. He sees your lowness, your tricks. He sees you with other men, yes, and married men too—you admit it yourself. So, say something now, try now to come between me and my dead!"

"Pa," she brought out, "Pa, I didn't mean, it's not—"

"No, nothing. I won't hear it. Not another word you say. Enough of your lies. I know what you are now."

The volume of her sobs rose; long, twisted reptile sounds snaked around him, enveloping him and crushing the flimsy coat of anger in upon himself so that he was suffocating with the actual, physical sense of their accusation. "Cry"—he made a desperate attempt to defend himself against them, but the very word was choked in his throat as he turned to flee from the contracting room. The ugly, broken wail of her sobs pursued him as he ran through the living room, the hall, and out of the house. As though invisibly propelled, he headed through the hot summer air, unaware of direction, scarcely aware even of the piston movement of his legs, and totally unaware that he was speaking his thoughts aloud to the night air around him.

At first they were jumbled thoughts, full of his grievance against Ruth, against the things she had said, against the sins of which she had accused him. But her words remained and curled themselves, like some monstrous growth, around all that he had thought was good in his life. And they were true. What things had he said to her? Even in defending himself he had degraded and besmirched himself, and now stood revealed by everything that had happened as something utterly different from that to which his soul had aspired. Never before had he quarreled like that, aiming his words like blows, not to enlighten or persuade but to maim, to hurt. How had he started; what had he meant to do?

Had he really been a man like that, selfish, thinking only of himself? What had Isaac thought of him? How had his dream appeared to them, his sons? Had they seen him as Ruth saw him, as he now saw himself? Was it for his own pride that he had dreamed his sons into heroes, so that he could boast that he was the father of such marvels? Was this why they had been taken from him? He had gone about, seeking only to know, to understand what had happened. Was this his answer, that not only the dream was lost but also the dreamer?

Abraham walked. He walked downhill to the very bottom of the flats, where the warehouses backed to the river. He walked upward again aimlessly, running sometimes with the urgency of his thoughts. He passed their house again, without noticing it. He passed Polsky's shop, where, although the butcher shop and the delicatessen had long been closed, a light still burned from behind the curtain of the kibitzarnia, where often the game went on till daybreak. Never before had he felt this way, this internal accusation that he himself was not worthy, that it had all been his fault. "I wanted everything for the best," he tried to reassure himself distractedly, aloud, "not just for myself, for them, for the world. If it was not meant to be, why did I feel it? Didn't he save the Torah? It's not true what she said. I made nothing up myself. I trusted."

Two late pedestrians turned to watch the bearded old man rush, railing, through the night. Once a motorist swore at him. But he was unaware. Not until his thoughts had worn themselves out completely in their frantic dance and lay in one throbbing, undifferentiated mass, aching in his brain, did Abraham pause to lean his head against a fencepost, as though he could no longer support what it contained.

The warm wind of a summer night, tugging persistently at Abraham's beard, pulled him gradually out of his stupor. Slowly he raised his head and looked around him. He pushed himself away from the fencepost and took a few steps forward. He stopped again irresolutely. Where? The stars, distant and cool, posed indifferently in the sky. There was no command. Only the wind, threading the hair on his face, whispered teasingly of life.

Gradually his surroundings assumed a familiar shape. His eyes focused on a window on the top story of a familiar house. There came to him the whole puzzling aspect of his life to which she, this woman, seemed strangely related. Hadn't she lurked always in the shadow of their new life in the city? A shadow moved now, past her lighted kitchen window. Somewhere must be the thread to unravel the knotted skein. Others had been led. He would trust. He would follow. He would even, if necessary, demand.

He crossed the street. He started the long climb up the stairs. He was tired in every part of him, and every separate movement seemed to require his complete concentration. He labored upward under a growing heaviness, as though he were carrying his whole life on his back up an endless flight of stairs. With each step the burden grew heavier, the stairs longer, the object dimmer, and the need greater. Slowly his limbs carried him. Several times he had to stop to catch his breath. But he could not remain for long in the vacuum of no movement. He pushed immediately on again, for it was absolutely necessary to reach the top, as though something important, after this arduous journey, must await him.

He stood for a moment in the dark of the landing, uncertain, with no more stairs to climb. Automatically then he groped for the doorbell. The sharp clamor of the bell was startling. He began to ask himself what he was doing here, but the incipient question lost itself in the dream familiarity of the moment. It had occurred to him at various times in his life that a scene seemed to welcome him back, as though he had been and was come again. All of it, Laiah's face framed in the doorway, the instantaneous change of expression from frightened suspicion to surprised pleasure, nudged for a moment at his memory, as though this had been promised or foreseen, and was gone. What remained was her immediate presence, the way she pulled him, after one swift glance behind him at the door across the landing, into the apartment, and his own surprise and lack of surprise that he should be here.

"Oh!" Laiah gasped, leaning for a moment against the closed door and holding tightly onto his arm with one hand. "You gave me such a fright. People don't usually ring my doorbell at this time of night. But come in, come in." She moved along beside him into the light of the kitchen. "You're welcome any time. I always tell my friends that they can drop in whenever they wish. But did you lose the key? Well, never mind. . . ." Laiah could feel that she was prattling but could not, for the moment attend carefully to what she was saying and deal with her internal feelings at the same time. The surprise, yes, she could have dispensed with the instant of fright when her doorbell had suddenly rung at this time of night. But his sudden appearance, disturbed—she could see he was disturbed; it must have been a struggle for him; she could understand that too. But here he was. She could hear herself chattering on, ". . . midnight snack. Sometimes I can't get to sleep without it, would you believe it? Every time—it seems to me that every time you see me I'm eating. That's where the weight comes from. But I was just saying to myself that in the old country we didn't care about weight, did we? Everything was more natural there."

Inwardly she exulted. He had to come! All of a sudden the weight that she was talking about seemed to fall away from her. Her body felt an internal glow of pleasure such as she had not known since— oh, since a time that might return again. She could feel herself almost blushing under the disturbing steadiness of his eyes, and her own eyes slipped modestly to focus on his beard. Her fingertips tingled to caress that beard, and the tingling spread, an almost invisible shudder, through her body.

Was this love that she felt? She had asked herself this question before in an ironic way when she realized how seriously she had begun to take what she called her "teasing" of him when they had tea together, a teasing which consisted of finding out, of probing to see what he felt and could feel. Not love, she had insisted then, but a kind of game. What else could you do with a man who took you so rigidly at your word? She had urged him to sit and talk sometimes, so he sat and talked sometimes. Often she had had to laugh afterward. But then it had occurred to her, wasn't this a sign of respect for her as a person? Well, now he was ready for more, and now, in an access of grateful emotion, she was willing to let it be love, let it be anything as long as she could go on feeling this way—young, alive, ready again to show the world. She had scarcely stretched out her finger really, she felt now, and he had come—not just anybody, this man. Look how he suffered from it, his face strained, his eyes dark—for her.

Laiah's eyes moved with pitying tenderness over his face. She had an impulse to lean forward and whisper those words, as though he might recognize and respond to them. "Little daughter," her bearded master had whispered as he had crawled in beside her on the stove. "Little father," she had whispered. But this was no Russian landlord to give her a pair of shoes and a hat with a feather. He would give her back more, all that had been taken since and all that had been freely given. Laiah felt suddenly voraciously hungry.

Abraham waited, not quite sure in his mind what he waited for, not quite clear in his mind what he was here for. Her vivacity confused him. It was not what he had expected. What had he expected? While she was making a whole pile of sandwiches, as if she expected guests at this time of night, he looked around him, examining the tiny kitchen, then turned his gaze through the door into the darkness of the bed-living-room and the hall, as though perhaps someone or something hid waiting there. Nothing. He faced the sandwiches again, which Laiah was urging him to eat. He noticed with a craftsman's twinge of disapproval that she did not wipe the bread knife when she finished slicing a tomato, but left it on the table with tomato juice and seeds clinging to it. He couldn't eat, but watched her orange lips fold themselves over a sandwich like separate, living, predatory things. Laiah, chewing, shook her head and made sounds to indicate that the sandwich was good and to encourage him to eat. Abraham shook his head again, picked up the knife, and with a paper napkin wiped it carefully dry. Beyond his uncertainty and his feeling that for some reason he had been brought into an alien place, he was conscious of a special awareness, of a reaching out of his senses. Sensations impinged on him sharply and separately. His eyes brooded on her face, on the masses of orange-auburn hair that lay on her shoulders now in little-girl fashion. This was so far removed from his own life, and yet— Her words had never sent him weeping into the streets. He felt an uprush of resentment against Ruth, and immediately a counterwashing sense of his own guilt, his own degradation.

"You won't have anything to eat or drink?" Laiah repeated. "Well, I won't press you." She wiped the breadcrumbs away from her mouth and pulled her chair closer to his corner of the table so that her knee brushed against his. Why didn't he speak? It flashed across her mind that he must have waited until his daughter-in-law and grandson were asleep and then sneaked out. How this must have been growing in him. And she hadn't even gauged it, really. She had thought that maybe— But who could tell, with him? Well, this secrecy was fine for now, for now it was all right. Later on— Already she could see herself dropping by the butcher shop to look in on her husband. Who would say anything to her in the kibitzarnia then? She might even consent to play a game occasionally if they would bite their vulgar tongues. And on the High Holidays she would go with him to the new synagogue they were building in the heights, to worship before the miracle Torah that her stepson had saved. She would sit with the richest women in town. But all that for later. For now— Laiah stretched her arms back; her breasts heaved forward momentarily. Then with a sigh she dropped her arms, wriggled her shoulders slightly, and leaned toward him, smiling.

"Well, Avrom, you've come to see me." She looked sideways at the table and added tenderly, "At last." Her voice was low, resonant. No use to be coy. He had come to her, distraught, disturbed. She would show him that she understood.

The words caught at his mind. He withdrew his eyes from her breasts, glancing at her guardedly, searching her face. Laiah put her soft hand over his, which toyed restlessly with the handle of the bread knife. "Yes," she began again as Abraham turned his eyes to her hand, which moved gently on his own—a soft, opulent hand with an odd red freckle here and there. The underlying throbbing in his fingers, on which was now superimposed the caress of her hand, seemed to draw all the nerves of his body to that hand. But this seemed to be taking place apart from him. In another region entirely his ears strained for her next words.

"Yes," said Laiah softly, caressingly, her words playing, like her hand. "I've waited a long time," she said a little chidingly.

"You have waited for me?" Now it seemed to him that she was beginning to reveal herself. If he listened now, if he could seize the right moment to ask the right question— It had been done in stranger ways. Something about this woman . . .

How tense he was! All she had to do was to lean over and pull his beard, and she would be in his lap in a minute. No, not yet—not with him. "Those times you've come here and sat with me for a few minutes, I could see that you knew, that you had felt it too, underneath. Further back even, from the first time I saw you in Polsky's shop, I could feel it. There was an affinity between us. I've always known that we'd be friends someday, good friends—maybe even more. Polsky"—Laiah gestured with the hand that had lain on his own—"even Polsky was—" She shrugged. "How could he understand me really?" Laiah said this with satisfaction, and her hand dropped back onto Abraham's hand and squeezed it slightly.

"You've known?" he repeated as though to himself. "You've waited?"—through all those years when he had suffered and labored and sweated to rebuild? He began to be afraid. Something he had expected, something he had wanted to know. Now he felt suddenly that it was late at night; he wished suddenly that maybe she wouldn't go on. All this turmoil in one part of him, while another was deathly still, intent, listening.

"How often I've thought to myself this last little while," Laiah continued when he said no more, "what a crazy world we live in. All this time that we've known each other, you and I, aware of each other; how often we've moved toward each other a little bit, feeling that somehow there was an affinity, that we were made to come together." Still he was silent. "I'm not hiding anything from you, Avrom. I know you must have heard stories. I was married once—better not to talk of that now. What do people understand? And besides, can you say"—she faced him challengingly—"that there are things you don't regret?"

"You have never had any children?" he said.

The statement—she didn't know whether it was a question or a statement—seemed so totally unrelated that Laiah was for a moment startled out of her train of thought and gave him a very puzzled look. But almost immediately another possibility occurred to her, and she laughed outright at the absurdity. Did he think she was a spring chicken? "I am not likely to have any accidents," she said. "Even if I had to worry I could handle that. I am not anxious for any more responsibilities either. I like children, mind you. But after all— And, you know, I'm not as young as I once was either." She couldn't help the coyness. Could he be so naïve? She felt again very young and carefree. She looked at him amorously, caressingly.

He could hardly look at her. It was as though he were seized up by something within himself, by a strong hand that gripped his insides tightly, then released them, gripped and released and gripped them again, each time more tightly, so that he seemed to rise and fall on a mounting wave of nausea, accompanied by a feeling of self-hatred that had grown on him from the moment, ages back, when he had left Ruth and the house.

"All my life," he burst out, "I have wanted only one thing: to grow, to discover, to build. Of all the voices that are given to a man I took the voice of praise; of all the paths I chose the path of creation, of life. I thought that merely in the choosing I had discarded all else. I thought that I could choose. One by one, with such ease, they were stripped from me. Wherever I look there is a shadow, a shadow that all my life I did not see, I tried to ignore. The shadow grows about me, filling in the corners of my emptiness, darkening my desire. You've waited for me, empty, all this time."

Laiah had listened patiently. She had heard, in an occasional word dropped around the kibitzarnia, that Abraham was not quite the same as he had been once, since his son had died. She could understand that. If he wandered off sometimes, as though trying to argue something out with himself, that was all right too. She could ignore it. But she was glad when his rambling took an understandable turn. "Yes, I've waited." He was right. What did the others really mean now? It was so simple. She gestured with her arms, empty and waiting.

"Why?" the question, momentous, was whispered from his throat.

Laiah didn't answer. Her eyes, large and moist, widened under his own. The game was deeply exciting to her now. Not since a very long time ago had she played it with such enjoyment, had it seemed so new, with whispered words and shadowy nuances. And he took it so seriously.

She didn't answer either. His impatience grew. "Why?" He was on his feet suddenly, leaning over her.

Startled at what was almost a shout, Laiah recoiled an instant. Then, looking up at him, conscious that her flimsy housecoat was open and that her nightgown was even flimsier, Laiah paused before she said defiantly, laughing a little, "Because." With a sudden gliding movement she pushed one hand through his beard, up his cheek and around to the back of his neck. At the same time she came to her feet and pressed herself up against him. "Because of this." She laughed deep, throaty laughter and moved against him. Abraham swayed against the table.

"Closer," Laiah murmured into his ear, "like one."

"Like one?" he repeated dazedly, feeling as though he really were sinking into the mass of her flesh. She was pressed up so close to him that it was almost as though she really were a part of him. "Why did you wait," he managed, "right from the beginning, watching me?"

She laughed again, brushing his beard with her lips.

"Because you knew?"

She laughed compliantly. "You ask so many questions. Haven't I told you? Of course I knew."

"Like one," he whispered. The other part of him—that was empty, unbelieving, the negation of life, the womb of death, the black shadow that yet was clothed in the warm, tantalizing flesh of life. Now she pressed herself closer to him, inward. She was bent slightly backward so that with one arm he was forced to support her, achingly, to keep her from falling. They swayed together, he back against the table and she falling now against him. His free hand reached behind him for support on the table. He felt a sharp pain in his palm as the blade of the bread knife bit into his hand. He moved his hand, which had suddenly become sticky, and brushed it feebly against his trousers before he braced it again on the table.

No matter what a man did, no matter how hard he tried, no matter how great his desire, was it all reduced to this, to a dream pantomime of life, a shadow of meaning? Did he come at last to accept the shadow, to embrace the emptiness, to acknowledge his oneness with the fruit without seed, with death, his other self?

Laughing, Laiah had reached up her other hand and was tangling her fingers in his beard. "Little father," she murmured in Ukrainian, "will you be good to me?" Her fingers gripped his beard, and she began to pull lightly. "Come into the bedroom," she whispered into his ear. Her fingers tightened. Her body undulating, she tried to pull him by its very movement after her.

"Don't!" he almost shouted. "Don't touch my beard."

"Shhhh." She giggled.

His beard, where she was tugging it, began to tingle in every hair root. His arm that was around her was painfully tensed, the pains shooting up and down raspingly from his shoulder. "Don't." He tightened his hold and pulled backward. Isaac had grasped his beard. The thought of Isaac made him pull his head back sharply and twist it frantically, trying to dislodge her hand.

"Does it hurt? Hurry, then." Laiah laughed. "You have to get home sometime, don't you? You don't want your Ruth to know you've been out all night. She'll be waiting for you," Laiah teased, "if you don't hurry. Listen, we can talk another time. I trust you. I'm not worried about you."

Her words brought back to him his scene with Ruth. His mind zigzagged back and forth from Ruth to the present moment, rebounding from the unreality of each. "I've hurt her," he mumbled.

Why did he hesitate? His hesitation caused a misgiving to stir inside of her. She didn't want any misgivings! She threw back her head and leaned against his arm, her hair flowing downward, her lips slightly parted, so that, she knew, he could see into the front of her housecoat. Then she raised herself slowly forward and, opening her eyes wide, looked into his. The nether part of her body moved all the while with practiced, lazy voluptuousness. "Do what you want with me," she urged. "I'm yours."

Abraham looked into the auburn eyes, the strange, indrawing, familiar auburn eyes. Again the sense, as of some past memory just beyond his grasp, nagged at his mind.

Still he did nothing. "Don't you love me?" she said, tugging his beard slightly to pull him out of his trancelike stillness. "Say you love me," she urged. "Come." Above everything else she wanted now that her moment should not become absurd. She stifled a resentment that was growing toward him for allowing it to begin to seem so.

He pulled his head back. Love—that word too played along his consciousness as though it belonged somewhere, and he could not quite place it.

"Come," she whispered. "I won't wait much longer." She gave a more violent pull that almost toppled them both over. He grabbed wildly back at the table again; bread crumbs glued themselves to his raw palm and stung. His hand grasped finally the smooth handle of the bread knife. He managed to keep his balance, but she moved a step backward, taking him with her.

"You want me," Laiah was whispering almost pleadingly, tightening the arm that was about his neck. "I can feel that you want me. I've known all along that you wanted me."

"All I have ever wanted," he protested distractedly, "is to build for my sons, to grow."

"Forget," she said impatiently, "forget all that. They're dead; we're alive."

Just like that she came out with it, just like that, as if it were something good, while her body heat glued her to him, stifling him, trying to stifle his memory. They were dead, and he was lost, and the present was as a dream in which he could find neither them nor himself but only this insidious excitement, urging him to forget.

"Avrom." There was an almost childish petulance in Laiah's voice that tried further to confuse him.

What are you? he wanted to ask her. Who sent you to mock me? Who? And the thought leaped, as though it had been waiting, electrifying, terrifying, to his mind. One he could seek who knew, who would speak if he asked, who would give if he offered—if he had the courage.

Suddenly Laiah sensed a change in him. She realized that she was no longer maintaining the embrace but that it was he who now strained her against him, holding her up. She felt a thrill of relief as his eyes moved with awareness over her. "Come into the bedroom," she murmured again. She let her eyes flutter closed under the ardency of his gaze.

Looking at her then, he was lifted out of time and place. Lifetimes swept by, and he stood dreaming on a platform, apart, gazing at her with fear growing in his heart, and somewhere his Master, waiting. As in a dream, the knife was in his hand, the prayer was on his lips. Praying over her, at some neutral point in time, he saw her as though for the first time, and yet as though he had always seen her thus, saw her as something holy as she lay back, a willing burden, to offer, to receive, as once another . . . From inside him a tenderness swelled toward her, and for a moment he forgot his fear and felt as though he were almost on the point of some wonderful revelation.

". . . *Eloheinu Meloch Hoaul'om* . . ."

Laiah heard with amazement the Hebrew words. Even over this he has to make a blessing. Her lips twitched to a smile.

. . She was laughing at him, still teasing him, his despair wreathed in smiles, the negation of his life. And yet there was something in him that ached to see how under her eyelids her eyebulbs were large and fine. Her forehead wrinkled and was somehow sad, like that of some time-forgotten creature that had crept out to seek the sun. Her hair flowed endlessly downward, falling gently over his arm. All this he could see, in the sacred place where he stood, and he could feel that it was trying to speak to him, to explain itself, for the moment was near.

Now, now was the time, in the stillness, as he stood once again, terrified, fascinated, on the brink of creation where life and death waver toward each other, reiterating his surrender; now was the time for the circle to close, to enclose him in its safety, in its peace. There must be a word, with them, in the room, hovering to descend. Almost it reached him there, beyond his mind, like the voice of a child, stuttering, excited, trying to break through the barrier of sound. He strained to hear.

"For God's sake!" In an access of impatience Laiah's hand tugged sharply at his beard. "Hurry up!" Her voice jarred like a harsh command. "My back is—"

Even as his arm leaped, as though expressing its own exasperation, its own ambition, its own despair, the Word leaped too, illuminating her living face, caressing the wonder of the pulse in her throat, flinging itself against the point of the knife. Life! cried Isaac as the blood gushed from her throat and her frantic fingers gripped first, then relaxed and loosened finally their hold on his beard. Life! pleaded Jacob as Abraham stared, horrified, into her death-glazed eyes. Life! chanted Moses as he smelled, sickened, the hot blood that had spurted onto his beard. Life! rose the chorus as the knife clattered to the ground, and the word rebounded from the walls and the floors and the ceiling, beating against the sudden unnatural stillness of the room, thundering in accusation against him. Weightier in death, Laiah pulled him to the ground.

Kneeling, he cradled Laiah in his lap. "Please," he whispered. With one hand he propped her head, which sagged grotesquely, forward to try to close the gaping wound in her throat. "Please," he repeated hoarsely. With the index finger of his other hand he moved her slack eyelids gently up and down. "Live!" he begged her. He tried with his hand to cover up the wound, shuddering at the sticky wetness of her warm blood. "Live," he pleaded, shaking her a little, and had to grip her head more tightly to prevent it from lolling over. "Please!" Anguished, he tried to breathe on her still lips. "Live!" He wept, his face against hers. "Live! . . . Live . . . ."

Very early in the morning Jenny, agog to find out who the visitor was that Laiah had had so late last night—she had been awakened by the doorbell but had rushed to her door too late to see—knocked, as was her habit, on Laiah's door. Then she knocked more loudly and tried the doorknob. The door opened, and Jenny, after wondering briefly whether she should just walk right in—after all, her friend might not be alone—giggled inside herself and decided that that would be the shock of her life. It was.

After she had cried herself out Ruth remained for a while with her head propped on her arms in a state that was close to exhaustion.

Then she raised herself wearily, unable to think any more of what had caused the outburst. She looked at the clock and saw that it was late and wondered fleetingly where the old man had gone after the door had closed. She shook off the thought of him. Still, after bathing her swollen eyes, she looked into the room where the boy slept, alone now. She went out into the front hall, thinking that perhaps he was sitting out front, too stubborn to come in and go to bed. But there was no one on the porch. From the porch she looked up and down the street, vaguely uneasy. But no shadow of his figure lurked. She came into the house again, leaving the outside light on for him. Wearily she undressed and fell asleep almost immediately.

About two hours later she awoke suddenly with a severe headache and the troubling knowledge that she had left something undone. She got up and went through the living room and down the hall to Abraham's bedroom, where the child still slept alone. Then she hurried to the front porch, where the night light still shone. Where could he be in the middle of the night? Leaving the front door unlocked and the light on, she lay down again.

When she awoke again she made the same rounds. By this time she could no longer sleep. Her mind unwound the scene of the evening before as she wandered from the kitchen to the front door and back again. In the re-viewing she lost much of her initial resentment. It had been such a stupid fight, a multiplication of errors. At any point they might have come together, reached a mutual understanding. But no, they had both been too busy pursuing their own devils. And she had hurt him, he who had been hurt so often before. She would have to be more gentle with him, make him understand that they were not enemies, that she had not meant so many of the things she had said in blind anger. And she would forget, would set aside the things that he had said. But why didn't he come home? In spite of herself she could not suppress her fears.

As the dawn began to relieve the night blackness she turned off the hall light, wrapped herself in her housecoat, and went out onto the porch to sit and wait. By the time the police came she already knew that something terrible had happened.

Chapter Sixteen

They were moving. Moses helped to uproot the furniture, pulling each piece out of its context with a kind of fierce pleasure and helping to push or carry it to the old wagon where it was piled crazily on with the rest. Though he resented old lady Plopler's attitude, meaningful, conspiratorial, he nevertheless moved with a feeling of furtiveness, of haste, glancing about him every time he came out on the porch with another bundle, to see whether there was any movement in the neighboring houses, any sign of the morning stirring other than in the cool dawning breeze.

Ruth had arranged for the cart to come to the house very early in the morning, while the street was still deserted. By the time they had piled on the last chair a wagon had passed, and several people, and Moses could sense the stretching that was going on in neighboring homes, the scratching, and the movements behind the blinds. Hurry.

His mother told them to go on ahead in the cart, while she took a last look around to see that nothing was left. Sonya Plopler settled herself beside the driver. Even though she told people privately how unfeeling it was of Ruth—how brazen, in fact—to be thinking of business while her father-in-law was in jail and the whole city was in an uproar over him, she nonetheless agreed that it was absolutely necessary to get the child away and insisted on helping with the moving.

Carrying the box with their remaining cat, Moses climbed up in the back, where he could crouch among the furniture, seeing but not being seen. "Clean getaway," he muttered as the wagon began creaking down the street and still none of the neighboring doors opened, none of the neighbor kids flew onto their porches. Yet he still expected that from somewhere their voices would blare out again. "Hey, Moishe, what was your granpaw? a butcher?"—from Tony. "Heeeeaaaaaaw"—braying laughter from Dmitri. "Some cow!" But they wouldn't come near.

His mother had turned almost immediately back into the house. The wagon rounded the corner and headed up toward the avenue. The most familiar houses disappeared. Maybe he would never have to see them again until the day came. He was not quite sure what day he meant, but he was sure that a day would come when things would be changed again, unless—and he could hardly bear to think of it—there were no good days left.

Though the driver showed less animation than was worthy of the subject, Mrs. Plopler, operating on the assumption that goyim were more likely to know about these things, persisted. "What are they likely to do with him?" she asked in Ukrainian, with a backward glance to make sure that the boy wasn't listening.

"They could hang him," offered the driver. "Of course"—he ruminated slowly—"if he was drunk when he did it—"

Wasn't that just like them? It was not bad enough to kill, but they had to be drunk yet, too. An everyday thing, to drink, to kill, to murder. Mrs. Plopler eyed the driver with distaste. Slumped in his seat and occasionally interrupting himself to flick the reins at the horse, he told in leisurely fashion about a man he knew who had got only five years because he was drunk, although he had often threatened to— He could have stood as a witness himself; he had heard him threaten. But who wanted to give evidence to one of those English judges?

But Mrs. Plopler did not want to hear about just any old drunk. She thirsted for more relevant discussion. Since what she referred to as "the day," she had risen above her own personal aches and pains, had blossomed forth into a new vitality. Her daughters kept telling her to keep away from that murderer's family, yet they came every day to hear what she had learned. Wherever she went a discussion began, or discussions paused and waited for her opinions on controversial points. She was able, by some miraculous act of synthesis, to hold simultaneously all points of view, rumors, theories, and judgments, no matter how contradictory, and believe implicitly in each one of them as it was voiced, bringing forth convincing arguments, based on her knowledge of the situation, as to why in each case it must indeed be so. Whatever the point of view, Sonya Plopler had gauged the entire range of possible emotions of those involved, and spontaneously re-enacted before her hypnotized listeners how it must have taken place. At least a dozen times a day she argued, condemned, pronounced, excused, emoted, until to some it seemed that her nose had indeed gone wild. At night she fell into bed exhausted, and blessedly without having had the time to stop and think all day.

"Say there!" Moses had just caught sight of the old man when Mrs. Plopler's voice called back to him. "Where are you, Moishele? Are you all right?"

He didn't answer.

"Stop, driver!" Mrs. Plopler cried. "Where's he gone?"

"It's all right, don't stop," he yelled.

"I can't see you there," she said. "Are you all right?"

"No, I fell off," he growled.

"Poor child," said Mrs. Plopler in Ukrainian, turning back to the driver, "he's so bewildered."

Crouched in his niche, Moses had not taken his eyes off the old man, who walked, with his prayer shawl in its pouch under his arm, in the direction of the green synagogue. With narrowed eyes he peered after the bent figure. Slowly, deliberately, he raised his finger and took aim.

Back in the empty house, Ruth walked from room to room. What was left behind? Nothing. Everything. The rooms resounded, hollow, to her footsteps. Yet she expected still in every room to see it as it was. As though two dimensions of being were imposed on each other, she actually felt for an instant that all was as it had been, and that she was really standing now in the middle of the ghost of the kitchen table and not in an empty room. She looked around for a chair to sit down on. She wanted very much to sit, but the kitchen was empty—four walls to lean against. She could hardly prevent herself from slipping wearily in a heap to the floor and burying her face in her hands. Instead she swayed on her feet.

If only—her mind played its insistent game. If only I had called out just as he was leaving. I was going to; I'm sure I was going to. It was on the tip of my tongue to call out. If I had got up from the chair and followed him, begging him to forgive me, telling him I didn't mean—flinging myself at his feet— If only . . . if only.

What if they should hang him? Hang Isaac's father, and because she hadn't called out, hadn't begged him to come back, hadn't dreamed— She had told them everything, about the quarrel, how he had rushed out, about Isaac, about how she had found him that day after Isaac had died. She had confessed to them that it must have been she who had given him this idea of his that he repeated over and over again, that he had killed Isaac, that he had killed his sons. During their quarrel, in her aggravation, she had said something— she had not had a chance to explain.

Did she do right? Did she do right to tell them all this? Better they should think him mad than hang him like a murderer. Of course he was mad. Thinking back, there were things he had said and done, things that she hadn't paid any attention to at the time. Wasn't this madness? And seeing him—was this a madman's, this haggard face? Yes, yes, it was no ordinary face. And madness can't be helped; it is no one's fault. A man sinks under the weight of his life finally. It is not a sudden thing caused by words said in haste and anger. But what did he leave them with? What had he done to them? The child— Mad or not, when a man is selfish—his own desires . . .

When they had let her see him she had held herself in, controlling herself against the desire to question, to blame, against all expression of horror, and against, too, the next moment's impulse to beg, to plead for forgiveness. Be with him; he is Isaac's father. Calm him. Pity him. What does it matter, the unanswered questions? Ask after his comfort—practical, important things. Bring him kosher food or he will starve himself. Above all, don't let him excite himself, upset himself. Comfort him.

She fought against the impulse to blame herself. Who knows, had he stayed, she herself or the child might have been— *No!* It had something to do with that woman. It was connected to her. Could he have been trying to break away from them all the time, to go to this woman, as Sonya Plopler had hinted? Had she misunderstood him all along? Was that why he accused her of running around with other men, because he himself wanted to be free? He hadn't the courage to say to her straight out, "Ruth, I have been living with this woman." When? When had he had time? Had he said, "I want to marry her," what could she have said? Instead he preferred to throw the onus on her, to make it as though she were to blame. Was that it? Who could tell, when all you could get from him was this confusion? She had tried to tell him at the jail, aching as she was with regret, with pity. "No, you never killed Isaac, Pa. I didn't mean that, Pa. I was upset. Isaac's heart was weak." But argue with a madman. What difference to him if you explained that he had not killed Isaac? He had killed. "All right, Pa. It's all right. Don't upset yourself. It doesn't matter."

Had there really been those years of laughter and argument? What did it matter now? Anything, anything to get the child away from here, to a new neighborhood, so that he could go out into the street without being hounded. Thank goodness Harry was kind. The house, empty, no longer held her as she moved toward the door.

For the first time in days Chaim Knopp pushed open the door of the green synagogue. In the movement itself there was comfort, and in the familiar sight of the interior of the house of worship. He moved slowly down the aisle toward the ark, drawing his prayer shawl out of its pouch and unfolding it, making ready to draw its protective folds about him.

Peace, Chaim was thinking, quiet and the knowledge that something still stands. Not to think too much, but to pray and perhaps to listen to the words of friends, exchanging doubts and the companionable nodding of heads. This was what he had needed the past few days as he lay in bed under the load on his heart, this, and not Bassieh's voice of recrimination, adding his friendship with murderers to his list of shortcomings, as if it was merely a new chapter in a long-standing family argument. How can one know a man?

"Chaim"—his friend Dreiman the shamus was greeting him eagerly—"we haven't seen anything of you lately. Where have you been? Come, it's early yet. Come sit and talk a minute."

Warmed by his welcome, Chaim let himself be led to where a group of his old cronies was gathered.

"They said"—Dreiman slowed down before they reached the others and spoke confidentially—"that you would give up coming to this synagogue. They said you were hiding from us."

Chaim stopped. "Who said? Why should they say? Just because I was not feeling so well . . ." Of course this was Dreiman teasing him again in his good-natured way about his well-to-do children and about the fact that he nevertheless still prayed with his friends in a not-so-high-class synagogue.

"Oh," Dreiman said, moving with him again toward the others, "we thought maybe because of that butcher business, because you and he were such good friends, you might feel that— Here's Chaim." Dreiman now addressed the group with an air of personal pride, as though he himself had conjured Chaim up. "And he has been sick. If I had known, I would have come to see you, Chaim."

"Thank you," said Chaim, "but one gets over it. Sometimes it's better to get up and forget about it."

"You weren't feeling well?" Pleschikov, shamus of the green synagogue, asked.

Chaim nodded. "Something was bothering me in here." He made a vague gesture toward his chest, pleased that they should be so concerned.

"You certainly don't look so well," Dreiman was saying.

"Gray," offered one of the others.

"A little tired," Chaim admitted and sat down.

"Maybe you shouldn't have come out so soon," said Pleschikov with a glance at Dreiman.

Chaim shook his head and waved his hand. There was no one left to whom he could say frankly that if he had stayed home with his Bassieh any longer he might never, heaven forbid, have got up again. As though he himself had taken a knife and— But he had told her finally; he had told her so sharply that she had stood there, scarcely able even to open her mouth, for a change. He had told her, all right, that it was enough, he had heard enough. If she opened her mouth about it again he wouldn't be responsible. He didn't care what she said to Ralph. And finally, when she had ventured to suggest in not such a shrewish voice that perhaps he should not upset himself like this, perhaps she should call George, their son-in-law the doctor, and he had said, "No!" because he was carried away by the unfamiliar sensation of being the despot in his own home, she had not insisted. She had even looked almost a little afraid. Well, she deserved to be afraid. After nearly sixty years, to suggest that he too might be making secret visits, as though she didn't— With what?

To compare him with a murderer! His own wife! It was true that he could not yet himself quite equate the Avrom he had known with the murderer he now knew about. But if all those things that they said were true—and he had not had time, and had not been well enough, and had not even felt able to sort them out in his mind for himself—if they were all true, then Chaim didn't know what to think. But he had frightened even himself when he had burst out at Bassieh that way, and so he had scrambled out of bed and into his clothes and had come to seek the peace of his old haven.

"Well, Chaim," said Dreiman, "what do you think?"

Chaim sighed.

"I mean," said Dreiman, "what do you think of your friend now?"

"I know what you mean, my friend," said Chaim softly, though for a moment he was tempted to pretend he didn't, because beyond the feeling of horror and revulsion he didn't know what he thought.

"Well, you can't deny that he was your friend," said Dreiman. "Wasn't it always 'Avrom this' and 'my friend Avrom that'?"

"That butcher!" said one of the elders vehemently.

"I don't deny," said Chaim. "The Avrom I knew was my friend." He shook his head. "Avrom the murderer I didn't know." And yet he knew that this answer was an evasive one. Why didn't he say right out what he thought? He thought as they thought, that the man had done a terrible thing, a dreadful thing. He wished fervently and deeply that he had never known him. That he, Chaim Knopp, who had always led an honorable life, who was respected—looked up to, even, by some—should have associated with a murderer! It was a blot on his old age. Thinking about it, he felt for a moment that if Avrom were to appear before him now he would spit on him publicly—or he would feel like it, anyway.

"There were two Avroms, then?" Dreiman asked. "Yes, you're right. Two men. One was the man he wanted us to see, full of big words and fine phrases; and the other, the real one, the woman-crawler, the knife-wielder, the God alone knows what."

The words fell with a flat unreality on Chaim's ear. He could not seem to connect them once and for all with the person they were intended to describe. But he wanted to acquiesce.

He has killed. Chaim shuddered. *Shun him.*

"When I recall him now," said Dreiman, "and it was just a week or so ago I spoke to him here, I wonder that I didn't see, that I didn't let myself see, really. I always had a premonition about that man."

Recall him. Chaim tried. Yes, he was one to give premonitions, more than premonitions—a man who walked toward his destiny familiarly, a man who had suffered. Involuntarily, he sighed. "Poor Avrom." No. Mentally he corrected himself— He would not have liked me to call him poor. No. Internally he corrected himself again — Who cares, who cares what he would have liked?

"Poor?" Pleschikov laughed with a certain scorn. "I should say it was poor someone else, wouldn't you?" The old men muttered various assents.

"True." Chaim agreed. He closed his eyes, and from the past a voice, familiar— "You too shall have a grandson by your son Ralph" —a voice confident of miracles, and the figure of a man, turning to him gaily, with authority— "Who can be my equal now?" The heavy feeling began to oppress Chaim's chest, and he sighed again.

". . . not that I can blame you entirely, Chaim." Dreiman was talking. "It's your nature. You are a little too quick to trust. You judge a man by his fine words. Often I used to watch you and think, Why is it that one of our leading members chooses to give his friend-ship to that butcher? But we can see now what mistakes even the wisest of us can make. A man goes around, thinking that he owns the world, chooses this friend, goes from here to there, retired, rich sons, doesn't have to worry where his next bite comes from. But the One Above has His surprises."

"My friend," Chaim felt himself constrained to say, "I did not give my friendship to a butcher, I gave it to a man."

"But what kind of a man?" asked Dreiman quickly, leaning toward him.

"A madman," said one of the elders.

"Ay, ay," said Chaim, "mad." He seized on the word. When a man is mad, then things he does become more understandable because they do not have to be understood. That madness should sneak up on a man so!

"Madness," said Pleschikov. "This is what I call a fine madness. A man who has the sense not to turn the knife on himself but on someone else is not my idea of a madman."

"In the papers it says," the elder continued, "that they are exam-ining his mind, and that the doctors think—"

"Sure, sure," said Dreiman, "a lot of things it says in the papers. A fine name he has given us. 'The first time,' they keep writing over and over again, as if he had discovered America, 'the first time in the history of the district that a Jew has committed murder.'"

"Mazeltov," said Pleschikov.

"They would have had to look a lot farther than this district." Dreiman snorted. "What Jew would kill? But no. He had to go and show them that we can have murderers too, just like them. And everybody knows he was from our synagogue, and now the congregation of this synagogue are complaining too. They too are given a black name because he came here after our synagogue burned down. I myself am ashamed. Is this the way we repay your hospitality?"

"It's all right; nobody blames you, Dreiman," said Pleschikov.

"I spoke to the rabbi himself," the elder persisted. "He too thinks that it could not be other than madness."

"So if he was mad why didn't he go bang his own head against the wall?" Dreiman turned on him.

"Does a madman know what he is doing?" asked the elder gently.

"I know what you're thinking of, Cohen," said Pleschikov, "but what has your son to do with this? Everywhere you push your son. It is true, your son was an unfortunate man, but does that make you a head doctor to tell us who is mad and who isn't? Who can compare him with this outcast?"

A powerful movement had taken place in the heart of Chaim Knopp as he listened to them arguing. Here was this man Cohen, a man who had scarcely known Avrom at all, looking at him through eyes made tender by the sight of his own mad son. And what did he do, who could almost feel the actual physical presence of his old friend, but turn with the pack, condemning, afraid to admit that he did not feel exactly as he himself expected he should feel. How to explain what he felt?

"Who knows?" Summoning courage, Chaim began. "Who knows? Even the papers don't know. He was not such a man— What he did — Madness, a madness of grief. He was such a man who couldn't stand, couldn't bear— It is a hard thing to explain, but a man like that—he could be pressed in, pressed in, but there was such a longing in him. You say just a butcher, but he was not, not like some others. He was not like me, afraid, treading the safe middle path. In his mind he was not afraid to climb, to soar, to walk the edge of the ravine. I would have liked to be such a one sometimes. But when such a man falls—"

"To hell," broke in Dreiman, "where he belongs. Does he have to drag the rest of us with him, through the mouths of the whole country?"

"Friend," said Chaim, "friend, what are you saying? It is a terrible thing. We all feel it is a terrible thing. But to curse in the House of God, when none of us knows where he is going—"

"He knew where he was going." Dreiman laughed scornfully. "In the dark he knew where he was going. I wish I were still young enough to sniff my way so well."

An ill-placed giggle from one of the elders was quickly subdued.

"Listen," said Chaim, "listen. They are looking into his head and finding out all kinds of things to say about a mad old man. But what do you think they would find if they could look where God looks, in his heart? What would they find? I myself cannot even bear to think of it." Chaim was surprised at what he was saying. It was almost as though someone else were speaking through his lips. And yet everything he said seemed right, unalterably, from the moment he heard himself say it, the moment even it entered his mind. It was as if his heart, ignoring the cautious warning in him that he should not antagonize these old friends, ignoring his own horror, had leaped to an understanding of what his mind could not grasp. "I know what they would find if they looked in his heart," he heard himself saying, and his whole being acquiesced in what he said. "They would find the knife!" In his excitement Chaim had started up. Now he sank back on the pew, his voice sinking to a whisper as he repeated, "The knife he used in his own heart."

Dreiman raised his eyebrows and looked knowingly about him, then back to Chaim. "You don't have to excite yourself so, Reverend Chaim," he said soothingly with the faintest irony in his voice.

Chaim became aware that there was an air about him in the synagogue, a tight feeling that was pressing in. The other men seemed to have formed a circle about him, their eyes pinning him around like a tight band. His head quivered nervously.

"All I am saying, Chaim," said Dreiman softly, relentlessly, "is that they found the knife elsewhere, remember? And who put it there, eh?" Dreiman appealed to the others. "How many places can a knife be at once? I am surprised to hear you, Chaim, defending him." Dreiman had adopted the deadly, patient tone of one who is speaking to a child, trying to force a confession of some misdeed from him. "You will excuse me if I say it right out. But I have always looked on you as one to respect, a man to come to for advice, more reverend, perhaps, than some of us. Not all of us have had the same opportunities for study. It is not that I—that we respect you any the less now, but here you come before us, sick from what has happened, and yet you will not admit that you have been wrong. In fact you still boast of your friendship with this murderer, and even compare him with yourself! What are we to think?"

"I don't know," said Chaim, "what we are to think. I too renounced him. In my mind I said, Pooh-pooh. He has more than sinned. Henceforth he is dead. But I cannot prevent my heart from aching. I cannot forget the years that we talked together and helped each other and gave each other the comfort of love. I weigh one thing against the other. Is this Avrom real? Or is that Avrom real? And the Avrom I knew is the real man for me, no matter what he did, no matter what madness his sorrow drove him to. He is the Avrom who said to me, 'Chaim, not to worry, be comforted.' I wish now that I had known how to say it to him so well. Whatever his madness is, you can be sure he does not need your curses; he suffers enough. Which of us has lost three such golden promises as he? I tell you he's sick." Chaim was pleading now. "Pity him, if only for the sake of his son, who saved your Torah."

It seemed to Chaim that in this last he had finally hit on the exact note that would soften their hearts toward Avrom. He looked around him eagerly, hopefully, when he ceased speaking. There was a moment of restless silence. The elders looked at one another, and finally at Dreiman and Pleschikov, avoiding Chaim's questioning glances. Chaim began to get the feeling that his was a trump card that had somehow been marked all along. Surprisingly, Dreiman was smiling, a rather sly smile.

"Some of us," said Dreiman after a long, deliberate pause, "have been thinking about this Torah-saving during the past few days.

How indeed, from such a family, can one be a murderer and another a hero? Oh, it can happen, no doubt, but is it likely? And then we began to wonder—have we been seeing things as they actually happened? Or have we been seeing them as your friend Avrom and his son wanted us to see them? There are so many unanswered questions about that fire. What man here really knows what happened? Do you know? Do I know?"

"What else is there to know?" asked Chaim. "I know, you know, we saw it with our own eyes. You yourself were shouting like a madman. All of a sudden, like a prophet, flaming, he came rushing out of that oven!"

"Oh, yes, you're right, you're right," said Dreiman. "We saw him rushing out, and I must admit that I myself was so overcome to see the Sepher Torah carried so that I cheered like the rest. It never occurred to me then to wonder what he was doing inside the synagogue at that time in the first place. How long had he been there? Was he in there before the fire started? Did he maybe have anything to do with the starting of the fire?"

"He was coming from work when he saw—" Chaim began. "He had a pupil—"

"Yeah, yeah," Dreiman interrupted. "In many ways I am like you, Chaim. I have a trusting nature. Even afterward, when people were spreading stories that it was all my fault because they could think of no one else to blame, and threatening not to make me shamus of the new synagogue—though there isn't a shamus in the city as conscientious as I, except my friend Pleschikov here—even then it didn't occur to me to wonder. All right, he happened to be around—fine, fine. There is no one more than myself who likes to see a man made a big hero. But now I am beginning to open my eyes. What do we know after all? It would be a fine thing, wouldn't it, if all this time we have been kneeling down and kissing his feet for saving the Torah, for being good enough to save the Torah though he burned down the rest of the synagogue?"

Chaim was too stunned to speak. He stared at Dreiman with unbelief and made one or two efforts to open his lips, but for a long moment nothing would come out.

"I'll tell them that too," said Dreiman, "if they think they're going to give my job away. I'm tired of whispering behind my back."

"Dreiman," said Chaim finally. "What are you saying? You know this isn't true. It doesn't make sense. Why should he burn down the synagogue?"

"Why should his father be a murderer?" asked Pleschikov.

"But he died from it," Chaim insisted. "If he hadn't rushed to save the Torah he might have been alive today."

"Who knows what he died from—perhaps a punishment from God?" Dreiman suggested.

"And besides," said Pleschikov, "he had a heart sickness. From a heart sickness you can drop off any time. He might have died anyway."

"But you saw, yourself. Dreiman, you are blackening your own face when you talk like this." Chaim looked around at the others, who stirred and shuffled uneasily. "Can you prove what you say? I believe in what I saw, a brave man who risked his life and forced even from you a cry of wonder. Now, now just because his death has driven an old man mad you will set on his memory, like a wolf. Beware, Dreiman, God hears, God sees." Strong in his sureness, Chaim stood up, looking around at the other old men. They looked uneasily from him to Dreiman.

"I am not afraid to be seen by God," said Dreiman. "I have nothing to fear. I say openly, perhaps you are right, perhaps he was a hero. But perhaps also you are wrong. Let God judge."

"What kind of a man are you," asked Chaim, "that casts a shadow where the sun was and hopes the sun is dead?"

"What kind of a man am I? What kind of a man is your friend Avrom, eh?" Grievance rang high in Dreiman's voice. "I am not that kind of a man, whatever I am. I am a man who watched while others were falsely exalted and bit my tongue and said nothing, though I myself was looked down on and maligned. But I see clearly.

Too often our people have sought false gods. You with your fine-speaking Avrom and his son for whom synagogues burn down. And when I speak up and say the truth you tell me I shouldn't dare, just because you have maybe a little more education than I. But I am as close to God as you. He will tell who is right."

Chaim shook his head. All of a sudden it seemed to be he himself who was on trial here, before these men who had always been his friends, had listened respectfully to his words, had even come to him, some of them, as they would have to the rabbi, for advice. He turned away from Dreiman and appealed to the rest. "Is it so much harder to turn to a man with pity than to turn away with loathing? He is sick; he has sinned; pity him."

"You look sick yourself, Chaim," said Dreiman. "You shouldn't have come out so soon. It's all right. Go home. Lie down. The synagogue won't fly away when you're gone. We'll take care of it, and if any miracles happen we'll let you know."

Chaim smiled a little. "If a miracle happens—" He shook his head. "Miracles could happen yet," he said. "Avrom used to say there is plenty of room for miracles."

"Our new prophet?" Dreiman sneered.

Chaim sighed and turned away from them helplessly. "There are many ways to kill," he said sadly.

"Go go," Dreiman called after him. "Go to your rich son. It isn't fitting that I should tell you in a synagogue; otherwise I'd let you know that the world knows how some men get rich."

Chaim had begun to move down the aisle toward the ark. Wounded by this final gibe, and by all that it seemed to betray of what men knew and thought, he moved now, doubled over almost in his haste, down and across toward the side door of the synagogue. Surrounded suddenly by enemies, he moved blindly, without pausing to listen to the voices that had raised themselves up in argument, or to glance back to see that some in that solid, hostile group had wavered in his favor.

"What are you talking about?" said Polsky with heat. "I'll tell you

in plain English what I think. The papers themselves don't know
from nothing. First they say he had a key to the apartment; then
they say he rang the doorbell to get in. At least that's what the dame
from next door says."

"Like I say," said Hymie, "maybe she had two visitors. Maybe
Avrom came up afterward and found the corpse."

"I'd think twice before I'd believe anything that dame said," remarked the barber. "Getting her mug into all the papers, smiling like
a priest at a pogrom."

"If he just found her," said Mandelknaidel to Hymie, "what did
he wait around for, sitting in a pool of blood, hanging on to her?"
Mandelknaidel sighed. It seemed like such a waste.

"For all we know," said Hymie, "the other guy could have
drugged him or hit him on the head or something. I'll bet it was one
of those gentiles of hers. And the paper said he was in a condition
of shock, or a shocked condition, or something, when they found
him."

"What I want to know is where and how he got his hand cut,"
said the barber. "He knows how to handle a knife."

"He might have come in in time to see this other guy knifing her,"
Hymie explained. "So he makes a dive at him, see? And he grabs at
the knife, but the other guy's quicker and pulls it out of the way,
and it cuts him that way."

"So if he'd seen the guy, you think he wouldn't have told by now?"
asked the barber.

"Maybe he did," said Mandelknaidel. "Maybe they wouldn't believe him. Or maybe they're working on it. You think they tell everything to the papers?"

"They could tell by fingerprinting the knife," said the barber musingly.

"Nah!" Hymie snorted. "You think he'd be dumb enough to leave
his prints? He wiped them off; then, while Avrom was still uncon-
scious, he put his fingers around the handle so Avrom's prints would
show. A perfect frame."

"I still say that if he'd seen the guy and the cops were working on it they'd have found out by now. Unless they'd rather pin it on a Jew," said the barber.

"Shock," explained Hymie. "Amnesia, see? He gets hit on the head and he forgets, see?"

"It didn't say anything about him getting hit on the head," said Polsky. "If you ask me it was self-defense. If you knew Laiahle's temper as well as I did, you'd know what I mean. He said something she didn't like, or he promised something he couldn't do, or something—or even she just plain wasn't feeling too friendly. Right away she grabs the knife and starts waving it at him. She likes a little scene occasionally, that one—liked, I mean."

"She was a wildcat," said Mandelknaidel fervently.

"Ah, how do you know?" said Hymie.

"Anyway," said Polsky, "maybe she even jumps at him, just to show she means business. Avrom doesn't know from any maybes. He tries to get the knife away from her. She cuts him in the hand; by her it would be a plaything—"

"Yes." Mandelknaidel glowed.

"Finally he gets hold of her wrist and grabs the knife," Polsky continued with relish. "But by this time she's really wrestling and her hair is flaming and the sparks shooting from her eyes, and I can tell you he's got a handful. And just when he thinks he's got her quiet she gives a twist and a jerk, and he forgets he's still got the knife in his hand and tries to hold her and accidentally—*zzzzzt!* her throat's slit. That's what she gets for playing around too much. Poor Laiah. I told her she'd burn her fingers someday." Polsky sighed.

"The police say it was a very clean, professional job," said Mandelknaidel respectfully.

"Well, there's no doubt about it, he was a good butcher," said Polsky. "But that's the only thing I don't understand." Polsky shook his head. "What was he doing there in the first place? I would never have thought that he would, somehow." He recalled how, long ago, after Laiah had quarreled with Hymie in the kibitzarnia, he had sent Avrom with some stuff, as a little joke. She had said something about it, though he couldn't remember what. Had it started then? And later, when the old man had taken over the afternoon deliveries . . . But so quiet, so hush-hush, not like Laiah at all. And he wouldn't have thought Avrom could be such a—such a sly one. He felt, almost, a funny kind of disappointment. Oh, she wouldn't have minded, there was no doubt of that. She would get a kick out of someone like him coming to her. That was maybe it; she had teased him. A man like Avrom is not easy to tease. Sometimes Laiah liked to be maybe just a little bit too smart. Why couldn't she leave him alone, someone like that. He would never have thought that Avrom would— "You never know with those religious ones." Polsky voiced his dissatisfaction morosely. "I don't know. There's more to it. I've known them both for a long time. You can be sure there's more to it. I'm not saying that he didn't have a case on her. He's only human, though he never seemed to be exactly her type. But there must have been a reason. She was probably teasing him, telling him she would, she wouldn't. And he's not the kind to play games with. If he wanted a little fun maybe, to forget his troubles for a while, do you have to pull your little tricks?" Polsky addressed an absent Laiah.

"If you ask me," said the barber, "he just went nuts. Read the papers. They're all saying he's nuts. They've got a bunch of head doctors from all over arguing over him now."

"I could have told them that a long time ago," said Hymie, "ever since Isaac died. The way he'd stand there, sometimes, the way he'd look at you. I told my old man—"

"What did you tell me?" said Polsky irritably. "Shut up what you told me. It didn't have anything to do with him being nuts."

"Ah, I didn't mean anything so bad. He used to be not such a bad old guy," said Hymie, "but you can say what you like, when I used to talk to him I had a funny feeling."

"So, can you blame him? A guy gets older. And he hasn't had such an easy life. Maybe he went nuts all right, but that didn't have anything to do with you trying to tell me how to run my business."

"I still think," said Morton, who liked his brother's earlier theory, "that there must have been somebody else."

"Guess he won't be at my wedding, anyway," Hymie said.

"Big joke," said Polsky.

"So what'd I say?" said Hymie. "All I said was guess he won't be —and he's ready to make a thing of it."

"You can say what you like," said Mandelknaidel, "it was still wrong for him to kill her."

"Of course it was wrong," said Polsky, scowling. "She was no diamond, but that doesn't mean you can kill her just like that."

"A maniac doesn't ask anybody's permission," said the barber. "A cousin of my wife is related by marriage to the wife of the man who interprets for them at the police station whenever they bring in —you know, a Jew who has maybe done something wrong. Not killings, of course, but you know what crooks some of these greenhorns are, and they can't even talk enough English to hire a good lawyer, some of them."

"You mean they have a man there at the police station just for that?" asked Mandelknaidel.

"Not just for Jews. He wouldn't make a living at it. But he's an educated young fellow. He speaks Polish and Russian and Ukrainian and Rumanian and I think German too, so he can help out quite a bit. Anyway it's not his real full-time job. He works besides for the welfare, spying on relief cases. Oh, he can turn his hand to a living, that one. Too good to talk to you sometimes. Of course he scarcely knows me. But anyway he told my wife's cousin that Avrom's stark crazy. He says—"

"Those filthy relief spies," said Mandelknaidel.

"Let him talk," said Polsky.

"He told her," said the barber, "that the first thing he thought about (they dragged him out of bed to the police station; at first they thought that Avrom couldn't speak any English at all) anyway, the first thing he thought was, Oh, God, I hope he isn't related to my wife. They're a big family. He could hardly wait to get home to make sure. But I was the closest she could trace, and I just work next door."

"So?" said Polsky. "What has this to do with it? What does he say about Avrom? What did Ayrom say?"

"Ah, he said enough," said the barber.

"What do you mean, enough? Did your cousin tell what he said?"

"It's not my cousin. It's my wife's—"

"Never mind," said Polsky. "I don't care what relative it is. I want to know what Avrom said."

"I don't know what Avrom said," said the barber. "Do you think they're allowed to tell what happened? He could lose his job. I just know that I'm glad I'm not related to that crazy family."

"They're not all crazy. Look what his son did," said Polsky. "Besides, there's more to it, I know. I wish I had that little Laiahle here right now. She'd tell me, all right."

"If his son hadn't done what he did, maybe he wouldn't have done this either," said Hymie. "Gone crazy, I mean."

"And if my grandmaw'd had balls she'd have been my grandpaw," said Polsky. They could say what they liked, but there was more to it. For all he knew, Hymie's theory about the other visitor might have something to it. The boy had a head. Poor Laiah. "Mort, watch the shop," he said. "Come on, let's have a quick game. I need something to take my mind off."

Mandelknaidel trailed behind them into the kibitzarnia. "What I want to know," he murmured wistfully, "is how he got that key."

"Still," Abraham complained, more to himself than to the man, "she won't listen to me. Still she keeps telling me, 'It's all right; don't upset yourself. I understand.' But it's not all right. What does she understand? I'm not afraid to be upset. Does she think it means something now, to be upset, not to be upset? Come closer to me, little Ruth, let me know that— I would gladly be upset— No." He shook his head and smiled a little, contemptuously. "Always I look for my own comfort. Even now I try to forget that I am cold and alone." He remained silent a moment. "Still," he resumed, "you see how she must have loved my son? Even now she clings to his father, when she should throw him out on the streets, when they should trample him at the door of the temple. The son works to redeem the father, though the father has— She says not to talk if it hurts me. She sees I cry. I shouldn't talk, she says. 'It doesn't matter!' Does she think I'm mad? Does she think I don't know? I can hear them calling in the streets, 'Moishe, what was your grandfather?' What will he answer? What can he answer? What will become of him?"

The man leaned forward after the interpreter had finished his brief mutterings. "You don't deny, then, what you have done, and you understand that you will have to be punished if you are found guilty in court?"

Abraham shook his head indifferently. "Sometimes to understand is punishment," he said softly. The interpreter shrugged slightly as he translated.

"We would like to help you," said the man patiently. "Can you remember—was there any reason? Was there an argument? What"— the man had an idea—"what exactly is it that you understand?"

The interpreter repeated the question in Yiddish, though Abraham waved him aside to show that he understood. "All my life I wanted only to build, to grow, to understand," he said in Yiddish. "That is what I thought." Abraham covered his face with his hands.

The man nodded when the interpreter had finished. He leaned forward and spoke to Abraham's bowed head. "But you understand that you have killed a woman, that you have taken a human life?"

"That I have taken life"—Abraham swayed—"that I have killed my sons, that I have made myself equal with my enemies, that it was in me, womb of death, festering, in no one else. Who was I? Who was I to demand, to threaten, when it was there, in my arms, breathing, alive. But no. It was in me. I was not content to be, as He willed it. I wanted more. I had to be creator and destroyer. Why did I weep, then, when I saw them hanging, swaying at the will of the wind? Why did I tear my hair when he lay there? When in me, all the time—"

The two men glanced at each other. Abraham was weeping long, rasping sobs. Always he came back to the assertion that he had killed his sons. When he had first been found, cradling the corpse in his bloodied arms and had insisted distractedly that they were dead, that he had killed his sons, it had caused a minor panic among members of the police force. Until they were able to locate Ruth they were convinced that a mass murder had been done. It was plain that in some way he confused the dead woman with his dead children. Sometimes from the way he spoke you could almost believe that he thought he had killed God Himself.

The man decided to make another try, to be brutal if necessary. "You understand"—he spoke clearly and distinctly—"that the punishment for murder is death. Unless you can prove extenuating circumstances, the murderer is hanged by the neck until dead." His words had an effect.

Abraham was suddenly quiet. He removed his hands from his face and looked uncertainly at the man with an almost childlike eagerness. "Yes?"

Slightly disconcerted, the man repeated, "Hanged," and made a gesture toward his throat.

The interpreter, also disconcerted at what was almost a smile that lit up the bearded face, leaned forward and hissed into Abraham's face in Yiddish, "They'll hang you." He dropped his head dramatically onto his shoulder and lolled his tongue forward in graphic illustration, to try to bring comprehension to the prisoner.

"Please," said the man, shocked, and the interpreter moved back, puzzled and a little ashamed of himself, but still irritated that the prisoner would not understand.

Tears had sprung again to Abraham's eyes. To suffer what they suffered; to pay, perhaps to atone. Oh, my God, it would be too easy, too merciful. "Is this true?" He addressed himself eagerly to the man, bending forward with more outward animation than they had yet seen in him. "Is it true they will hang me?"

"Well, if they find you guilty, yes," the man stammered and froze with horror, for the crazy old man was crying and kissing his hand.

Chapter Seventeen

Moses laid down the novel as in the distance a cluster of yellow lights popped open and peered from behind the Mad Mountain's hump. Once that had been the signal for him to close his eyes and rush quickly into his disappearing act. His hand would push the bow gently across the violin strings and disappear after it into the open music. His arm would follow, and his shoulder, his side, his back, his hips, his legs. All of him in one fluid turn would flow into the music and remain, invisible, untouchable, floating in sound. Only a mistake could render him visible again while the piece he played lasted. The trick had been never to make a mistake, to be safe at least for a little while. But he was no longer a child. He nodded, instead, at the lights of the asylum. "Hello, Grampa," he murmured sardonically, and wondered again in which one they had the old demon chained.

He heard his mother come in through the store entrance and fiddle around in the shop before she came up the three stairs that separated the shop from their living quarters. He could tell by the slow way she moved that there would be no good news. He got up quickly and turned on the light and sat down again, pulling his book closer to him. Whatever it was, he didn't want to hear.

"Hello, Moishe," she called from the kitchen.

"Hello," he answered shortly.

"You didn't go out anywhere?" she asked.

He didn't reply.

"You should go out sometimes—more." He heard her speaking the familiar plaint, half to herself. She had come into the room with him. He tried to pretend that he didn't notice that she was moving about, touching things and making a noise so that he should raise his head for her to talk to him. And it would not be good news. It was

328

not just the news itself that he would hate, it was what she would say inevitably, the comment that would depress as much as the news, and the way he would feel afterward. Already he could feel the heaviness descending on him and with it the need to surrender, to listen. He raised his head. "Well?"

"Well?" His mother shrugged and ran her hand in a familiar gesture through her hair. "She's very sick." Sighing, Ruth lowered herself into a chair. "Perhaps it'll be better. The way she's suffered the past year. And lately, from day to day, she's fallen away. You can see how it eats her, from inside, sucking away the flesh. It's a terrible thing to see what becomes of a person. You wouldn't know her." Ruth shook her head slowly from side to side; her double chin waggled gently.

Moses watched the bright, chubby bloom of his mother's face, imagining the flesh being sucked away, the skin pulled back against the bones. He recoiled from the thought. Don't tell me any more. You've told me; I've heard.

"Mind you, she recognized me, I think. It's hard to tell. She's so full of drugs to kill the pain. Ah." Ruth opened her hands, palm upwards, raised them, and dropped them again to her lap. "I said to myself, So this is what becomes of a person."

"Will she die?" He had to ask, in spite of himself— Her nose will be forever still. Idly he began to draw, with his finger, a long, pointed nose on his book. He had never much liked her. As a child she had frightened him. And yet . . .

"Nothing is sure till it's done," said his mother. She shook her head. "Her two daughters"—she laughed a little, sarcastically—"like twin mountains, sitting there, with their chairs pushed a little bit farther back from the bed than they should have been, as though they are afraid that death is a catching thing."

Moses bent toward his book as though he thought she had finished and he wanted to get back to it again. Heavily her words weighed on him, dragging down his spirits, forcing him into a presence of which he was afraid, making him think of things he hated. It had been the same when she used to turn on the radio to hear the war news, or when people told of the horrors of the concentration camps. Why did she talk to him of these things? Each time she spoke she laid another load on him, and yet her words held for him a sort of fascination, so that though he sank under their burden he could make no real move to escape.

"She is afraid, too, I think." Ruth seemed to be half musing, softly, yet loudly enough for him to hear. "I wouldn't be." Her voice rose, and she looked her son straight in the eye. "I wouldn't be afraid to die. What's there to be afraid of? Do they think death will serve them worse?" Ruth gestured and nodded fatalistically. "Only one thing I pray for." Moses knew what was coming and was tempted to say it for her. Instantly he was smitten with horror that he should, even in thought, for a moment, have had the impulse to mock what she was saying.

"I only pray that I should live long enough to bring you to the shore," his mother continued earnestly. "If I could only live to see you safely grown and happy, that's all I'd want."

"You don't have to die," he mumbled in an agony.

"What, do you think we're immortal? We all have to die," Ruth said firmly, "when the time comes. But—" She saw that her son was distressed by the elementary truth. He might as well know about life. Better it shouldn't take him by surprise. "Don't worry," she added. "We've got time yet. Your mother won't leave you for a long time yet, God willing.

"Certainly"—Ruth reverted to the Ploplers—"he's thinking of living, old Plopler. If he waits out his year before remarrying I'll be surprised. And you think she doesn't know? It eats her more than her sickness."

The iniquities of men. Having watched him through the various quickenings and awakenings that revealed themselves not only in his added inches of height and the passing awkwardness of his limbs, but in the molded changes of his face and the deepening, secretive awareness of his eyes, what could she say to him in warning? It was necessary, she felt, sometimes, because he had no father, to throw out an allusion that was almost a veiled threat or an accusation, about the nature of man, the dangers of manhood, about those undisciplined fires which a man, selfish, or perhaps not in control of himself, can unleash, bringing tragedy to others. This much was Ruth's concession to the theory that the old man's crime, to which she now never openly referred, was one of what the newspapers called "midwinter passion."

It was a mountainous weight that dropped on him when she talked like that, of death and the evil of men, like an old mountain of his grandfather's stories, settling, crushing the giants of his childhood over again, breaking them into splinters that tore him apart inside.

He picked up his book again.

"Have you practiced?" she asked.

"A little," he said. "More later."

Blessedly, she was silent. He looked covertly up at her face as she gazed abstractedly past him. He remembered a time long ago when he had looked at her, and just like that it had come to him how beautiful she was. Now she stirred in him a sort of pity and an obscure indignation. Who had done this to them? There was one that he wanted to accuse, to name right out, even to swear at. Instead he snapped his book shut.

"You know whom I saw today," said Ruth, "on the way to the bus? You'd never guess. Little old Reb. Chaim Knopp. Oh, how old he's grown, and small."

"He always was," said Moses.

"But now he's like a little *kneppaleh,* not a *knopp.* I stopped to say hello, and he had to come right up close to me, peering into my face, before he recognized me. His eyes aren't what they were. But he's all there otherwise. Right away he was asking all kinds of questions. It made me ashamed that I haven't had a chance to visit him at the Home. But I promised him I'd come. I'll bake him something. He asked especially after you."

"He remembers me?"

"Oh, his mind is clear. Mine should only be so if I live to be his age. Only sometimes, whenever he mentions his wife, his Bassieh, he looks around him in a funny way, as if he still expected her to be there. I think it must be five-six years already since she died. But for an old man like him it would be hard to get used to the idea that his lifelong partner is gone. Anyway, he said he would so much like to see you, to see the kind of boy you had turned into. Of course I told him what you'd been doing."

"I can imagine what you told him."

"What did I tell him? You think I sang your praises? I know you too well. The truth may be hard for a mother to get used to, but I've learned to bear it."

Moses smiled at his mother affectionately. "Pity."

"So I told him that you'd like to visit him sometime too," Ruth continued complacently.

"Hell, Ma!"

"Don't swear."

"Well, why do you have to go making dates for me? I don't want to go see him. What'll I say to him? I won't go."

"You'll find what to say to him. You don't go running around that much that you can't find a few minutes to give an old man some pleasure."

"Pleasure, what kind of pleasure? What kind of pleasure do I look like?"

"To me you're a pleasure," she said. "Anyway, you don't have to go," she added reasonably. "I just said— Well, he reminded me of so many things. He asked me about— Do you remember, or were you too little, the day that your father saved the Torah?" Ruth was smiling. "The way he talked about it—and then when he said he would like to see my Isaac's son, what could I say? I don't think he gets that many visits from his rich children in the high-tony districts."

Moses remembered, all right. But he also wanted to say the other thing, the unspoken thing. I also remember what my grandfather did. But he held it in and didn't say it, feeling, as he controlled himself, that he was being immensely protective toward her. How he would like to— He didn't know quite what it was that he would like to do for her. He pulled his chair around closer to hers. "I don't know what you want from me," he said, giving in gracefully.

Ruth felt with pleasure the warmth of his face with its tender young bristles pressed against her cheek and chin. "What I want? I want you should be—" She hugged him. This watchful boy—almost, this young man—about whose thoughts she sometimes puzzled, was still her little boy after all. For how long? She held him to her very tightly.

To his embarrassment, there was another visitor with Chaim Knopp when he was shown to the old man's room, a boy of about his own age. And Chaim's eyesight—or was it his memory too?— was even less keen than Moishe's mother had led him to believe. He was forced to repeat his name several times, growing each time more embarrassed as he bent forward to give the old man a chance to get a good look at him. Finally the other boy repeated Moishe's name more loudly. Moses glanced at him with less than gratitude, furious with his mother for having put him in this position of making a fool of himself in front of people who obviously didn't know who he was or what he wanted. He was about to drop the parcel of food his mother had sent and bolt, when Chaim answered the other boy.

"I know, I know, I heard him all right. I know who it is. I just couldn't believe that you had come, and he too, on the same day." Chaim brushed his hand across his eyes. "Tell me, you know each other, then?" The boys, forced to look at each other, exchanged wary glances.

"No," said the other boy.

Expensive clothes, Moses observed; rich. He began to wonder whether Chaim Knopp was as clear-headed as his mother had thought. He was introducing Moses to his grandson Aaron as the grandson of his best friend. And yet he knew who he was. He mentioned Avrom by name.

"Your grandfather Avrom would be so pleased to see you here now," said Chaim, peering from him to Aaron. "It was a dream of his, and mine too, that someday the two of you would be friends."

The two boys looked at each other unenthusiastically, though in each there was a certain carefully concealed curiosity.

"Your mother sent me something?" Moses had handed him the parcel. "Bless her. I don't need anything. But thank her."

"For Rosh Hashonah," mumbled Moses. "She's sorry she couldn't come herself. She said Happy New Year."

"Thank you, thank you, and the same to her, and to you, and to all of us." Chaim beamed. He wrinkled his nose. "You know what? We shouldn't stay in this room. We should go outside in the fresh air. We will sit on a bench. Here it smells like death. You two boys bring life. Come, come, it's not for you here. That doesn't mean"—Chaim turned to his grandson—"that I am complaining. They take good care of me. There's plenty of food. I have a room to myself, bigger than most. No, tell your father I have no complaints. I'm happy here, happy," Chaim repeated. "Only maybe they could come more often. Of course I understand, I understand they're all busy. They live far away. But you came, Arnie, and by yourself too."

Aaron looked embarrassed.

"You're a big boy now," his grandfather continued. "Maybe you could—more often. But why am I complaining?" Chaim was leading them down the long corridor to the front door, with a hand on the elbow of each, bobbing and nodding and saying a proud hello to elderly people who stood watching yearningly at the door of every room. "My grandson," Chaim called several times, pushing Aaron's elbow. "The grandson of my friend"—he pushed Moses' elbow—"come to see me." The old people nodded and mumbled. The boys glanced helplessly at each other over his head and found themselves smiling awkwardly and nodding as they walked along. It did smell.

Chaim seated them on a bench right beside the front entrance so that people could see and he could explain who they were. There were some who would not wish to intrude, but would nevertheless ask later. "Little did I dream," said Chaim, "little did I think when I stood by the river this morning, emptying my pockets and asking God to wash away my sins for the New Year, that I would right away receive such a gracious gift. Your grandfather would be proud too." Chaim turned to Moses. "Proud," he repeated softly, nodded his head, and sighed. "Ay, ay," he murmured.

Moses glanced at the other boy. The reference to his grandfather didn't seem to mean anything to him.

Chaim brightened. "Did you young fellows empty your pockets too this morning? Not that at your age there are many sins. But it's best to look forward with clean hearts to Yom Kippur, when our fates are sealed."

Aaron made some unintelligible reply. Moses did not answer at all. Chaim did not seem to notice but was explaining loudly to a deaf old lady who nodded and smiled enthusiastically that these boys were his grandson and the grandson of his friend, come to visit him. But Moses, whose eyes met Aaron's, realized with a quickening of interest that this kid didn't believe either.

The old man asked them questions, embarrassing both by singing the praises of each in turn so that they moved more and more to the edge of the bench until they both decided, almost simultaneously, that it was time to go. Chaim walked them to the corner and stood waving so that they were compelled to keep turning around and waving back until they saw him joined by another old man, with whom he turned back, talking animatedly.

The boys walked along, perforce together, in silence. Each one separately pondered the question. The old man had seemed very happy. Neither was quite sure why. Of course people should visit more often. He seemed to think they were friends, or that they should be friends. He talked about some miracle. Friends—not likely, thought Moses bitterly, observing his new acquaintance out of the corner of his eye. Funny the old man had said nothing about —about the other thing. Could you forget even that when you were old?

"You look familiar," the other boy said in English. "Did my grandfather say you play the violin or something?"

"Yeah," said Moses.

"I've heard about you," said Aaron. "Your picture in the paper. You won some prize."

"Yeah," said Moses.

They walked along in silence. Finally: "What else did you hear about me?" Moses asked.

"Why? You got more talents?"

"No—yes." Stung, Moses was determined that this rich smart aleck wouldn't get the verbal best of him. "I have all kinds of talents. But I thought maybe you might have heard that I'm kind of peculiar, too. I don't know why, but people always think I'm odd, because my grandfather was—nuts and killed that dame; you probably heard, slit her throat. They always say, 'He's queer, but he sure can play the violin. Look at all the prizes he's won. It's a pity it wasn't my little Pretzel with all that talent. Now, Pretzel, don't get too friendly with him. He's liable to take his bow and—' "

"Stick it?" asked Aaron coolly.

Involuntarily the side of Moses' mouth twitched, though his eyes met Aaron's suspiciously.

"I know a couple of women," said Aaron in an offhand manner. "They like odd types. Maybe they'd like to meet you."

"Women," he called them. Fast. All right. "Heights women?" Moses adopted the word, speaking contemptuously and daringly. "Well, they can't have my million dollars. They'll have to take my nice firm bow."

Aaron grinned, good-natured, showing him that he had scored. "Maybe they'll even pay you," he suggested.

Moses was still suspicious. "Not necessary," he said coolly. "Free gratis. Satisfaction guaranteed or you can try again. And again. I'll die trying." He heard himself with amazement. A hot sensation was burning the back of his ears. What kind of women were they? What kind of fast crowd did this rich kid run around with? Well, he needn't think they were that hot.

"Do you know any?" Aaron asked.

"Women?"

"Yeah."

"Sure," Moses shrugged and looked away.

"How do you know my grandfather?" asked Aaron abruptly.

"You heard him, he was my grandfather's best friend." Let him swallow that.

"The one that killed the dame?"

"Yeah."

"Why'd he do it?"

"Search me," said Moses. Then: "Oh"—as though he knew more than he would say—"there were reasons."

"I was just a kid," said Aaron, "but I remember something—my dad and mother talking to my grandmother. Did they hang him?"

"No." Moses squinted up and around automatically. "He's up the hill."

"Doesn't seem to bother you much," said Aaron with a certain cautious admiration.

"Nah, not much." He almost believed it, it was so easy to say. "I even hope it's hereditary sometimes." He watched his companion as he said it, with a certain enjoyment. He had succeeded. Aaron looked startled but recovered quickly, so that when Moses added, "In fact, I think it is," his words produced no visible effect.

"Ever been up to see him?" Aaron challenged.

"No," said Moses. "Till now I was too young. But I'm planning a little visit."

"Yeah, when?"

"Soon. Couple of weeks."

Aaron was silent and, Moses felt, unbelieving. Did he think he was afraid? It suddenly seemed to him that all his life since that day he had waited for this. "Not exactly a couple of weeks," he said with sudden inspiration, "more like a week. I'm going up there on Yom Kippur day. Thought I'd like to see how the old boy spends the Day of Atonement." He could see that his words, the bitterness and cynicism of them, had taken effect.

Aaron glanced at him with respect and with a certain feeling that almost bordered on fear—maybe queer, but he sure was smart in a diabolical way. "Well," he said, "if they let you out let me know what happened."

"You may think I'm pretty queer," said Moses, though he tried to stop himself from saying it, "but I've always felt, ever since it happened, as though he were still around. Not just up there, I mean; almost—watching. It was so—unfinished. Lot of things never seem to get finished—just rag ends. Sometimes I feel like talking to him." Moses glanced back at the mountain with narrowed eyes. "All kinds of things I'd like to say to him," he added bitterly. He glanced at Aaron defiantly. "Maybe it's because they took him away in such a hurry. I woke up one morning, and he was gone. We never even had a chance to say good-by." He spoke with exaggerated mock regret. "All he left me were a bunch of crummy old stories and the facts of life."

They walked along in silence. Aaron was beginning to realize that this kid didn't care so little after all. Finally he spoke cryptically. "There's a killer in my family too."

"Oh?" Moses, afraid that he had revealed too much, was prepared to be amused at whatever joke the other made, to cover up, to show he didn't care.

"There's more than one way to kill," said Aaron. "Some kill slowly." Aaron stopped, not knowing if he should go on further, almost regretting that he had begun. What if he got laughed at by this kid who knew all about murder and talked with such laughing ease about doing things with women and such casual fearlessness about visiting the madhouse? Moses was watching him.

"My old man," said Aaron, throwing it out, "has been slowly killing my mother for years."

Moses remained silent, watchful.

"He sleeps with other dames," Aaron burst out, coloring, "and she knows it, too. Maybe it's not the same as taking a knife, but it's cleaner to take a knife. And when you take a knife you've got a reason. Sometimes I feel like doing it myself."

"How did you find out?" asked Moses quietly.

"I've heard them! All my life I've been hearing them. They don't care who hears them. 'What's the matter, you've got your big house, haven't you?' he says to her. When I was a kid I didn't understand.

I just felt as if I were rolled up—tight—and couldn't get loose. Now —that's one of the things—"

He didn't sound so sophisticated and rich now. Moses was surprised to detect tears in Aaron's voice. He didn't look. It had been a long time since he had cried in public. His defenses melted a little. He could feel sorry for this kid, who felt so bad even though he didn't know what it was to have, all of a sudden, everyone against him, the whole world turn over and nothing be the same. "Tough," he said quietly.

Aaron swallowed. "Yeah." Warmed by the short word of sympathy, he couldn't help going on, though he hadn't intended to tell the rest. "That's why I came down to see him today, my grandfather. He's a straight old guy. You have to know there's someone straight close to you sometimes. You see, he never said anything bad about yours. Besides"—he hesitated—"it was maybe like saying good-by."

"Going someplace?"

"Can you keep your mouth shut?"

Moses shrugged. "Sure. Whom would I tell?"

"There's a war on in Palestine." Aaron looked straight ahead.

Moses whistled softly, eying him with tentative respect. They walked for a while again in silence.

"We'll start a new country," Aaron went on finally. "Start new, build new, clean, get rid of all the dirt—"

"I don't know," said Moses. "We've had a country before. Remember what happened?"

"In those days the people were still pretty wild," Aaron pointed out. "They didn't have our modern forms of government. They knew a lot, but we've been around since. We won't make the same mistakes."

"In those days the people were still pretty wild," repeated Moses. "They used human children for their sacrifices."

"What?"

Moses laughed shortly. "Nothing. I keep remembering bits of crummy stories. I don't know if you'll change anything."

"You're pretty cynical," said Aaron respectfully.

Moses shrugged. "Tell me something. Are you scared—I mean to go and fight?"

"I don't even know if they'll take me," said Aaron. "They may think I'm too young. But I figure if I got a head start without my dad finding out, and got out of the country, they'd have to take me. And then— Sure I'm scared."

"I am too," said Moses. "I mean about that." He nodded toward the mountain. They walked on, more relaxed now, until Aaron stopped. "You turn off here?" Moses asked.

"Yeah. I never told anybody else about— I mean—" Aaron hesitated.

"You never told anybody, period," said Moses, eyes still on the mountain.

Aaron grinned. "Say, give me a call, why don't you? I'd like to hear more about that crazy old coot of yours."

"You phone me," said Moses. "The dry-goods shop under our name, in the book. We can talk about your old man. I haven't read any dirty books lately."

"All right. Tomorrow?"

"Sure." Moses watched while Aaron rounded the corner and ran for a streetcar. He seemed—pretty nice, for a heights kid. It almost seemed as though he had been trying to make friends. But he probably had all kinds of friends. Well, he'd see. Tomorrow, if he phoned, okay. If not, okay too. It was hardly likely; he wasn't going to bank on it. Moses pushed the hope out of his mind. The other thing crowded in. Yom Kippur. What had he let himself in for? But it was so. He felt as though all along he had known it would have to be. In a sudden panic he prayed that the old man would not die first, before the reckoning.

Now that he knew what his intention was, it seemed to Moses that all those years of waiting, of listening and watching, all those years that he had spent alone, that core of him that had crouched behind locked doors had waited only for this. Often, in the daydreams of his childhood, he had journeyed to the mountain, confronted a shadowy old man. "See what you've done!" His grievances, his accusations, the fury of his attack had finally brought the giant old man crashing to his knees, pleading with him, weeping torrents of rain that tore up the grass by the roots and swept the mud down the hillside, begging his forgiveness. Sometimes the old man finally revealed to him and only to him some amazing secret that explained everything, that showed him to be a hero, as his son had been. That woman had been a part of some evil plot; he had been sent to save the world; secrecy was necessary, and now he was in hiding on the mountain until the time came.

For a while he had been absolutely certain that his grandfather was a hero in hiding, because after they had found out that Harry was a black marketeer he had heard his mother telling Mrs. Plopler that Avrom had warned her. But this dream had faded too.

In the more aggressive moods of his early adolescence he had often thought of facing his grandfather sneeringly with his own disbelief, his own impiety, his own rebelliousness. His words would slash at the old man. If he ever asked him, "Moishe, do you go to the synagogue regularly?"— "Nah, I'm synagroggy."

Not that he believed any more, not really, at any rate, that a revelation awaited him. He knew—oh, he knew all right what "unfit to plead" implied. He knew that if the old man had not been brought to trial it did not mean, as he had at times imagined, that there was some plot in it, some darker purpose. And yet he had to see for himself. Almost he looked forward to seeing his grandfather a senile old man, slobber-lipped, unkempt, vacant, or even a still raving maniac. That would be that.

It was not surprise he felt, exactly, that his grandfather was not chained in a padded cell in the madhouse but was standing just over there, beside the path. In a dream there are no surprises, and time stretches and shrinks, as now. Moses floated toward him. Unmistakably it was he, though his clothes hung limply about him in a way the boy didn't remember. He measured himself, as he went forward, against the familiar figure that faced away from him, eastward. His first sharp sensation was a curious pleasure that he was almost as tall.

Now he was at the old man's side. The beard was there, though in memory it had been whiter. And it was the same profile, though more elementally, more austerely so, with the skin cleaving more closely to the cheeks than he remembered. A voice that was loud, yet somehow weaker than he remembered, startled him by breaking suddenly forth in prayer, intoning to the eastern air. The old man thumped his chest—the prayer on sin.

Though he stood right beside and only slightly behind his grand-father, the old man seemed totally unaware of his presence. The height of the mountain might still be separating them. There was his deafness, of course, and his complete absorption in prayer. So he prayed still!

Moses was rather pleased that he could stand so close and so un-emotionally, so automatically, register details. He would be able to tell Aaron that he had felt—practically nothing, just this almost otherworldliness. He could not remember in his grandfather this frailty. The old man swayed in the breeze of his own words; the crack of his fist on his chest echoed hollowly; his clothes flapped about him in the gentle autumn wind.

A murderer. Moses tried to comprehend that this was the mur-derer. But the word was something remote.

"Grandfather." He was annoyed at the thumping of his heart as he had to repeat the word in the old man's ear. Slowly the old man raised his head. For a long time the deep eyes gazed at him out of the still face. Then Abraham dropped his eyes and bent his head to look at the ground. At last—"Isaac?" he asked, and in his voice there was such a yearning that his grandson trembled.

"No, it's I, Moishe."

"Moishe," repeated the old man, his head still bent.

"Moishe Jacob," said Moses, not sure that the old man under-stood.

"Moishe, Jacob, Isaac," the old man repeated slowly, nodding his head, closing his eyes, and climbing over each name as though it were an obstacle.

Moses stood there beside the path and tried to make himself realize that this was the adversary.

"Yes, yes," said the old man half to himself, "it's the little Moishele." He nodded to himself several times while Moses tried to digest the pleasure that he felt in the fact that his grandfather had recognized him after all.

"Sit down," said his grandfather and sank rather suddenly onto the bench. Moses sat. "You've come to see me." The boy noticed that his grandfather still kept his face slightly turned away from him. Now was the moment for accusations, for harangue, for the imposing of his will, the reckoning. Where were all these notions now? There was the longest silence, during which the boy searched his mind desperately and could find nothing, nothing to say, almost nothing to think. None of those thrusting things that he had thought of, those brutal things, seemed to have any place here on the bench under the trees. Every thrust would turn in his own side. How could he wound without being wounded? He wanted to say, Don't turn away. Foolish words he wanted to say, of pity and comfort, that he did not even understand. Instead he kept very still.

"I have built a crooked house for you," said his grandfather finally.

Moses didn't answer. There was another long silence, into which memories of his early childhood came rushing and frolicking so that Moses had to bite his lip and mutter inwardly, Soft, you're soft. Bawl, why don't you?

Again his grandfather spoke. "You lay in my arms, beautiful, alive. You called me 'little father,' and still I did not understand."

Moses stiffened and glanced around him. The old man said "you," but whom was he talking to? He seemed to be looking through things, into a different world. His madness . . .

"You spoke of love," his grandfather said gently. Moses repressed a shudder. "And still, though something in me reached out, I did not understand. Nothing was necessary. I could have blessed you and left you. I could have loved you."

` Was he talking to—that dame? Whom he had killed? From the way he spoke he sounded almost as if he had loved her, real love, not just—whatever it was. And yet Moses had the feeling that, though he was addressing someone else, his grandfather was somehow addressing him, too.

"I took what was not mine to take," said Avrom, "what was given to me to hold gently in my hands, to look at with wonder. Moishe—" Moses started. "When a human being cries out to you, no matter who it is, don't judge him, don't harm him, or you turn away God Himself. In her voice there were the voices of children. Do not harm her, lest you hear them weeping." His grandfather shook his head. "He wouldn't let me die. What right had I to die, like the innocent?"

Moses wished his grandfather—wouldn't—cry—like that. "Grandfather" he said loudly. Anything to stop him, before—he himself—

"Do you hate me?" Abraham asked painfully. "I think of you; I think of her, of how I have wronged you. How you must hate me."

Moses shook his head violently from side to side, though he could only whisper, "No," from his tightly clogged throat. He hated himself for being soft like this. All right, so he was sorry for— Did he have to start bawling with him too?

After a moment the old man spoke again. "Ruth says you will be a fine fiddle-player."

Moses shrugged almost angrily, still unable to raise his head.

And again, with a curiously positive note in his voice, which was vaguely an echo from another time, almost as though he were thinking of something he was afraid to rediscover, Avrom added, "God willing, you will grow." Almost timidly he reached out his hand, finding Moses' own hand that lay in his lap. The boy started a little at the initial contact. He looked down at the hand that lay warm on his own, only partly hiding it—a large hand, with the knuckles swollen and reddish, coarse with the signs of many years' labor, thin with fasting. Underneath he could see part of his own, effeminate by contrast, white and cared-for. He could neither move his own hand nor look away from his grandfather's. This was the hand of a murderer. His eyes, fascinated, saw that the hands were not really different in shape, one from the other. And for a moment so conscious was he of his grandfather's hand on his own, of its penetrating warmth, of its very texture, that he felt not as though it merely lay superimposed on his own but that it was becoming one with his hand, nerve of his nerve, sinew of his sinew; that the distinct outlines had disappeared. It was with the strangest feeling of awakening that he saw their hands fused together—one hand, the hand of a murderer, hero, artist, the hand of a man. He could not for the life of him pull his hand away, nor did he want to. It was as though he stood suddenly within the threshold of a different kind of understanding, no longer crouching behind locked doors, but standing upright, with his grandfather leading him, as he always had. Avrom. Impulsively he brought his other hand down on the hand that held his own, and squeezed tightly, feeling his eyes swell up and the tears burning hotly down his cheeks. His insides ached, and he could not really think of why this should be so, except that his grandfather's hand trembled between his own two hands, and his grandfather's face, still partly averted from his own, wore an expression of joy.

Even afterward, as he sat in the bus that rattled its way down toward the city, with his hand shielding his swollen eyes from the possibly curious glances of the other passengers, he could not understand exactly what had come together for him. Nothing had happened, really. He had not wrenched from the past a confession or a cry for forgiveness; he had not won an exoneration or wreaked some petty revenge. He did not even know concretely, in any way that he could explain to himself as yet, any more than he had known. And yet he knew that he was a different person from the boy who had gone up the hill.

He knew that when Aaron asked him, as he was bound to ask him when he met him at the bus depot, if it had been as bad as he'd expected, if he still hated his grandfather as much, expecting him to say yes, so that he could then go on to tell him again how much he, too, hated his father—"Listen," he would say. "No, no, there's more to it." All kinds of sentences and words and thoughts that he would say raced through his mind. He wondered if he would have the nerve to say right out, "I love him"—just like that. Funny about his grandfather. He could still hear his voice raised up, addressing a power that he himself had long ceased to believe in: "You Who have shown him to me, beautiful and straight; Mysterious, Merciful, bless him!"

Again he tried to formulate the things he would say to his friend. "Listen—"

"Depot!" the driver called.

With a gesture that was vaguely reminiscent of his grandfather of another time, Moses lifted his hand away from his face, straightened up in his seat, and looked curiously about him at his fellow men.